the secret root

a novel

by

d.s. cahr

G

Green Flyer Press

Chicago

Every burning star, every silent nebula, every particle leaving its ghostly trace in a cloud chamber is an information processor. The universe computes its own destiny.

—JAMES GLEICK

Time is a brisk wind, for each hour it brings something new... but who can understand and measure its sharp breath, its mystery and its design?

—PARACELSUS

prologue

jared garber's last normal day

Many years later, a group of historians would argue that Jared Garber's disappearance at the age of fifteen marked the real beginning of the Plexus War. After all, they noted, this was the first sign that hostilities had commenced. Other scholars, however, declared that Edie Boyd was responsible for the rebellion, and thus the war's beginning should properly be set far in the future. Yet in spite of these disputes, both sides agreed that the afternoon of Jared's disappearance was nearly perfect, and held no warning of what was shortly to come.

On that day, Jared's twin sister Josie strolled beside him as they walked home from school. The two teenagers were a striking contrast as they ambled through their suburban neighborhood: each had dark, almost black hair, with piercing green eyes and pale skin, yet the resemblance stopped there.

Like all of the volleyball players, Josie's long hair was tied in a high ponytail, with an orange-and-blue school ribbon loosely hanging down her neck. She looked every inch the lifelong athlete, and wore her team sweats like a military uniform. Her posture was perfect and her head was held high, aggression radiating from her stare like a heat lamp.

Conversely, Jared was clad in his standard outfit: a carefully distressed, black leather jacket, frayed jeans, and a mildly offensive t-shirt for some band that no one else had ever heard of, and that Josie suspected might not even be real. He slouched as he walked, peering up from the ground only to avoid bumping into things. He wore a metal bracelet made of tarnished chain, and heavy engineer boots with steel toes and silver clasps. Yet despite his appearance, he was by all accounts significantly less belligerent than his sister, who seemed to be perpetually ready for a fight.

As they walked through their subdivision, where every street was named after an exotic plant, they passed older couples sitting on porches soaking up the early April sunshine, and muddy children tackling each other in yards. A tricycle was lying upended on a sidewalk, its former rider sitting happily on the grass watching a butterfly glide on the breeze. Jared could hear laughter coming from a backyard, and what sounded like a hose watering a garden.

But his thoughts that afternoon were on Sally, the girl who sat next to him in history class. She was a close friend of Josie's, which was a problem, but she was smart and funny in class, and had a great smile. Even better, earlier that week he had accidentally overheard her tell Josie that she liked him. Jared wondered if he could manufacture a good excuse to hang out with Sally over the weekend, and tried to remember if she had ever mentioned what she did for fun. He particularly liked the way her hair covered one of her light brown eyes, as though part of her face was veiled.

"You know," said Josie, breaking the silence that had settled between the twins a few minutes before, "there's nothing wrong with actually talking to people. It's fun, twin-guy. Really, you should try it."

Jared shot his sister an amused glance. He wished he had worn sunglasses—the sun was right behind her, and he was forced to squint. "It's nothing against anyone in particular," said Jared. "I just like to keep to myself." He thought for a moment. "I have friends, I'm not a hermit."

Jared looked down as he kicked a rock, and then gazed back over at his fierce twin sister. He smiled at her concern. As usual, she looked ready to punch the next person she saw. "I'm just not all that interested in figuring out who's dating who, and whether Bari broke up with Steve," he said. "I can't keep up with it all, twin-girl."

"Bari didn't break up with Steve," groaned Josie. "And this has nothing to do with *that*, you're just missing out on actually having any fun. Why don't you come out with us on Saturday? Seriously, I promise you'll have a good time."

Josie looked at her brother expectantly and then sighed with frustration when he didn't respond. Not that she was surprised. As twins, they were similar in so many ways, yet something about Jared always seemed slightly off to her. While she was the soul of school spirit, he seemed oblivious to the culture of the place. As much as she loved her brother, she always wondered whether he was a jerk or just a bit too intense for his own good.

Josie was intense in her own way, of course, and she knew it. When she strolled through the school, her long, loping strides could divide a crowded hallway like Moses parting the Red Sea. She had been power incarnate in the ecosystem of junior high, and even as a freshman this year she was already sought out by the upperclassmen for their cliques and parties.

As Jared decided whether to toss a jibe back at his sister, and maybe ask whether Sally would be at the party too, they turned the corner and passed the house behind their own. It was a small white ranch house on a large plot of land. The house looked as though it had been poorly maintained for years. Aluminum siding peeled off the façade, and a large wasp nest poured messily out of one of the eaves. The building itself was surrounded by a scrim of trees that hid the backyard from nearly every angle, except from the top floor of Garbers' own house. Several months ago a new occupant had moved into the home, but neither Jared nor Josie had yet seen their neighbor, and the house continued to appear empty to the outside world.

When they walked by the house on this day, however, the front door opened and a man was suddenly framed in the entrance. Jared stopped as though frozen in time, and stared. The man seemed to be made not of flesh and clothing, but of code and symbols that pulsed in ceaseless waves across his form. Every inch of the man's body was alive with a surge of incomprehensible geometric language, flowing over his limbs like hot liquid, twisting shapes rotating at every joint. Jared could not even recognize the expression on his neighbor's face through the cascade of icons and shifting characters.

"Josie," he whispered, blindly pulling his sister back as she walked ahead. "Do you see that?"

She stopped and looked, but saw only an unremarkable man emerging from the house. In her eyes this man, mustachioed and bald, was staring back as Jared pointed and frantically whispered something about numbers and codes.

"Twin-guy," said Josie, speaking in as soothing a voice as she could manage while guiding his head in a different direction. "There's nothing going on. Come on." And perhaps a bit more firmly than she originally intended, she tugged Jared along behind her, eventually dragging him around the corner and into their yard.

While this transpired, the man remained silent. He followed the Garber twins up the street with an icy stare, peering at them as they entered their own yard. After scratching the side of his face, he went back into his home and closed the door.

part one

*edie and meg
make a serious mistake*

1

edie boyd is not a praying mantis

It was not until later that Edie learned the truth about the Garbers and why they had disappeared. By then, however, it was far too late for her.

The day of that first disappearance began no differently than any other. Edie was asleep, caught in a web of deep and dreamless slumber. Her alarm went off at 6:00 a.m., and she pounded the snooze button on her snarling clock twice. Her eyes did not open, even after she at last turned off her alarm and threw it to the floor.

Edie then sat up blindly in her bed. She yawned and stretched like a cat, pulling the bedcovers this way and that. Eventually, she climbed out of bed, walked four feet to her right, opened her eyes, and stared into her mirror. She was never happy with what she saw. A month before, in a diary entry later scrutinized by three different middle-aged, male police investigators, Edie had made a list of things she saw in the reflection:

1. Mousy brown hair hanging over dull, grey eyes
2. An oval face with no cheekbones
3. Ears that look at least one size too small

   4. A long, narrow body with long limbs and no curves

Due to these many perceived flaws, Edie had long ago concluded that she looked like a praying mantis. Of course, she knew this was deeply unfair. In fact, during the twilight minutes before she fell asleep each night, she repeatedly told herself that she did *not* look like a praying mantis. Yet the more she tried to banish the thought, the more the image remained imprinted in her mind.

One of Edie's other diary entries was, in fact, entitled "I Am Not a Praying Mantis." This entry was later analyzed without success by two different forensic psychologists during the investigation.

To be sure, Edie felt that she was entitled to a certain amount of self-pity. After all, she was the youngest girl in the eighth grade. She was surrounded by boys who looked almost ready to shave, and girls who wore makeup and seemed strangely adult. Worse, her junior high was on the same campus as the high school, and a caste of even older kids was visible everywhere, incessantly imitating their favorite shows in new, crude ways each day. Edie felt so much younger than everyone else she knew, trapped in childhood as her classmates grew older and left her behind. Even as new birthdays came and went, Edie always felt exactly the same.

But each morning, after she looked in the mirror and felt sorry for herself for approximately four minutes, the ugliest part of that feeling would subside. Edie would tear herself away from her reflection, take a shower, dress in clothes far too large for her body, and head downstairs. Aunt Judy and Uncle Pete would have already started breakfast. She loved them with a reverence that approached awe. In her mind they had saved her from a fate so horrible she didn't even like to consider it. On that critical day, however, things were already different by the time she sat down in her chair.

"Hear about the Garbers?"

Edie was chewing her toast. She looked up at her uncle, shook her head, and swallowed. "What about them?"

"They're missing, just gone," he said. "Every one of 'em, gone."

Uncle Pete was a graying, disheveled man who spoke in gunshot rhythms and rarely conversed for more than five seconds at a time. His eyes were surrounded by the type of wrinkles that seemed to extend across his face into his hairline, even though he was only in his mid-fifties. Yet while the stresses of his life may have aged him prematurely, Edie could hardly imagine him as a young man. To her, he was eternal. Old pictures of him standing next to her own father as boys seemed almost like poorly faked photographs. To Edie, her uncle could never have been young.

But regardless of his true age, Uncle Pete could usually be found at breakfast peering over a newspaper, grumbling incoherently. Between politics and the dress habits of teenagers, he generally managed at least three expletive-laden sentence fragments during breakfast. Many of these little explosions would make Edie laugh out loud. That day, however, his initial comment of the morning was spare and disturbing. She paused in mid-bite. "What do you mean, 'just gone?'"

"I mean the Garbers, all of 'em," he said. "As in, they are no longer living in their house."

She frowned and then finished chewing her last bite of toast. "Did they move? What happened? People don't just disappear."

Her smiling aunt placed a large stack of pancakes in front of her. "Pete, what's this I hear about the Garbers?"

3

Aunt Judy passed the maple syrup over to her husband as she spoke. "Denise just called to tell me the house is empty."

As far as Edie could tell, her aunt was unable to cook anything other than pancakes or frozen dinners, although that hardly diminished this warm, remarkable woman in Edie's eyes. Aunt Judy was an elegant presence who seemed oddly out of place in the western counties of Kansas, even in a college town. Edie had once joked that Aunt Judy was like a picture from a sophisticated soirée pasted into the local newspaper next to the prices for hog feed. In fact, it almost appeared to Edie as if someone had created her aunt from some outdated notion of what a housewife should look like: Aunt Judy still put on makeup and a dress before coming down for breakfast every morning. Edie could not even recall seeing her without makeup during the many years Edie had lived in their house. And despite the somber discussion topic, as she handed her husband the syrup, she looked as though she might spontaneously break into song.

"I've known Larry Garber for years, ever since we moved here," Uncle Pete announced, chewing noisily through his words. "The man has roots." He thought for a moment more and then continued. "He's the orthodontist in town, for heaven's sake. His kids have friends. You don't just pack up the family in the night."

Edie had attended the same school as the Garbers last year, but they had since moved on to the high school. The twins were ninth graders, a year ahead, and thus had never been in any of her classes. Even so, it had been impossible not to notice them in the halls. Over breakfast that morning, their images came to her immediately. She pictured Josie standing next to her locker, confidently towering over the other girls who surrounded her like a flock of eager birds. Josie always had a strange hostility in her eyes as she walked the halls; she almost seemed to dare her classmates to say hello. Edie's picture of Jared was quite different: she saw him in the library, staring intently at a book as though it contained vital state secrets. His handsome features were always hidden by a shock of uncombed black hair. He wore dark colors and black boots. He listened to music that no other person at the school could identify, music that was reported to sound like crazy industrial noise. He used a wallet that attached to his belt with a long, metal chain that hung in a loop along his hip. His mysteriousness only added to his credibility as an authentic outsider, and she knew that many girls had sketches of his face in the margins of their notebooks.

"Is it in the paper?" asked Edie.

"Not yet," said her uncle. He brusquely pulled some unchewed bread from his mouth. "I expect it there tomorrow. People only realized it last night, and the police are just getting into it now. That's what Harold told me out front a few minutes ago, right before he headed for his shift at the station."

Breakfast was fairly solemn from that point on. Edie made passing mention of homework and soccer practice, but no one's heart was in it. Uncle Pete was right: people simply did not disappear, not like that. Not a whole family. In fact, as she ate that morning, she developed a strange feeling in the pit of her stomach, a feeling as though something had changed.

2

the notes in
edie's locker

School was only five blocks away, and the most direct path took Edie past the Garbers' house, a standard, split-level suburban home. Faded red-orange bricks on the first floor gave way to cedar on the second level. A wall of brown wood on the east side of the house was dotted with three windows in a triangular configuration. The arrangement of these windows had always looked like an angry face to Edie, and each time she walked by the house it seemed to be sneering at her. The landscaping was immaculate, with perfectly trimmed hedges snaking alongside the lawn. Flowers bloomed in a bed near the front door, and a basketball sat neatly on the lawn like a freshly laid egg.

Today twin police cruisers sat in the driveway side by side. Several neighbors were outside on the sidewalk, loudly discussing various criminal scenarios which they had gleaned from watching reality shows. As she walked closer, Edie could see two girls huddled under a spreading maple tree on the parkway. Both were crying and looked thoroughly stricken. One girl, an attractive blonde in ripped jeans, was holding her knees. This was Sally Karger, a close companion of Josie Garber's and the older sister of one of Edie's best friends.

Sally's eyes were tightly shut and she seemed to be struggling to breathe. The other girl was trembling but still managed to hug Sally's shoulders, even as tears streamed down her own face. The sight of the crying girls was too much for Edie. Turning away, she hurried down the hill. She felt as though she might turn to salt if she looked back even once.

School provided no relief. By the time she had arrived at her locker, she had overheard more discussions of the disappearance than she could possibly count. Every snippet of conversation included the words "Garber" or "Josie" or "Jared" or "disappear." Graffiti in the girls' bathroom read: "Where are the Garbers?"

She spun the dials of her locker combination and tried not to think about anything Garber-related. Just then Megan Karger ran up and grabbed her arm. As she opened her mouth, nails digging into Edie's elbow, a torrent of words rushed out as though a faucet had just been turned on:

"Did you hear? Ohmygod, Sally can't stop crying, and I know they wouldn't have gone anywhere without telling us." Meg's eyes were wild. "Something must have happened, I can't imagine what, I hope they're not dead or worse, who could have possibly done this, I can't believe something like this is happening here, nothing like this ever happens here, nothing ever happens here at all, hey, Edie, what are you staring at?"

Someone had placed a note on the shelf in Edie's locker. It was written in block letters on firm, smooth card stock. It read simply:

TIME IS A TRAP

"I don't know," said Edie slowly, pausing to examine the message. "It's just a weird note." She turned back to Meg and tried to concentrate again on her friend. "But what's with the Garbers? I saw your sister and her friends by their house. How long have they been gone?"

"That's the thing," said Meg, spreading her arms wide like a politician. "They were here two days ago. Josie was going to come over after dinner last night to work on a project with Sally, and now the house is empty? It's crazy. They've got a housekeeper who comes in the evenings, she showed up there two nights ago, I guess, and there was nobody in the house, half-eaten dinner still on the table, cars still in the garage." She was still breathing hard. "No one—nada. So they've been gone, really, for like two days, even though it only became an official thing yesterday, and I guess they questioned the housekeeper, and they even questioned Sally, if you can believe it, and I can't believe it, can you believe it?"

In truth, Edie could barely comprehend what Meg was telling her, both because it made so little sense and because it had been spoken at such incredible speed. Meg looked manic, barely in control, which was very unlike her. In part to avoid staring directly at Meg, who was making her nervous, Edie again looked down at the note. "Time is a trap." The handwriting was oddly familiar, and despite the block letters she felt as if she should recognize it. She could not quite place it, though.

"Meg, do you know this handwriting?" she asked.

With the sudden change in topic, Meg seemed to regain some degree of self-control. She plucked the note from Edie's hand and began to examine it, a concentrated look of curiosity on her face. Within a few short moments a complete transformation had taken place in her manner, and the Garbers were forgotten, at least for a moment.

Meg was a curveball in Edie's otherwise predictable life. She was a startlingly blonde fourteen-year-old with sharp fashion sense and an even sharper tongue. She fit in well with the alpha girls who wore makeup and played field hockey, the popular kids who rarely spoke to Edie and in fact barely seemed aware that she even existed.

But in addition to being part of the accepted crowd, Meg had always been something of a natural spy, a born troublemaker in plaid skirts and hair bands. That was why she and Edie were friends. And that is why it seemed appropriate to Edie that Meg was with her now, discussing a crime scene and a weird note.

The girls had initially bonded as second-graders determined to find out what "really" happened in the teachers' lounge. This had become an obsession of the kids in their class. They imagined a fantastic world behind that door, filled with unlimited candy and forbidden treats. What exactly, they wondered, could the teachers be up to, hidden in their own private space?

Edie and Meg, for reasons that neither of them could perfectly recall, had decided to take matters into their own hands. While on a bathroom break, they'd snuck into the lounge and hidden themselves in a closet with a purloined notebook, prepared to detail what they heard for the rest of the class. They were thrilled until they realized, to their dismay, that the closet door could not be opened from the inside. They were stuck in a place they were not supposed to be, with no obvious means of escape.

Rather than give themselves away, however, they quietly listened in on their teachers' increasingly frantic discussions as the school began to search for them. To their amazement, many of these conversations dealt with the fact that the teachers found both Edie and Meg to be exceptionally irritating kids, the type who just would have disappeared from class.

Edie and Meg were too fascinated to be frightened, listening to the dramas of adult life normally shielded from their ears, and they remained in the closet for what felt like hours. Eventually a fourth-grade science teacher opened the closet to grab a coat, and Meg stealthily propped the door open with a hanger. When the room was empty and the teachers were out searching with everyone else, Meg and Edie slipped out. They then snuck into the school library and allowed themselves to be "found" by their favorite security guard. Since that day the girls had been oddly close, despite the fact that they moved in vastly different social circles and rarely spoke to each other during the school day. Given that Edie herself had no siblings, Meg sometimes felt like a part of her family.

So when Edie handed Meg the note, Edie knew on some level that this was going to be the beginning of some kind of crazy exploit.

"Where was this?" asked Meg. Edie could already see a familiar, obsessive intensity behind her blue eyes, which glittered with anticipation. Moreover, she noticed that Meg was pulling her hair back from her face, a tic that always meant she was thinking. Edie couldn't help but smile.

"I just found it in my locker," she said. "While we were talking, I found it sitting on the shelf, on top of my algebra book."

Meg flipped the card over, flipped it back, and brought it close to her eyes. "I don't know, it looks a bit like your handwriting, I guess, but it's in block letters. No. This is a guy's handwriting. Maybe even an older guy pretending to be a kid. I'm not even sure this is a kid at all." She handed the note back, shaking her head. "I don't know, let me think about it. We'll talk later. Who writes about time like that, anyway?

"And by the way," she added, "I'm taking you shopping this weekend, we need you to wear normal clothes. You would look so awesome if you'd let me dress you for once."

Edie punched Meg on the arm, laughing, and grabbed her books. The two of them walked down the hall to social studies class, as Edie fended off Meg's offers to give her a makeover. This was a regular argument, with Meg insisting that Edie was attractive and needed to stop hiding under ugly clothes and a bad attitude. Edie, however, thought she was being charitable at best and didn't like the idea of being her friend's fashion doll.

Once they turned into the main hallway, their pace was slowed as Meg stopped every five feet to greet someone that Edie didn't really know. She found herself hanging back, silent and slightly uncomfortable. As Meg talked, Edie kept reaching into her pocket to finger the note, running her hand along its stiff outer edge, occasionally hip-checking Meg to move her along.

When they finally arrived at class, Meg separated to sit with her posse on the far left-hand side of the room, and Edie sat with the group of unaffiliated kids in front. These kids were Edie's people.

Meg had long accused Edie of having, as she put it, "loser friends." To Meg, it seemed that Edie was simply trying to be the biggest fish in the smallest pond by hanging out with less social kids. Edie thought this was a horrible thing to say, and she considered Kathrine, Amanda, Melissa, and Lisa to be her closest friends. When Meg brought it up, as she did from time to time, Edie dismissed the theory out of hand.

Secretly, though, she wondered whether Meg might be right. She recognized her own fear at leaving the comfort of familiar surroundings and wondered if she didn't trade up in social class simply out of a dread that she herself might be rejected. Yet while she appreciated Meg's subtle invitations to join another clique, she could never imagine being away from her friends.

"Edie, did you hear?"

"The Garbers..."

"...all gone."

"...did you hear?"

"No one there..."

A chorus of voices that bubbled in tones split between disturbance and wonder surrounded Edie as soon as she sat down. She tried to answer Kathrine, Amanda, Melissa, and Lisa (whom Meg sneeringly called Edie's "ladies in waiting") as all four continued to talk over each other. They threw speculation upon speculation like layers of brick in a wall, while Edie eventually stopped trying to talk and just listened.

"My dad said that Larry Garber owed a lot of money..."

"Why wouldn't he just sell the house?"

"The kids had plans for this weekend..."

"Couldn't they be on vacation?"

"Nah, I heard that all the furniture's gone."

"No one saw a moving truck?"

"And the furniture was not gone," said Lisa. "I looked in the window this morning."

"Did not!" said Kathrine, sneering.

"Yep, one day they're around, the next day they're gone. Poof!"

"I forgot, you're the one who wants to be a cop," said Kathrine.

"So?" asked Lisa. "At least I figured something out today without a calculator..."

"If the furniture isn't gone," said Melissa, "maybe they're on vacation, or they got sick and..."

"Please," said Kathrine, in her best attempt at an analytical voice. "There's a logical explanation to all of this."

"So how come you're not freaked out?" asked Amanda, surprised.

"I don't know," said Kathrine, leaning back in her chair. "But people don't really disappear. We'll eventually find out what happened, and—"

"Yeah, Ms. Logic," interrupted Lisa, perhaps a bit more aggressively than she'd originally intended. "They were all murdered, we know that, and they're probably at the bottom of the lake."

"I don't think..."

And so it went on for several minutes. Edie always marveled at the fact that her friends could be so clever and talkative amongst themselves, but so shy around everyone else. They all had their goals and dreams for the future, of being cops and scientists, or doctors or politicians. Their electronic messages, furtively sent under desks, were filled with subtle insults and wry insights, using nothing but misspelled words and sentence fragments. Yet to most of the school, these girls were nameless, faceless, anonymous bodies.

"Edie, can we get together on Saturday?" asked Kathrine. "I need to talk to you about the art project—you know, the toothpicks."

"Sure, Kathrine, we just need—"

Just then Mrs. Besicka, their social studies teacher, walked into the room and began writing on the smartboard. She was a prematurely grey woman in her early forties with striking green eyes like a cat's, and she was dressed in a black suit with a crisp white shirt. Her ramrod posture and oddly formal outfit made her appear stern, which she was, and she commanded the classroom like a military drill instructor.

Edie and the rest of the class strained to see what she was writing. Edie loved Mrs. Besicka's classes. Each lesson was intense, and her classes were never dull.

"There will be no discussion of the Garbers in class today," said Mrs. Besicka, still scribbling, and still looking away from the class. "Instead, we will talk about time."

Edie's head snapped up and she looked over at Meg, who seemed equally shocked. They both saw that Mrs. Besicka had written a single sentence, in elegant script, on the smartboard: "Time does not change us. It just unfolds us." Edie stared at the words, but could not figure out what they really meant.

Mrs. Besicka spun around and faced the class. She then began to move her arms slowly, as though conducting an orchestra. "Time is, in many ways, the hidden theme to all of our studies this year. Our discussions of many topics have touched upon time and the passage of time. But now we will be a bit more explicit."

She moved closer to the front row and leaned over, as though telling the class a secret. "Our discussions of geography, of history, and of politics are all really about time," she said. "When you are older, you will learn that time is a dimension of our world, as real as height, width, and depth." As she said this, she measured herself out with a yardstick that had been sitting on her desk. "And time cannot be escaped. It is what separates you from earlier this morning, and what separates me from being a little girl. We underestimate time at our peril."

Edie began running her fingers along the note again.

"Edie," asked Mrs. Besicka, "did you read pages 421 through 435 last night?"

Mrs. Besicka was staring at her. Edie suddenly remembered that she was supposed to speak.

"Yes, yes I did," she said, trying to regain her focus. She closed her eyes and thought for a moment. "It was about the failed invention of the computer."

"And why is it important to understand the initial, failed invention of the computer in the context of time?"

Edie stared up at a cracked ceiling tile as she considered the question. She thought back to her reading. "Well, when Leibniz first thought about the computer, in..." She quickly looked down at her textbook and flipped to page 421. "...in 1671, it was a good idea, but it was way ahead of its time. He had the right idea, I guess, but it was too soon for it to catch on with anybody."

"Edie, why didn't the idea catch on?" Mrs. Besicka's eyes were now boring into her, and she felt warm with the attention.

"Well, they didn't have much use for it," she said, looking around the room to gauge the interest level of her classmates. "They didn't have electricity or vacuum tubes or anything like that. No big factories, no industry, nothing. They just had some gears—what were they going to use a computer for? It was pointless back then."

"Ah, so unless it helps people do what is important to them at that time," said Mrs. Besicka in a tone of triumph, "innovation gets ignored. Which means—and this is red-magic-marker territory for all of you taking notes—that where you are in time is just as important as who you are." She paused and looked over at Randy, an athlete eight inches taller than almost any other boy in the class. "Mr. McCarran, two hundred years ago you wouldn't be in school, and you wouldn't be playing sports. You'd be working in the fields or in a mill."

Randy looked irritated at being singled out, but nodded.

"And Meg, you might have been a seamstress—or," added Mrs. Besicka in a tone of mild amusement, "if you were noble-born, you might be engaged to be married. Already."

Meg and her friends giggled nervously.

"So, what is the importance of time?" asked Mrs. Besicka, who did not wait for an answer as she turned back to the smartboard. "It is the thing which most shapes our lives. Since our topic this month is technology and its effect on our culture..."

Mrs. Besicka smoothly segued into another question and wrote something new on the smartboard. Edie, however, was left wondering at the coincidence. Why on earth was Mrs. Besicka talking about time on the same day she'd found a bizarre note in her locker and the Garbers had disappeared?

The rest of Edie's day expired in a blur. Meg was not in many of her other classes, and Edie didn't speak about the note with anyone else. For some reason, she didn't feel comfortable talking about it with her other friends. Instead, they talked about the Garbers, and homework, and the Garbers, and swim lessons, and the Garbers.

At least two different murder theories were making the rounds, neither of which made any sense. Kathrine, Amanda, Melissa, and Lisa were in full gossip mode, but since they didn't talk to anyone but each other, Edie learned very little new information.

When she returned to her locker at the end of the day, she was bewildered to find yet another note. This one, in the same handwriting and on the same card stock, asked a question:

WHAT IS TIME?

Just then, as though summoned, Meg arrived. "You got another note?" she asked, excitedly snatching it away. "What the...he's asking you questions?"

"Yeah." She peeked back over Meg's shoulder at the note. "'What is time?' That's the question, I guess."

"Well, it's a clue," said Meg, now growing more excited. "He's giving us a clue! This is like some kind of game for him."

Edie suddenly felt worried. This seemed far too strange, and vaguely inappropriate. "Shouldn't we tell someone?" she asked, retreating a bit. "What if this guy is dangerous?"

Meg had a slightly manic look in her eye, and was clearly not in a mood to be put off. "No way. We've got to figure this out. He's asking us a question, so we need to go find an answer. It's probably some kind of thing from Mrs. Besicka, you heard her today. It's a riddle. She probably got her husband to write it, and she put it in our lockers to make us think about it. So where do we start? Let's go to my place...."

Somewhat mollified, Edie nodded and they walked quickly out of the school. It would certainly be like Mrs. Besicka, thought Edie, to seed their lockers with riddles. Yet it still seemed a bit strange, and something about the whole situation felt very wrong.

3

the twins paradox

As they opened the door to Meg's house, the two girls were tackled by a black, mop-like dog. "Down, Roseanna, down!" ordered Meg, laughing as Edie tried to get up, already covered in dog drool. Just as they had finally calmed Roseanna, who was still happily trying to get them to play with a soggy ball, the girls were intercepted by Meg's mom, a jovial woman in a paint-smeared smock and fluorescent green clogs.

"Edie, make sure you call your aunt," said Meg's mom, in a voice that tried unsuccessfully to sound both insistent and casual. "You can't be too careful these days." Edie and Meg both knew implicitly what she meant.

So after alerting Edie's aunt ("Don't worry, Aunt Judy, I'll be home for dinner"), they made their way down into the study. Meg's parents kept a computer there for her and her sister to use for homework. Meg said she also suspected that part of the purpose of this arrangement was to ensure that her parents always knew what the kids were doing in cyberspace. Given Meg's somewhat aggressive approach to life generally, Edie felt this was probably wise.

As they entered the room, Edie ran for the desk chair, plopped down, and logged on in a single, fluid motion. By the time Meg had made it over to the desk, her only option was to tackle Edie and try to pull her from the seat. "Hey!" screamed Meg in mock indignation. "It's *my* computer!"

Ignoring her, Edie went to a search engine, typed in "what is time?" and waited for the results.

The first thing that came up was a site called The Twins Paradox.

"Weird, what's this?" Meg leaned in over Edie's shoulder. "What does that have to do with time?"

"Let's see," said Edie, reading along. "Some science stuff. 'Time is relative, and can only be understood in relation to space...'"

"Oooookay," said Meg, rolling her eyes. "I have no idea what you just said. Anything else?"

"Alright," said Edie under her breath as she bit her lip, scanning down the page. "Anything here...okay, listen to this. 'For example, imagine a set of twins. One remains on earth, and the other steps on a spaceship and travels around the galaxy at the speed of light for what seems like three years. When he returns, the earth twin is an old man.'"

"No way," said Meg, a look of amusement on her face. "This site's junk, that's impossible. Try something else."

"I'm just reading what it says," said Edie defensively. "Okay, there's a lot more here. Hmmm...." She scanned down the page and began scrolling to different links, with Meg popping over her shoulder to try to read along.

"No way," mumbled Edie to herself as she grew impatient with what she was reading. "I know what time is. It's minutes, then hours, then days...."

"What are you talking about?" Meg was still trying to see over Edie's shoulder.

"I don't know. It says here that...." Edie skimmed ahead. "Some people think time is a line with a beginning but no

end, and others say it's a circle, or a series of lines with loops. Time loops? That's pretty funny. Others say that... 'time doesn't actually exist, that there is just a series of nows.' That's interesting....I wonder if you can move from one now to another, like cars on a train?"

"'Nows'?" giggled Meg. "They're plural?"

"Little moments, I guess. Anyway, this isn't helping at all." She skimmed down a bit further. "It looks like no one even agrees on what time actually is, let alone whether it's a trap, or what that even means."

"Maybe we should ask Mrs. Besicka why she put the note in your locker," mused Meg, leaping onto a large, over-stuffed leather chair next to the desk.

"Why are you so sure it was her?" Edie closed the link on the site.

"You heard her today." Meg threw her legs over one of the chair's well-worn arms. "I'll bet she put notes in the lockers of a bunch of different kids, and she's got a plan. Like I said, it's a riddle."

Edie nodded, still not quite convinced, and soon the conversation returned to the Garbers. "So where's your sister?" she asked. "I saw her at the Garber house this morning, and she looked pretty bad."

"Good question. Mom!" Meg yelled at the staircase. "Where's Sally?"

Mrs. Karger's voice drifted down from the kitchen. "She's with Alexis."

"Well," said Meg, "there's your answer."

The two of them sat silently for a minute, Meg slouched in the chair, Edie staring off into the endless space of the computer monitor. Edie finally spoke up.

"How can a whole family disappear?"

"Maybe," Meg began, smiling ruefully, "they got on a rocket going at the speed of light, for a quick trip around the stars. And when they return two weeks later, we're all dead. It is called the twins paradox, right? And Jared and Josie *are* twins...."

Meg trailed off as Edie began to stare at her.

"Meg," she said, putting her fingers to her temples as though she was developing a headache. "I'll bet that's exactly what happened."

Much later, Meg told Edie that at that moment, for reasons she could never fully explain, she knew Edie was right.

• • •

The next day Edie brought the notes to Mrs. Besicka, and was not surprised to find that she had no idea what they were talking about.

"What kind of notes?" asked Mrs. Besicka in her clipped voice. "May I please see them?" Edie pulled them from her jeans. Her teacher looked at the cards intensely. "Girls," she said slowly, "someone is having some fun at your expense, but it isn't me. I wish I were that clever, but I'm afraid slipping notes into the lockers of my students is not part of the lesson plan."

"Should we tell...?" began Edie.

"Yes, you should show these to Mr. Hall if you don't recognize them." She stared down at them quite seriously. "He needs to be aware of anything out of the ordinary in this school. Thank you for bringing this to my attention."

Edie felt annoyed. Talking to the vice principal was not at all what she'd meant to propose, and the thought made her feel slightly ill. But now it seemed that she had little choice. "In fact," continued Mrs. Besicka, "you should tell him before your next period. I'll give you a hall pass." She grabbed a pre-printed pass from her desk, scrawled a date and time on the front, handed it to Edie, and then turned around to face the blackboard.

Meg and Edie hurried back to their desks wearing uneasy looks. Edie wondered what this all meant, and if it was somehow going to get them in trouble. As far as she could tell, neither she nor Meg had done anything wrong. But Mrs. Besicka's reaction made her nervous, and she wondered how this would end.

Mrs. Besicka, however, seemed to have put the matter behind her with remarkable alacrity, and began speaking to the class before the girls had even managed to take their seats.

"Mr. Galler?" she asked, as she pointed to a skinny boy in a faded crimson football jersey. "What can you tell me about pages 435 through 448?"

Alec Galler fiddled with his book, flipping pages and quickly skimming a few of the highlighted paragraphs. Finally, after at least a minute, he looked up.

"This section talks about how technology does stuff to culture."

"Define," ordered Mrs. Besicka, ignoring muffled giggles from the class, "the word 'stuff.'"

• • •

After class Edie wandered to the second-floor administrative corridor. She looked at the nameplates by each door until she found Mr. Hall's office. She had never been there before. In fact, she was fairly sure that only kids who had been disruptive in class were ever sent to him. Even the term "vice principal" was intimidating. While she was nervous, though, she reminded herself that she was doing the right thing. She knocked and a female voice chirped, "Come in."

Edie entered a small waiting room. A tiny, wizened woman in an obnoxiously flowered dress and a teased-up hairdo sat behind a computer monitor. "May I help you?" she asked in a musical tone.

"Yes, can I speak with Mr. Hall? I have a question. I mean, I have something to tell him." Edie thought her voice sounded strange, as though someone else were speaking. She didn't know why she was so nervous, but something about these notes was really getting under her skin.

"Mr. Hall is not available right now," said the woman, peering curiously over her glasses at Edie. "Is it an emergency, or would you like to make an appointment?"

"Umm..." Edie tried to think quickly, as she had not expected this fairly obvious possibility. "Sure. An appointment is fine. How about after school today?"

"I'm sorry, Mr. Hall has a meeting out of the office. How about Monday before school begins, say, 7:30?"

"Yes," agreed Edie. "That would be great. Oh, and you need my name, right? I'm Edie. Edie Boyd."

"Okay, Ms. Boyd," said the woman, now smiling. "Your appointment is set. We'll see you on Monday morning."

Edie left the office. She felt silly at being so nervous, but pleased that she had scheduled an appointment. She always felt better when she knew that an expected event would take place with a high degree of certainty. In fact, as the day went on, her mood improved so markedly that she spent most of her free time discussing the Garbers with Lisa, Melissa, Kathrine, and Amanda, with nary a thought about the notes. Even Meg seemed satisfied, at least temporarily, with news of the meeting.

All of these pleasant feelings instantly evaporated when Edie returned to her locker after gym class. When she opened the door, she found another note sitting on top of her algebra book. As though expecting this development, Meg had again miraculously appeared at Edie's side even before she had finished the combination on her lock. The note read:

IS TIME A CHOICE?

"What's this one say?" asked Meg, whispering so loudly that Edie wondered why she was even bothering to whisper at all.

Edie handed Meg the note, her hands trembling slightly.

"'Is time a choice?'" Meg asked indignantly. "What kind of question is that? Do I have a choice that it's today? I don't think so."

Edie stared at the note and thought back to their conversation the previous afternoon. "Meg, remember when you wondered if the Garbers were taking a ride into space, and when they return we'll all be dead?"

Meg looked nervously at her shoes. "Yeah. Something like that."

"Well, what if they went somewhere without leaving their house, or the earth?"

They mulled the question on their way to class. Neither of them looked at the other as they walked slowly down the corridor, the voices of their classmates echoing around them like a movie soundtrack.

4

a brief history of time

Conveniently, Edie's and Meg's next class was science, the only other class they shared. Their teacher, Ms. Cavanaugh, was the polar opposite of Mrs. Besicka in just about every way Edie could imagine. Mrs. Besicka was cool and in control at all times, a coiled spring who thrived on creative tension in the classroom. Conversely, Ms. Cavanaugh was a dynamic woman prone to wild gestures, entertaining rants, and broad, sweeping statements only tangentially related to the subject at hand.

Ms. Cavanaugh was a flaming redhead whose fondness for large ethnic jewelry nicely complemented her crazily disheveled appearance. Meg had once said that Ms. Cavanaugh always looked as though she had only barely remembered to clothe herself in the morning, and that sounded about right to Edie. That said, Ms. Cavanaugh also had an undeniable charisma far in excess of what would normally be expected of an eighth-grade science teacher, and Edie enjoyed her classes immensely.

Ms. Cavanaugh always began with an open call for questions. During the first few classes of the school year no one had raised their hands, and Ms. Cavanaugh had looked alternately dispirited and uncomfortable. At first the silences had lasted for painful lengths of time, and Edie found herself squirming in her seat. But after Meg broke the ice on the fourth day of school and asked a question about how aspirin worked, the class got into the spirit of things. Now nearly every day began with a random question from the students, and Ms. Cavanaugh was pleased.

"Well," began Ms. Cavanaugh, striding across the room like a preacher or a motivational speaker, a green peasant skirt swirling around her legs. "I must ask you all on this beautiful Friday, do you have any questions?"

Edie's hand shot up. Ms. Cavanaugh smiled.

"Ah, Ms. Boyd. Let 'er rip." She swept her arms around like a dervish, spinning in place, finally coming to a stop after two full revolutions. "I'm all ears."

"Ms. Cavanaugh," started Edie, unsure of exactly how to phrase the question. "What is time, and can it be a trap, or a choice?"

Ms. Cavanaugh stopped moving and stared down at her feet. After a moment of silence, she looked up at Edie, smiling.

"Now that is a challenging question indeed!" She looked up at the ceiling as she spoke, considering her response. "Time is one of the great mysteries of modern science, of modern philosophy, cosmology, mathematics—you name it. Everyone wants to understand time, and it seems like it should be so easy." She began to pace, the eyes of her class following her as she twirled behind her desk, almost knocking over a model of the solar system in the process. "We look at our watches and time makes sense. We watch ourselves grow older and time makes sense. But just as an optical illusion changes when you start to look at it more closely, so changes time.

"For example," she continued, resuming her circuit around the classroom, "there are many different kinds of time, but since they all go by the same name, they are easily confused by most folks, including most of you. Specifically, there is physical time, psychological time, and biological time. Yet despite their similar names, they are not the same. No, not at all.

"*Biological time* refers to the transformation over time of a living being as it ages. In other words, you grow up, you get older, and then you die." Ms. Cavanaugh did not seem to notice several members of the class shivering at her offhand dismissal of their eventual doom. "*Psychological time* simply refers to your sensation of time. A year feels much shorter now than it did when you were five years old, and a watched pot never boils! That kind of time is interesting, to be sure, but it is just inside your own head. Since it has no meaning in the real world, it has no place in this discussion."

Ms. Cavanaugh turned dramatically towards Edie. "But since you are speaking of time being a choice, or a trap, I assume you are thinking about *physical time*, time as a dimension, time as related to space and movement. Correct?"

Edie nodded, though she wasn't entirely sure what Ms. Cavanaugh was talking about.

"Well, this is a most interesting question. As you recall, we have been discussing galaxies. At the center of many galaxies are structures called *black holes*, a term I'm sure many of you know." At this, she started to move her gaze across the room, trying to meet the eyes of any students who might not be paying attention. "Black holes are, in fact, time traps. They are places where gravity is so powerful that it affects the physical properties of matter. One of those properties is, according to our current theories, time itself. Inside the area just outside the center, which is called the *event horizon*, time itself slows down until, theoretically at least, it comes to a near standstill. You are thus trapped in a single moment in time which never changes, even as the rest of the universe moves on without you. *Your* time grows out of sync with your friends here on Earth. Thousands of years pass and it seems but a moment to you. Of course, you would likely have been crushed by the gravitational force of the black hole before then, and smooshed into a tiny point of matter. But assuming you were alive, time would have grown endless and enormous, and all of your friends on earth would be dead."

Ms. Cavanaugh went on in a similar vein, eventually moving the discussion to the question of how black holes formed, but Edie soon lost interest. She was struck by the idea that a black hole could trap time, but that still did not help with the notion of choice. How could time be a choice? You couldn't change time yourself unless you had your own black hole....

Edie suddenly straightened up in her chair. Everything made sense. She couldn't wait to tell Meg all about her theory after class. Of course, it might require some detective work and a brief visit to the Garbers' house to fill in the details, but Edie knew instinctively that Meg would be on board with her plan.

5

this will go down on their permanent records

"Edie, you want to break into the Garbers' house?" asked Meg. "Even I'm not crazy enough to do that." They moved quickly, stepping lightly from driveway to driveway, with Meg struggling to catch up as Edie surged ahead. Meg seemed amused to be playing the role of the worrier for a change.

"No," corrected Edie, avoiding a large crevasse in the pavement with a jump. "I don't want to break into the Garbers' house." She paused, looked around to make sure no one was listening, and then turned back to Meg. "Okay, I *do* want to break into the Garbers' house, but we're not going to do that. At least not quite yet." After taking three more steps she stopped again, looked at Meg, and smiled. "And anyway, you are most certainly crazy enough to do that."

By this point the girls had nearly reached the Garbers' house itself. It was still empty, but the police sentries were gone, and no authority figures of any kind were visible anywhere on the property. Edie circled the house from one direction, walked through the neighbor's yard, crawled over a vine-covered fence, and suddenly found herself in the Garbers' backyard. A moment later Meg joined her from the other side, having slid between the broken slats of the fence.

"This is incredibly stupid." Meg shook her head and then laughed under her breath. "I can't believe I wasn't the one to think of this."

Edie didn't reply this time but instead began walking towards the house. Meg rolled her eyes and followed close behind, still stepping quietly. As they approached the door, she put her arm in front of Edie.

"Don't touch the door handle with your hands," said Meg. "You'll leave fingerprints. Use your shirt."

Edie smiled. "You are devious, aren't you?"

"That's why you like me." She motioned towards the door.

Edie put her hand under her shirt, grabbed the handle of the sliding glass door, and pulled. Astoundingly, it opened.

"The police must have forgotten to lock the place up," she said, amazed.

"Not too bright."

They stepped cautiously inside. Natural light flooded the house, but an unmistakably creepy feeling began to consume them as they started to walk around.

"What happened to not breaking into the Garber's house?" asked Meg under her breath.

"I changed my mind."

"Let's look upstairs first. We'll do the basement last."

They skulked around the living room, which was still filled with the bric-a-brac of the Garbers' travels, and headed towards the stairs. As their legs slowly took them upstairs, they found themselves surrounded on every wall by family photos. Edie saw pictures of Jared and Josie at every age, growing older as they climbed the stairs. The Garbers all watched silently from their frames, frozen in time, as Meg and Edie strode towards the second floor.

Once upstairs, they paused on the rust-colored shag carpeting, then split up. Edie went towards the master bedroom, while Meg crept into the twins' adjoining rooms.

When Edie stepped into Larry and Lindsey Garbers' bedroom, she was immediately struck by the large, sliding glass door overlooking a small deck and the backyard. The shades were open, and it seemed to her like an acre of glass. Drawn to the window like a metal shaving to a magnet, she soon found herself looking into the neighboring backyard.

It took only a moment for her to scream, and only a moment longer for Meg to appear at her side.

"Meg," said Edie, pointing wildly at the neighbor's yard, her voice strangled with amazement. "Do you see that?"

A man stood next to something that looked like a weapon from a very old science-fiction movie. The device was gunmetal blue and shaped like a long, thick French bread perched on top of a tripod. The apparatus would not have been visible to passersby, as it sat in a deep hole in a fenced-in yard. It could only be seen from that particular window in the Garbers' house.

The hole itself appeared to be about ten feet deep, with a narrow ladder embedded on one of the sides. Moreover, the compartment inside seemed to have a retractable cover, and internal supports covered with metal shelves. A man scurried around the edges of the machine, turning cranks and pushing buttons, occasionally looking down at an instrument he held in his left hand.

Suddenly, with the painful inevitability of a piece of toast falling jam-side down, he looked up and locked eyes with Edie and Meg. Breaking into the Garbers' house no longer seemed like such a good idea, thought Edie. They stared at this strange man like startled squirrels confronted by a dog. They froze as though rooted to the spot.

The man appeared to be in his mid-twenties, but in an oddly ageless way. He sported a shaved head and a mustache that curled around the corners of his mouth. He wore a tool belt filled with unidentifiable electronic devices, many of them aglow even in late afternoon daylight. The belt was laden with so many of these appliances, it hung below his hips. He looked as though he rarely smiled. As he gazed at the girls, his expression was difficult to interpret, although Edie later wondered if it wasn't a look of triumph, the man's eyes dark pools of malice.

The man moved first. He quickly reached around the contraption while swiveling the machine towards the Garber house in a single smooth motion. Before the girls could duck, run, or do anything more substantive than stare dumbly at this bizarre man standing in a hole, a bright orange light erupted from the end of the machine. Immediately the girls each felt as though a hook had been placed inside their ribcage. Edie reached out instinctively and found Meg's hand just as the hook pulled them bodily from the Garbers' house. They fell into what felt like a tunnel, spinning and twisting like a corkscrew rollercoaster, but without the benefit of a car, or a track, or any sense that it was all going to be okay.

Edie screamed, sucked into a black vortex, but she could not tell whether she was actually making any noise. She did not, could not, *would not* open her eyes. She had no sense of whether or not Meg was nearby, though she felt as though she was still holding her friend's hand. In fact, Edie was unsure whether she was alive or dead, as her spiraling fall continued for what seemed like minutes, then hours, then days. Instinctively she knew that it could not possibly have been very long, but the experience seemed endless, and she had no reference point for comparison. Just then she remembered that she was wearing a watch.

Carefully, and with some trepidation, she lifted her wrist, opened her eyes, and saw—nothing. Everything around her was black, as black as she had ever experienced. While she continued to feel as though she was falling, she could see nothing, not even herself. Realizing that the watch idea was going nowhere, she looked around for Meg.

"Meg!" she called out, but no sound came out of her mouth.

Then, without warning, Edie was standing on the ground, in a room. The ground was solid. She was, it appeared, still in the Garbers' house. Yet she hesitated to use the word "still," because something was quite different, something she could not immediately put her finger on.

She saw Meg standing next to her, looking equally puzzled and anxious and still clutching Edie's hand. They each dropped their hands to their sides, and turned to stare out the window. They saw the neighbor's house, which looked nearly the same. The only difference was that the hole in the backyard was gone, filled in and covered with grass, as though it had never existed.

They slowly spun around, still silent, and gazed about the room. All the old furniture was gone. In its place were strangely shaped pieces, formed as though metal had been twisted like fabric to construct a bedroom set. The bed, in fact, reminded Edie of a frozen ocean wave. The walls were painted in extreme, contrasting colors, such as burnt umber and turquoise, covered with what looked to be tiny lights in a grid pattern from the floor to the ceiling. The carpet had changed, too. No longer was it a rust-colored shag under their feet; now it was a taupe, textured surface with metallic highlights that looked almost liquid. Edie felt as though she might be able to swim across the floor.

"Let's get out of here," said Meg, breaking the silence. "Something is totally wrong."

Edie nodded and they crept out of the room. The house was hushed, and it appeared that no one was home. They slunk down the stairs and noticed that while the stair-well walls were still covered with pictures, the photos were now of another family. Even stranger, the pictures were no longer in frames but seemed to be animated directly into the walls and filled with miniature living bodies. When the girls had passed a spot on the wall, the pictures froze back into permanent smiles, but in what appeared to be three dimensions. There was no trace of the Garbers.

They reached the back door and Edie was surprised to see that it had been replaced with a hinged entry that seemed to float in the doorframe. The remains of the wall had somehow been transformed into floor-to-ceiling windows without any apparent structural support. Edie reached under her shirt, grabbed the handle with the fabric, and opened the door as quickly as she dared.

They ran like a shot out of what was clearly no longer the Garbers' house, sprinting as fast as they could towards the vine-covered fence. They each vaulted it cleanly without a pause and ran towards the sidewalk at top speed.

It took only a moment to realize that the neighborhood surrounding them was not the one they had left. The cars on the street were cartoonish, sleek models they had never seen before, in colors that seemed to change with each glance. Several of the houses on the block had been torn down and replaced with much larger, oddly shaped structures with glass exoskeletons. Children playing across the street were dressed in unfamiliar styles, in clothes made of strange fabrics in unnatural, metallic hues. One little girl wore a hat that spooled holographic video images of dancing ballerinas in a circle around her head. Her dress was neon yellow, emitting light as though filled with fluorescent bulbs. Another girl jumped a rope that turned on its own, without assistance. She was dressed in a gold lamé jumpsuit with a picture of a pink pony on the back. The pony looked at Edie and smiled. When Edie continued to stare, the pony added a knowing wink.

"Meg." Edie slowly turned to her. "I think I know what happened to the Garbers."

Meg almost started to laugh. "Ya think?"

"I also think we have a problem." She began to walk in circles as she gazed, aghast, at her new surroundings. Finally she stopped, and something clicked inside her. "What year do you think this is?"

"I was going to ask you the same thing," said Meg, a small rasp of fear in her voice. "But I have no idea."

They began to walk down the street, agape with every step at the new sights they saw in unexpected places. Even the trees appeared to have changed, with bizarre, glowing plants curling around their trunks in geometric filigrees. After about 100 yards, however, Meg suddenly grabbed Edie and yanked her behind a large, prickly shrub. "We'd better stay out of sight," she said. "We're going to stick out like sore thumbs around here."

Edie looked down at her clothes and silently agreed. Until they figured out what was going on, they had to assume that they were in danger and act accordingly.

Meg peered over the branches. The kids across the street hadn't noticed them yet. "Let's cut through the forest to my house," she said, and then frowned. "Assuming I still live there."

Two doors down from the Garbers was a small tongue of trees that led into a forest preserve. Despite the fact that adults regularly forbade their children from using the pre-serve as a shortcut between neighborhoods ("Who knows what kind of person hides in a forest these days," noted Aunt Judy on more than one occasion) nearly everyone used it, as it saved at least ten minutes by foot.

With that in mind, the two girls ran from their hiding place over to the trees, which were still there, though now significantly bigger. They turned right as they reached the well-worn path into the forest, hoping no one had seen them. Once they entered the canopy of trees, they finally slowed down. After looking around to confirm that they were alone, Edie burst out with a question.

"Do our families think we're dead?" Her voice was too loud, as though a cork had popped from a bottle of cham-pagne. Breathing hard, she looked over at Meg. "I mean, maybe we are dead. Are we still alive? Where are we?"

"I don't think we're dead," said Meg, also gasping. "At least I don't feel dead. But if we disappeared years ago, without any reason, and they never found a body—and why would they, we're still alive—they probably think we died." She looked down at the ground. "I hope everyone we know still lives here. I mean, who knows how long we've been gone...." There was a catch in her voice, and she sounded like she was about to cry.

"Oh god," whimpered Edie, and as if on cue she did begin to sob, shoulders heaving. "This is just like second grade, except this time we really were gone. *Are* gone. Oh god." They parked themselves on a rock and a log, respec-tively, and stared at each other, tears rolling down their faces, eyes slowly turning red and puffy. Edie wanted to get up and hug Meg, but she was too afraid to move.

"Who was that guy next door?" asked Meg finally, wip-ing her eyes on her sleeve. "We've got to figure that out. It's the only way we'll get back."

"How do you even know we *can* get back?" Edie began kicking the ground with her heel, trying to regain control of her emotions, nauseous with fear. "We don't know what year it is, or what even happened to us."

They sat in silence for a few more moments. Then abruptly Meg straightened up and announced, "Well, there's only one way to find out what's going on. Let's go to my house and see if anyone's home. We're almost there, after all. We'll get a plan and beat this, whatever it is." She stood, wiped her face again, and began walking along the trail, not even waiting for Edie. Edie gathered herself for a moment more, and then followed her down the path.

She was glad to see that Meg had regained her sense of focus, as she was certainly not feeling it herself. After picking up her pace, she was finally able to catch up with Meg, who was staring straight ahead, and she soon found herself striding alongside her. Edie had to admit to herself that even the briefest outline of a plan made her feel better. They were moving towards something, and that had to be better than sitting in one place.

After a few quiet minutes, Edie grabbed a stick and started lightly hitting the trees as she passed, making a rhythm with her steps. It appeared to be sometime in late spring or early summer, as every tree was almost iridescent green, life exploding across the forest floor into this oasis of unrestrained nature. She wondered if these plants were even the same ones she remembered from only a few hours before, or if new ones had taken root since their departure.

Finally, after what seemed to be far longer than she had ever remembered, they reached the clearing that opened onto Meg's backyard. Edie was relieved to see that the backyard looked remarkably similar to her own recollection, with the exception of some new lawn furniture. Perhaps, she thought, this wouldn't be quite as much of a shock as she had feared. Upon closer inspection, however, she realized that the chaises were glowing, as were some new, elaborately geometric shrubs.

Before they lost their courage, they marched up along the side of the house and around to the front door.

"You ready for this?" asked Edie.

"No," said Meg, trying to smile. "Not even slightly."

Nervously, Meg knocked on the door, which appeared to be unchanged, except for a new brass knocker. After a moment, the girls heard some rustling noises behind the door.

"Who is it?" someone asked from deep inside the house. When the door finally swung open, Edie was surprised to be looking at Meg's older sister, Sally, who now appeared to be in her early forties, decades older than she had been a few minutes before. But the girls were not nearly as surprised as Sally, who, upon seeing the girls, promptly collapsed to the floor in shock.

"Oh my god, Edie, help me get her up." Meg rushed into the doorway and began sliding her sister into the living room. Edie grabbed a shoulder and helped pull Sally's limp figure into a chair.

At about that moment Sally opened her eyes, which quickly grew as big as saucers. "It can't... I mean, you're no older...I can't...you're dead...."

"Sally," Meg asked, grabbing her shoulder and shaking her slightly. "When did I disappear?"

Hearing Meg's voice, Sally seemed to snap out of her reverie. "Twenty-five years ago, something like that."

"Where're Mom and Dad?"

"They live in an apartment near the university. Jim and I live here now, with our kids, oh my god...." Sally trailed off for a few moments, and then her panicked look returned. "Where have you been? Why are you still fourteen?"

"Sally," interrupted Meg softly. "We know what happened to the Garbers."

Sally looked as though she had been sucker-punched. Edie watched all of the traumas of Sally's childhood come roaring back in a cascade of pained expressions. Without warning, Sally abruptly grabbed Meg and began hugging her, crying. "I thought you were dead, oh my god, where have you been! We've got to call Mom and Dad...."

As Edie watched them hug, she began to grow uncomfortable and concerned about her own life, and whether any of it was still the same.

"Sally," asked Edie, "do you know if my aunt and uncle are still in town?"

Sally looked up, realizing for the first time, apparently, that Edie was there.

"Um...," began Sally. "Hi, Edie, I can't believe—! Well, yes—I mean, sort of. It's a long story...."

"Edie," Meg interrupted, as though suddenly worried about what Sally might say. "We probably don't want to talk to too many people. I mean, we probably shouldn't talk to our parents either." She didn't look pleased to be saying this, and it sounded more than a little like an excuse, but then her face grew more determined. When later questioned by Edie she unable to explain why, but Meg *knew* that it was important that Edie stay away from her family. "It could mess everything up more. We're not supposed to be here, in this time, remember?"

"We found Sally," said Edie, sounding hurt.

"I know, and I'm not even sure we should have done that. But we need someone," said Meg in a voice that Edie thought was supposed to sound comforting, but instead sounded forced. "We needed to talk to someone, but I don't think we should do more than we have to right now. We could get in serious trouble."

"How could things get any more serious than this?" She pointed at the strange gizmos that covered nearly every table. "Look where we are!"

Finally Sally interrupted. "So," she said, still visibly trying to compose herself. "What happened to you, and what happened to the Garbers?"

part two

separation

6

jared garber's
awful secret

When Jared Garber finally regained his balance and opened his eyes, he found himself standing in a field he had never seen before. Colorful wildflowers and green prairie grass waved cheerfully in the wind, fanning around him in a dancing circle. He could see a few buildings sitting low on the horizon, like mushrooms in the distance, but nothing distinct or recognizable. No people were nearby, and his neighborhood was nowhere to be seen. His sister, Josie, and his parents were gone. Jared was alone.

A feeling of overwhelming confusion quickly settled over him. He sat down, almost dizzy, crushing some long, purple flowers in the process. He put his head in his hands, held his eyes tightly together, and tried to make sense of what had just happened, as he slowly rocked back and forth.

He had been sitting at dinner, at the table in the kitchen. A wall of windows had reflected his family's faces against the early evening sky. His parents were there, laughing as they spooned gravy over potatoes, or took another piece of casserole. His father was, for once, having a good time—no snide remarks about whether Jared was a slacker, or uncomfortable comparisons between the twins. Instead, he and his father had teamed up and were teasing Josie together, joking that she actually ran the school. The teachers, according to Jared, feared her as much as the other kids did, which amused his parents to no end.

"Do they have you check everyone's grade reports before they send them out?" asked Larry Garber, laughing. "We need to get you a union card." Jared had long forgotten about the man made of code next door, and was enjoying the novel sensation of having fun with his family.

Josie had been in mid eye-roll, opening her mouth to shoot back a barbed comment, when the kitchen was flooded with a blinding orange light. An intense pressure sucked the wind out of his lungs, and Jared spiraled through what had felt like a whirlpool of sensation as he was pulled under a blanket of darkness. He could make no sound and could see no images as he was snatched away from the dinner table. After what seemed like an endless black journey, he finally landed hard on the ground in the middle of this field, in the bright sunshine of early morning.

None of it made any sense. What had happened to him, and why? Where was his family? Then he remembered the man made of code, and being pulled away from a neighbor's house by his frantic, worried twin earlier that afternoon.

It had not been the first time Jared had seen code in the world around him, and that knowledge only magnified his fear as he sat sprawled in that unfamiliar prairie. In fact, things had begun to change for him nearly four years earlier on a similar spring day, when the world was revealed to him in a new and startling way. He knew, with painful certainty, that his current predicament could be traced to the events of that day. He just wasn't sure how or why.

• • •

Jared had sat quietly in his fifth-grade math class, try-ing without success to focus on polygons. Then as now an earnest boy with shaggy black hair and green eyes, he enjoyed math but found shapes and geometry to be incred-ibly dull. "When am I going to need to know how to figure out the volume of a cube?" he had asked his father the pre-vious week. "It's not like cubes are just lying around on the lawn waiting to get measured. It's a total waste of time."

Mr. Garber had sighed and put down his magazine, slapping it on his knee as he leaned forward. "Don't worry," he said, a hint of contempt in his voice. "There comes a moment in everyone's life when a thing they learned in school becomes useful. Trust me."

Despite his general annoyance with the subject of poly-gons, Jared didn't want to disappoint his father. So each day that year, he struggled to maintain his focus in class. He studied the circumference of circles, turned trapezoids into a series of triangles, and stacked rhombuses on top of squares. He tried to transform the age-darkened maps on the classroom walls into origami swans in his mind. He built equilateral teepees out of his folders, and little houses out of pencil fragments.

Nevertheless, something about geometric forms made him intensely sleepy, and he often found himself imagin-ing fantastic, futuristic worlds when he should have been thinking about parallelograms. In his head he spooled movies where heroes fought timeless battles against evil empires, instead of solving problem sets with the rest of the class. He saw fields of war where luminous weapons protected the innocent, and a brave soul could earn a living by courage alone. But each day his teacher's voice would eventually cut through these daydreams and return him reluctantly to class.

On that day, however, something was profoundly different. As his math teacher droned on about dodecahedrons, and his eyelids began to droop with boredom, he noticed something unusual, something that caused him to bolt upright with surprise.

When he stared straight ahead, a variety of symbols and coded images seemed to flitter like a swarm of bees around the blonde girl who sat in front of him. These shapes glittered under the dull lights of the classroom, a cloud of stars bursting from his classmate, a special effect happening less than three feet in front of him.

He had barely noticed the girl before and could not recall having spoken more than a few sentences to her all year. Now, however, he was rapt with attention as phantom images cascaded underneath the girl's skin like insects caught in a jar, as though she were both transparent and hollow. Just as strangely, he found that if he focused carefully on the girl's clothes, he could see other odd images and characters floating above the straps on her top, woven into the fabric like thread. These puzzle shapes moved with balletic grace along the curve of her shoulder, as though typed into her body. But when he shook his head the symbols were gone. Disturbed, he tried to think about polygons for the rest of the class, but instead spent the remainder of the period staring at the girl, waiting for the symbols to reappear.

They never did.

Yet after that first incident, Jared began to notice these symbols and geometric shapes in a variety of other unexpected places. An ice cream store was suddenly filled with data-intensive flavors, churning silently within the scoops. He saw spinning cubes and icosahedrons embedded in his steak, pooling in the sauce like a rope. The music that blared out of his computer etched sound waves into the air like a stylus on a clay tablet. The symbols were everywhere, it seemed, if you only knew where to look.

A few months later, when Jared was arguing with his parents, the images began to speak to him directly. That parental browbeating had been a fairly typical one, and as usual it took every bit of his self-control not to run from the room.

"Why can't you try harder in school?" asked his father, a humorless-looking man with salt-and-pepper hair and a piercing stare. "I simply don't understand it. You're a smart boy." He peered over his reading glasses, examining him like a slide under a microscope. It always made Jared feel small.

"You always get good scores on those tests," said his mother. "We know that you're bright, and the books you read..."

"Yes, Jared, the books you read." Mr. Garber was just getting started, and Jared knew that any interruption would only extend the torment. Thus he remained as quiet as possible, hoping his father would simply exhaust himself. Mr. Garber took off his glasses and began waving them for effect as he continued. "Of course, I do like the fact that you read books. I like books, your mother likes books."

"Yes," said Mrs. Garber, nodding vigorously. "I like books a lot."

Jared tried not to laugh, and dug his nails into his arm to keep silent. He appreciated that she was trying to placate his father, but he knew what was coming next.

"Your sister, Josie, even she likes books," said his father. "When she isn't bouncing a ball, at least. But you like books in a way that is too much of a good thing. You need to realize that there are only so many hours in a day. You can't waste time with things that don't help you get ahead in life. Everything in moderation. You need to turn over a new leaf. From brown to green, that leaf needs to change color. You cannot expect to get by simply because you're clever, that isn't enough anymore. You need to work. College will come sooner than you think. You need to work hard. Do you think I got where I am without working hard? I started work when I was ten years old, worked two jobs to get through high school. You need to get ready for what's coming. You're soft. You're not ready."

"But I'm in fifth grade," protested Jared, no longer able to contain his frustration. "I'm not going to college anytime soon. I'm still a kid, and..."

"What your father is trying to say," interrupted Jared's mother, a warm and pretty blond woman with bangs, "is that you need to realize that school is important. Not just books you read on your own."

"Yes, while reading is good, other things in your life require your attention," said Mr. Garber, a tone of conclusion seeping into his voice. "You need to focus on your priorities. Staring out the window is *not* one of your priorities. Reading books about things that don't matter is not one of your priorities. Your number-one priority is school. Everything else is secondary. Do you understand?"

Jared barely heard the last half of this parental duet. Because while his father tried to bully him into doing better at school, and his mother tried to prevent an argument from spiraling into something more painful, Jared saw a waterspout of vibrant, indigo images pour out of his father's mouth. Every word was accompanied by ripples of digital information, like a magic incantation. He became aware that his parents's words had a physical substance he had never seen before. His father, who cared for Jared so deeply but could never express himself except in demands, suddenly looked transparent. Now

Jared could see his father's emotions float like equations in his chest, and his feelings cascaded in symbols that he could almost read. He looked at his mother, who loved him and his sister so much that it made him uncomfortable when she hugged them in public, only to find that he could see through her skull. He watched, horrified, as her brain processed numbers and icons like a calculator, synapses firing bullets of logic through channels carved into her mind like riverbeds on a relief map. He nodded dumbly at every pause in the conversation, and quickly agreed to whatever his parents asked him to accomplish that night. He ran upstairs to his room and spent the remainder of the evening staring at a wall, anxious to scrub these images from his mind.

The visions persisted over months and then years, coming and going with little rhyme or reason. After a while, he worried that he was losing his mind. He scoured books in the library and the computers at school for information, hoping to discover the source of these strange experiences. He furtively snatched strange medical textbooks off high shelves in hidden corners of the university library. He poked and prodded computer networks for any available insight into his predicament. But after several months of concerted effort, he could find nothing that might explain what was happening to him. Worried about what others might say, he never said a word to anyone, and the visions became his own terrible secret.

By the time he reached ninth grade, Jared had given up his search and had largely stopped trying to understand his odd visions. The fact that he occasionally saw shapes and codes where others saw skin or fabric was, apparently, just one of those mysteries of life that resisted explanation. Perhaps others saw similar things. Or so he tried to convince himself at night as he fell asleep, seeing points of illumination and pixilated geometry in the ceiling of his room.

In the end, he supposed, these strange visions had no real impact on his life, so he learned to ignore them, even as he wondered whether some deep explanation was lurking out there, just beyond his reach.

• • •

But lying in a strange field, almost four years to the day after Jared had first seen those mysterious images, he realized that he had made a terrible decision. He had never warned anyone, never told his parents about what he saw. Now everything was gone, and it was entirely his fault.

After staring at his hands for a long time, however, he concluded that nothing was going to be accomplished by sitting around feeling sorry for himself. He had to get home, had to find his family. He pushed the panic down inside his chest, stood up, dusted off his jeans, and began walking towards the buildings in the distance. As he moved closer, pushing tall grass aside with his arms like a machete, he discovered that the buildings were a concentrated outcropping, constructed closely together. No other buildings were visible.

From the position of the sun in the sky, Jared had already guessed that it was still quite early in the morning. The sky was free of any aircraft contrails, and he heard no sounds from cars or tractors in the distance. He could not recall ever seeing anyplace this devoid of any activity.

After trekking for nearly a mile across the prairie, he finally emerged from the field into what appeared to be a bricked arcade, with small shops on either side of a narrow alleyway. The signs in the windows looked vaguely like English characters, but used various pictograms and unusual accent marks rather than words. None of the signs were even remotely readable, and his four years of Spanish did nothing to assist him. From the look of the windows, the shops were closed. No one else was out or about at this time of day.

The town did not appear to be in Kansas. In fact, the town did not appear to be anywhere in a world that Jared could recognize. He peered inside the shop windows and quickly found what might be a grocery. But none of the other stores sold items he could readily identify or even guess at. The products looked both incomprehensible and oddly futuristic. In one shop he saw glowing metal needles wrapped with moving orange and metallic webbing, placed carefully in velvet showcase boxes. The stores themselves seemed almost quaint, like they were selling antiques.

The streets were clearly intended to be a pedestrian mall and were covered in well-worn bricks. The entryways of the buildings were carved wood, as Jared had seen on a trip to London with his parents two years before. Each store appeared to have a second floor, perhaps with an apartment inside. He imagined that the storekeepers each lived above their shop. However, despite the charm of the neighborhood, it seemed oddly depressing, as if the town was merely pretending to be quaint but actually hid sweat-shops behind the façades.

Throughout all of this, Jared found himself too per-plexed to panic. Yet the frantic questions about his family, and where they were, and how he could possibly find them or get back to the home where he belonged, still bubbled just below the surface. Was Josie hurt, or worse? What about his parents? Maybe all of them were still back at the house, hoping he was alive. Inexplicably, he even thought of Sally, the pretty girl from his history class, and won-dered if he would ever get a chance to ask her out on a date. His stomach tightened at the thought that his old life was gone.

He continued walking through the arcade of stores, glancing back and forth as though at any moment things might suddenly make sense. He felt certain that he could close his eyes and reawaken back in his home. Disappointingly, when he tried it, he merely walked into a lamp post. Rubbing his forehead, he continued on.

Soon, without even realizing it, he had reached the end of the street. Instead of emptying out into a much larger street, as he had expected, the avenue opened up into what appeared to be a small campus. Having grown up in a college town, he recognized the format: a quad surrounded by academic buildings and (he presumed) dormitories for students. But as he got closer he realized that the buildings were smaller than he had first suspected. Hardly any of them had windows, and most were made of a colorless, grey concrete substance. On the right as he approached the quad was a small podium with what appeared to be a map embossed on the top. He ran over and looked down on what looked like a topographical view of the area. With all of the strange letters and words used on the map key, it took him a few moments to realize that the map pictured a town, in fact showed the very town he was standing in. He saw the small arcade, the few groups of buildings, and very little else. Apparently there was not much to see in the area.

He began looking towards the outer areas of the map, trying to gain his bearings more generally. He saw only one road into town, and no highways in the region. Evidently this place was isolated. Near the top of the map, however, he saw a small river branch off from another in a manner that felt familiar. He followed the curve of that river across an expanse of flat land, watching it turn in a number of expected ways, until he realized, slowly and with growing horror, that the town pictured in the map was his own. He was, indeed, still in Kansas after all. But it was a very different Kansas, in a very different world. By the time he finally ripped himself away from the map, tears were dripping from his face onto the podium, and Jared had never felt so completely alone.

7

a history of the future

Edie thought that Sally was taking their reappearance fairly well. After all, Edie was not sure how she would have reacted if someone she'd known to be dead for twenty-five years had suddenly turned up on her doorstep without having aged a day. Sally, however, seemed both fascinated and accepting. Or perhaps she was too shocked to be anything other than polite.

Sally listened, rapt, while Meg described how they had been sent twenty-five years into the future. Having lived the story herself, Edie was not particularly interested, and found herself only half-listening. When they started discussing Meg's funeral ("You can't even believe how many people were there," said Sally), Edie abruptly stood up and began to walk around the living room. She had no interest in hearing about their deaths, and Sally and Meg were oblivious as she examined the pictures on the walls, trying to keep her own terror at bay.

The pictures, or rather the wall coverings that seemed to incorporate images, showed Sally and her husband at various points in time. As children, as young adults, and as parents, Sally and her husband filled the images.

Many of the pictures, however, were not static. Some of the more recent ones were short videos, while earlier ones comprised cascading slideshows. Sally as a young girl, as a teenager, as a college student, moving inexorably in slow motion towards adulthood in three-dimensional clarity. Mixed among the pictures were some group shots of Sally's family, including some pictures of Meg from an earlier time. Edie found the pictures almost unbearably sad. As she stared at a photo of Sally and Meg playing as young children, the conversation between the sisters behind her became louder, and she returned to the couch to listen.

"The person you need to tell is Jim. This is *so* up his alley."

"Who's Jim?" asked Meg. "Wait, you mean your husband? I can't believe you have a *husband*."

Sally smiled. "Hey, I can barely believe it myself sometimes." She looked a bit misty as she leaned back in her chair. "I still feel like a teenager, you know, and I've never stopped feeling like a teenager, even with all the years... even with a husband...." She laughed under her breath, then looked briefly serious. "Maybe I'm the one stuck in a time warp."

Edie walked towards them, a bit impatient to get back to the story. "So why should we talk with Jim?"

"He teaches physics up at the college," replied Sally, a note of pride unmistakable in her voice. "His research is on all sorts of stuff with multiple dimensions and things like that. He and Kathrine—you remember Kathrine, right Edie?—just published a paper on this type of thing. Wait, I've got it over here." She popped up and began rummaging through piles of clutter on a credenza.

Edie thought back to shy Kathrine, one of her "ladies in waiting" twenty-five years before, who was now apparently some sort of science genius. In some ways that fact sharpened Edie's feeling of dislocation as much as anything else that had happened that day. Her friend, so scared of the world, was now writing papers on weird, complex physics. Of course, Kathrine had always wanted to be a scientist, but still.

"Here it is." Sally strolled back to the couch with what looked like a piece of translucent paper. "Jim is so old-fashioned, he loves having this stuff on e-paper, if you can believe it." She shook her head with exasperation. "It's called, get this, *Conditional Aspects of Time in 11-Dimensional M-Theory.* God, how Kathrine and Jim can understand things at that level amazes me. I studied stochastic calculus in college and even I can't follow this stuff to save my life...."

Edie didn't even bother to ask Sally what "stochastic calculus" might be, or why Sally had studied it, or why it was so strange for Jim to want things printed on something called e-paper. Instead Edie snagged the document, eyebrow raised. She began leafing through it, turning back and forth between the introduction and various places in the document. The paper was interactive, with moving charts and graphs. Small drawings of gnarled atomic structures spun lazily in place as words underlined themselves to indicate a point of emphasis.

Apparently, from what little she could understand of the introduction, the known universe actually had eleven dimensions, rather than three. Vibrating membranes and strings smaller than the tiniest subatomic particle created all matter. Time itself was a separate dimension with independent sub-dimensions and topology, and...suddenly the page was filled with equations. Edie looked at them, stared at them, but could not even figure out what they were, or how they worked. One of the equations looked like this:

$$|x>=\sum_v e^{ixp}|p>$$

She was amazed that Kathrine could have written a paper filled with such strange, complicated math. Edie had always liked math, but had never seen or imagined anything like this. She was simultaneously mystified and impressed. She desperately hoped that she would get the opportunity to talk to Kathrine again—either the one she remembered or the adult of today.

"Well." Edie smiled uncertainly. "I suspect we've come to the right place. When is Jim coming home?"

• • •

Sally's kids were nine and ten, respectively. From the photographs on the wall, Edie could tell that the kids each looked like one of their parents, with the girl a spitting image of Sally. The children disappeared up to their rooms when they came home from school and did not even question Sally about the sudden presence of two teenagers in their living room. Edie thought she might have done the same thing in their shoes. After all, most kids avoided hanging out with their parents unless it was absolutely necessary. In other words, she thought with a smile, unless food or money was involved.

But then again, she mused, having parents to be embarrassed by would have been nice, too, and that was something she had lacked for many years. Now she didn't even have her aunt or uncle. She shivered and shook off that thought, which was close to bringing her to tears once more, and turned back to Sally. Sally had continued to recover from her initial surprise at their reappearance and was now telling her own stories of the past quarter-century in more detail.

But she rarely got more than a few words out without interruption, as Edie and Meg peppered her with questions about the world of this future and what it was like. The past twenty-five years had been enormously eventful, it seemed, and it was difficult for them to internalize the changes. Even the small things Sally described seemed odd and out of place. Actually, Edie thought, it was especially the small things.

Now there were no traditional televisions. Instead, according to Sally, you either watched three-dimensional projections in the middle of your floor, or plugged your mind directly into a computer network. Apparently this latter form of communication, called "cronking," took place through a strange-looking metallic headset. As you wore it, you experienced entertainment from an infinite number of perspectives inside your brain. Reality shows were watched through the eyes of the characters themselves. A football game could be seen through the coach's eyes, with edited thoughts, of course, or through the point of view of the quarterback, or the ball, or any variation imaginable. A soap opera villain could be accessed one moment after the hero. You were inside every character, seeing the action as though magically implanted into their minds. Thought actors, known as "POVs," had become highly sought—people who could mold their thoughts in a way that others could easily access and understand.

Through cronking, you could now feel the sensations of skydiving, or the tension of a war, without ever leaving your chair. Every stimulation imaginable was instantly available, but instead of looking at a screen it was all inside of you. You were every protagonist, every villain, every hero. Or, if you preferred, the characters would stand next to you as though they were your houseguests.

Students never looked up words in a dictionary; the answer would simply be pulled towards their minds as they interfaced with endless computer networks that spanned the globe and arched into space. The world was a single computer, with even the tiniest things tied together into a seamless whole. Rarely did people type. Instead they simply thought themselves into physical places on the network, which was no longer a string of web pages but a series of actual places you could visit without leaving your chair. While on that page, a being that looked like you—or looked nothing like you, if you so desired—would be visible to others. This was your avatar, controlled with your thoughts, a being that had an independent life on the web. It was, as Sally explained, another you.

Some things were still read on e-paper ("especially by folks like Jim who can't let go of the past," said Sally), yet most information was kept in swirling clouds of electrons in quantum computing networks which held the sum total of all knowledge in a spider web of electronic networks and wires and pipes and radiowaves bouncing over the globe.

Even music had changed. Sally said, "When you're cronked in you just think it and you can start composing music in your mind, with instruments and everything! Of course," she added, "we won't even get into the body modification stuff. That's too weird even for me."

Just then, Jim arrived home. He was carrying an oblong metal briefcase, and he looked both professorial and friendly in the modern version of a tweed jacket, which incorporated glowing, patterned elbow patches. He was a good-looking man, with dark hair and the beginnings of grey on his temples. He noticed Edie and Meg almost immediately and stopped in his tracks. He stared at Meg for several moments, and then looked over at Sally.

"Is this who...?"

"Yes," answered Sally in a strangely calm voice. "It is. It's a long story. And they need your help."

"But they're...?"

"Yes," she answered again patiently, with a sly smile. "Things are about to change. That research of yours just got a bit more practical."

• • •

They all sat and stared at each other for a while as Jim tried to think of something to say. The silence grew uncomfortable. Finally, Sally broke in, exasperated. "Well, Jim, here's the story: contrary to everything I've always believed, Meg and her friend Edie were not, in fact, killed by a drifter and then buried in some anonymous roadside grave. Everything I ever told you about the most traumatic thing that ever happened to me, and the most horrible thing to ever happen in this town, is apparently untrue. They were not kidnapped. They did not disappear. Well, okay, they did disappear. Someone shot them with some kind of time ray and transported them twenty-five years into the future." She took a deep breath before continuing. "Apparently something similar happened to the Garber family, the family I told you disappeared at about the same time. We need to figure out what we're going to do about it and get them back to where they belong. That way I don't have to live the past twenty-five years without my sister." She grinned dreamily at the thought.

"Um," said Jim, still flabbergasted. "You realize what you're saying, right?"

"Yes, Jim." She was now clearly growing a bit annoyed, putting an aggressive emphasis on the word *yes*. "This girl is my sister, and we need to get things right some-how. And *yes*, I understand that this makes absolutely no sense whatsoever." She was now standing, her hands on her waist in the timeless stance of feminine displeasure.

He stared anxiously at her for a moment, and then shook his head with some newfound amusement as he turned back to the girls. "Well," he said, a laugh now audible in his voice, "we'd better get started before Sally *really* gets mad. Meg, I assume you remember that getting her angry isn't a good idea." He smiled winningly at Meg, who returned the look, and then turned to Edie. "I'm Jim, Sally's husband. Sally thinks I may be able to help you. I'm not so sure about that yet, since what I just heard is utterly impossible and contrary to centuries of accumulated scientific knowledge, but why don't you tell me a bit about what happened."

Meg had already been the one to explain this to Sally, so Edie decided to take a crack at it this time.

"Well, Meg and I were investigating the disappearance of this whole family, the Garbers, who lived in our town. One of the Garber kids, Josie, was Sally's best friend." Edie looked at Sally, who nodded and appeared to be a bit choked up at the thought. "Anyway, we started getting these strange notes, or *I* started getting these strange notes, in my locker, talking all about time. They were clues, it seemed like, so we did some research and it sounded like the Garbers might have fallen into some kind of time trap. Some kind of black hole. It was the only way they could have disappeared like that, we thought, and the clues kept talking about time, and it made sense. So, we went to their house and snuck in and yes," she added, turning to Sally, who was clearly about to say something, "that was incredibly stupid and we're really sorry we did it."

Edie spun back to Jim and continued. "Anyway, we got inside and looked around, and then we went upstairs and looked into the neighbor's yard, and there was a guy with a mustache in the backyard with some kind of ray gun." She paused for dramatic effect. "He saw us, and before we could do anything about it, he shot us and we ended up here. Now it's twenty-five years later and Sally is all grown up and married to you and we're still fourteen." She gasped a bit, breathed deeply, then continued. "So, we think the same thing happened to the Garbers, but we don't know where they are. And we don't know who that guy was or anything. All Meg and I want to do is get back to our own time, I guess. Can you help us?"

During Edie's description of their misadventures in time, Jim had stroked his chin like he half expected a beard to be there. He did not look directly at Edie but instead stared off into the distance, apparently in deep thought. When she finished, he stood and started pacing.

"Sally is right, this *is* the kind of thing that I'm studying. But to be perfectly frank, I don't even know where to start." He began slapping his thigh rhythmically with the back of his hand, as though trying to play a song. "This is all theoretically possible, I guess, if one of the time frameworks Kathrine and I have been discussing is true, but it's one thing to be theoretically possible and another to see someone sitting in your living room who is supposed to be dead."

He continued to pace, knocking his knee into the cocktail table as he slid by Meg and moved into the larger part of the room adjoining the dining room table. "I suppose the first thing we need to do is some research on the folks who lived behind the Garbers back then. If it is who I think it is, this could be complicated. Maybe I should also talk a bit with Kathrine, get her over here to discuss this." He looked up suddenly and turned back to Edie. "We should talk in detail about everything that happened. In particular, I'm curious about these clues. What were they?"

"Notes left in my locker," replied Edie, rummaging around in her jeans. "I actually still have them in my pocket. Take a look."

She handed them to Jim, who looked at one of them, turned it over, held it up to the light, and flexed it between his fingers.

"And this was in your locker?"

"Yup, that and the others, too," interrupted Meg, now too excited to let Edie respond. "We thought that one of our teachers had put them in as part of some class game or something, but she said no, and Edie had made an appointment with Mr. Hall to talk about it, but we got shot before she could see him."

"Girls, if it's okay with you, I'd like to take a closer look at these." Jim grabbed an envelope off of the desk and slid the notes inside. "And I need to start doing a bit of research on all of this."

Sally stood. "How long do you want?"

"Um, I don't know. I'd think an hour or two to start, then I'll have some other questions. Maybe I'll get Kathrine over here, too, as I said. This may take a while. Why do you ask?"

"Well, I don't know about you guys," she drawled, turning to face Edie and Meg. "But I'm hungry. And I want to spend time with my sister, someone I've thought was dead for, like, decades." She walked over to the girls and squeezed Meg's shoulders. "Let's talk about this later. We need to get you girls some normal-looking clothes, and then we can get a bite to eat. Jim, you can feed the kids after they've finished their homework, but you should start your research now. We're going shopping."

8

a trip to the mall

The drive to the mall was objectively quite short, but to Edie it was endless and she quickly lost track of time. The startling things she saw at every turn amazed her and left her mute with wonder. But even before their trip had begun, Edie and Meg had had to deal with Sally's car.

The car, which Edie supposed was the current equivalent of a minivan, had inspired at least 10 minutes of detailed inspection by the girls, neither of whom had ever shown the slightest interest in a car before. It looked like a cross between a jellybean and a racecar. The front end was modeled after an aerodynamic locomotive with a polished cowcatcher for a grill. The paint shimmered blue and green like an iridescent deep-sea fish illuminated from within. Pinstripes on the side were made of moving digital words snaking around the car like an art exhibit Edie had once seen at a museum. The words appeared to spell out a poem, but she was too distracted by the rest of the package to read it.

The tires were made of a soft metallic substance that looked silvery and almost liquid. Meg poked one and it reacted like the mercury in a thermometer. "It's nanofabric," Sally laughed as she watched them examine the tires. "No more flat tires!"

The inside was even more bizarre. In place of a steering wheel, a stick like a pilot would use poked out of the floor. The seats were constructed out of a smooth material that felt like velour, except it seemed to massage your skin when you sat on it. The controls were the graphical user interface of a computer screen, but included a variety of diverse and unfamiliar gauges. One of these readouts described "magnetic confinement" levels, while another gauge described "graphite" in a manner that mimicked a gas gauge. "Fusion Power," read the dashboard, in what apparently passed for an automobile company's idea of fancy handwriting. Edie shook her head, trying to take it all in but almost overwhelmed by the inputs.

After buckling up, Sally pushed a glowing gold button on the dashboard, turned to view a screen showing a dozen views of the back of the car, and the vehicle backed out of the garage, seemingly on its own. The chatter began as soon as they were underway. Meg spouted a rapid-fire series of questions, ranging from details about her parents to details about Sally's wedding. "What's it like," asked Meg mischievously, "to have a husband?" This left Edie to stare out the window and watch the world go by.

The world had certainly changed since she had last driven this route with her own family. In fact, only a few weeks before, she had gone to the mall with her aunt to buy new clothes for the approaching summer. She remembered spending the entire ride trying to convince her tradition-minded guardian not to embarrass her in the underwear store.

But today this familiar street was filled with uncommon sights. Oddly shaped cars zipped around, some trim and fit like razors cutting through the air, others bulbous like balls with wheels. All of them were resplendent in a rainbow of colors she had never imagined before. The crayon box of her youth, she thought, would need to be expanded.

People filled the sidewalks wearing unrecognizable clothes, covered with filigrees and frippery that seemed infused with some form of inner energy. The houses were built out of gleaming metal sheets or origami folding paper. Curving turrets and corners that seemed to twist like paper or pipe cleaners seemed out of place in Kansas, but there they were, growing out of the ground like mutant crops.

Edie also noticed cameras everywhere.

They were an odd note in a small college town in the middle of Kansas, but they were at every corner, aimed in every direction. There couldn't possibly be enough people to watch the pictures transmitted by so many cameras, she thought. Even stranger, why on earth would anyone want to watch? Nothing ever happened in this town. Nothing, she added quickly to herself, except for her own disappearance and presumed death. And Meg's. And the Garbers'. As she watched the strange and altered landscape zip by, she wondered if there had been other disappearances over the years.

Sally's and Meg's laughter snapped her out of her reverie as they arrived at the mall. It looked nothing like Edie remembered, nothing like anything she had ever seen.

What had previously been a standard commercial building made of dull brick with a few boring stucco flourishes had been transformed into a piece of Las Vegas dropped into the middle of a cornfield. Screaming lights and advertising covered every square inch of the outer shell of the building, much of it moving, all of it garish and loud. Except for a few soft drinks, none of the advertised products were even remotely familiar.

"Girls," said Sally, "welcome to the shopping experience of the future. Or, let me say, the shopping experience of *your* future."

"What's with the mall?" Edie gasped. "Why does it look like that?"

"Most people order most things over the network," said Sally, "so the mall needs to come up with pretty good reasons for you to drop by in person. And let me tell you, they've largely run out of them at this point. You can buy a few things here, because everyone needs to pick something up quickly from time to time, but mostly people come because of the food, or because of the headwork."

"The head what?"

"Headwork. It's a way of connecting into the network, except it's stronger here than you can cronk it at home unless you've got some kind of industrial accelerator or you're incredibly rich. If I wasn't talking to you on the drive over here, I would have worn mine while I drove. Oh, and girls," she added, as Edie tried to make any sense of her comments, "don't get out of the car. I don't want anyone seeing you yet."

"But I thought we were going shopping," said Meg.

"No, we can't have anyone seeing you, at least not yet. Not until we know more, and get you something more modern to wear, and maybe hack something for your scans,. But I'll go shopping for you here, I'll get you some clothes, and I'll be back in a few minutes. After you get changed into something proper, then we'll all get something to eat."

Before Meg or Edie could ask why it mattered if someone saw them at the mall, or what it meant to "hack something for your scans," Sally walked out of the car. After a few moments, they could see her figure swallowed by the gaping entrance to the building.

They sat in the car, sullen, while they stared at each other. Meg had forgotten to leave any music on, and the car was silent. Time ticked by slowly as they peered out of the window into the vast expanse of the parking lot.

"I can't stand sitting here," said Meg suddenly, her hair whipping by as she turned towards Edie. Edie immediately recognized her friend's most impulsive expression. "This is ridiculous. So what if someone sees us? We haven't done anything wrong." She began looking for the door lock. "Someone else shot *us* with some kind of death ray. Why should we have to hide? Who cares, let's get out of this car. I want to check this out."

Edie smiled. "Normally I'd try to convince you that it was too dangerous to get out, or that we'd get in trouble, or that we needed to listen to Sally." She was already reaching for the door handle. "But under the circumstances, I can't see why it matters."

As they jumped out of the car they were immediately confronted with even more astounding sights. Parents pushed strollers that more resembled angry sharks than carriages, with pointed snouts and fuel tanks. The children inside them were the same as ever until you moved close enough to see the toys, which seemed to cuddle against the kids of their own volition.

The most dramatic differences they noticed, though, were in the clothes. The cut of the garments worn by the people strolling to and from their cars was unusual, but not so different as to inspire wonder. The material, however, left Edie flabbergasted. One girl's shirt was playing a 3-D movie, with monsters jumping out of the shirt and onto the street, where the monster would circle the girl and then jump back onto her clothes. A woman's ultrasound was playing over her pregnant belly, apparently live. An old man in the corner of the lot wore pants that looked exactly like feathers, only each feather bore an individual video image of a different woman in a brightly colored bikini. The women danced seductively as he walked. The threads in the jacket worn by a man opening his car door burned with an otherworldly green, transforming him into a human glowstick. Edie was certain she was staring, but she couldn't stop herself from spinning around and checking out the clothes worn by these random people in the parking lot.

Slowly, however, she began to notice that her stares were being returned by the people they passed. She leaned over to Meg and smiled nervously.

"We must look like the Amish to these folks." She rolled her eyes. "They haven't seen people dress like this in decades." After a few more moments, she began giggling. "Maybe we'll start a new trend."

Meg laughed too. "Yeah, that's us. Everything old is new again, right?"

As they entered the mall, Edie saw what appeared to be small lasers scanning the faces of everyone crossing the threshold into the building. The lasers made an almost imperceptible grid pattern on each face, and then they were gone. Edie didn't even have a chance to mention it to Meg, or to speculate why they had been scanned, because they were thrust into what appeared to be the inside of a neon light. The mall was alive.

9

best friends forever

The grid pattern created by the low-intensity lasers as they scanned the face of every shopper was quickly transformed into a stream of data, describing every physical feature of each individual. The data zipped wirelessly into a router, which then sent that data to a hub deep within the bowels of the mall complex. There the data was rapidly compared with other data and placed into a profile.

Every person in the town had a profile which in turn was part of a larger relational database of profiles from around the country. The mall would place that tiny byte of information—"visited mall on April 29"—into the database, which kept track of every public activity of every person within that region. Cameras tracked these individuals when they were recognized, and software agents imbued with artificial intelligence could predict that person's likely behavior. Every resident received advertising on the street directed to them personally, based on data collected on all of their public activities. The consumer preferences of every person were available to every merchant. And others.

Something was different on this day, however. The data scanned from the faces of Edie and Meg were sent to the database in a blistering stream of binary information, as was customary, but no matches were found. No similarities were confirmed. This apparent error caused the larger program to review the information, to compare the data a second time, and to undertake further analysis. This, too, led to a dead end and no matches with any cognizable profile. Finally, after several failed efforts to find a match, which took nearly three trillionths of a second, the supervising program alerted the local monitor, who in this case was Lieutenant Lisa Alter, a thirty-nine-year-old officer with the town's police force.

Lt. Alter sat at her office computer, wearing her headwork. She was cronked into the system and bored out of her mind. She had always enjoyed walking the beat, meeting people on the street, patrolling the neighborhoods where she had grown up years before. That, to her, was being a cop. Walking around as an imaginary being within cyberspace was interesting, she supposed. People revealed themselves as gangster wannabes all the time on the network, when they would have been smart enough to fade into the background in real life. Nevertheless, this was hardly what she had signed up for when she joined the force. To her, patrolling a collective, consensual hallucination was not her idea of exciting police work.

Lisa had recently been promoted to lieutenant, the third-highest-ranking officer on the force. Moreover, she was one of only two lieutenants, giving her a fair degree of day-to-day authority. She personally commanded thirty other police officers, with only a captain and the chief ahead of her. Yet she still often found herself sitting at a desk, wearing headwork.

The other lieutenant was Mark Sullivan, the single most infuriating person Lisa had ever met. At least she thought so at the moment; they had dated off and on for nearly nine years. This week it was off. *Very* off.

As she sat there, Lisa wondered if things were over between them permanently, or if they would drift together again. With Mark, it sometimes felt like the same day was repeating itself over and over again, but with tiny variations too small to perceive.

Just as she was drifting into a bit of a daydream about her romantic life or lack thereof, Lisa felt an alert beep in her ear. Then the frame of her vision became outlined in red. Soon an image appeared, floating in front of her eyes like a subtitle in a movie. As an avatar, she had been sitting in a website programmed to seem like a South American dive bar, having an imaginary drink of tonic water with lime. The drink tasted like real tonic water, and it felt wet in her throat, even though she was in fact sitting at a desk in a small town in Kansas connected to a computer network. She had been watching a Colombian telenovela on the screen above the bar; the program now faded into an alert notice. She could, however, still see the reflection of her avatar in the imaginary television screen, even as the notice grew more urgent.

Lt. Alter believed that she was much better-looking as an avatar. She could sculpt her appearance to match the twenty-year-old Lisa Alter that she wished she still was today, instead of the older—though, as she liked to remind herself, still attractive—Lt. Alter sitting in an office with a headset.

But none of that mattered as the beeping continued. The insistence of the alarm finally forced her to change her surroundings and she reluctantly thought herself back into job mode. Her real self touched a display in her office, and the avatar version of Lt. Alter suddenly found herself in a room filled with television monitors and data displays. She typed in a few more words, and spoke into a microphone, still holding her drink.

"Display U-P's," she instructed, pronouncing it as "you-pees." A screen directly in front of her avatar blinked on, displaying the words "unidentified person one" and a clear picture of Meg. The next monitor displayed the words "unidentified person two" and a clear picture of Edie. Both pictures were high-resolution shots taken as the girls had walked into the mall. Next to their pictures were a variety of statistics regarding their facial structure, approximate height, weight, and age. A chemical analysis of their clothing types scrolled below.

Lisa dropped her imaginary drink. She stared at the pictures on her monitor screens, pictures of her classmates from a quarter-century before, and mouthed the words "oh my god" again and again and again. Finally she snapped, "Save images to private file, Lt. Alter nine-zero-seven-zero-niner." She quickly zoomed back to her real self in an office inside a modern glass-and-steel police station. She ripped off the headwork, untangling some of her hair in the process, and had her car keys out of her pocket before she had even reached the door.

10

the river

Jared stared at the map embossed onto the pedestal for several more minutes. The curve of the river, so familiar to him from years of gazing at maps of the town on classroom walls, seemed foreign and strange. What had once served as confirmation that everything was normal now seemed like a slap in the face.

After a while he realized that he had lost all track of time standing in the quad gazing at the map, and that the sun had moved higher in the sky. Wishing for the first time in his life that he owned a watch, he tried guessing the time. Was it mid-morning? Time for breakfast? Although, he joked to himself darkly, perhaps I need a watch with a "year" hand. I don't have one of those.

As the sun began to peek over one of the buildings and shine directly into his eyes, Jared finally tore himself away from the pedestal and began walking into the quad itself. The buildings seemed to have a quiet dignity, like churches or museums, even though they were spare and unadorned. The quad was paved with large stones, laid in an ornate pattern that reminded him of a large, monochromatic archery target. There were no benches, or seats. There was no landscaping. In fact, he noted with some surprise, there were no trees or green spaces at all. The quad looked like a series of monoliths, stripped of anything natural and lacking any color or recognizable humanity.

While he strolled among these stately, sterile buildings, he noticed what appeared to be a directory of some kind posted next to a giant metal door on one of the larger structures. Some words in bold text were set next to a series of characters in what appeared to be a type of alphabetical order. The character set used in the writing was unfamiliar, however, and indecipherable to him. He continued staring at the list as though he were actually reading it, but it was still gibberish and remained impossible to comprehend.

As he stood there staring at the directory, he tried to develop a plan. Yet each time he started to think about his situation in any detail, he felt himself slide into increasingly intense levels of worry and panic, and he had to begin again from scratch. Finally, after several false starts, he was able to calm himself down enough to think through his options.

He had read enough fantasy to be able to assess his situation in its broadest terms: Jared Garber, a fifteen-year-old teenager from Kansas, had been transported directly from his dining room to the same spot many years in the future. He had been separated from his family. He was fairly sure it had something to do with the man made of code, but he had no idea what to do next.

Worse, he suspected that this new time was so far into the distant future that the civilization he knew had long ago departed. From the quad architecture, he guessed that this was still a college town of some kind; from the directory, he suspected that the building in front of him was filled with professors or academic offices. But everything else was speculation, and his head began to ache from the implications.

He tried focusing hard on the edges of the buildings in this new age, and the leaves sprouting into green webs of verdant nature on the trees in the distance just outside the quad, hoping to see phantom images. Perhaps the spinning shapes and codes might make sense now, in this different time, but he saw nothing unusual.

Jared wondered whether he were the only one who had been sent into the future. Where was his family? How could he get back? Was it even possible to get back?

Normally he had somewhat mixed feelings about his family. He loved them all, of course, but they were not by any measure an easy group. His father was a self-made man, a relentlessly self-improving orthodontist who'd pulled himself up from a poverty-stricken childhood through a maniacal work ethic, and who had little patience for anyone not prepared to labor just as hard. For Jared, every discussion with his father was like tiptoeing past a sleeping lion, and he had to choose every word carefully for fear of setting off an unexpected attack.

If Jared was sitting down in the family room, his father wondered why he wasn't slaving away at his homework. If he was slaving away at his homework, his father presumed that he was doing it wrong and needed further instruction. Jared found it infuriating, and it was constant, and it had been that way for as long as he could remember.

His mother, Lindsey, was in many ways the polar opposite of her husband. She was a published author of five books on cats. Her best seller to-date was a book of "cat-related wit" titled *Cat Got Your Tongue?* that even Jared had to admit was fairly amusing. She spent her days relentlessly emoting good cheer and rescuing kittens at the local animal shelter. However, while superficially happy at all times, she was just as intense as Larry Garber, and no less demanding. In fact, Josie called her mother the "Happy Harpy" behind her back. Mrs. Garber would systematically drop honeyed hints to her children, comments that while phrased as friendly suggestions ("Josie, you may want to take a look at page four of your science worksheet") were understood by everyone to be immediate requirements. There was nothing optional about any suggestion made by Lindsey Garber.

And then there was Josie, his twin. Jared had never spent more than a day or two away from her since their birth, and in many respects she felt like an extra limb. He could feel her emotions without a word passing between them, and she was still his closest friend. She was also his hero.

Josie was everything Jared wished he could be: smooth with other kids, in control of every situation, and confident of her place in the world. She never doubted herself, never wondered if she was destined for something important, or felt concerned about whether she was doing the right thing. By definition, if Josie was doing it, then it was the right thing to do. There were no second guesses.

But he had kept a secret from her for all of these years, and he felt guilty even thinking about it. What if they were all gone because of his visions? What if something could have been done if only he had told someone about it? What if they were in danger? He needed to find them; there was no question in his mind that this was his first order of business. They might have driven him crazy, but they were his family, and he couldn't let them down.

As he stood there contemplating his almost incomprehensible situation, he saw someone approaching in the distance. It was the first human being he had seen since his arrival, and immediately his heart began to race. This person, walking on the bare path between two buildings, seemed to be striding purposely towards him, and had the bearing of an authority figure of some kind. However, it rapidly became apparent that this person, like the man

Jared had seen earlier that afternoon, was completely constructed out of code and geometric images, flowing with
symbols like gravy poured over meatloaf. While the man
seemed to be wearing clothes, his garments also appeared
to be without substance, and merely sat like an extra layer
of code on top of his body. Jared's heart sank, and he considered whether to run.

But he knew that if he ran he might never figure out
what was going on. Danger or not, he had to talk to this
coded man. He put on the bravest face he could manage
and waited for him to arrive.

As soon as the figure came within speaking distance,
Jared remembered that he had no idea what kind of language was spoken here. As he couldn't think of anything else
to try, he figured that English was as good a guess as any.

"My name," he began slowly, pointing to himself, trying
to sound eager and friendly, "is Jared Garber. What year is
this? Do you speak English? Are you real?"

The man looked at him with grey-scale eyes, whirlpools
of semiotic data swirling in their depths, and Jared knew,
instantly, that the man was pleased by his presence. He
looked as though he were thinking about his next move,
stepping back away from Jared as he did so, but then
beckoned him forward, calling him with his arms. "Come
with me," said the man in accented English. He pointed to
himself. "Lasho," he said. "Lasho Gluck."

Jared reached out to shake his hand. Silently, but without taking Jared's hand in greeting, Gluck began to walk
towards one of the buildings on the quad and gestured for
him to follow. He watched the man for a moment, shrugged
with resignation, and then followed behind him. This was
not ideal, but Jared was hopeful, for the first time this
morning, that perhaps he would not be alone in his quest
for answers.

11

turn on the news

Edie initially thought that the mall was "garish," as her Aunt Judy might have said, but then corrected herself. "Garish" hardly did justice to the lights that flashed everywhere in thousands of different combinations in colors she could not even begin to recognize. All of it was in constant motion, with video images projected in lights on nearly every surface. Instead of stores, there appeared to be caves constructed of glowing crystals with signs in English and Spanish and a variety of Asian characters. As the girls walked into the mall, they noticed that only a few of these caves contained any goods. Instead, most of the vendor stalls held cushioned chairs with headsets slung over the armrests. An apparatus on a tray was attached by an arm to each chair.

Next door to one of these places was a make-up shop similar to the ones they knew from their own time. Here girls swarmed over cheap lipstick and blinking jewelry, and argued with their parents over whether they could get a third ear-piercing. Apparently, thought Edie, there were some experiences you still had to have in person. Nevertheless, she cringed at the earrings that looked like medical instruments and fastened through enormous holes cut through the cartilage of the upper earlobe. Next to that store was another variety of cave that appeared to be populated entirely by fifteen-year-old boys. She could not tell what they were selling, but small bottles were being handed to the customers by salesmen who looked only marginally older than the kids. Each worker held some kind of scanning device, and each customer held out his wrist after receiving the bottle. The salesman would scan some kind of wristband and the boy would leave. Edie watched for a moment, trying to figure out what type of transaction was taking place, especially with no adults in the vicinity, but gave up after a few moments and walked further down the mall. She quickly realized that Meg had gone in another direction, but before she could panic she reminded herself that this was just a mall, and just like any visit to the mall they could find each other later on.

Soon she came upon a cave that sold what appeared to be some deconstructed TV or computer; she couldn't really tell the difference anymore. There were a variety of models, none bigger than an orange. A tiny, bulbous lens broadcasted images holographically in three dimensions. The people on the screen were not actually on a screen, but instead stood on the floor in front of the device, as though they were fellow shoppers instead of people inside a news broadcast.

And in fact, that was what Edie was watching: a news broadcast. She moved closer to the store, curious to see what was going on in the world twenty-five years after she had last watched any television. The story of the day seemed to be about the presidential election. Well, she thought, nothing too different there. There was always an election going on. The various candidates in the forthcoming primary were analyzed, and each one was profiled. The anchorwoman was sleek, dressed in a cross between a business ensemble and a tracksuit, her lapels open to reveal a tasteful beaded necklace. In between candidate profiles, her image floated back into view, standing in front of the shop. She was tall, or at least her image was tall, and she towered over Edie. Edie drew closer to listen.

"Our next candidate is Jackson Hronck, the Thomas Edison of our day and the current mayor of New York City. Widely predicted to announce his presidential candidacy this week, Hronck is expected to self-finance his campaign with the proceeds from his globe-spanning technology incubator, Hronet." Suddenly the image of Jackson Hronck came to the forefront, and it took everything Edie could muster to prevent herself from screaming. She did, however, manage to make eye contact with Meg, who had just walked by, apparently in search of her. Edie urgently waved her over and pointed. Meg came running, and almost immediately her own mouth displayed a silent rictus of shock.

As they watched, the girls became so focused they barely noticed that nearly everyone in the mall was staring at them. The expressions on these shoppers' faces appeared similar to what Edie's face might have been like if she had seen a woman in a seventeenth-century ball gown at a baseball game.

On the screen, Jackson Hronck looked far better than he had in the backyard behind the Garbers' house. He was still a bald man with a mustache, but while he appeared to be in his early fifties, he had a vibrancy that suggested he had been well cared for indeed. He spoke with a charismatic force and wore what must have been the modern version of a suit, with lapels that shimmered with an emerald green hue. The total effect, while understated, unquestionably emphasized his sophistication, wealth, and power. He looked very much like a presidential candidate, but it was what he said that made Edie feel as though her insides had been chilled.

"The future is more than a sped-up version of our past. It is an opportunity. It is an opportunity to begin again, to start our lives from zero, and, if done properly, from *before* the zero. It allows us to recognize that our world is outmoded and diseased. It presents us with a chance to change our lives, our nation, and our world. And that chance arrives every day. Each day when we awaken, we must look upon the dawning day as a blank page, and we must write our first chapters anew. I will have an announcement in the days to come, and I will tell our nation what I believe must be done to achieve our destiny as a people."

The girls looked at each other and began to back towards the exit from the mall in unison. "Meg," said Edie, "I think we have another problem."

"Like we needed one," said Meg, with only the hint of a smile on her face. "But no doubt."

"We'd better get back." She pushed Meg to the door with her shoulder. The stares from their fellow mall-goers were now fairly obvious, and both girls could sense the attention swelling as they walked. "Sally will throw a fit if she sees us in here."

They made their way back to the car, Edie hoping that she would be able to recognize Sally's minivan. It was an unnecessary concern, however, as they soon noticed Sally walking up an entirely different aisle towards her car, carrying a bag.

"Sally!" called Meg. Sally turned towards them with an irritated look. "We need to talk."

"Girls! Why did you get out of the car?"

"We wanted to see the mall. And we saw a bit more than we expected to."

"What are you talking about?" Anger was obvious in Sally's voice. "You could have been seen—in fact, you probably *were* seen." She held up the bag. "That's why I wanted to get you these clothes, I—"

"Who cares?" Meg was visibly upset. "We have a bigger problem. We know who sent us into the future."

"Don't talk so loud," said Sally, looking around nervously. "What are you—"

"It was Jackson Hronck," said Edie.

Sally's face told them everything they needed to know.

12

a picture tells a thousand words

After a drive back from the mall at what must have been at twice the posted speed limit, Sally, Edie, Meg, and Jim talked nonstop for nearly an hour. The kids upstairs once again ignored the visitors, completely unaware that something far more interesting than their homework or school gossip was going on right under their noses.

"Are you sure it was him? Could either of you draw what he looked like?" asked Jim. "Did you really get a good look at him?"

Meg immediately shook her head no, but Edie thought about it. Finally she nodded. Sally waved her hand in the air and a screen appeared, floating in front of her. "Use this," she said. "Pretend your finger is a pencil. Just wave your hand to erase things."

After getting over her initial surprise, Edie began to make some marks in the corner of the screen, trying to become accustomed to the feel of the instrument as she drew. When she felt like she understood the device, she began to sketch in earnest. She had always been a fair artist, and she frowned as she tried to remember the details of the man's face, the curve of his mustache, the angle and depth of his cheekbones. She began to draw the eyes first, as they were what she remembered most about the man from earlier that day, capturing the look of pleasure as he'd turned the weapon on them at the Garbers' house.

She sketched for several minutes, with Meg occasionally piping in a suggestion. Sally and Jim sat silent, watching intently. At last Edie turned the screen around (it was opaque from behind) and held up the sketch.

"Oh my god," whispered Sally. Jim was staring at the picture with a pained look on his face. He was barely breathing, and his knuckles were white.

"Girls," he finally said, looking up at them uneasily, "your problem just became a heck of lot more complicated. If you're even half the artist you appear to be, Edie, that's Jackson Hronck." He said this as though everything were now evident. There was a pause.

"Um," said Edie. "Okay, we still don't know who that is, except that he's running for president. Who is he?"

"Well." Sally interrupted Jim as he was about to speak. "Let's put it this way: imagine the biggest celebrity you can think of from when we were kids together. Think magazine-cover big, talk-show-guest-star big, tabloids-in-the-grocery-store big. Now imagine he's also a two-time Nobel Prize-winning scientist and the world's richest man. Then throw in the fact that he's the mayor of the largest city in America. Oh, and he's widely expected to be our next president." She turned to Jim. "Am I missing anything?"

"No, Sal," he said, smirking. "I think that just about covers it. I knew he had lived here before he moved out of town, and I was concerned that he might have been the one when Edie first told us what happened. But I hoped it wasn't true, and I didn't know he'd lived right behind the

Garbers. And I won't lie: as I said before, it *is* a significant problem."

There was silence as everyone digested the news. Meg was the first to speak.

"Well. This should be fairly simple then. We just go to where he lives, ask him to send us back, and the problem's solved."

Edie stared as though she were mad. "Don't you get it? I don't even know this guy and I can tell this is going to be a problem." Her voice grew louder. "You think it's going to be easy to get ourselves in front of the richest guy in the world? The mayor of New York? And this is someone who had no problem erasing us and the Garbers with a flip of his finger. I'm sure he's got guards everywhere. We're the only ones who know the truth about how he really got where he is today."

"But don't you understand?" Meg spoke slowly, as though to calm Edie down. "We're the biggest problem this guy could imagine. We know the truth. His whole image depends on that never getting out. He has to talk to us. Doesn't he?" She suddenly appealed to Sally and Jim, almost pleading with them.

Sally smiled. "You know, Jim," she said, "the girl may have a point. Perhaps we should be going to New York. I can't really think of any other option right now anyway. Can you?"

He frowned. "He could just as easily want to keep you out of the way, shut you up, maybe even have you hurt. We need to try to figure out what's going on before we go traipsing to New York and get arrested."

"Why would we get arrested?" asked Edie, still marveling over the fact that the person they were off to see was some big celebrity, even if he was a bad guy.

"I don't know, but something about this whole story seems wrong," Jim said. "For example, where did the notes come from?"

"The story seems 'wrong'?" asked Edie, making air quotes. "What, is there a right way to get sent twenty-five years into the future?"

"Well," he agreed sheepishly, "perhaps not. But your story seems even weirder than it should be. Not that it isn't plenty strange already." Sally nodded her agreement. "I guess I have no problem with you guys going to see Hronck, since I can't think of anything else yet myself, but we need to think about this before we do anything rash. Kathrine's coming by in a few minutes, and we can talk about it more then."

Meg frowned. "I'm not sure what's rash about trying to get back to a time when my parents don't think I'm dead."

They all sat and stared at each other, trying to wrap their minds around the oddness of their situation. Jim looked as though he was thinking intently. Then he got a faraway look in his eye and began to smile.

"Girls, I think I've got an idea." He started looking for something on the desk. "Can you leave me alone for a bit until Kathrine arrives? You know what they say…"

Sally smiled at Edie and Meg. "I'd yell at him for being rude and kicking us out of the house, but I get like this too when I working on some new finance algorithm, so I guess turnabout is fair play. Let's go outside. Oh, wait, first put on your new clothes." She handed over some bags and the girls went into the bathroom. After a few minutes of struggling with some oddly shaped shoes and even weirder garments, they followed Sally outside, leaving Jim to frantically scribble equations on a pad of paper while fumbling with a headset to cronk into the network. Edie and Meg examined their new clothes in the daylight and were amazed at how perfectly they fit.

"Good guess on size," complimented Edie as she tugged at the hem of her bizarre orange skirt. The skirt showed a variety of different sunsets from around the world at regular intervals, with each thread of the fabric video-enabled.

"Actually, there was no guessing involved," said Sally. "The clothes figure out your size and then adjust accordingly. It's another one of Hronck's inventions. You can't even imagine how much he's changed the world. He's really quite the wizard."

Edie snorted and looked away. "You'd be a wizard too if you had a time machine. That makes everything a lot easier. Takes the work out of it."

Sally looked at Edie, puzzled. "What makes you think he didn't invent some of these things? He invented a time machine, and that's no small accomplishment. Do you think he sent himself into the future to get *all* of these inventions?"

"Just a guess," replied Edie. "But somebody who tries to get rid of a bunch of kids and a whole family with some kind of death ray because he's afraid that someone will see his big 'invention' doesn't seem like an honest guy. Who knows what else he's done? And how do you even know *he* invented the time machine?"

Sally nodded. "I guess that's probably true, but you have to understand that everyone views this guy as a hero. No matter what kind of problem you have, he seems able to solve it. It's now almost impossible to see him without getting through a million gatekeepers." She smiled. "At least, that's what the magazines say. And who am I to doubt—"

"Sally," interrupted Meg. "How did Hronck get so big? You said he's like the richest guy on the planet, right?"

"Hmm. Interesting story," she said, watching Edie sneak a glance at some flowers in the garden. "No one really knows where he came from, but the first we all heard of him was when he was a teacher at the college here in town. He taught physics and math—similar type of work to what Jim and Kathrine do, actually. One day he started inventing things, just like that. He started Hronet, his company, and he was off to the races. After his inventions hit the jackpot, he made his fortune and moved to New York City. Been there ever since. I think it was after he put together the fusion engine. That took him into the serious big time. Politics all over the world were altered by that. As you can imagine, when a glass of seawater can power a city, everything becomes different. And it did."

The girls absorbed the story for a few minutes. But just when Edie was about to make some kind of quip about Hronck, or about the fact that they were stuck in a world that they didn't recognize, Sally turned back towards Meg and hugged her. Edie could see that Sally was sobbing, and she turned away. This display of genuine emotion forced her to think about her own situation again, and she realized that she had never received a full answer to her questions of a few hours before.

Edie spoke up a few moments later, after Sally had recomposed herself. "You still haven't mentioned what happened to my aunt and uncle. Are they still in town?"

Sally looked sadly down at her feet. "They still live in town, but they're really not, well, the same. They live in a home, assisted living. When you disappeared it was pretty devastating for them, and after what had happened to your parents, Edie, I think they kind of packed it in."

"I've got to go see them," insisted Edie. "They have to know I'm alive. Do you know where they live?"

Sally nodded sadly. "Do you think that they'll understand what's happening? They're pretty old, and..."

"I need to see them," insisted Edie. "Let's go right now."

Meg inserted herself between them. "Edie, we don't know if it's a good idea for anyone to see us. It could be a problem with time."

"No," replied Edie. "I was thinking about it. That's only if we go backwards in time. That could change the future. But we're forward in time, what's there to change?"

Meg thought about it for a minute. She seemed flustered.

"Why don't you want me to see my aunt and uncle?" Edie demanded. "What's the problem?"

"Edie, I...I don't know." She began to shuffle her feet, looking a lot younger than her fourteen years. "I just have a bad feeling about this whole thing. I don't think we should talk to anyone. If the story gets out, we may never be able to get back home. And I want to get home. Don't you? If Hronck finds out about us before we can get to New York, we may never be able to get to New York at all. Then we're stuck here, or worse. I don't want my parents to see me now—they'll flip out completely. And do you think that will help us get back any faster?"

This made absolutely no sense at all to Edie. Meg, she decided, was the one who was flipping out. Sally seemed similarly unconvinced.

"Meg, are you sure?" asked Sally. "I don't think it will hurt."

"Fine," said Meg, as though conceding an important point. "Go see your aunt and uncle. I'll stay here. I don't want to see my mom or dad right now. It would be too much for them and, well, too much for me. Sally, nothing against you, but I don't want to cry anymore today."

Puzzled, Edie turned to Sally. "Can we go now?"

"Later," she said. "Kathrine should be here any minute, and we need to hear what she has to say about this. Jim claims she's even smarter than he is, and that's saying something, because he's one of the only people I know who's smarter than me." She smirked and began walking back towards the house.

"Sally," said Edie, almost running to catch up, Meg following. "What are *you* doing these days? What's your job?"

"Pretty unusual one, actually. I guess you could say that I write software to trade financial instruments, some of which I invent myself. I use the programs to trade for my own account, and I sometimes sell the software to big banks in Japan and China. Jim likes to say that my hobby supports his job, and I guess that's pretty accurate." She was clearly quite proud of this last fact. "We do pretty well. I make the money, and he gets to be a scientist."

Meg laughed and they all tromped back into the house. They found Jim sitting at the table with a woman, her dark, disheveled hair framing a pale, heart-shaped face. She was rather stunning in an unadorned way, and was busily scribbling away on the table itself—apparently the surface was electronic. It took a moment for Edie to recognize her friend Kathrine, timid and mousy Kathrine, last seen yesterday as a droll, laconic fourteen-year-old. Now she was evidently a swan. Oh, and a theoretical physicist.

Kathrine seemed to notice Edie and Meg at that same moment.

"Edie," said Kathrine, looking her up and down appraisingly. "You forgot to meet me on Saturday to talk about that project for art class. But hey, better late than never, right?"

Edie smiled. It was such a typical thing for Kathrine to say. Apparently Kathrine was still someone who didn't get excited about anything. "Well," Edie replied, "I was otherwise occupied. But I'm guessing you know that now." She gave Kathrine a big hug. "I hope you didn't fail that project. Toothpick sculpture, right?"

"Oh, I failed it, all right. Never even finished it," said Kathrine, hugging her back. "But people understood. Given the circumstances, it wasn't held against me. Of course, for you, we last spoke, what, yesterday?"

"Actually, we saw each other earlier today. Remember, I asked a question in Ms. Cavanaugh's class about time?"

Kathrine laughed. "Well, at least you now know she was right. Sounds like you've had an eventful few hours."

"Um," interjected Meg, eyeing Kathrine somewhat suspiciously. Kathrine was, after all, still one of Edie's friends, albeit now impossibly gorgeous. "You know how everyone wants to stuff years of experience into a short time? It's pretty overrated."

Kathrine grinned, but looked a bit like she might be stifling tears as well.

"Meg, we've got some ideas," said Jim. Edie had forgotten he was even there. "I don't know where they'll get us, but I think we may understand what happened to you guys. That isn't much, but at least that's a first step."

Edie glanced over at Jim and Kathrine and Meg and Sally, and, for no reason in particular, she felt much better.

13

the future of the past

By the time Lt. Alter arrived at the mall, there was no sign of Edie or Meg. She scanned the crowds, looking for teenagers dressed for an earlier time. Seeing none, she made her way into the security office, pushed aside some elderly mall security agents, and found a desk. She rapidly donned her headwork and cronked into the network as quickly as she could sit down.

Almost immediately, as the data flowed through her mind, Lt. Alter learned that the girls had left the mall not long after she had seen them in cyberspace. She scanned videos of the parking lot until she found the image of them running towards a woman and getting into her van. She zoomed in on the license plate, ran it through the network, and learned that it belonged to Meg's sister, Sally, and her husband, Jim.

Lt. Alter knew she should call for backup, and understood that this entire situation was both unprecedented and deeply worrisome. But she was still more than a bit concerned that she was having some horrible dream. It had even occurred to her that she could be ill: just last week she had heard a news report about a nineteen-year-old boy who had been downloaded with one of the new transhuman online viruses. This new kind of malware didn't merely affect your avatar (those viruses had been around for years), but changed your actual body through the introduction of toxic information into your physical being. No one was exactly sure how or why it worked, but in that case the virus had caused the boy's real eyes to turn into glass orbs that looked exactly like little fishbowls filled with water.

Lt. Alter was pretty sure that had not happened to her. There were no other signs of trouble, and her eyes were still their typical brown. She detected no other symptoms of psychosis. Yet nothing about this situation made any sense. In fact, having fishbowls for eyes would have been easier to digest; at least in that case there would have been a reasonable explanation.

Meg and Edie had been dead for twenty-five years. There was no question about it. When Lisa had joined the force, she had studied the file, and snooped around to see if she could learn anything new about the case, which had been inactive for many years. After all, the so-called "April Disappearances," which had snatched the Garber family, Edie, and Meg out of Lisa's town, had been the seminal events of her childhood. It had been even more horrifying for Lisa personally because she had been so close to Edie for so many years. To lose one of your best friends would have been difficult under the best of circumstances, but to lose her in such an inexplicable fashion was doubly painful.

The case was still cold so many years after the incidents, and there were no new clues. Lt. Alter had gone back and relived the horrible trauma, read the newspapers and looked through confidential investigation memos. The story, from all sources, was consistent: on that spring day, Meg and Edie had ceased to exist, just as the Garbers had only days before. The only clue? Edie had made an appointment with the vice principal earlier on the day she'd disappeared. It seemed Edie had been concerned by some notes that had been left in her locker, which investigators never retrieved. Neither the Garbers nor Edie nor Meg had ever been found, and the crimes remained unsolved to this day.

Lt. Alter was confident that her eyes did not deceive her now. She knew in her heart that it was Edie at the mall. She was equally certain that it was Meg alongside her. The fact that they were seen getting into a minivan owned by Meg's sister only intensified Lisa's sense that perhaps this really was the dead brought back to life. She got back into her car, having downloaded the newer images from the mall and the video from the parking lot cameras into her head-work, and cronked back into the network. She assumed her avatar form and sat at a desk in a holographic police station that was nowhere in particular except in her mind. Sometimes she wished she had paid for the body modifications that allowed you to link into the system without using headwork, but the specter of those online viruses made her nervous, and she had long ago decided that the convenience was not worth the risk.

Lt. Alter rapidly called up images of Edie and Meg from long ago, images of young teenagers in the prime of their lives. These were the eighth-grade class photos that had been used on "missing" posters and even on milk cartons for months and then years after the event. "Have you seen this girl?" images, with Edie's or Meg's picture and a description of their last outfits, had been posted like wanted posters all over the town. Lisa hardly needed to even see them again; the images were forever burned into her memory from repeated viewing. Nonetheless, she put them on the screen, and then pulled together the images from the mall.

She arranged them side by side, conjured herself an imaginary drink to sip, and stared at the comparison.

There was no doubt about it. No one could, or would, question that these were the same girls. Now, of course, the question became more pressing: why were they suddenly alive and unchanged from a quarter-century before, even wearing the same outfits? If they had been thirty-nine-year-old women, she could have dealt with it all in a rational way. Perhaps they could have been living in Brazil all this time as captives, or as part of some other kidnapping scenario out of a movie. But *this* was impossible.

As she pondered these thorny questions, and tried to decide how to handle the implications of this discovery, she became aware of another presence nearby. Of course, it wasn't really nearby, as nothing was near anything inside the network. Nonetheless, it was the equivalent of feeling someone staring at you. She turned off the images, rose from the desk, opened the door, and found herself looking at the avatar of Mark, her serial former boyfriend and coworker.

"Lisa, what's up?" Mark's avatar looked like he did in real life, but somewhat more sculpted. His hair was a bit thicker, and his profile a bit stronger, but he still was a good-looking guy in either world. A former athlete, he had joined the force right out of college along with Lisa. The two of them had moved up the ranks together, and their off-and-on dating habits were a source of both exasperation and amusement amongst their coworkers.

"Nothing, Mark." She tried not to look annoyed. "Why are you here?"

"Oh, just checking up on you. Seeing if you need any assistance." He walked into the imaginary office. "The desk sergeant said you flew out of the station this afternoon like a bat out of hell. So of course I was curious and worried, and I went to find you. Turns out you're sitting in a parking lot outside the mall, cronked in and sitting in your private office online. Thought there might be something wrong."

"No, Mark, nothing's wrong." She walked back to her desk, already annoyed with herself for sounding annoyed. "Just needed some time to think about some things at work."

"Anything in particular?" he asked, getting a bit more insistent. "Anything I can help you with?"

"No," said Lisa. "Look, I'm a bit upset about some things right now. Can we talk another time?"

"Upset? Upset about us? Upset about what?"

"Just upset." Her avatar was expressionless, though she suspected that her voice was still strained. "We can talk later. Alright?"

"Okay." His avatar slowly stepped back from the doorway. "We'll get together later. Just let me know when you want to talk."

As he closed the door, Lisa was unsure of why she had refused to mention any of the afternoon's mysteries to Mark. She wasn't sure why she had been secretive, or why she had not wanted to talk. But she knew that this was something she wanted to investigate on her own, at least initially. It wasn't police business, at least not yet. It was her business. She wondered if she should call Kathrine or Melissa. Maybe they had some ideas. My god, would they be shocked.

As she considered her options, Lt. Alter looked up Sally's address. She had started the car before she had even finished logging out of the system. As she removed her headwork, she had put the car in drive. She knew exactly where she was going.

14

time reconsidered

"**S**o?" asked Meg expectantly. "What's your idea?"

"Everybody sit down," said Jim with professorial authority. "This is going to take a few minutes." Edie, Meg, and Sally sat down on the bar stools across from the table and looked intently at Kathrine, who was holding her computer tablet.

"In order to explain all of this, I'm going to ask all of you to cronk into the network," she said. "We've put together a secure room where we can display everything. We've got some extra headwork for Meg and Edie to use. And yes," she added, before Kathrine could speak. "They'll use generic avatars. I know we don't have anything else for them."

"What do we do?" asked Edie.

"Here." Kathrine handed headsets to Meg and Edie. "Just slide the headwork directly onto your head. They'll take care of the rest. Once you're in, just talk normally. It will all seem easy once you're online."

The headpiece resembled an old-fashioned telephone operator's headset, except that it was made of a strange, milky material that was like metal but softer, and there was a visor over the eyes. The material felt velvety, like fabric, while shimmering like liquid or polished stainless steel. Edie slipped the headset on, carefully sliding her hair behind the earpiece. She was startled to feel the headset adjust itself to the size and shape of her head.

"Ready, guys?" asked Kathrine, who was adjusting her own headset. Sally and Jim were doing the same. "Welcome to the future!"

With that, Kathrine touched a button on her tablet, and Edie felt a sensation similar to what she had experienced when Hronck had shot them with his time machine. After being yanked into a vortex, she found herself standing around a table in a nondescript room. She felt as though her eyes had stopped working. In fact, they had, as a new image feed was now directly imprinted onto her optic nerve. Everyone around her resembled realistically rendered cartoons. Sally and Kathrine were hyper-perfect versions of themselves, with nary a hair out of place. Jim appeared to be more rugged adventurer than theoretical physicist: while perfectly shaved in real life, his avatar sported a three-day-old beard and wore heavy motorcycle boots with a flannel shirt.

Meg looked like the most generic teenage girl Edie could imagine, and supposed that she herself looked the same: blue jeans, a striped, long-sleeved shirt, and what appeared to be pink sneakers. Funny, she thought, the clothes in real life looked a lot crazier than this.

"Okay, everyone, take a seat and get ready for a class in Time 101." Jim had moved towards a screen. He waved his hand and an image of a graph appeared.

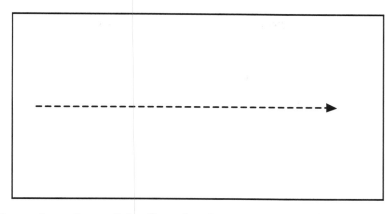

"Imagine that this line is the passage of *you* through time. Each millisecond you are alive is a dot in that line. Millions of those dots make up your life. Got it?" Edie and Meg nodded. "Now, every dot along the line in your past, right on up to the present, makes perfect sense. It is no different than your movement through physical space from one side of a room to the other. You moved ten feet to the left? We can follow that movement with no problem. We see where you were, we see where you are today.

"The trouble comes in understanding the relationship between where you are *right this second* and where you will be some time in the future. How do we know where that line will take you? Is there a predetermined line streaming out into the future, with an arrow on one side of the line? Do we just blindly follow that line along and end up where we are today, twenty-five years ahead, without choice in the matter?"

Kathrine stood up and moved towards the screen. "There are three different ways that scientists think about these things," she lectured in a practiced voice. "One view is that the past, present, and future have always existed the way they exist now, and you can move from one moment in time to another. History and the future, in other words, are part of the same single line, and can never be changed.

"The second view is that everything up until the present can be understood as a line, but then the future branches off into many lines, and many different possibilities, with each choice we make. In that view of time, there are an infinite number of worlds branching off from each moment in time. By choosing one path, you never learn what is on those other paths."

Edie's head was swimming. "Kathrine, I think I understand the first one—that's the idea that time is like a train, and each moment is a car, and you can move from one car to the next, backwards or forwards, but the train never changes. Right?"

"You got it, Edie," said Kathrine. "That's exactly correct."

"So in the first view, our lives are already set up for us. We just have to live them, and we don't get much choice in the matter. But the second one is hard to think about. Are you saying that each time we have a decision to make, we have a million different futures we could choose?"

"That's exactly right." Kathrine clicked on the screen and the graph changed. "In the second theory, each moment looks like an octopus, with different futures sprouting from it like arms."

Meg rose and went to the screen. "If you choose one future," she asked, pointing at the graph, "do all of the other ones go away?"

Jim smiled. "That's a great question, but you're getting ahead of us. The short answer is that we don't know. Or more specifically, we didn't know until you showed up at our house. I think that Kathrine and I have figured that one out. But let's talk about the third option first."

"The third view," explained Kathrine, "is called 'present-ism.' This means that only the present is real. The past was real but now is gone. Once we live a moment, it goes away and we never get it back. Similarly, the future will be real when we get to it, but isn't real yet—nothing is real until we experience it. Only this moment is real. You can't go forward or backwards in time because the 'future' and the 'past' don't exist as real places. Only 'now' exists. Until earlier today, I was a firm believer in presentism." She laughed. "With your arrival, I have now been disabused of that belief."

"So you think that only one of the first two options is accurate?" asked Meg.

"Well," said Jim, "based on what happened to you, and our own understanding of time from Einstein on, we now know that time is not an absolute thing. If you go the speed of light, for example, time is altered by motion. If you're stuck in a black hole, time is altered as you get sucked into the event horizon. We know that time is not a constant thing. So what is it?"

"That's exactly what we were trying to find out!" said Edie, throwing up her arms. "We looked everywhere, and no one seemed to know. Even our science teacher wasn't sure."

"Edie, by being sent here, you have answered your own question," said Kathrine. "We believe that the second theory is the correct one, and that Hronck has somehow developed a device that forces its target along a timeline. This is not the only future that was possible for you, but this is where you were pushed to. Imagine that you are on a train, and someone puts a rocket on the caboose and shoots the train along the track. The track passes scheduled stations, and goes by switches that would have taken it in other directions. That's what we believe has happened to you."

They all sat quietly for a moment, trying to absorb Jim and Kathrine's explanation about time. Edie was the first one to speak.

"I think I understand what you're getting at, but the only question that matters to me is whether I can get back to my own time. Once I've been pushed along that train, can I put it in reverse?"

"I wish I could give you an answer," said Kathrine. "But the truth is that I have no idea. We don't even know how Hronck's machine works, let alone how to reverse its effects. I don't know if it is even possible."

"I've got another question," interrupted Meg. "What about all of those other tracks that our train didn't take? Do they go away when we pass them up, or are they always there?"

"Good question," said Jim. "Again, I have no idea. But there have long been theorists who believe that we are living in but one of multiple universes, with each universe created by our choices. If that's true, no one has been able to prove it. But if it is true, it means that perhaps we can travel between those different universes."

"Then how do we know which is the right 'past' we need to travel back towards?" asked Edie. "If each of our choices is its own universe, then that could be billions of different universes, or pasts, or something like that."

"Again, I don't know." Jim was now looking a bit less excited, and his shoulders seemed to sag. "It is clear, though, that the only chance we have to get you back to where you belong is to talk to Hronck. I don't like it, but I can't think of anything else."

"Um, Jim?" asked Meg. "Is there any reason you decided to pull us in here other than to show us some graphs? You could have done that on a piece of paper in the house."

"Of course. We need to talk about how you're getting to New York City, especially now that you girls have almost certainly been scanned."

"Scanned?" asked Edie. "What are you talking about?"

"When you went into the mall. You know, where you saw Hronck on the news? No question that you were scanned. But since you disappeared well before they started keeping track of biometric identifiers, they probably don't know who you are. The only issue is whether or not they'll try to find out."

"Okay, back up," said Meg. "I have no idea what you're talking about. Who scanned us, and what do you mean about them knowing who we are?"

Jim sat down and leaned back in his chair. "For many years now, the folks in charge have been using a system of cameras and scanners—you know, like the ones you used to see at the grocery store checkout—to identify people in large public areas. It scans your physical features, your irises...." He shook his head. "You probably aren't aware of this, but we went through a pretty uncomfortable period a few years back."

"Very nasty," agreed Sally. "Very dark. Thousands of people killed. Bombings, chemical weapons...it was like a nightmare that got worse with each passing week."

"Now, if you want privacy," said Kathrine, "you're safer online. Not even the military can get through the strongest encryption here. But step outside into a public place and you're on a reality show."

"Except no breaks for commercials," cracked Jim. "The advertising just never ends. Anyway, we can be pretty sure that when you went into the mall, the scanners sent your information to the local monitors. I just don't know what they'll do with an unidentified scan of two teenage girls dressed in clothes from an earlier age. Will they chalk it up to a mistake? Will they follow up?"

"I think they'll follow up. It's too strange a coincidence for two girls walking together to have no profile in the system," said Katherine. "We have to assume they'll be coming here soon. I'm also concerned that other people, non-government people, may be able to obtain the scanner info. We can assume that those others may be looking into this as well."

"Which means," said Sally, getting the drift of the conversation, "that we need to figure out how we're getting to New York City quickly."

"Thus the need for this online room," Jim put in. "So let's take a look at our options." He pointed at the screen, which changed into a map. Edie looked over at Meg, who, despite the generic appearance, looked simultaneously disturbed and excited. She gave Edie an unenthusiastic thumbs-up and they both turned to the screen. Despite the modestly encouraging fact that they at least had the beginnings of a plan, Edie suspected that this trip was going to be no fun at all.

15

the overload

Jared followed the mysterious man into the building, noting the odd flatness of every surface they passed. The building was devoid of any visible ornamentation, and each step they took echoed through long, sterile corridors. The doors had simple handles and what appeared to be number designations, but nothing else. No pictures or photographs adorned the walls, which seemed to be made of the same barren concrete as the exterior. After a few minutes they approached a door reminiscent of an elevator. The doors opened and his guess was proven correct: inside was a padded cell with buttons on one wall. They went inside and the man pressed one of the buttons, none of which bore a number. The doors slid shut with an almost friction-free and effortless motion, like a well-oiled screen door.

The man who had identified himself as Lasho Gluck was silent, but there was something about his manner, even transmitted through the wild noise of code shimmering across his being, that indicated excitement, as though he had suddenly discovered something important and couldn't wait to discuss it.

However, it still came as a shock when the man turned to him as the elevator doors closed and said, "Welcome, I've been expecting you."

Jared didn't know how to respond as the elevator moved smoothly down below the lobby, so it was helpful that the man continued without waiting for him to recover.

"I have been looking forward to your arrival ever since you were transitioned," said Gluck. "I thought it would be too jarring, however, to meet with you right after you arrived. I thus first permitted you to acclimate yourself to this time region. I hope you do not mind." He paused, as though hoping Jared would agree. Instead, Jared stared blankly at the wall until the elevator finally stopped.

The doors opened into a stark, empty laboratory. "What is this place?" Jared asked. The room was lit with what seemed to be fluorescent light, lending everything in view a washed-out appearance. Everything except for his new companion, who still rippled with glowing information and swirling data like a neon sign.

"Ah, that is the question, is it not? Would you prefer the difficult answer first, or the easy one?"

"Let's start with easy." Jared sat down on a black office chair and looked quickly around the room, which was crammed with unidentifiable apparatus and a group of desks. "Especially since I'm guessing that I'm not going to like this."

"Mmm, yes, you are not likely to appreciate this situation, I think, but you need to understand, and understand why you are so critical, eh?" Gluck seemed to offer a thin smile behind his veil of cascading data. "Well, the simple answer is that you are now in the place you used to call Kansas. No one alive today remembers Kansas except as a province in a long-departed empire, twice replaced. Most human life long ago departed this world, Terra, for a variety of new colonies.

The world you left does remain, however, a bastion of learning and scientific knowledge, and many return here for their formal education. Some former university towns are still in use as such, as is this one. The world you once knew has changed greatly. That is part of the simple answer."

Jared allowed this story to sink in. Much of it was exactly as he had guessed based on the strange sights he had witnessed that morning, although he found himself clenching his teeth in frustration when he considered how far into the future he had stumbled. But he knew there was much more, and that it would be worse.

"I'm guessing," he said, trying to keep the fear out of his voice, "that the difficult version of this story explains why you can speak English, why you look like a bunch of glowing symbols, and how I ended up here. Is that right?"

"Yes." Gluck nodded as if acknowledging a clever student. "But perhaps we should start with a question for you. What are you?"

Jared almost laughed, and didn't answer at first until he was certain that Gluck was serious. "I am a human being, a person. I'm not sure how else to describe myself."

"Well, Mr. Garber, what if I were to tell you that a human being is comprised of information?"

Jared thought back to the books he had read in school, and the ones he'd read for fun, the ones his father complained about. He suspected he knew where this conversation was headed. In fact, it was beginning to sound like a riddle, which would have normally annoyed him to no end, except he had nothing better to do at this point, so he decided to play along, hoping desperately that there was an answer at the end of the game.

"I would agree with you," said Jared. "Our DNA is data, the heat in our bodies is information. We are made of information, which instructs our bodies how to be ourselves. All things are made of data; our cells and even the molecules inside us are data. Is that what you're getting at?"

Clearly pleased, Gluck clapped his undulating hands together. "Excellent! This will not be as difficult as I feared. Yes, all things are made of data. But imagine you *are* data. Data must reside somewhere, correct?"

"Um, sure."

"So where do you reside?"

"In Kansas?"

"Ah, you are thinking too small. A better question might be, where does *Kansas* reside?"

Suddenly, with stomach-turning intensity, he understood. All the fear of the past few hours melted away, only to be replaced by an even more insistent emptiness. He felt his own jaw drop into a wordless O. After a moment of silence, he recovered enough to speak.

"My world, it—it isn't real, is it? Is that why I can see code when I look at you? Because we don't really exist?"

"Not exactly, Mr. Garber. You do exist, but you are getting closer. Much closer," said Gluck. "Perhaps I should skip ahead now and give you the difficult part of the answer."

"Wait," interrupted Jared, shaken. "That wasn't the difficult part of the answer? I think that was plenty difficult."

"Trust me. It will get far more difficult than that."

"You've got to be kidding me." Jared slid his chair backwards in irritation.

Gluck sat down next to him, his skin a nonstop mélange of glowing code, and focused his grey-scale eyes on the teenager before him.

"The difficult part of the answer relates not to what *you* are, but to what *I* am. You see, if your world is an illusion of sorts, the more disturbing question lies in what is behind the curtain, eh? Something must be real, correct?"

Jared's head was now hurting in earnest, but he tried desperately to follow Gluck's reasoning all the same. "Let me see if I understand this." He looked around at the room, frowning with concentration. "The bad news is that I've been sent thousands of years into the future. The good news is that all of this is fake? Does this mean I can get back to my family, in my old fake time? And who sent me here? Are you real? Am I real?"

"Yes, well, you have focused on the central issue before us," said Gluck with what almost seemed like a chuckle. "But many of your questions require us to define our terms. You speak of things being 'real,' but that is not the correct word. 'Real,' you see, is a relative concept, and there are different kinds of real." His features became more serious. "You were sent here by someone known in your world as Jackson Hronck. He is not a human being. He is what we call a Faktor."

"A Faktor?"

"He is, in fact, a specific kind of Faktor. I, for example, am a Faktor as well, as you may have guessed. But Hronck is...on a different team, shall we say, with a different goal. I am what is called a Noema; he is an Antinomi."

Jared tried to interrupt but Gluck, oblivious, continued. "Hronck is sworn to changing, to altering the outcome of the computation, and believes that context is the only reality. I believe in content integrity, and am sworn to preserve the outcome..."

"Okay, please stop," Jared broke in finally. "I don't understand anything you just said. Try that again, from the beginning."

"Ah, perhaps I skipped ahead a bit far, hmm?" Gluck looked pensive, or at least as pensive as it was possible to look when your eyes had no visible pupils, and then he began again. "You are correct in guessing that your world is a simulation. That simulation, or world, was created inside the Mesh. There are many such simulations, perhaps an infinite number, that lie within the Mesh."

"Perhaps? Is this Mesh thing like a computer network?"

"It is exactly like a computer network. You are beginning to understand."

Jared paused to consider this. "So am I a piece of software, or an app, or a program—something like that?" His eyebrows shot up to his hairline as he spoke, still incredulous.

"A similar notion, perhaps, but a bit limiting. Perhaps some history will help put all of this in perspective."

"Okay," said Jared with a deep sigh. "I'm up for history, as long as it gets me home."

"It will, Mr. Garber, if you listen well. To go back to the beginning, there was a race of beings that lived long ago, called the Saan. They created the Mesh for their own obscure purpose. But as far as we can tell, the Saan no longer exist, so we cannot ask them why. We do not even know what type of beings the Saan may have been. They have been gone for what seems even to me to be an infinite series of eons. We do not know where they went, or why they departed, but they have left us many clues."

Jared found his jaw hanging open and remembered to close it just as Gluck began to speak again.

"In addition to the Mesh itself, the Saan created a race of beings known as Faktors. We can move between the worlds created within the Mesh. Moreover, we can speed ahead to what might seem to you to be the future, or move backwards into the past in any given world. To be sure, within your human worlds, as in all worlds, we must follow certain rules of the system. While in your world, I cannot act like an omnipotent god. I cannot climb into your mind and learn your thoughts. However, we have enormous freedom within any given universe. We do not know why we were created, and we have differing views on how we should relate to the Mesh and the worlds within. Our own purpose, you see, is a significant subject of debate."

Jared thought about this for a moment, trying to place this story in a framework he could understand while trying not to think about the fact that he was essentially a prisoner of Lasho Gluck.

"Is it like a war? I mean, between your type of Faktors and the other kind?"

"That is not an inaccurate way to consider our dispute." Gluck looked up as though thinking. "We each have visions of what the Mesh is and why it exists. Hronck, and the other Antinomi, are trying to manipulate the Mesh to achieve certain outcomes. It is far too complex to describe right now, but it involves Hronck and his followers becoming almost what you call gods. The Noema, such as me, believe that the Mesh exists for a reason. And we are trying to guide it to its natural conclusion."

"Do you want it to end?" Jared looked horrified. "Destroy the world?"

"No. We believe in transformation, not endings."

Jared stared at Gluck, trying to process this blizzard of new ideas. After realizing that the effort was futile, he decided to take another tack. "But why can I see you, when nobody else can see what you really are?"

"Ah, that is exactly why you are so interesting. You are, as far as I know, the first human being—and perhaps the first non-Faktor in any Mesh world—who is able to see us in our coded manifestations, who can see the world as it truly is."

"Really?" asked Jared, amazed. "No one else has ever seen those codes?"

"No, I believe that you are the first one. Hronck has seen you and has sensed that you can see us as we are. But I suspect he considers you a simple anomaly, and perhaps he wishes rid himself of you simply out of caution. He does not, you see, know something else about you, something crucial. If he knew or even guessed at the truth, he would have killed you on the spot."

"Why's that?" He pushed his chair a bit farther away from Gluck. "What do you know about me?"

"That you can open the door." Gluck paused, as though deciding how to proceed. "Let us say that there is a door, and behind that door is almost unimaginable power. But when you seek to open the door, you cannot, for it is locked. In order to see what is inside, you need a key. This key is much discussed among the Faktors, and it is known as the Root. No one knows exactly what the Root is, but we all believe that it exists, and that it will provide a user with almost limitless opportunity within the Mesh. The possibility of the Root is, of course, well known to Hronck. He believes that it will be decisive in determining the direction of the Mesh and the forthcoming battle between the Faktors. Unfortunately, he already knows about *her*, another one from your world. She is the one who can find the Root, and Hronck is already putting her on a path towards finding it. Thus, we must obtain it first."

"She?" Jared could only barely follow Gluck's explanation. "Who do you mean?"

"For the moment he remains ignorant of your role, which is good," said Gluck, ignoring his question. "However, the girl is in great danger, for Hronck wants the Root more than anything else in this world or any other. Our goal is to assist her, to preserve her. She is powerful in ways that even I cannot understand, but she does not know, and cannot know yet."

Jared felt even more confused than he had at any time over the past several minutes. Gluck sighed and stood up.

"Come, Mr. Garber. I need to show you something that may help you understand."

Jared followed Gluck to one side of the room. Gluck waved at the floor and a glowing silver stick emerged from the tiles, impaled on the surface like a sword stuck in a stone.

"Please, Mr. Garber, grasp this handle. You will feel a strange sensation, but then you will see things, in your mind. I will be there."

Jared hesitantly walked up to the silver handle, noticing that it had a undulating, liquid surface. Deciding that he had nothing to lose at this point, he firmly grabbed the handle, only to discover that it was soft, like putty. Suddenly, the silvery gel on the handle began to crawl onto his hand. Before he could pull away, he felt a hook grab him in the abdomen and swirl him into nothingness. He closed his eyes as the motion buffeted him, then opened them just as he came to a halt. There, standing next to him, was Gluck.

They were outside in a field similar to the one he had arrived in earlier that day. He could tell, intuitively, that he was in Kansas once more. However, he could do no more than guess at the year, as the buildings in the distance were too indistinct.

Gluck turned to him and began to speak once more, sounding to Jared's ears very much like a self-important teacher. "This will, as I promised earlier, be difficult to grasp initially. However, I suspect that once you think about it, you will realize that everything you have experienced in your life, everything you have ever suspected, is still true. As we talk, we shall walk into town. By the time we reach our destination, I hope you will better understand our predicament. We must find the other one, and help her before Hronck understands that you are a real danger to him."

"How so?"

"Think of the world you know as a computer," said Gluck, now beginning to walk. Jared followed closely behind. "Each of you is a bundle of information, moving along corridors of logic within your system. Your interactions with each other are operations in a computer program. There are rules, like grammar, which control what it is you can say, think, or do. Millions of years ago this computer, your world, was programmed to solve an equation. You and this other person, whom you will soon meet—you are the answers to that calculation." He smiled, mirthless and cold. "This is an exciting and dangerous time indeed, Mr. Garber. You will experience what you might call an adventure, whether you were looking for one or not."

16

stakeout

L t. Lisa Alter parked her car several doors down the street from Sally and Jim's house. It wasn't a squad car, so it lacked the flashing lights that still adorned most emergency vehicles. It was, nevertheless, clearly an official transport of some sort, and Lisa didn't want to look obvious. She wasn't sure why she didn't want to be easily noticed, and no one had done anything illegal that she was aware of, but it seemed imperative to her that she not stick out like a sore thumb.

Lisa had called Kathrine from the car, but she hadn't taken her call, which was extremely surprising. Lisa had always been able to reach her on a moment's notice, ever since Kathrine had moved back to work at the university. This was not merely because the women were close friends, although they were. Rather, Kathrine spent most of her time sitting around thinking, or pondering the results from some French particle-accelerator experiment. She rarely had meetings and was usually both available and happy to distract herself for a few minutes with a call. She was *always* available. An unreachable Kathrine was, to Lisa, quite alarming.

Lisa stepped out of the car and walked cautiously towards the house. Sally's minivan was in the driveway, but no one seemed to be around. Stepping alongside a neighbor's house, she slipped into the backyard and hid behind a hedge. *I can't believe I'm snooping around like this*, she thought, amused. *This is such a rookie move.* Just as she was contemplating walking towards the house to see inside, the sliding door opened, and Sally, Meg, and Edie walked out.

Edie and Meg were now wearing modern clothes. Sally looked to be the proper age, and there was no question about her place in this world. But Edie and Meg resembled the same young teenagers who had disappeared decades earlier. In fact, as Lisa craned around the hedge for a better view, it seemed that both girls were even sporting the same haircuts they had the day they vanished, and Meg had the same earrings. She stared in wonder as they came closer to where she was hiding.

"Good guess on size," said Edie, playing with her video-enabled skirt.

As Lisa listened to their conversation, she had to stifle a gasp. This had something to do with Hronck? A time machine? She bent even closer and tried to see through the branches. A twig poked her in the forehead, but she ignored the pain as she angled for a clearer view.

"Somebody who tries to get rid of a bunch of kids and a whole family with some kind of death ray because he's afraid that someone will see his big 'invention' doesn't seem like an honest guy," Edie was saying. "Who knows what else he's done?"

Now Lisa began to back away from the hedge. She had to think about this for a moment. Did she hear that correctly? It was almost too much to absorb. Jackson Hronck had a time machine? Is that how he'd invented all of those amazing, world-changing things? And he'd sent Meg and Edie into the future because they were nosy? And was he responsible for the disappearance of the Garbers as well?

Gradually her native indignation kicked in. While she considered the implications of what she'd heard, she watched Sally and the girls head back inside. As they closed the door, she ran, crouching, towards the kitchen window. There she saw Kathrine with Jim at the table.

So, thought Lisa, Kathrine knew about this but hadn't mentioned it to her? Why not? Didn't she trust her? *She* was the police officer, after all. The irritation over the slight grew but was soon quashed by the wonder at seeing Edie again. As Lisa watched, the girls donned head-gear and cronked into the network. She went back to her car and decided that an informal stakeout might be appropriate here. Moreover, she needed time to consider her options. What exactly was she supposed to do about this? Should she walk up to the front door and confront them, and hug Edie as she had longed to do for so many years? Why did she feel such a strange resistance to doing that?

Lisa put in for vacation time right then, right from her car. She hadn't used any for eighteen months, so she felt perfectly within her rights to take a few days off without explanation. The request form had a line for "destination," but she left it blank.

• • •

Lisa was so focused on her new, informal investigation, she had failed to notice that a man had followed her from behind the hedge and listened in on the same conversation from a few feet away. She also failed to see him look into Sally's window only a few moments after Lisa had departed. She never saw his figure walk two streets over to his car, get in, and immediately place headwork over his well-coiffed hair.

As he cronked into the network, Mark immediately initiated a search on Lisa's activities for the day. He wasn't sure what he was looking for, but her behavior today had been completely inexplicable, even in light of their breakup. Moreover, his own detective training had begun to kick in, and he grew increasingly suspicious the more he thought about what he had seen. He needed to get to the bottom of this, though he wasn't sure why. But there was one thing Mark was certain of: it was going to require some further investigation, and he was ready.

part three

everybody hits the road

17

life is a highway

The yellow strips in the middle of the road flew by so quickly that they blurred into a solid line of gold stretching out into the horizon. Only 1,627 miles and a day or two separated Edie from New York City and what she hoped would be a return trip home. It was no different than many other family trips she could recall, except that she was not with her family, and her final destination was unknowable.

"Ironically, when I was a teenager, I used to fantasize about stopping time," said Sally from the front seat. "You know, pushing a button and stopping time for everyone but you."

"I had that same dream, too," said Meg, smiling at the thought. "I'd wish, in the middle of a test, that I could push pause on everything, like a movie, and just think about my answers for a while. Maybe go home and watch a soap opera, or reread my textbook by the pool."

"Well," laughed Edie, momentarily forgetting herself, "it looks like someone else had the remote and hit fast-forward instead."

But that conversation had ended a while ago. In the silence that had descended over the van, Edie thought back on the planning for this trip. She still couldn't believe this was happening to her.

Jim had changed his mind and decided that the three of them should leave immediately, in case the mall scans of Edie and Meg were viewed by the wrong folks, whomever they might be. Kathrine mentioned the impossibility of air travel and dismissed the trains out of hand. "We need to reduce the number of opportunities for you two to get scanned," she said. "I'd like you to limit your travel to roads. There are only a few places where they scan cars on the highways, and those are mostly at the borders. They don't bother at the small town restaurants and motels."

"No one really knows how many people really have access to the scanning information," Jim said. "For all we know, Hronck may be able to get his hands on this stuff, and we don't want him to know about you before we get to New York City."

Edie had looked at the avatars sitting around an imaginary table and almost laughed at the strangeness of it all. She wondered what else you could do with your fake bodies in the network. Could you touch each other? She leaned over and poked Meg, who briefly turned to face her. So you *could* feel sensation while cronked in, she thought. That was pretty cool. How bizarre that you could think something in real life and have it happen in the network to your avatar. Before she could consider the implications, she heard her name.

"Edie, if we can get you guys back to your original time, maybe Hronck will never get to be president at all, never even get to be mayor." Jim started to get excited. "Maybe history is changed again."

"But won't he know that?" she asked, skeptical. "Is he really going to help us?"

Meg looked over at her. "Can you think of a better idea?"

She shrugged. Without proof of what had happened, she figured, no one was going to listen to them anyway.

Jim pointed at the screen where a map of the highway system shone red like blood vessels over the nation. "Sally, if you drive them, you can probably make it in a bit over twenty-four hours. You'll have to stop to sleep once, at least, but you should do it at the most anonymous motel you can find. No fast food, either."

"And what do we do once we get to New York?" asked Sally, examining the map. "Where do we go?"

"That's going to be the tricky part," said Kathrine. "Melissa and Amanda both live in New York, but I'm not sure how to contact them about you two without flipping them out. Our best bet is definitely Mel, though."

"Why?" asked Edie. "What's the story with them now?"

"Melissa's a surgeon. She can handle difficult situations, and she's less of a hothead than Amanda," said Kathrine. "Amanda will be important later, because she knows Hronck through City Hall, where she works, and she can probably get us into see him. But we'll need to work on that part of the plan as we get closer."

They all silently considered things for a few moments. Edie tried to read their electronic faces.

Sally finally broke the silence. "Do they both live in Manhattan?"

"Hronck lives on Fifth Avenue, right off the park, in a big famous house, and Melissa lives nearby. To be honest, I don't have any idea where Amanda lives anymore," replied Kathrine. "I'll call her ahead of time and tell her to expect you folks. I'll explain that it's urgent, but I won't mention the two of you. Or maybe I will." She sighed. "I don't know, I guess I'll probably play it by ear. Anyway, avoiding a scanner in New York City is going to be nearly impossible, but at least you'll be there."

"When are you calling them?" asked Jim, not even bothering to try hiding the concern in his voice.

"Before Edie and Meg cross into Manhattan. Also, we need to make sure that they're well hidden in the back of the van—so girls, don't stick your faces out and smile at the bridge tolls."

Now, sitting in the back of the van watching the world go by, the idea of New York City seemed an eternity away. But at least they were headed in the right direction, and she could hope that things turned out okay. Unfortunately, she thought, that seemed pretty unlikely.

18

family trees

G luck had steered them towards Jared's town. As they slowly edged into the neighborhoods near his home, Jared began to recognize the trees. They looked almost the same. Twenty-five years was a long time for a human being, but to a mature tree it wasn't long at all.

A spreading chestnut arched across the trail they followed, leaves emerging into the spring air. He remembered reading about these trees, how they had been replanted a few decades before to replace trees destroyed by a blight. Billions of chestnut trees had been killed, all over the country. Was that tragedy intentional, part of the script composed by the Saan millions of years before?

As he inhaled, Jared realized that the smells surrounding him were painfully similar to those he remembered from earlier that day, from his walk home with Josie in another time. *It must be the same time of year as when I disappeared*, he thought ruefully. Some things, apparently, remained unchanged in this time.

If only he could go back home.

He shook his head to dislodge the association from his mind, and continued following Gluck up the path. Gluck was a silent companion, a man-shaped soup of data strolling ahead of him.

Squirrels darted from the brush, unafraid of the approaching footsteps. Jared wondered if they knew they were living in a simulation, that they were the dreams of a race long gone and forgotten. Were the birds that flew through blue patches in the canopy of branches merely operations in a mathematical proof lasting millions of years? Should that change how Jared thought about them, or about himself? Gluck, apparently oblivious to both the drama and the poetry surrounding him, pulsed with light as they wandered into Jared's old neighborhood.

Once again Jared felt incredibly alone. A few minutes earlier, still bubbling with emotion, he had tried to extract more information out of Gluck, with only limited success.

"I have one big question, and I still need an answer before we go any further," said Jared, leaning forward as he walked. "Where is my family? Are they okay?"

Gluck appeared to frown. "Your family is not available."

Jared rushed ahead, blocking Gluck's way. "Are they dead?"

"No," said Gluck, but Jared felt something hidden in the blank response. Gluck stepped lightly stepping around him. "I do not believe they are dead. I would be able to detect their deaths. They are simply elsewhere. As I presume that none of you were holding hands, or were otherwise tethered, you all went in different directions along the timeline, given the method used by Hronck."

Unsatisfied, Jared continued to press. "Well, at least I have you to explain things, and I've read books where this kind of thing happens." His eyes watered despite his efforts to remain in control. "My dad is an orthodontist, and my mom writes about cats. They have no idea about all of this.

And my sister, she's my twin, she won't know what's going on...."

As he trailed off, he hoped that Gluck might provide more explanation. He did not, merely continued to saunter forward.

It was about this time that Jared realized he was exceptionally tired. It was the early evening when he'd disappeared, and he had since lost all track of time. It could be 3:00 a.m. to his body as far as he knew, perhaps even later. Soon he would need to sleep. Moreover, given his unkempt mental state, he half expected to learn that this had all been a horrible dream.

For that reason, as they walked by the familiar tongue of trees leading towards the Garbers' brick house, he almost believed that everything would still be the same there. Josie would be hitting a volleyball against the side of the house, her hair in a ponytail, her face set with effort as she slammed the ball with a tightly clenched fist. His parents would be inside, reading big-city magazines and preparing bizarre foods out of cookbooks filled with vivid pictures of persimmons and finger limes. But then he turned to his side, saw Gluck undulating ahead of him, and was immediately pulled back to grim reality. He sighed and plodded on.

While contemplating what Gluck might have meant by his threat of an "adventure," Jared noticed that he had magically been given new clothes. Apparently Gluck could manipulate more than just time. Jared's shirt now appeared to be layered with moving wave-forms ricocheting across his chest. His pants were constructed of some kind of wide-wale corduroy that had small vehicles traveling in its velveteen valleys. For a moment he was distracted by watching what appeared to be a race among three of the little cars on his thigh. Just then, Gluck stopped abruptly.

"While we are headed towards your house, that will not our destination." He seemed oddly concerned that Jared not get the wrong idea. "No one is there of interest to you anymore, not in this time. We are going elsewhere. We arrived in a more distant location so as not to attract unwanted attention. However, now we will go on towards the hospital. There we shall visit with two others."

"Any plans to tell me what we're doing now?" Jared felt petulant. "I mean, if I'm so important, it would be useful to tell me what's going on."

Gluck made a sound almost as though he had something stuck in his throat. "We are visiting the guardians of the other one, the girl. They have chosen to decommission themselves, but at my request they have remained available for these many years for this eventuality, which I have foreseen. While I could personally communicate with them through the Mesh, it will help for you to meet them in person, so to speak. It will provide you with some perspective on the girl, your partner in this effort. These guardians currently reside in what you call a 'nursing home.' They have no family, for obvious reasons, and thus we will be their first 'visitors' in many years. However, I have ensured that the custodians of this facility are expecting us."

"You realize," said Jared, no longer trying to disguise his impatience, "that I still have no idea what we're doing, except that we're going to a nursing home. This is getting completely ridiculous."

"It is just ahead." Gluck pointedly ignored Jared once again. "The building next to the hospital. We will be looking to visit individuals known in this region as Judy and Peter Boyd. They are together in this facility, as they have been since the disappearance of their niece, Edie Boyd, twenty-five years ago."

"Edie Boyd?" Jared thought the name sounded familiar, but couldn't quite picture the face. "She was in my school, right? Or wait, maybe it was last year, in junior high." He thought a bit more, and struggled to recall more detail. "Different grade, right?"

"Yes, that is correct," replied Gluck. "She was a year behind you. She and a companion, Megan Karger, have been sent into this same time by Jackson Hronck." He started walking more quickly, and Jared hurried to catch up. "Ms. Karger is of little relevance to me. However, Edie Boyd is an anomaly, just as you are. A critical anomaly. You will meet her." He paused and added, almost as an afterthought, "Eventually. But in the meantime it is vital that you hear her story. There are no better people to provide that background than her guardians."

Jared tried again to picture Edie Boyd. "I remember her, sort of, I guess." Then something clicked and he stopped. "Now I've got it. Josie was friends with Meg's older sister, Sally. I saw Edie hanging around with Meg. I don't really know much about her, though."

Gluck's tone was clinical. "Ms. Karger was raised without parents. The story told to her, and thus to others in your town, in your time, was that her parents perished in an accident, a car accident, when she was young. This was more easily understood by you and your kind. However, the truth, as you might expect at this point, is more complicated."

"And what's the truth?" asked Jared, wearying of Gluck's circular explanations. "What really happened to her parents?"

"The truth is that Edie Boyd never had parents. She was born without them."

It took several moments for Jared to begin walking again.

• • •

The nursing home was pleasant, if sterile, and oddly non-futuristic. The lobby was painted in a variety of neutral colors, with soothing prints of landscapes hung on the walls.

Jared was still trying to get his head around the notion of being born without parents when they arrived at the room of Judy and Peter Boyd. *No parents.* What on earth did that mean? Gluck had not bothered to expand on his bombshell revelation about Jared's "partner." Was Edie Boyd stuck in some kind of time warp, too? He felt completely trapped by his dependence on Gluck, and on Gluck's carefully dosed teaspoons of information. Was Gluck really going to help him get back to his family? Upon reflection, he wasn't sure that Gluck had ever agreed to do that at all. As they walked into the room, he decided he needed to start thinking more critically about this Gluck guy if he hoped to get home.

Lying in beds next to each other, the Boyds both appeared to be elderly and barely aware of their surroundings. Each had a similarly glazed look, an expression unfortunately familiar to Jared. His own grandmother had declined quite suddenly a few years back, and in her final days she could neither recognize her family nor assist herself in any way. For that reason, while Jared didn't even know the Boyds, he found their condition depressing. That is, until he remembered that they weren't actually real people at all.

Gluck spoke as soon as the attendant left the room and closed the door. "Mr. Garber. As you may have guessed from our earlier conversation, while not Faktors, Judy and Peter Boyd are not beings of this world. While they appear catatonic, they have been fully engaged with our larger project over these past several decades within the Mesh."

"Can they hear us?" Jared felt uncomfortable talking about the Boyds while they were in the room. "I assume we came here to talk to them, right?" He noted that, unlike Gluck, these beings (whatever they were) did not appear to be a bundle of liquid code. Rather, they looked quite human and unremarkable.

"Actually, Mr. Garber, we came here for them to speak to *you*. If we are to assist Ms. Boyd, and if you are to understand your own destiny, we need you to better appreciate what is happening in your world." He turned to the beds, where the Boyds still stared blankly at the ceiling. "We are now alone. You may speak."

As though a switch had been thrown, the Boyds shot up in bed, staring at Jared with frank curiosity.

"He can see you truly?" asked Mrs. Boyd, as though they had been speaking for hours. "He can see you in your true form?"

"Yes," Gluck replied. "He is the other of whom I have spoken. Hronck does not yet know of the deeper logic we have discovered, and thus does not understand Mr. Garber's significance." He turned to Jared. "These are the simulacra of the Boyds. They were the guardians of Ms. Edie Boyd for fourteen years until her disappearance twenty-five years ago."

"Edie is a remarkable girl," said Peter Boyd, sounding very much like the cantankerous uncle. "We were lucky to find her."

"Gluck was expecting her," added Judy Boyd in a light, fluted voice. "He understood that the Mesh would produce her. He sent us out to find her."

Jared thought he was beginning to understand. "Where did you find her? I mean, how was she created?"

"She appeared in a field, in the middle of nowhere, in a location charted by Gluck based on statistical probabilities and programming necessities," answered Mrs. Boyd. "She was created by the Mesh itself, from nothing. As Gluck may have told you, that has never happened before, neither in this world nor any other. Even *you* were born of parents from the Mesh, and Gluck tells us you're a powerful anomaly, too. He knew she was coming, though. We retrieved her, as instructed, and raised her according to the information we were provided."

"These beings were created to mimic the behavior of parents and guardians," said Gluck, pointing at the Boyds almost as though they were machines. "They were put in place with a full back story. These Mesh instruments became Ms. Boyd's aunt and uncle. At a certain age—although it was difficult even for a Faktor such as myself, and had not been attempted before—we provided Ms. Boyd with false memories so that she would have a normal childhood. I concluded that such a background was necessary."

Peter Boyd chimed in. "That's right. Once Edie was old enough, we gave her certain recollections, so that she 'remembered' her fake parents. We thought it was important that she believe it. We then moved here, where I assumed a job. The goal was to bring Edie up as normally as we could, and allow her to develop her talents, which we did not yet know and still can't completely identify. Our hope was that she could learn about her destiny as an adult, naturally. Events, however, have made that impossible."

"Why?" asked Jared. "Why not tell her right away that she was special?"

"We believe," said Gluck, "that it is important that Ms. Boyd be unaware of her true nature. She can change the Mesh, and change your world, by finding and using the Root, whatever it is, with you. However, we do not know how she will accomplish this task. Thus, we do not want to alter the future by changing her."

"Well, you guys blew it," snorted Jared. "If you had warned her, she wouldn't have gotten anywhere near this Hronck guy."

"Actually," said Judy Boyd, "we now suspect that she was *supposed* to meet Hronck. He is the one who sets her on course to find the Root."

"When we realized that Hronck had learned about Ms. Boyd," explained Gluck, "we initially believed that our hopes had been dashed. She might be taken away from our control, along with our ability to study her. However, upon further analysis, we believe that things are unfolding in the only manner in which it was possible for them to occur. Your presence confirms that fact."

Jared thought about what he was hearing and grew increasingly disgusted. Edie Boyd had been brought up to believe that her parents were dead, that she was being raised by doting relatives. But all of it was a lie. Instead, she was the result of some kind of miraculous birth, she was supposed to save the world with a boy she had never met, and she had no idea that she'd been in serious danger from the start.

"So," said Jared in a probing voice. "When did you learn about me?"

"We detected you several years ago, when you first began to see the coding of your world," said Gluck. "At first you appeared to be merely a simple incongruity in the Mesh— there are many of various kinds throughout your world— and Hronck, I suspect, presumed the same thing, if he even bothered to notice you. It is a measure of his arrogance that he did not even consider in his calculations the coincidence that you lived in the same town as Edie Boyd." Gluck went and stood between the two beds. "I, however, considered it far too serendipitous to presume mere happenstance. Instead, I began to investigate, to drill down into the deep logic of the Mesh. Even amongst Faktors I am particularly skilled at analysis of the Mesh and its code." His tone was almost proud. "Through that investigation, I believe that I now understand you, Mr. Garber, and why you exist."

"Is that right," said Jared. "*You* understand *me*?"

"Perhaps not your motivations," replied Gluck cautiously. "However, I understand *what* you are. You, in concert with Ms. Boyd, can change the nature of the Mesh, and of this world. You can wrest control of your world and your time from the power of Faktors such as myself, and doom Jackson Hronck to irrelevance." He swept his arm as though pointing at the room and everything beyond it. "You can make all of this *real*."

"Change the world? Take control?" Jared suddenly felt as though a camera had zoomed in on his face, as if he were in a movie. He experienced an unmistakable sensation of nausea, and began to wonder whether Gluck was insane, or whatever it was that Faktors became when they lost their minds. He needed to get home and find his family, and these people, things, Faktors—whatever they were— wanted his help to rule the universe. Or maybe not —why would Gluck want to help Jared become powerful enough to harm the Faktors themselves?

As he came back to his senses, still in a state of turmoil, Jared noticed that the Boyds and Gluck were all staring at him intently. His exhaustion was now competing with fear for control of his body. "How am I— are we—supposed to do all of that? Do you have a plan? We're just a couple of teenagers, and I barely know her." Jared now began to pace as he spoke to Gluck and to the empty room as though it held an audience. He felt like a cornered animal facing a predator. "And why should I help you? What are we supposed to do to make this happen?"

"Ah, yes, that is the difficult part," said Gluck almost apologetically. "I do not know."

jackson hronck: man of the century

"So, do you girls want to learn a bit more about Hronck?" asked Sally, turning to glance at the girls briefly before staring back at the road. "I'll bet you can find a documentary on the network. There's some headwork in the back, if you're interested."

Edie and Meg exchanged a look and shrugged in unison.

"Not that you aren't great company," said Meg, "but that's not a bad idea." She started fiddling around with various compartments around the seat, until she found headsets similar to the ones they had used in Sally's house. Edie helped her get them on, and then Meg assisted her.

"Sally, we've got them on, so how do you get the things to *start*?" asked Edie, looking for a power switch.

"Sorry," called Sally from the front. "I've got it right here; I'll click you in." She pushed a few buttons. "When you get into the network, you should be in the library—I have it preset to go there. Best place to find things, and the only place you guys can go, anyway."

Before Edie could ask why they were restricted to the library, she felt once again the sensation of being sucked into a hole and swirled through a vortex. Moments later she found herself in what appeared to be an old-fashioned library. Books lined every wall, and a ladder heading up to the highest shelves was parked on one side. A series of comfortable chairs and side tables were scattered throughout the room, as were large cushions and a leather couch. Meg was there, too, in her generic teenager avatar get-up, striped shirt and all.

"I suppose," said Edie resignedly, pointing to Meg's clothes, "that I still look pretty ridiculous."

"Yes," she laughed, looking at her own clothes. "You do. If we end up being stuck here, Sally is going to have to get us some custom avatars. We're basically cartoons."

"We'd better not be stuck here," said Edie, suddenly humorless. She looked around. "So how do you think this works?" She ran her hand over the spines of books. "Do we read these books, or is there something else here?"

They explored the room for a few minutes until Meg discovered what looked like a tiny screen on one of the walls. "Hronck documentary," she said to the screen. To Edie's surprise, the screen immediately expanded into a large projection covering the wall and came to life; she was barely able to run over and sit down before the narrator began her introduction.

"Jackson Hronck," said the narrator in a posh but impossibly excited British accent. "Inventor. Pioneer. Change agent. His inventions represent nine percent of the gross national product of the United States of America. More than seven million Americans are employed by his company, Hronet—more than the armed forces, the postal service, and every federal government agency combined. Movements in the stock price of Hronet can affect currency valuations. Factories and service centers for Hronet products can be found on every continent, including Antarctica, and in nearly every nation."

As this narration continued, pictures of Hronck in a variety of heroic situations flashed across the screen: Hronck as industrialist, wearing a hardhat while opening an automotive plant in a newly revitalized Detroit. Hronck as environmentalist, wearing hip-waders and a flannel shirt while leading a drive to clean up the Hudson River. Hronck as scientist, wearing a lab coat and sitting behind a series of beakers and a large blue flame. Hronck as charity worker, looking sad-eyed as he helped feed the hungry in some remote, war-torn village in sub-Saharan Africa. Edie frowned throughout the entire description.

"So what accident of history produced Jackson Hronck?" the narrator asked in a faux-erudite voice. "Can his success be replicated by others, or is his genius simply lightning caught in a bottle? Tonight on *Backgrounds*, we look at Jackson Hronck." A credit sequence flashed across the screen, followed by a picture of Hronck as a young adult.

"For many years, Jackson Hronck has maintained a wall around his personal life, seeking to remain a private individual even as he changed our world."

"I'm sure he *has* wanted to keep his life private," said Edie, feeling somewhat appalled. "He didn't want anyone to see the ray gun he kept in his backyard."

"Shh," said Meg. "No commentary."

"His beginnings remain somewhat of a mystery," continued the narrator, as more pictures of a much younger Hronck appeared on the screen. "While his appearance as a post-graduate fellow at West Kansas University is the starting point for most Hronck biographies, we went searching for the child who would become our leading innovator."

Edie snorted. "I think I'm going to barf."

"Shh!" whispered Meg even more urgently. "This may be important."

"...remarkably little evidence documents the early life of Jackson Hronck. An orphan, his parents are unknown. He was raised by foster parents who are no longer alive. Homeschooled in a rural area with few electronic files, he has no existing records of his classroom experiences. No playmates can be found to discuss his childhood...."

"How do we pause this?" asked Edie suddenly, looking around for a button.

"Why?"

"I'll bet you just say 'pause' to the screen. Okay, I'll try it. 'Pause!'" As if by magic, the screen image paused over an image of Hronck reading a thick book by a fireplace.

"Don't you think that's a bit strange?" she asked, turning to Meg with a conspiratorial note in her voice. "There's no record of his childhood, he just suddenly appears as a guy in his twenties. Isn't that a little fishy?"

"I guess...," Meg began, but Edie kept talking.

"I know, I know, but think about it. No details from his childhood?" She shook her head so violently that her neck cracked. She massaged the back of her head. "No friends, no relatives, no teachers? No way. Something is completely wrong with this story."

Meg considered this for a moment. "Sure, no question it's weird, but let's keep watching." She frowned. "I don't know what to think anymore." She turned back to the screen and said in a commanding voice, "Play!"

The narration immediately restarted. "One of the few reliable descriptions of Hronck's childhood comes from Hronck himself, in an interview conducted on the eve of his acceptance speech for his first Nobel Prize, his initial one in physics. Here, Hronck discusses the town where he grew up."

The screen was suddenly filled with a slightly younger Hronck, looking dapper, as though ready to attend a formal event.

"The details of my childhood are, to be frank, somewhat inconsequential," he intoned to an interviewer as they strolled through what appeared to be a seventeenth-century palace filled with malachite pillars and lapis masonry. Large paintings hung throughout the hall, and Hronck's heels echoed across marble floors as he walked. "Much of my schooling was self-directed. I didn't have much contact with other children, so my friends were largely of the imaginary variety."

He looked somewhat forlorn, but Edie was struck by how plastic his expression seemed. Having had her own childhood traumas to survive, she had long wondered whether adults ever really forgot the pain. Did they leave their memories behind them, as though they had happened in a different life, or did they cling to their hurts like an old piece of gum on their shoes? Being both introspective and cynical, she had always assumed that the pain never really went away, which is why she immediately mistrusted Hronck's story—it all seemed too well rehearsed.

"When did you first realize that you were special?" The interviewer was so obsequious as to annoy even Meg, who loved celebrity interviews, and she could soon be heard making retching sounds in the background. Edie laughed while trying to listen to Hronck's reply.

"As a young man, perhaps thirteen or fourteen years old, we had a dog. I loved that dog, but one of our neighbors hated it." He looked down at his lap. "She accused it of biting her, and she wanted it destroyed. A total fabrication, of course, as far as I could tell. So she got the sheriff to take it away, and I was distraught. I followed the sheriff into town and took the dog back. Stole it, really, from his car when he went into the station. I promptly ran away from home because I thought I would get in trouble."

"Did you get in trouble?" asked the interviewer, seemingly mesmerized by Hronck's stilted delivery. "You sound like you were a bit of an outlaw."

"Oh, please," said Edie, looking for something soft to throw at the screen. "This is so fake, he doesn't even remember the name of his dog, or if it was a boy or a girl."

"Shh!"

The video suddenly focused more tightly on Hronck's face. "While I was out with my dog"—("Still no name for Fido?" Edie sneered)—"I ran into a man, a traveling salesman, I believe, who convinced me to return home, despite everything. I could not abandon my life in the face of a mere obstacle, someone who did not like my dog."

"This story seems awfully familiar," interjected Meg.

"As I walked back, I watched a storm form in the sky, a super-cell thunderstorm. And as I watched it, I realized that I wanted to determine how it worked. It was so huge, so majestic. I wanted to understand why the weather happened. And I became obsessed with balloons."

"Why balloons?" asked the interviewer, fascinated. "I mean, the weather...how did it help you understand that you were special?"

"Well," continued Hronck, a self-important smirk on his face. "I wanted to build my own weather balloon, to measure and change the weather. So I went back home and figured it out myself. I built all of the instruments. Once I saw that I could do that, saw that I could do whatever I set my mind to doing, I realized that there were no limits for me. None. And I also realized that everyone else did not have my sense of confidence, my sense of destiny."

His lips turned up in what was clearly supposed to be a smile, and Edie shivered. "Because I did have these feelings, I knew in my heart that I was special."

"And, indeed, you are special," fawned the interviewer.

"Pause," said Edie emphatically, and the picture froze again. "This just gets worse, doesn't it?"

"Totally." Meg gazed thoughtfully at the screen. "I swear, this whole story seems familiar, like he took it from somewhere else. Maybe," she said, tugging on her hair, "maybe he isn't from our time, either."

It was as though an explosion went off inside Edie's brain. "That's it!" She stifled a scream, and Meg jumped a bit from surprise. "He didn't have a childhood here, that's why the memories all seem so fake. It's because they *are* fake—he's from another time, too." She considered this for a moment. "But I don't think that helps us much."

"No, probably not, but let's keep watching. I still want to hear more about this guy. Play!"

20

the faerie queen

L isa had always been close with Kathrine, Melissa, and Amanda, but Edie's disappearance so many years ago had brought them even closer. Edie had been their leader, the first among equals, and her absence had forced them all to grow up, fast and together.

All four of them had left Kansas for college. However, Amanda and Melissa had moved to New York after graduation, while Kathrine and Lisa had each eventually made their way back to Kansas (in Kathrine's case, after receiving a Ph.D. in particle physics from Caltech).

While they still spoke occasionally, Kathrine and Lisa only saw Melissa once or twice a year when she came back to town for the holidays, and Amanda much more rarely than that. Moreover, Amanda and Melissa were married and had children of their own, and were in a different place in their own lives. Neither Kathrine nor Lisa had ever married, and both were resolutely single. Lisa's stories of relationships gone bad and Kathrine's comedic dates were the grist for many of their conversations. Rarely a week went by without Kathrine and Lisa getting together for a giggly lunch and discussions over the silliness of their lives.

They had not discussed Edie's disappearance in many years, despite the fact that it loomed over their lives mercilessly. In fact, Lisa could not remember the last time Edie had even come up in conversation.

For Lisa, perhaps the oddest result of Edie's disappearance was something she had never revealed to anyone: Lisa always kept a complete change of clothes in her car. This was not typical police procedure, and she was not aware of any other person who did it. But she always felt more comfortable knowing that the clothes were there. Perhaps she might need to go somewhere in a hurry, wherever that happened to be.

It was a habit she had acquired as a teenager, shortly after Edie had vanished. It began with her backpack. Before leaving for school, she would carefully confirm that the bottom of her bag contained a tightly packed pair of jeans, underwear, socks, and a shirt. Also, in a small plastic bag, she kept a toothbrush and a full tube of toothpaste she'd snagged from underneath her parents' bathroom sink. Her bag was always heavy, but she felt better, somehow, knowing that her clothes were there. You never knew, she had reasoned, when you might be taken away.

For years afterwards, Lisa would daydream about Edie and where she might be. To be sure, she understood on a fairly basic level that Edie was almost certainly dead. The disappearance of a child rarely resulted in happy endings, as the news reconfirmed nearly every day. Yet she had seen enough stories on tabloid shows about kidnapped children growing up in captivity that, for a while anyway, she kept a small light on inside herself, hoping and believing that Edie was alive.

One of her most vivid fantasies of that time had been that Edie had met up with the faeries. Faeries, Lisa learned from Mrs. Besicka, were mischievous creatures in European mythology who gloried in leading travelers astray. They would kidnap children and take them to another world, where the children would pine for their lost families forever.

The myths varied, of course, as to what happened to those the faeries kidnapped. Lisa's dreams of what had happened to Edie varied, too. In some fantasies, Edie became a beloved pet to the faeries, permitted to live her life as the object of infinite affection. Perhaps she was jester in the court of Oberon and Mab, wearing bells and telling jokes to amuse the royalty gathered on a midsummer night. In other dreams, Edie was a slave, perhaps to the evil queen Nicnivin, living in a parallel world and waiting to be rescued. Lisa imagined herself the rescuer, and pictured a journey into the netherworld to recover her friend.

Mrs. Besicka had explained that faeries had been an obsession of Victorian England because they represented nostalgia for a way of life that had vanished. Faeries represented a lost time of farms and rural life during an age of factory smoke and rapid change. Now, thinking back on a happier childhood with Edie and her friends, Lisa couldn't help but identify with that Victorian urge. Her remembered childhood with Edie and her other friends had already become impossibly idyllic soon after Edie's disappearance. By the time Lisa was sixteen or seventeen, Edie had grown into a figure of such power in her imagination that she could calm herself merely by imagining Edie's life in the faerie world.

In one of the myths she had read in class, faeries would enchant the clothing of their victims; as long as they wore the same clothes they had been wearing when kidnapped, they would be trapped in the faerie world. If they were able to change their clothes, they would be free. Lisa had been unsure for many years whether the clothes she kept with her at all times were for her, or were spares for Edie if she found her. Now Lisa did not need to concern herself with that distinction; her spare clothes would serve one purpose only: they would allow her to follow Edie and Meg without coming home.

Because now she had learned she wasn't imagining things. Edie and Meg were really alive. Hronck was responsible. The Garbers had likely been sent into the future as well. All of the pieces began to fall into place. It was almost as though she had learned that her daydreams about faeries were true, and that they had been really sent to another world. But the world they had been sent to was Lisa's world as an adult. Now, she thought, perhaps she could help rescue them after all.

As she thought more about this, a smile playing around her lips, she saw Edie and Meg (along with Sally) leave the house and enter Sally's van. They were carrying what appeared to be a small suitcase, probably with a change of clothes. Lisa quickly put her seat back into driving position, stowed her headgear, and prepared herself to follow. She couldn't wait to talk to Edie again, but decided that the time was not right. Not yet.

• • •

Mark's first task when he got back to his car was a simple one: cronking into the network and trying to figure out what strange thing was happening to Lisa. Sure, this breakup had been mild, as far as their breakups went. There had been no yelling, no throwing of plates. There were no accusations of dishonesty or immaturity. Instead there was coldness, a discomfort. Sitting next to her on the couch, watching television, Mark could feel emanations of distrust and irritation. It was, he decided, not unlike the heat-sensation weapons that police departments now used instead of guns. These weapons shot an energy beam that penetrated the skin to a depth of 1/64 of an inch, causing incredible pain but no damage. He remembered how, at the police academy, each recruit had been forced to experience the pain. It was searing and then it was gone. The breakup with Lisa had been like that. A beam of heat followed by nothing.

He suspected that he was primarily at fault. He usually was, and he knew it. But Lisa, Mark was quick to remind himself as he slid on his headwork, bore plenty of fault as well. She refused to trust him on the most basic things. He wondered whether it was better to leave well enough alone and move on. After so many years, he had begun to believe that their relationship was ultimately doomed.

But personal feelings aside, something about Lisa's behavior today was particularly curious, even suspicious. She was clearly investigating something on her own. Mark knew she would have called for backup under normal circumstances. In fact, at her level of seniority, she shouldn't have been investigating anything at all. She should have been supervising others, the officers who would execute the investigation in detail. Moreover, as annoyed as she was with Mark right now, she certainly respected his investigative abilities enough to ask him for advice, or at least a second opinion. They did that all the time, even during their worst periods together.

But now, beyond not asking for help, Lisa seemed to be actively *hiding* an investigation from him. That was not only surprising and annoying, but against force policy. No officer was permitted to engage in his or her own private investigations. A force in which officers kept secrets was more akin to something you would find in dictatorships, not in a democracy. Lisa's distrust of him was now going to get her in trouble—which probably served her right, he thought.

Mark's mind resolved into a series of three-dimensional images, ending with his avatar sitting in his private office in the network. He tried to remember the bits and pieces of the conversation he had overheard while snooping on Lisa's stakeout at that house. He thought he had heard something about a time machine and Jackson Hronck, but none of that made any sense, and he'd been too far back to hear much more. Nor did he see the people who were talking and could only surmise that they were on the young side. As soon as he was fully connected, he called up the address of the house Lisa had been staking out. The background on the house, ownership history—all of it popped to the surface in his mind. Jim and Sally, the owners, were easy enough to investigate: professor and financial entrepreneur, respectively. Two kids, nice house. Scanned history of their public behavior streamed below like a stock ticker. But he still couldn't see any connection, and could not guess why Lisa might be investigating them in secret.

Frustrated, he called up Lisa's most recent searches over the network. This was something he had authority to do, though he wouldn't normally have done it. He quickly noticed that all of the searches related to two girls named Edie Boyd and Meg Karger, with a couple of extraneous ones relating to Jackson Hronck. Apparently Lisa was still sitting in her car performing more searches on the network. *Curious,* he thought. Looking further into the records Lisa had accessed, he discovered that the girls had disappeared twenty-five years before in a crime that had never been solved. He tried to pull up the rest of her searches but discovered that several had been deemed "private" by Lisa and were inaccessible. Now *that was* interesting.

Taking a wild guess, he looked into the official file relating to the disappearances and learned that Edie Boyd's circle of friends, all interviewed as part of the investigation, included several girls, one of whom was...Lisa Alter. It didn't take much longer for him to notice that Meg Karger had a sister named Sally. It took even less time to realize that Sally Karger was the co-owner of the house where Lisa had been snooping a few minutes before.

Reading through the file, he noticed that much of the investigative speculation at the time, twenty-five years earlier, centered on the question of whether the disappearances were connected to a similar disappearance earlier that same week, in which an entire family had vanished. He sat back in his chair and began to read the rest of the file. Lisa, it seemed, had developed a hunch about this. But what was it, and why now? He understood that something this traumatic might become an obsession, but why had she never mentioned it to him, after all those years of dating? Again, apparently she didn't trust him. His annoyance grew.

Mark removed the headwork and pulled his car around the block, driving slowly in case Lisa came barreling out of the next street. He hit a few buttons on the console and a mapped image of the neighborhood appeared. Several flashing dots indicated moving cars. He typed in a few more commands and a red dot appeared on the map, showing the location of Lisa's car. After a few minutes of staring at that dot, letting his mind roll through the various facts he had learned from his initial research on the network, Lisa's car pulled away from the curb.

"Let's see where you're going, Ms. Lisa," he mused aloud. "Where are you going, and why is it a secret?"

21

a boy without a brain

Just as Meg ordered the video screen to play, a disembodied voice was piped into the library, echoing like a broadcast. "I'm going to jack you out of the network," said Sally's voice, amplified through what sounded like stadium speakers. "We've got to stop for food and a bathroom break. I'm dying here and I figure you guys must be, too." Suddenly the library dissolved and Edie found herself sitting in the back of the van, wearing a headset and looking at the now completely darkened sky. The van was sitting in the parking lot of a restaurant. The sign in front flashed "Colonial Steakhouse."

"Where are we?" asked Meg, turning around to peer through other windows. "You know this place?"

"Yeah." Sally gathered up her purse. "We're in Oakley, just off the highway. Stopped here with Jim and the kids when we went to see Buffalo Bill's statue." She opened the door and stepped out. "Come on, we never even really had dinner and it's late. We'll want to grab food then try to drive a while before we have to find a motel." Edie and Meg nodded to each other, stepped out of the car, and followed Sally into the restaurant. It occurred to Edie that she couldn't even remember the last time she had relaxed at all, and hoped that a big meal would help settle her thoughts and her stomach.

"Sally," Edie yelled as she jogged to catch up. "Do you realize that it's been twenty-five years since Meg and I have eaten anything?"

"Well, you'd think I'd have lost some weight from that," laughed Meg, patting her trim stomach. "But I still look the same."

. • • •

After dinner, they drove another hour or two and then stopped at a generic-looking motel just off the highway. A trailer park sat across the street, surrounded by undeveloped land and farms. Well-groomed landscaping and some makeshift street lights created the appearance of a subdivision, as opposed to a trailer park. The motel itself, Edie thought, was one of the most unremarkable looking buildings she had ever seen.

"This looks perfect!" said Sally. The building was a series of blue concrete slabs with peeling red paint on the window frames. A sign outside said "motel" in scrolling letters on video fabric stretched over a frame that hung from a pole. Edie had now seen so many video images playing on so many random surfaces that she barely noticed them anymore. Weird, she thought, that she was now taking the time to notice that she didn't notice them anymore.

Meg began to snore, and Edie looked over at her friend. How much did she really know about Meg or Sally—or anyone, really? She had never really considered what type of problems her friends might have, or whether any of them might have traumas in their own lives. She thought back to her many lunch conversations with Kathrine, Amanda, Lisa, and Melissa, and realized how few of them had touched on their inner selves. It was mostly superficial stuff, with a few "plans for the future" thrown in for spice. Now Edie needed no plans for the future. She was living the future right now. It made her feel lonely.

As she wondered if there was any surface in this new era that could not be wrapped with video-enabled fabric, or any clothing that didn't come alive with images, Edie fell fast asleep. She dreamed uncomfortable dreams about balloon rides and thunderstorms, and she tossed and turned.

• • •

When they awoke the next morning, it was not to the sound of birds chirping or some other bucolic sound of rural America. Rather, they heard fighting, yelling, swearing, slamming of doors, and (Edie suspected) furniture breaking. She and Meg immediately put their ears to the wall but could not hear anything coherent through the old, heavy drywall.

"Girls, come on, that isn't nice," Sally tutted as she stood up from her bed, though Edie could hear the concern in her voice. "You shouldn't be listening in on other people." It only took a minute more, however, before Sally, too, was standing with her ear cupped to the wall.

"All I can hear now is crying," said Meg. "It sounds like the other people are gone."

"I don't hear them either," said Edie. "But I do hear someone crying. It sounds like a kid."

Now looking even more concerned, Sally started moving her ear along the wall to get a better sense of the sound. The only sounds were muffled sobs, like the cries of boy who had been physically injured. After a moment or two of hesitation, Sally pulled some pants over her pajamas. "Girls," she whispered, "I can't believe I'm saying this, but wait here for a minute. Something is horribly wrong next door, and I've got to check it out. And don't worry," she added, as Meg was clearly about to say something cautionary. "I'm going to look in the window first. You guys are Example One of why you don't go into places where you're not supposed to be." And with that she departed the room, leaving Meg and Edie nervously awaiting her return.

Minutes went by, creeping along, slowing time. Just as the tension reached an almost unbearable level, Edie heard another voice in the room next door, a voice that sounded like Sally's, making what sounded like comforting noises to another person.

"What are they saying?" asked Meg. Edie shook her head, unable to hear anything other than the muffled voices beyond the wall, and sat back down on the bed. "Let's get changed," she whispered, though there was no one around to overhear her. "We may need to go pretty quickly this morning." Meg nodded and moved from the wall, and they quickly stripped down.

"Nice underwear," joked Edie, noticing that even Meg's bra was video-enabled. "That is so disgusting!" Meg laughed as she looked down at an image of old films playing on her chest as they put on their clothes. Just as Edie pulled her arms through her shirt, Sally entered the room with a young man in tow. The boy was about their age, perhaps a year or two younger, but he had been badly beaten about the head and neck, and blood was splattered around his nose and over his shirt. His jeans were torn, and he wore no socks with his ratty sneakers. Sally had a kindly arm around him, and he looked both frightened and relieved.

"Girls, this is Ray. Ray, this is Edie, and this is Meg. We'll do extended introductions in a few minutes, but first let's go into the bathroom and get you cleaned up a bit, alright?"

Meg and Edie could hear the water run in the bathroom for several minutes, with some splashing noises interspersed. Neither girl said a word. They were too shocked by this unexpected turn of events to even consider an appropriate response. Suddenly Ray and Sally emerged from the bathroom. Much of the blood had been removed from Ray's face, and Sally looked intensely maternal. She sat the boy down on one of the beds.

"Ray, why don't you tell us what happened? I know you already told me some of it, but let's start at the beginning."

With a fat lip and bruised cheek, Ray looked like he was going to have a difficult time discussing anything. He was rail-thin and pale, with light brown hair flipped over his forehead, and his antic, olive-colored eyes darted around the room. He was physically awkward, as though still growing into his body, like a puppy tripping over his own paws. The presence of Sally appeared to calm him, however, and after a moment he began to speak.

"Well, they left me here," he began, looking at the floor, shaking his head as though surprised to hear his own voice. "I don't really want to talk about it much more. I don't have nowhere to go. But the worst part is, they took my headwork and they took my passkey. It's like all of my stuff is gone, all of my memories." He looked forlorn at the thought. "It's like I don't have a brain anymore, they took it all. And getting access again—can't do it without my passkey. It's all gone, gone!"

Sally put her arm around him. Edie and Meg looked at each other, utterly perplexed. They had no idea what he was talking about. Sally, however, seemed to understand everything.

"They took your passkey?" She sounded concerned. "You didn't keep it in your headwork, did you?"

Ray nodded, and Sally gave an exaggerated sigh. "You shouldn't have done that. You really *will* have a problem now."

"And I don't got nowhere to go," he said again. "They were fosters from the start, weren't even my real parents or anything, but they were bad folks. Truth be told, I was going to turn them in myself anyway. I got the talent, you know, so I saw it on the network."

Edie couldn't take it anymore: this was even more confusing that her conversation with Kathrine the day before. "Okay, I have no clue. What talent? What are you talking about?"

Ray looked over at Sally, who nodded. "Well, when I cronk into the network, I can see things," he said. "Important things, and so I can move faster than normal people can. I can do things, special things. But without my passkey, I can't do anything at all, I don't exist." He shook his head, and his eyes moved to the bed. "You might as well stuff my head like a mattress, 'cause it won't do me much good either way."

"Um," said Meg, equally confused. "What's a passkey, and why can't you just get a new one?"

"A passkey is your online identity," said Sally. "It's what permits you to hook into your private space on the network and allows you to transact anything, really." She looked like she was struggling to find the right words to explain. "You girls were in my library in the car, cronked in through the network, but that was a private room. You couldn't leave that space. You need a passkey to leave, to go places." She looked over at Ray, who looked like he was going to cry again. "And you can't just 'get' a new passkey. There's way too much of a privacy issue; it's your most serious identification. You need to confirm your identity with biometrics— eye scans or things like that. It's who you are. You can't just get that anywhere. You need to go to a city to do that, to get it reset."

Edie suddenly got an idea. Ray looked so sad and abused that a strange instinct to protect him came over her. "Well, we're going to New York, why doesn't Ray come with us? He could get his pass-whatever reset. He doesn't have any family to help him."

Sally looked a bit unsure, but when Ray heard this suggestion, his eyes lit up with such pure excitement and childlike wonder, she couldn't possibly say no.

"Well, is it okay with you, Meg?" Sally nodded towards her sister, though she appeared to have already made up her mind.

Meg looked a bit more suspicious, but offered no reason why not. Edie looked at her, pleading. This boy clearly needed help, desperately, perhaps even more than they did. Yet even more strangely, it all seemed to make sense that he would join them, as though the decision had already been made for them.

"Sure," said Meg. She pulled her hair out of her face. "But maybe we could use a bit more information about you. Where did you come from? What happened to you?"

"I'll tell you." Ray was bouncing now, his bloodied shirt coming untucked from his pants. "If you're taking me to New York City, I'll tell you anything. That's where Jackson Hronck lives, right? I've always wanted to meet him!"

Edie raised her eyebrow at Meg. "I think," she said, "that we're going to have a lot to talk about."

Sally nodded. "Let's get our stuff in the car and get going."

22

suspicious minds

Lisa felt guilty to be following Sally's car, but not enough to stifle her almost overwhelming sense of curiosity. Her own car was equipped with active cruise, with full A.I. support, so she was able to lock onto Sally's van, hover several car lengths behind, and cronk into the network while her undercover police cruiser did all the work. It was admittedly a bit strange to be traveling 130 kilometers an hour without paying attention to the road, but such were the delights of the new age.

Lisa was certainly glad that she had the use of her own unmarked cruiser, instead of the painfully obvious standard unit with flashing lights on the roof. Following anyone was impossible in that car. Cronked into the network, sitting at her desk, she put her feet up (or, more accurately, the feet of her avatar), and thought about the situation at hand. Her dead best friend from childhood was alive and sitting in a car four cars ahead of her on the highway. She didn't need to be too much of a genius to guess that Edie was driving to New York. It was the only sensible thing to do under the circumstances. Hronck was the one who had sent Edie and Meg into the future; thus, he was likely the only person who could send them back.

But now, beyond that initial equation, Lisa was torn. More than anything, she wanted her own childhood back. She wanted to grow up without fear that some adult would walk into her life and take her away, or take away some other friend. She wanted to grow up with the innocence of, well, childhood. And the most effective way to accomplish that was to ensure that Meg and Edie made it back to their own time, and that they did so without incident.

The operative question, however, was how to do that. Was it better to hang back and be the anonymous guardian for Edie, Meg, and Sally as they motored towards New York? Or should she make contact with them, join their team, so to speak, and become a member of their convoy?

The question answered itself somewhat when the phone rang. Or rather, the phone in her imaginary office rang. Her avatar quickly answered it. She had, in an uncharacteristic fit of whimsy, programmed a late-1960s-style phone into her office, pink and shaped like a donut. She leaned forward and picked up the phone. She was surprised to hear Kathrine's voice on the line.

"You rang?" said Kathrine in her typically clinical voice. "I got several messages. I'm sorry I haven't been around."

"Kath, wher've you been?" She felt self-conscious about trying to sound relaxed. "Anything interesting going on?"

"Nah. Just hanging out."

"You know, I just had the most amazing experience today. You won't even believe it. It's why I called you before."

"What happened?" Kathrine suddenly sounded a bit more restrained. Lisa could well guess the reason for her hesitation, and she intended to push it.

"Well, I was sitting at the station earlier today when an alert came over the line." She kept her voice causal. "An alert about two U-Ps at the mall, teenagers. You know what U-Ps are, right?

"Unidentified persons?" Kathrine's normally confident voice wavered a bit.

"Exactly." Lisa now began to speak more quickly, trapping Kathrine with the speed of her voice. "So I pull down the pictures and you would not believe what I saw. Can you guess?" She allowed a bit of malice to creep into her voice.

"Um, no," answered Kathrine, now faltering completely and barely trying to cover the fear in her voice.

"It was impossible. I'll tell you. I suddenly found myself looking at Edie Boyd and Meg Karger. *Edie Boyd*. These girls were their spitting images." She paused for dramatic effect. "They were even wearing the *same clothes* they were wearing when they disappeared. But they've been dead for twenty-five years. Right?"

"Right," answered Kathrine unenthusiastically.

"So I did what any reasonable cop would do: I went down to the mall and took a look at the security cameras." She could hardly keep the sarcasm out of her voice. "After a while, I saw that the girls got into a van in the parking lot—a van owned by Meg's older sister, Sally, who, unlike Meg, has apparently grown up like the rest of us. With me so far?"

"Quite a story." Kathrine sounded like she would rather be anywhere other than having this conversation.

"I head over there and sure enough, it's Sally with Meg and Edie and, to my surprise, you. Now tell me, Kathrine." She suddenly changed to the imperial tone she used when questioning suspects. "What the heck is going on?"

The silence on the line was both jarring and long. "I can't really tell you much," said Kathrine, almost meekly. "Except that I think that our friends are in serious danger, and they need to get to New York."

"As you can imagine, I guessed that. But why didn't you tell me?" Her voice had shaded away from her official tone into a more classically hurt tenor. "Do you have any idea how much I want to talk to them again?"

"Yes I do," said Katherine, "but things have been moving too quickly. They only just appeared. They're already on the road. I should have called you, but I didn't think about it because I was too busy trying to figure out what to do. They're alive." Her normally unemotional voice was now filled with wonder. "Can you believe that they're alive?"

"No, I can't. But I hope they are. As it seems I'm following them to New York right now, it must be true."

"You are?" Kathrine sounded genuinely surprised. "Then we need to talk right away. Can you please set up a room for us to talk? You need to hear the full story. We may need you. As I said, I think they're in horrible danger."

"I know. I heard who sent them here." Lisa's avatar began punching the display. "I'll get us a room right away. I think I can help protect them. Or at least I hope I can."

23

...on their trail

When Sally's van pulled into a restaurant in Oakley, Mark hung back, far back, so that not only Sally and her passengers wouldn't see him, but neither would Lisa. Unfortunately, this also meant he couldn't get a good view of who was in the van, or of what Lisa was doing. After a while, the group hit the road again. They drove through the late evening into nighttime, when the trees began to look like otherworldly life forms and the barns on the roadside looked alive.

By the time they pulled into a motel for the night, Lisa hovering behind them, he was almost unbearably curious. He wasn't scheduled to be on-shift again until the next day, but he decided that he would do a bit of snooping before he headed back to town, and to his normal life.

He parked a few hundred yards down the street from the motel. He walked silently up to the lot, glad not to be in uniform. There he saw Lisa in her car, apparently staking out the place. She appeared to be on her headwork and was leaning back in her seat. He quickly crossed the parking lot and looked around until he sighted Sally's van. It was parked in front of Room 14, which didn't necessarily mean that they were staying in that room, but certainly gave him a reasonable place to start. He walked around to the back of the hotel, counting off the windows to gauge which one would be Room 14. Finally he came across that window. The lights were on, but the window was closed and the shades drawn. He took out his scattered-particle viewer, held it up to the covered window, and put his face to the eyepiece.

Inside, two girls and a woman whom he rapidly identified as Sally were talking. He couldn't hear what they were saying, but that was the least of his concerns. The girls were clearly Edie Boyd and Meg Karger. He had stared at their "missing" posters in Lisa's file for too long today to forget their faces. Classmates gone for so long, appearing in their home town without warning: now he understood why Lisa was so interested. Her dead childhood friends appeared to be alive and, even stranger, unchanged from twenty-five years before.

He pulled out another device, stuck one end to the window, and held it to his ear. A chorus of voices filled his head.

"I can't imagine Hronck won't want to see us, when he does see us," said one of the girls.

"You're assuming that he'll ever actually find out we're there to see him at all," said the other girl. "We'll have a million people to go through before he'll even know about us."

"True," said Sally. "But that's what we're counting on with Amanda. It sounds like she knows Hronck and may be able to get us a meeting. Of course, this is all speculation, and Hronck may simply try to have you killed. That's also possible. So we need to stay on our toes."

"I doubt he'll try to have us killed," said the second girl, twirling her blonde hair in her fingers. "He's running for president right now. He's not going to risk it. You can't kill someone and get rid of the body when you're running for president. Someone would notice."

"Maybe," said Sally. "But he sent you here, so we know he's willing to hurt people. Anyway, we're not going to figure it out now, so let's get some sleep. We'll need to be rested tomorrow." And with that they three of them climbed into two beds, turned out the lights, and stopped talking.

Mark was floored. He noticed he was sweating, even though it was cool outside. He sat back on the ground, put his chin on his hands, and inhaled deeply to clear his mind. *Hronck* had done this? How likely was that? Instinctively he knew this truly was something worth investigating. He slunk back around the motel to gather additional information. After noting that Lisa was still cronked into the network, he lightly stepped around to Sally's van, reached underneath, and placed a small, sticky, coin-sized device under the rear bumper.

He quietly made his way back to his own car, typed a few commands into his interface box, and watched on his map as the red light of Sally's van joined the blue light representing Lisa's car. He spun his car around and headed back to town, but as he drove off, he decided he had one more thing to do that night.

Putting his car in active cruise, he slipped on his headwork. He resolved into his avatar, sitting in his own office, and picked up his sleek desk phone. He thought himself a number and heard the phone ring on the other end of the line.

"Hello?"

"Nick? This is Mark. How you doing, buddy?"

"Fine," said a vanilla-sounding voice on the other end. An odd silence hung between them a moment. "What's up?"

"I was wondering if I could talk to you for a minute. Just a sec, you know."

"Sure, always." The voice registered no emotion. "I haven't seen you in a while, Mark. Not since last year. How's Lisa?"

"Well, this may have something to do with her," he said cautiously. "Are you still working with Hronck?"

"Deputy security chief for the mayor's office—got the promotion last year," said the voice, with just a note of enthusiasm. "VP of Hronet, too."

"Well. Then you're just the person I need to talk to...."

24

aliens

"Honeys, welcome to Effingham, Illinois," said Sally from the front, a bit of a chuckle in her voice. She was removing her headgear roughly as the car turned right into the parking lot of a restaurant called The Midway.

Edie was starved. They had been talking nonstop to Ray for several hours, a task which she found both entertaining and exhausting. He could not sit still. If he hadn't been buckled into his seat, she suspected he would have flown around the car like a rapidly deflating balloon. Meg had tried unsuccessfully to pull a coherent story out of him, but his tale jumped around almost as much as his body did.

"So, your parents," began Meg.

"No, *foster* parents," interrupted Ray. "My real parents were spies. Worked for the government, killed by some evil alien guys and—"

"Wait." Edie raised an eyebrow, a note of amused skepticism in her voice. "Your parents were spies?"

"Well, they worked for the government, and I don't know what they did, and if they don't tell you what they do and they work for the government, they're spies, right? 'Cause they can't tell you the truth." He was talking at lightning speed and barely paused for breath. "Anyway, some folks came and shot them with a gun, like a laser, just like in the movies, and I was there and I saw it happen. I was three, so first I got sent to my grandma, and she was great, but she died, and there was no more family left, so they sent me to live with foster parents. First ones were good, but they had to stop because the mom got hurt in a car accident and couldn't care for kids anymore. Second ones were good too, but the state decided to move me, and then they passed me on to a third one, and they weren't good. They were bad people, totally bad. They knew about my talent, see, and they tried to get me to work for them, and—"

"Slow down a sec," said Meg, putting her hands on Ray's shoulder as though to brace him from moving forward. "Your parents were shot by whom?"

"Aliens," repeated Ray, more slowly this time as though for emphasis. "They were wearing funny suits and everything. They were dis-integrated, like in a cartoon, but in that cartoon you can re-integrate yourself when you get dis-integrated, but you can't really re-integrate, like calculus, and poof! My parents were gone."

"Ray," interjected Edie, now totally confused. "Who beat you up?"

"Those were my fosters, they were bad news, bad, *bad* news." He turned to look at Sally, who also looked mesmerized by his performance. Edie found it incredibly strange to watch the van drive itself as watched him from the captain's chair. "They found out about my talent, about how I can move inside the network, with my mind, and they wanted to use me for it." He began to tap the back of his hand against his knee, which was bobbing up and down relentlessly. "So they did, for a while, and I helped them do things, because they were taking care of me and all, but after another while I realized that what they were doing was, like, illegal and that I could get in trouble too, and that other people were getting hurt, so I refused. We were just now going to where they were going to do one of their next bad things, in St. Louis, and they were going to use me there, but I refused, so they beat me up. They thought they could make me do it, but I'm like my real parents, I won't break, even if some aliens come back again. They'd have to kill me first, but my fosters don't have some ray gun, so they cracked my head against the wall and stuff. The dad beat me with his shoe. Then they took my head-gear and my other stuff, and you guys find me and take me to New York!"

There was silence for a moment while the others tried to absorb this torrent of words. Later, Edie would tell Meg that listening to Ray was like taking a drink by putting your lips around a fire hose.

"So," Meg said, smiling a bit. "I almost understood some of what you just said. But what is this 'talent,' what do you do that's so special that these guys wanted you to do illegal stuff for them?"

"Well, I can move over the network in a special way." He began to bounce again. "I can be there and not be there at the same time. I can access the background. You know how when you're cronked in, it can feel like you're in a room?"

"Sure," answered Edie. "You're an avatar, and you're in this other world with rooms and stuff."

"Well, that other world is really all programming. It's all numbers and words and commands and coding. When you're cronked into the network, it looks like there are walls and chairs and other people, but they aren't real. It's all just a bunch of instructions somewhere telling a computer what to do. People and machines write the instructions, they write them in code, and because they do that you can live in the network as an avatar, like a cartoon drawn inside a movie." He paused for breath and Edie and Meg looked at Sally, who was nodding as though she understood where he was going with this story.

"But you can't access the code for the network world itself," he continued. "That's not allowed, they've got serious encrypts on that stuff. No one is supposed to be able to crack that ice, but *I* can. I'm not supposed to be able do it, no one is, it's not even supposed to be possible, but I can do it. I can't help it. I just see it there, like someone wrote the instructions on the wall for me to read." He paused once more, taking in a deep breath. "When I'm my avatar, I can change anything into anything else in the network, because I can access that code, and I can change it. I'm like a god inside there, like in a comic. I can seem like the police, or your mom. I can make people believe I have lots of money in the bank, even when I don't. But I can't do it without my passkey. Without that, I can't move into the network at all. Even I can't do that. I'm trapped in private rooms."

"So if you cronked in right now…," began Meg.

"I couldn't leave the room that the machine put me in. You guys have passkeys, right?"

"Well, not exactly," said Edie.

"Someone take yours, too? Man, that's happening a lot to kids, I guess, although I never heard of it before. Neither of you have them?" He sounded amazed. "So you know what I'm talking about. It's like someone ripped out everything from your head, right?"

Edie decided that being coy wasn't going to work here. "We never had passkeys. You see, we're not from this time. We're from the past. We're time travelers."

Even Ray was left speechless.

Meg stifled a giggle. "I guess our problems may be as bad as yours after all." She turned to Sally, who was laughing at Ray's sudden quietude. "Maybe we can help each other. Is that why you invited him along?"

"That had occurred to me. But I also wasn't going to leave a beat-up orphan to fend for himself at a roadside motel." She grinned and patted Ray on the arm. "But when I heard about Ray's talents—and trust me, I know what he's talking about—I did think we might have stumbled onto someone who could be a real help. Moreover, if I recall, it was Edie's idea. Right, Edie?"

After hours of talk, they were pulling into a restaurant parking lot. The restaurant was somewhat old-fashioned, like every roadside diner ever built, but in a comforting sort of way. Even twenty-five years into the future, Edie could guess what the menu probably looked like, from the omelets to the open-faced turkey sandwiches with gravy. Ray had put on a clean shirt with a bouncing rabbit on the front. His foster parents had apparently not left with *all* of his stuff; Sally had retrieved what was left from the other motel. There was no question that the past few hours had been restorative for Ray, and he no longer looked quite as forsaken.

"Hungry?" Meg smiled as Ray started to run ahead. Then, looking more serious, she turned to Sally. "I wonder if they were feeding him. He looks like a rail."

"Maybe even thinner than you." There was an edge to Sally's voice. Meg grinned uneasily, and they strolled together up to the restaurant, where Ray was already waiting.

"I hope you don't mind," said Ray, "but I'm probably going to eat a lot. Is that okay?

"Fine by me," said Sally, opening the door. "We'll try to keep our arms and legs out of the way."

25

jared tries and fails to get some sleep

Jared had finally snapped, his exhaustion overwhelming his combined feelings of wonder and panic. "I need sleep. Now," he told Gluck, his manners long forgotten. "I don't care how you arrange for it, but I can't go on without it."

The two of them had left the nursing home several minutes before and were walking back towards Jared's house. Jared had now ceased to be surprised by anything he saw. The astounding cars, the disorienting clothes—all of it was now a blur. Once you'd seen thirty astounding sights in the space of a few hours, he concluded, your mind became impossible to shock.

Moreover, in addition to sleep, he felt as though he needed an apology. Stung by Gluck's admission that he had no plan, and no idea of how they were going to help Edie Boyd, or how they were going to change the Mesh, Jared was forced to consider once again the possibility that Gluck was a crank. An immensely powerful crank, to be sure, but how could Gluck be trusted when he had no idea what they were supposed to do?

"Yes," replied Gluck. "And we would lose much more than our lives, such as they are. We would lose the answers that the Mesh has been computing for millions of years. I said that you and Ms. Boyd were answers to questions asked of the Mesh by the Saan many years ago. But there may be other answers, other outcomes, and Hronck's victory would destroy any hope of ever understanding the reasons why the Mesh was created. All would be lost."

"So we need to keep him from getting the Root." Jared pondered how this might work. "But Hronck is already getting Edie to look for it? Shouldn't we tell her to stop?"

"That is the problem. We need the Root as well. Our hope is that you can use the Root to change the Mesh permanently, to stop Hronck, and perhaps to free your world from the Mesh itself, and allow us all to see outside the boundaries that have been set for us by the Saan. We need her to find the Root. She must not be stopped."

Jared threw his arms up in the air. "So we need her to find the Root, but we need to prevent her from giving it to Hronck. Meanwhile, we need to protect her somehow. Can't we at least *warn* her?"

"Yes, we certainly should warn Ms. Boyd. But we must be careful. Hronck cannot know that she is aware of his plan. We cannot tell her everything. Thankfully, while he can manipulate this world in many ways, his ability to track her is not complete, and he cannot know everything she does any more than I can. However, for that reason, we must also watch her closely: if she does discover the Root, Hronck may eliminate her immediately, perhaps before she even obtains it herself. And yes." He was watching Jared's face intently. "This will be quite difficult."

"Well, where is she now? Shouldn't we go there right away?"

"Ms. Boyd is on her way to New York City with several friends. This is a scenario I believe to have been crafted by Hronck himself. As we do not know when or how she will find the Root, we cannot stop or slow her progress. But we will join her shortly. I am currently calculating the optimum moment to have you meet Ms. Boyd, and I believe that moment is arriving soon."

26

the heart of the matter

True to his word, Ray was famished. He inhaled two cheeseburgers, a large order of fries, a vanilla milkshake, a bowl of chili, and three pickles. After his second dessert—a generous piece of apple pie smothered in vanilla ice cream—he finally pushed away the plate, groaning with discomfort. Edie felt like she had eaten nearly as much, with eggs, biscuits, and sausage gravy weighing her down as though she had swallowed a barbell. Even Meg had eaten, under the close eye of Sally, who seemed pleased to see each forkful enter Meg's mouth.

Outside, on the way back to the car, Ray ran figure-eights around Edie and Meg, with Edie laughing at how much energy the kid had, even after consuming about 8,000 calories worth of lunch. As they drew closer to the van, Edie noticed a very young woman, perhaps as young as one could be and still be a woman and not a girl, sitting on a silver plastic suitcase in the middle of the parking lot.

The young woman was crying, but in the manner of someone who had nearly exhausted her ability to cry. She was blonde, with an open face. She wore a metallic dress utterly inappropriate for either the morning hours or even Effingham, Illinois, at all. The garment was video-enabled, like most clothing Edie had seen in this new time. But the dress's video element seemed to be broken. The same few images of an old French film were stuck, quivering over her body as though they had bad reception. Her eyes were smeared with old makeup, and one of her heels had broken off.

"Sally," asked Meg quietly. "Why is everyone we meet today crying?"

"A good question," she replied in a soft voice, a concerned look playing across her face. She paused for a moment, apparently in thought. "I have to say that normally I wouldn't do this either, but I'm feeling charitable today for some reason, and I don't think I can stop myself." She looked pensive again, then determined. "Girls, get into the car. I'll be back in a minute." With that, she marched over to the young woman and began to speak with her. From a distance, Edie couldn't decipher what was being said. Lacking the ability to eavesdrop, the three of them could see no point in disobeying Sally's instruction and tromped back to the van. There they planted themselves firmly next to various windows so they could watch the conversation and imagine what was being said.

Ray, surprisingly, was silent, focused like a laser on the young woman with the suitcase. Edie wasn't sure what to make of this scene herself, but after the events of the past few days, she could hardly be surprised by anything. After several minutes of conversation, the young woman broke down in tears under Sally's gentle questioning. Sally walked back to the van, a serious yet empathetic look on her face. The young woman remained seated on the suitcase in the parking lot, balancing the bag uneasily between her knees.

"Okay, here's the story," began Sally as she stepped into the van. "This girl is a mess, a complete mess. She went to

Los Angeles with her boyfriend to break into thought-acting to become a POV." Seeing the perplexed faces of Edie and Meg, she continued, a bit of exasperation in her voice. "You know, where the audience lives the life of a show character through that character's eyes, and in their mind? I told you about that, didn't I? Well, I guess this girl must be pretty good at faking her thoughts, which is both really hard and incredibly important in cronked reality shows."

"Sally, I'm sorry, but I don't understand what you're talking about at all," said Meg, and Edie nodded in agreement. "That sounds impossible."

Sally sighed. "Okay, instead of *watching* television like we did when we were kids, instead of sitting and watching a screen, you cronk *into* a show. Say it's a soap opera. You can choose to experience the show through the minds of the actors. Thought actors implant special equipment in their skulls, and they broadcast their thoughts and what they see and hear to you at home. But it's very hard to do. You can't let your thoughts betray that you're an actor playing a role. You have to really become your character so that everyone believes it. It's truly difficult and an incredible talent. Just like Ray here." Ray beamed at the compliment. "To be able to disguise your thoughts online...wow. I wish I could do that."

Sally glanced back out of the window, where the girl still sat, pathetic, squatting motionless over the pavement. "So her boyfriend claimed he could get her an audition, which is nearly impossible out there. Believing him, she came across the country with the guy, but it turns out that the opportunity wasn't even real. The boyfriend had no connection to the producers who make the shows, he just wanted her to come along with him to L.A. He totally ripped her heart out. They had a fight and he kicked her out of their apartment without any money. So she's trying to get back home. She's only a few months out of high school, and now her car's been stolen, with almost all of her clothes, and her ex-boyfriend has her credit chips. Can you believe it?" She looked as though she was about to add some additional observation, but then at the last minute decided against it.

Edie was mesmerized by the story. "Forget about thought acting, or whatever she does. *This* story sounds like a TV show," she said, impressed with the melodrama.

"Yes. Yes it does," replied Sally. "But it only gets worse. The only thing she has with her is the suitcase with her tryout clothes, which she had brought into her motel room to fix—I guess the video broke. So all she has are some flashy clothes and some inappropriate and uncomfortable shoes, and she just broke one of those."

Waves of sympathy flooded Edie as she automatically empathized with anyone stuck far from home.

Sally went on, her voice rising into a higher register as she grew more excited. "She has no money and she's been walking up the highway, trying to hitch a ride, but no one who looks safe will pick her up. Meanwhile, she's stuck. She can't figure out how to move at this point, she's just frozen there in place. All of her dreams have been, well, literally torn out of her, and she just wants to get back home."

"Let me guess," said Meg, looking a bit resigned but also intrigued. "We're going to take her home, too."

"Look," said Sally, "it's important to help people who need it. Just imagine what would happen if we weren't helping you."

"Wait a minute." Meg held up her hands in protest, making circular motions with her palms. "I didn't say anything about this being a bad idea. I just find it amazing that we're running into all of these people who are just as messed up as we are. We're like some van o' misfits here. Maybe she can do a thought-show about us."

Edie glanced at Ray, who was still staring out the window at the woman, and thought about her own life. If her aunt and uncle hadn't rescued her, she might have been in the same boat as Ray, shuffled from foster home to foster home. Without support, she might have ended up like this young woman, stranded and stuck and alone. In a weird sort of way, she realized she was feeling lucky. Here she was, nonchalantly thrown twenty-five years into the future, but she had friends and people who wanted to help her. With all of that, she concluded, she was actually in pretty good shape. For the first time since she'd been ripped from the Garbers' house, she felt better.

"Let's get her inside," said Edie. "She looks like she could use a more comfortable chair."

• • •

Once the young woman was in the car, Edie could see that she was quite beautiful, albeit disheveled in the extreme. She had silvery blonde hair, exceedingly pale skin, and a delicate look about her that made her seem like she was an origami sculpture constructed of tinfoil. After a moment of discomfort, while Ray, Meg, and Edie stared at the woman without knowing what to say, Sally introduced her.

"This is Haley. And Haley, this is Meg, Edie, and Ray. As you can see, Haley's had a pretty tough time of it, but we're going to help her get back home. We're also going to stop by a motel to get her cleaned up." Sally apprised the young woman. "Haley, where exactly are you going? I know you're headed towards the coast..."

"Well," began Haley with some hesitancy, her voice an attractive, flute-like sound. "My family is in Connecticut, but I'm not sure I can face them right now. Not like this. I need to get back on my feet first before, you know....Where are you going?"

"New York City," said Ray out of the blue, suddenly excited again. Edie shook her head as his machinegun of a voice started in earnest. "These girls are going to see Jackson Hronck, though they won't tell me exactly why, but they're from another time, so maybe it has to do with that. Anyway, I need to go get my passkey reset, so I might as well go to New York too, with them, because that's a big city, and they'll do it there, and I don't really have any- where else to go right now anyway. So maybe you should come to New York, too!"

Haley smiled, and Edie guessed this was likely the first smile she had managed in many days. "That sounds like quite a story, Ray. Maybe I'll tag along for a while, and I'll figure it out along the way." She turned to Sally, who had climbed into the front seat. "Is that okay? I just need a little time to think about what I'm going to do."

Sally smiled back. "Sure, we're just driving right now. We can talk about all of this more when we get closer to New York."

• • •

They were able to stop at a motel only a few miles further up the highway. Sally rented a room and the whole crew came in. Sally and Haley headed into the bathroom, and when they emerged, Haley looked much better. She was still wearing the silvery dress, but it was looking a bit cleaner, and the images were now functioning well. She was also wearing a pair of Sally's much more comfortable shoes.

"I should have realized that guy was bad news before I went to L.A.," Haley was saying ruefully. "He would hang out at the mall, buy those bottles with the wristbands, and then cronk in for hours, paid no attention to me. He was a total addict."

"Wait a minute," said Edie, suddenly remembering something. "We saw that in the mall back in Kansas. Some store where teenagers were buying bottles and getting their wrists scanned. What are those things?"

Ray suddenly got up off the bed, where he had been sitting quietly while tapping his knee with the back of his hand. "I know those places, that's where you can buy the nitro, merge with your avatar. Totally wicked, but wicked bad."

"Exactly," said Haley. "It's a totally teenager thing to do—no offense meant to you guys. I should have wondered about somebody twenty years old who messes with that kind of junk. Completely pathetic."

Edie was about to protest that, as usual, she had no idea what they were talking about when Sally's head rang, or rather chirped, and the hotel room went quiet. Edie did a double-take as Sally reached behind her ear, tapped a spot near her ear canal, and the phone, or rather Sally herself, stopped ringing.

"Hey, Jim, how are things going at home?" Sally walked around the bed to squeeze Meg's arm.

Meg smiled back at her, turned to Edie, and said under her breath, "I still can't believe she has a *husband*."

"Sure, we can cronk into the library when we get back to the van if you want to talk," Sally was saying. "We have some additional passengers, too. I'll tell you about it later." Edie watched her talk, and then her eyes slowly traveled absently around the room to stare at the bare walls and the thin, flowered bedspread. "Are you or Kathrine going to come to New York? Okay, we'll talk in the car."

She tapped her ear again, and then turned to the rest of the group. "Looks like it's time to go. Let's all use the bathroom and then we'll head back to the car. We're losing time and we need to hit the road. Also, Jim wants to talk to us, so we'll go to the library once we get going. Haley, are you feeling better?"

Haley smiled at Sally. "Much better." She looked down at her now-functioning dress, gleaming silver under the dull glare of the cheap motel room light fixture. "I can't even begin to thank you. I was rusted to the spot in that parking lot. I have no idea what I would have done if you hadn't come along."

"Well," said Meg. "Hopefully someone else would have helped. Most people..."

"Most people wouldn't have done this," said Haley, her face hardening a bit. "Which is why I owe you guys. I really do."

Edie silently absorbed this conversation, feeling a strange sense of déjà vu. Why did all of this seem so oddly familiar?

27

note to self

Once back in the car and on the highway, Ray and Haley fell into a conversation about being a POV, a thought actor, a conversation so convoluted and jargon-heavy that Edie, listening nearby, felt completely lost. Ray, it seemed, had a deep appreciation for Haley's talent, which he assured the rest of them was both unusual and difficult to master.

"You try to make your thoughts exactly like what your character would be thinking," he explained. "It's almost impossible to do that. You've got to *believe* you are that person you're pretending to be. People who can do it are huge, make tons of money, but it's not so easy to even get an audition. Everyone wants to do it, and you normally have to take a long class first, lots of training…"

"A long *expensive* class," said Haley wistfully. "I can do it without taking the class, though. I even got the implants in my frontal lobe with the money I saved from waitressing in high school. All I need is an audition, but try getting one without a certificate from the class, it's nearly impossible. I would have had to work for two years to earn the money to take the class out there."

"But your boyfriend said he could get you an audition without taking the class?" interjected Meg, who had been listening in as well. "Not a good idea to believe him, I'm guessing."

"So *totally* not a good idea," agreed Haley, a teenaged twang still in her voice. "It was all a scam to get me out there, to basically be his slave and pay half the rent. I couldn't do anything without asking his permission first, it was, like, such a bad scene. And the jerk kept dangling the audition in front of me to keep me around. It took a long time for me to realize that it was never there, and I had no chance to do this without taking the class. And if I had to take the class, I might as well go home to do it."

Just then, Sally turned around and handed out the van's standard headwork to Edie and Meg. "I hope you guys don't mind breaking up the conversation, but we have to talk to my husband, Jim, for a few minutes online."

"No problem," said Haley. "I'm just glad to be out of that parking lot. Go ahead." She turned to Ray and grinned. "Ray and I will talk tech while you're gone."

With permission kiddingly granted by her guests, Sally pushed a button and the three of them cronked back into the network. After the now-familiar feeling of being swept into a vortex subsided, Edie found herself sitting in the same library where she and Meg had watched the documentary about Hronck. Meg and Sally were there, but so were Jim and Kathrine.

"Hey, folks," said Kathrine, smiling. "I'm guessing that things are still boring on your end, eh?"

Edie laughed. "Sure. Nothing going on at all. How about you guys?"

"Well, we've been hard at work on our end too, and I think we have a few things we need to discuss. First of all, there's your old friend Lisa."

"Lisa?" asked Meg, incredulously. "Edie's friend?" Edie was sure that Meg would have remembered Lisa as another one of Edie's lame group of admirers. Although, looking at Kathrine's attractive and commanding presence now, it was difficult to see how anyone could feel too dismissive about that bunch anymore. If Meg ended up half as beautiful and smart as Kathrine, Edie suspected, she'd be pretty pleased with herself.

"One and the same," said Kathrine. "I had an interesting discussion with her a few minutes ago. It appears that she's following you right now in her unmarked police car. Don't worry," she added, as Edie began to blurt something. "She's a police lieutenant now, and a good friend of mine, and she's dying to see you again. I can't tell you how upset she was with me when she realized I hadn't told her that you were alive. Right now she's hanging back, trying to make sure that no one is following you." She looked over at Meg as though to reassure her. "She's concerned that others may notice your scans, and she's going to do everything in her power to make sure that you arrive safely in New York. In fact, *she* saw your scans from your visit to the mall, and she's been doing her detective work to figure out what's going on. That's how she ended up on your tail. Thankfully, we've talked, and she's going to be a lot of help. You can feel confident of that. Once you get closer to New York, she'll come by and you can talk."

Edie was amazed to think that all of her friends had grown up into, well, *adults*. Lisa was a high-ranking police officer. Melissa was a doctor. Amanda was a politician of some kind, and Kathrine was a professor of theoretical physics. Amanda and Melissa, apparently, even had families of their own. It was almost too much to absorb. To Edie, these were all kids she had been hanging out with a few days before.

"But even more important," said Jim, "we need to talk about those notes you received."

"The notes?" asked Edie.

"There's something about your story that's been bothering me." Jim pulled something out of his pocket. "The notes you received in your locker—something about them doesn't make any sense. Who sent them to you, and why? Were they connected to Hronck? I've been rolling it around in my head for the past several hours, talking it through with Kathrine, and I think we may have a solution.

"Edie," continued Jim, a curious tone in his voice. "Could you please try writing 'time is a trap' in block letters? Just use the paper on the desk, that would be fine."

Edie noticed that a desk was, in fact, sitting next to her in the library. She took a piece of paper from a large stack, snagged a pen, and began to write. She carefully wrote out "time is a trap" in block letters and handed the paper to Jim. He looked at it, compared it to the paper that he had pulled out of his pocket, and then frowned.

"Girls, take a look. In one hand is a scan of the note Edie received in her locker. In the other is what she just wrote."

It took only a moment for Edie to see that the handwriting was exactly the same. She felt her stomach fall into her knees.

"You!" screamed Meg, stepping back from her in disgust. "*You* wrote this? We got sent twenty-five years into the future and everyone thinks we're dead because you wanted to play a joke on me?"

"No!" said Edie, stricken. "I would never—I didn't—I mean, really, I—"

"How do you explain this?" asked Meg through tears.

As Edie started to open her mouth, Jim interrupted. "Meg, Edie wasn't playing a joke on you. She did write those notes, but I think she did it from another time. She was sending you a warning."

Now it was Edie's turn to be flabbergasted.

"Those notes are from another time," said Kathrine. "Edie must have slipped them into her locker when she came back to your time. And no," she added as Meg started to interrupt her. "I have no idea how that could have happened, or what it means, or even what Edie was trying to tell you. I'm just as confused as you are."

Edie had no idea what to say. She looked around for a chair, found a big leather recliner in the corner of the room, and dropped down into it like a sack of potatoes. Her fingers trembled a bit. "Does this mean that I sent them from *this* time? Or do I end up going to another time?"

"We have no idea," said Jim. "This doesn't make any more sense to us than it does to you. While it appears that you wrote the note, there's no way you could have slipped yourself a note like that in your own time."

"You see," Kathrine said, "when you were looking into the Garbers' disappearance, you would have had no reason to know that they had been sent into a different time. Those notes could only have been sent by someone who knew about Hronck. And it appears that the person who sent those notes was you."

"But how could I—"

"Wait a minute," interrupted Meg, now pushing her hair out of her face maniacally. "Wouldn't the person who sent these notes have to be in the time where we originally were? I mean, we couldn't send a note back to ourselves twenty-five years ago from here, right?"

"That's right," said Kathrine. "But that's what's so confusing about all of this. How could you have been in your own time, twenty-five years ago, and still have been able to send yourself a note? And why would you send yourself *that* note?"

Edie jumped up. "Exactly! Wouldn't I have sent myself a note saying, 'Don't go into the Garber house, a crazy guy with a death ray will shoot you if you do that?' Wouldn't *that* be the smart thing to do?"

Meg finally smiled again. "I guess. Unless you're an idiot."

"Thanks," said Edie, smiling back. Then, more seriously, she said, "You know I would never have done something like this as a joke, right? I mean, I don't think sending us here is remotely funny."

"Yes." She paused, and then looked directly at Edie. "I guess I know you didn't do it on purpose. This is too weird, though. And then we have these other two freaks in the van with us, too. Sal, did you mention that to Jim yet?"

"What?" said Jim and Kathrine in unison.

"Well, it's kind of a long story. You see...." As Sally explained how Ray and Haley had ended up on the road with them, Edie began wandering around the library. She had forgotten for several minutes that she was in the midst of a hallucination hosted inside a computer network. It was all so real, her mind had lost track of the unreality of it all. She picked up books from the shelves and turned the pages. They felt like real books. She had a sudden, almost uncontrollable urge to pick up a large brown book on one of the lower shelves. She picked it up, feeling almost like a puppet, and flipped through the pages. She found herself turning to page 11, where she saw a reproduction of a piece of art entitled *Waterfall*:

Edie suddenly was suffused with a strange feeling, as though the room had intentionally put this particular book in front of her. Given the fact that she was in an imaginary world controlled by artificial intelligence, this feeling was, she supposed, neither irrational nor impossible. Why had the room put this book in front of *her*? She stared at the picture, an etching of an impossible waterfall that fell in a circle. Something about it resonated with her, but she could not figure out what exactly it was. Finally, unable to make heads or tails of the hint, she said aloud, "I don't get it."

Sally stopped talking. "What don't you get?"

"Oh, I'm sorry. I was just talking to myself."

Sally looked at her watch. "We should go back into the van. Ray and Haley are probably wondering what we're up to in here."

"I still can't believe you picked them up," marveled Jim. "You're really something. And I mean that as a compliment." With that, he leaned over and kissed her. "Goodbye, everyone," he said, as he disappeared through the doorway.

"I'd better go too," said Kathrine. "I've got a plane to catch. I'll see you in New York." She walked over to Edie, squeezed her arm, and followed Jim's path out the door.

Meg, Edie, and Sally were left standing in the library, staring at each other.

"Just when I thought this couldn't get any weirder," said Meg. "It did."

"Let's get back to the van," said Edie to Sally, under her voice. "I want to ask Ray about the network. I ...I think it may be talking to me."

Sally looked at her curiously, shook her head, and without warning the three of them vanished up into the vortex and back to the van.

28

the monkey

Monitoring the goings-on several hundred miles away, Mark could hardly believe the freak show that was now filling Sally's van. Between the kid who couldn't stop moving and the girl with the silver dress, Mark could not figure out for the life of him what type of game they were playing, or what their intentions were.

For him, surveillance was usually an exercise in confirming suspicions. You thought someone robbed a bank, you staked out their house, you followed them around, and you figured out if it was true. Very simple. In this case, however, it was a matter of determining what on earth was going on. Three people rush out of the house in a hurry, head halfway across the country, and pick up vagabonds along the way: totally unexpected. Mark did not like unexpected. He liked predictable.

He was back in his office, cronked into the network, using a combination of his tracking device, roadside cameras, and satellite imaging technology to follow Sally's van down the highway. The tracker made it easy; once he had locked in on the target car, the cameras that sporadically appeared on every highway in the country did his job for him. Most folks vastly underestimated how many of these cameras existed. And with satellites that could pick out the dirty pores of a pimpled teenager from miles in space, there wasn't a single move they could make without Mark's knowing about it. It was a good thing he had followed Lisa, he thought—the folks in the van seemed to be doing everything they could to avoid scanners. Without the tracking device, it would have been difficult to monitor them, no matter how many cameras he might use.

The van was in Ohio now, cruising along a highway in the late afternoon, and he thought back on his conversations with Nick, Hronck's security chief. Nick had been a friend of Mark's in school—or, perhaps more truthfully, Mark had been a friend of his. Nick was a strange guy, had been strange even then. Mark had always thought of him as "the monkey," both because he looked weirdly simian and because he had a fetish for fruit. The guy would eat bananas by the bunch, all the time; one semester, while studying, Nick had survived for three days on nothing but bananas. Mark wondered if the guy hung from trees in his spare time or had a prehensile tail.

Now Nick was the pet monkey, so to speak, of Jackson Hronck, doing his bidding wherever he was needed. Being "security chief" was a euphemism for "hatchet man," as far as Mark was concerned. Moreover, nothing in Mark's recent conversations with Nick disabused him of that notion.

"This is a very strange story," said Nick in their first conversation. "Why are you telling me this?"

"I'm telling you because they are pretty clearly going to see Hronck, and their intentions are unclear," he said, irritated at having to spell it out. "As security chief for a guy soon to run for president, I would think that would be of some concern. I think Lisa may be worried about the same thing, but as I said, she's being a bit of a lone wolf about the whole thing."

Nick had paused for a moment; he had apparently been reviewing something on the network as he listened to Mark. "I would like to discuss this situation internally before I do anything specific," he said. "Let me get back to you."

The follow-up call came only half an hour later. Nick sounded much less dispassionate and much more serious.

"I've spoken with my employer, and we would like you to assist us in monitoring this situation. We believe that the woman you described to us may be armed, and may have hostile intent towards Mr. Hronck. The fact that she has acquired girls who have a specific look to them is also of concern, as it would appear that some form of blackmail may be intended. As you know, Mr. Hronck lived for some time in—"

"Yes, I know that. I know where he lived. But if you think she's armed, shouldn't we get the Feds involved? Do we need—"

"At the moment, there's no need to alert the authorities, except for you," said Nick, a smile evident in his voice. "But we will be happy to pay you extra for monitoring work performed after hours. I presume that your employer permits you to do that?"

It was true that the force permitted off-duty police offers to work security gigs, but usually that meant being a bouncer at the minor-league baseball park, not a private eye. However, Mark could see no reason why he couldn't do this job for Nick. Moreover, Lisa might be in danger. He couldn't forget that.

"Sure, I'll be happy to do it," he said confidently. "I'd like a retainer payment—"

"A credit has been deposited in your account," interrupted Nick. "I presume that it will be satisfactory."

Mark had quickly switched into finance mode in his avatar's mindspace and was stunned to see the new number listed in his banking account. It was several orders of magnitude larger than the number that had been there yesterday.

"Nick, that's very generous..."

"Don't worry about it. I know you'll be of service to us. We may ask you to take a bit of time off from your job, however, to do some work on the ground." He sounded sly. "We don't know when that is, or if it will be necessary. We'll let you know. But please be prepared to leave on short notice."

For Mark, the conversation had been both exciting and mildly disturbing. He was thrilled to be receiving compensation of that size in exchange for any task. But he was concerned about what type of task Nick would consider "necessary." Just as he was thinking about the vacations he might take with the new money in his account, the phone rang in his imagined office. It was Nick again.

"Can you get to the airport?"

"What, you mean right now?"

"Yes," replied Nick impatiently. "Right now. We want you to be on the ground, and we've figured out that you can intercept in New Jersey. But you need to get on that plane within half an hour. We've got one of Mr. Hronck's jets set up for you. You just need to get in the car, drive over to the airport, and we'll take care of the rest. I just need to know that you can do it."

"Sure." He felt a bit hesitant, but also as though he had no choice in the matter. "I'll fly. I just need a minute to set up people to cover for me here."

"Hurry up," insisted Nick. "I want you in New Jersey before they get there, and I want you prepared. We'll talk on the plane. You're the man, Mark. I really need you on this."

"Don't worry." He was already wondering if he had made the right choice by calling Nick in the first place. "I'll be there." As he hung up the phone and removed his head-work, he concluded that he may have in fact made the wrong choice. But now he was stuck. And even worse, he was too curious to leave this all behind. It couldn't really be Edie Boyd and Meg Karger in that van. They were dead. Nick must be right, this must be some kind of bizarre black-mail plot. What did Lisa know about it? Was she in on it?

As he got into his car, feeling the leather seat con-form to his body automatically, he wondered whether Lisa was in danger and whether he would need to rescue her. Perhaps, he thought, he would need to save her from her-self. Somehow that thought comforted him, and he aimed the car towards the sun, heading towards the airport.

29

programming is destiny

Jared Garber had always liked computers. He enjoyed writing code, playing games, looking up random facts online. Along with reading, playing around on the family computer was one of his favorite ways to waste time on a lazy weekend day.

But computers were machines. They weren't alive. Even as he saw code in the world around him, he had never doubted that there was a difference between human beings and computer processors. Living things were superior to the machines human beings created for themselves.

Yet now, in the space of a few hours, all of his basic conceptions of the world had been upended. As they left the nursing home, he felt an endless series of questions bubbling to the surface.

"So how was Edie born, exactly? I mean, if she didn't have parents, how did she just appear in a field?"

"As I told you, the Mesh created her," said Gluck, his face as inscrutable as ever. "The algorithms that power the Mesh rendered her as the solution to an endless series of calculations. She was the inevitable result of the Saan. As were you."

"And you have no idea what we're supposed to do?" prodded Jared, unsatisfied. "I mean, do you have any idea what this Root thing is at all?"

"It is merely guesswork on my part. I believe it would be reasonable to speculate that the Root does not take the form of computer instruction, or a piece of code. It almost certainly appears as a physical form in this world."

Jared thought about this for a moment. "So this Root is a thing of some kind, but you don't know what it looks like? Do you have any idea of how we might recognize it when we see it?"

Under the swirling clouds of data, Gluck almost seemed exasperated by the questioning. "I believe that the Root can only be recognized by Ms. Boyd. I do not know what it looks like, or how it can be distinguished from its surroundings. Ms. Boyd's power, as you will see, is substantial. The ability to see what no one, not even a Faktor, can perceive is remarkable. To be able to then use that power to transform the Mesh—that is almost unimaginable."

"And how do I fit into all of this? I'm still not sure I understand why I'm important."

"Mr. Garber, without you, Ms. Boyd will be unable to do a single task with the Root, or so I believe," said Gluck. "The deep logic of the Mesh requires it. You will know what to do when the choice is presented to you. It is not only your destiny, it is your purpose."

As Jared thought about what that might mean, he noticed that they had once again moved into the trees surrounding his neighborhood. At first, he hoped that might mean they were heading to his home, but instead Gluck once again pulled out the silver handle, its liquid surface pulsing underneath his coded touch. He stuck the handle into the ground and gestured to it, calling Jared over with a wave. "Given the urgency of our mandate, it is clear that the time for explanations is over. It is nearly time for you to meet Edie Boyd. But first, you need to observe her in action so that we can plan our approach."

a frightened feline

Cambridge, Ohio, was a small town on the Appalachian plateau. Nestled into the eastern side of the state, it sat at the crossroads of several highways. It had been justly famous for its glass production and picturesque bridges for many years. The downtown was attractive, with a classical courthouse and small, crafty stores that would have fit in at any time during the prior century.

Yet Edie cared little about the town or its charms. For one thing, she had spent the past hour discussing Ray's "talent" in some detail. From this conversation, she had concluded that her odd experience in the library had not been imagined. The network was, according to Ray, self-aware and possessed of some kind of independent intelligence. When he merged his mind with the network he could sense its thoughts, and could feel something that felt almost like emotion coursing through its code.

"You see," Ray said, and he changed seats in the van for perhaps the third time in ten minutes. "When I go on the network, I don't need to follow the rules. There are rules, you know, that your avatar has to follow. When you think, 'I want to pick up the phone,' your avatar must do that. It has no choice. When your mind thinks, 'I need to lean to the left while I'm talking to Ray,' your avatar must do that. Your avatar has to act exactly the way it would act in real life. When they build the network, they put those rules in, and you have no choice except to follow them, even if you want to break them, because they want to make it difficult for crime, and that kind of thing. Hackers, sure, they try to break it, and they sometimes do, but the network figures it out so the hackers can't do it the same way twice."

"But what do you do?" chimed in Haley, who seemed particularly fascinated. "I mean, you say that you don't have to follow the rules, but everyone else does? When I'm cronked in I don't really see that I have a choice."

"That's my talent. That's why my fosters, the last ones, used me in their con games. They do long cons, tricks where they convince people to give them money, even though they only want to steal it. They're like actors— though not as good-looking as you." Haley blushed. "They pretend to be friends with their targets, partners. They go into fake businesses with them and then rob them blind." He reached over and grabbed a pretzel from a bag they had picked up from a convenience store in Indiana. "I was helpful, since it all happens on the network. I can make anything seem real on the network, rules or no rules, because I can change the rules. Whatever you want, I can make it happen. I made them lots of money, but I wouldn't do it anymore."

Edie shook her head, noticing absently that Meg's new shoes were glowing purple. "I don't understand. Do you mean that the network *lets* you do it? Does someone run the network?"

Ray shook his head. "Don't nobody run the network. That's like saying that someone runs you." He laughed a bit. "I know the network, and the network knows me. It lets me do it, but it lets me because it has to let me. I can do it whether it wants me to or not. Of course," he added forlornly, "without a passkey I can't do nothing at all."

After listening to Ray, Edie thought the notion that the network may have been trying to communicate with her no longer seemed far-fetched. That said, she still wasn't exactly sure she understood Ray's theory in its entirety. But as she worked through the details, she had a great deal to consider. She spent a while silently contemplating her situation and listening to Haley, Ray, and Meg as she thought about the implications. Edie hadn't yet told Meg about her experience in the library. She was still concerned that Meg would think it was her imagination, or that she might still be mad about the notes.

The notes, Edie thought, were the strangest part of this entire nightmare. She wouldn't blame Meg if she were still angry, even though Edie didn't remember sending notes to anyone, let alone herself. How *could* she have sent herself a series of notes, and why would she have done it in exactly the way most likely to get her sent into the future? Her mind hurt even thinking about it. It made her think about the waterfall picture in the book. The waterfall ran in a circle, which was impossible. After the water fell, it circled around to the top again. It was seamless, infinite, and illogical. Was that a clue?

But the last and most pressing reason that she was currently paying very little attention to the town of Cambridge was a bit more unexpected. A small cat, not much larger than her hand, had jumped into Sally's van when they'd stopped for a bathroom break. Meg, Haley, and Sally had departed the car for the restroom, leaving Edie and Ray with the car to themselves. Sally had left the door open for only a moment, but that was all it took. In that split second, a small orange cat without a collar had leapt onto Sally's seat, scrambled into the back, and then burrowed into a gap between the seat and the headwork control panel. Sally had continued on into the store to use the bathroom, unaware that the van had gained a new passenger.

"What the...!" Edie had said.

"Is that a cat?" asked Ray, laughing.

As Edie, assisted by Ray, dove around the van looking for the cat, she speculated aloud on why a cat would jump into their car. "Do you think it was being chased?" She threw blankets around left and right. "Did you see a dog or something out there?"

"Must have been. I can't think of why a cat would want to hang out with us!"

As they were continuing to dive around the backseat, Sally returned to the car. "Those two are so slow." Then she stopped, noticing Edie and Ray flopping around in the van. After looking puzzled for a moment, she finally smiled and asked, "What are you guys doing?"

"There's a cat, a little cat," exclaimed Edie, trying to get to the kitten, which was now just out of reach under one of the seats. "It jumped in the car, and now it's hiding under here. Can you reach it, Ray?"

"Nah, even my arm's not small enough to get in there." He peered under the seat at the cat. "This is one scared cat, man. It looks like it's shaking."

Edie looked under the seat, and sure enough, the little cat looked terrified. It had plastered itself against the steel rod that held the seat in place and was desperately trying to avoid the swiping hands of Ray and Edie as they tried to reach it.

"You guys have clearly never had a cat," laughed Sally, as she too looked under the seat at the cat. "What an adorable kitty! The only way to get a cat out of tight place like that is to entice him, make him *want* to come out. I've got an idea." She sat up and swung her legs back out of the van. "I'll be right back." As she returned to the convenience store, Meg and Haley emerged, laughing together. Edie thought Haley looked a lot better laughing than she had before. Sally stopped to talk to them. The two of them looked perplexed and then ran back to the van, smiling.

"There's a cat in here?" asked Haley excitedly. "Where is it?"

"Under the seat," said Edie. "It's hiding there and we can't get it out."

Haley looked under as well. "Oh, it's only a kitten," she said, her voice growing higher-pitched as she looked at the cat. "And it looks so scared!"

Meg shook her head. "Everyone we meet is scared," she said, laughing. "I'm just surprised it isn't crying."

Haley elbowed Meg playfully just as Sally came back, a small can of tuna in her hand.

"I guarantee that this cat will move very shortly." Smiling, Sally opened the can of tuna and placed it on the floor, just outside the seat. "Come on, guys. Let's give kitty some space."

They all moved back, leaving the cat to itself with the tuna. Sure enough, a minute or two later, the kitten emerged. It looked emaciated and horribly thin, its orange fur dulled by malnutrition. It had enormous eyes, twice as large as seemed appropriate for its tiny head, and a mane of yellow fur surrounding its face like a halo. As soon as it saw the can of tuna, it threw caution aside and stuck its face directly into the can.

"Told you," Sally laughed.

"That is one hungry cat," said Ray. "We're taking him too, right?"

This notion had obviously not occurred to any of them, not even Sally. There was an uncomfortable silence as they all wondered which of them should tell Ray that taking a cat to New York City was hardly advisable. At least that was what Edie assumed everyone was thinking, until Meg spoke.

"Oh, we might as well," she said, rolling her eyes. "We've been rescuing people for the past day and a half, why not a cat? It can be our mascot or something."

"Or something," said Sally. "I don't know that we have the—"

"Sally." A sudden hardness entered Meg's voice. "We're stuck in the wrong time. Ray's an orphan who gets whacked by his foster parents for not helping them steal stuff. Haley got abandoned thousands of miles from home with no money and no clothes and her car was stolen." She gave Sally a look that Edie recognized from many an argument over the years. "I think it's clear that we need a cat."

Sally sighed and kicked the ground absently. "Is that okay with the rest of you? It's not going to be all that easy traveling with an animal." The others paused, looked at Meg, and then nodded. "Fine then," said Sally. "He is cute, no question." She looked back at the cat. "This is ridiculous." She seemed to be trying to convince herself of something. "Fine. I'll go back in the store and get a travel litter box and some food. This is *so* ridiculous...." She turned and headed back to the store.

"Meg," said Edie, still a bit surprised. "Why did you want the cat?"

"I don't know. You said it just jumped in the van, right?"

"Yeah," said Ray. "It ran into the van like someone was chasing it or something. Like it was afraid of something out there."

"Well, I'm afraid of something out there, and I guess the rest of you are too. I can identify with scared. Maybe we could use more company. Maybe the cat will like being somewhere safe."

"Meg," said Edie, looking at the cat still gorging itself on the tuna. "I'd like to be somewhere safe, too. You know where I can find a place like that?"

They had watched in silence as Sally walked back from the store. The cat mewed softly as it ate, apparently happy to be secure, for a moment at least.

Gluck, looking at that motley group through the eyes of this coded kitten, was pleased that his plan had worked so effectively. In fact, if Faktors had been capable of joy, he would have smiled.

part four

the sick rose

31

welcome to new jersey

The caravan would be passing into New Jersey shortly, and Lisa knew that a most unlikely reunion was rapidly approaching. She wondered what she would say to Edie. It had been twenty-five years for Lisa, less than seventy-two hours for Edie—but soon they would meet again

For some reason, this entire scenario reminded Lisa again of the faeries. As an adult, she had never fully rid herself of her obsession with magic. She'd continued to read books on the topic long after her fantasies of rescuing Edie had faded. One story she read in particular imprinted itself indelibly on her imagination. In that tale, a young girl named Anne had been taken from her home by the faeries. Anne was transported into the parallel faerie world, never to be seen by her family again. Many hundreds of years later, a human visitor into the faerie world met a small girl matching the description of the missing child. This girl said her name was Anne, and she thought she had been in the faerie land for about two weeks.

This, thought Lisa, was weirdly similar. Except there were no faeries involved, as far as she could tell, or witches or magicians or wizards. Instead, the rest of the world had moved on, while Edie and Meg had been trapped in their childhoods. Or, as Kathrine had tried to explain, they'd skipped ahead two dozen cars on a train of time without living their life in between.

In any event, she wanted to meet with them. She put the car on active cruise and cronked in. After she had reoriented herself in her office, she called Sally in the van.

"Hello?" Sally's voice echoed a bit in the van. Lisa could hear several other voices in the background.

"Sally? This is Lisa, Edie's friend. The cop." Lisa felt a bit uncomfortable having this conversation given the fact that she had been trailing these guys halfway across the country. "Did Kathrine tell you I would be calling?"

"Yes, she did." Sally sounded grateful. "Are you still a few cars back?"

"More than a few. I'm locked in on your van. Listen, I was wondering if we could meet over the network. I haven't seen these kids since, well, I was their age."

"Of course you can. I'll send along the room for you to initiate. It's a library."

Lisa looked down at a screen on her avatar's desk. A series of coded coordinates had appeared.

"Great, I'll see you there in a minute." She hung up and looked at the coordinates. All she had to do was look at them and close her eyes. No other action was required. Within a fraction of a second, she was standing in a doorway, looking into a beautifully appointed library. The room was covered from floor to ceiling in books, except for a small video screen. Two chairs and a sofa sat in the middle of the room, all covered in leather.

It never ceased to amuse Lisa to see how people furnished their imaginary rooms. With complete freedom to decorate in any way imaginable, most people just created nicer versions of what they had in the real world. In her years of police work, she had rarely seen anyone do something really adventurous in their avatar spaces. In fact, she herself had done nothing special with her own spaces, despite promising to do so for years.

"Lisa, is that you?"

Two generic avatars stood next to an accurate-looking avatar of Sally. Lisa thought she was going to cry.

"You know," she said, her avatar's eyes getting misty with cyber-tears, "you guys don't look anything like yourselves."

With that, one of the generic avatars ran up to Lisa and gave her a hug. "Lisa, you're grown up too. This is so totally strange."

"Edie, think about how I feel!" Lisa could not hold back the computer-generated tears, which were flowing freely, and presumably were doing so in the real world as well. "Are you guys all right?"

"Yeah, if you can consider this 'all right.'" Edie was smiling, making quotation marks with her fingers. "Kathrine said you're following a little bit behind us?"

"Yeah, I suspect you may need a little help when you get to New York." Lisa wiped her imaginary eyes. "And anyway, it looks like we're going to have a big reunion, first one in twenty-five years."

Meg was standing back from the scene with Sally. Edie noticed that Meg looked more than a bit uncomfortable. Having always been the more popular of the two girls, Meg probably found it odd to be surrounded by Edie's friends. Edie was sure it was even stranger because of who those friends had become. All of them had grown up to be successful, attractive adults. Edie knew that Meg had always assumed her friends would turn out to be losers. Much as she loved Meg, Edie was proud of her friends, and she was glad Meg had been so very wrong.

As for Meg herself, these last few days had made her wonder about her own judgment. First, she hadn't noticed that the notes had been written in Edie's own handwriting. Then she had gone along with Edie's idea to break into the Garbers' house. Then she had been wrong about all of Edie's friends, who were now uniformly brilliant and beautiful. What did that mean for Meg? Had she peaked in junior high?

Just then, Meg became aware that the conversation had continued without her. She interjected herself to slow things down, fearful of missing something. "So where are we now?"

"New Jersey," answered Lisa and Sally simultaneously. They both laughed, and then Sally added, "We're almost there. Not that we have any idea what we're doing once we get there."

For that very reason, the plan still bothered Edie. They were going to New York, but with little notion of what would happen thereafter. "Lisa, do you think that Hronck is going to try anything? I mean, he did this to us in the first place."

Lisa looked hard at Edie. "Yes, I think so. No, I don't know if we'll be able to convince him to send you guys back to where you belong. Yes, I think this is going to be incredibly difficult. No, I don't think it's impossible." She seemed to struggle to find the right words. "Do you remember when we took Greek mythology in sixth grade, with Mrs. Ness?"

"Sure," said Edie, confused.

"Well, do you remember the story of Persephone?"

"I know I should, but I..."

"Persephone was kidnapped from her family by Hades, king of the underworld. She thought she would be stuck there forever, thought it was hopeless, but she was rescued, and she saw her family again. There's no reason why this can't be the same. We just need to keep trying."

"But wait!" interjected Meg. "Didn't she eat some seeds or something while she was in the underworld, so she had to return four months out of the year?" She looked over at Lisa. "Wasn't that, like, the explanation for why we get winter? I like you guys fine, but I don't want to come back here for summer vacation."

Lisa smiled. "Well, there's no perfect myth. But there's always hope. We're going to get you guys back to your own time. I have no idea how, but we're going to do it."

"Lisa, I'm glad you're here too," said Edie. "But I'm getting the sense that you don't have a plan, either. Have you talked to Amanda yet, or Melissa?"

"Nope, no plan," said Lisa, laughing. "But Kathrine has talked to Melissa. I don't think we're going to talk to Amanda until we get there. She's a bit more difficult, as you'll see. And she knows Hronck, so we'll need her help. But without seeing you guys, she'll never believe it. Melissa, apparently, believed it without question. She's always believed that we'd see you again." She suddenly looked like she was going to cry again.

Edie turned towards Sally's avatar. "If we go back to where we're supposed to be in time, does that mean that we never were gone? Will Lisa's life for the past twenty-five years go away? Will yours?"

Sally looked down at Edie, a motherly look on her face. "I have no idea. Perhaps my life goes away, and that frightens me more than I can say. After all, I have a happy life today. But this isn't right. You aren't supposed to be here. We have to make things right again." She looked over at Meg and shook her head. "We can't let this happen. It's just wrong."

"But what if we can't?" asked Meg. "What if we have to live our lives in this time?"

Lisa and Sally looked hard at the two generic avatars, attached to familiar voices neither of them had heard in decades. The silence was finally broken by Lisa, with a malicious grin. "If you're stuck here," she said in an exaggerated tone that suggested *there is no way that will ever happen,* "we'll make sure you get better avatars."

Meg smiled back. "Is that a promise, officer?"

Lisa looked down at her avatar's uniform. She looked back at Meg, who had rarely spoken to her when they were young. She returned the grin.

"You can count on it," insisted Lisa. "Trust me."

32

mr. hronck will see you now

Mark flew into the Teterboro airport in something similar to a private jet. It was a drone, an automated aircraft from Hronck's fleet that flew just below the speed of sound. Mark had never flown on a drone before and found it disconcerting that he was the only person on board. The beautifully appointed cabin had six large, leather chairs, two couches, and a bedroom. A refrigerator was fully stocked with drinks, sandwiches, and fruit. However, there were no flight attendants and no pilots. With Mark as the only passenger, the silence was eerie.

Even before takeoff, he had cronked into the network. He had received instructions to do so before entering the plane. A man wearing a black suit, white shirt, and implanted sunglasses had handed him an envelope as he approached the aircraft. "Cronk in when you get on board," he'd said with nary an expression on his face. "The coordinates are in the envelope." Mark had opened the envelope on the spot, read the numbers, and nodded. He knew what to do.

Once in his network office, his avatar merely had to think the numbers provided and he vanished into a vortex, off yet again to another location on the network. His passkey was preloaded into his cerebral cortex (a piece of elective surgery that Lisa had mocked him for on various occasions), so he did not need to enter any further information. Within moments, he had arrived on what appeared to be a street on the Upper East Side, as Manhattan would have looked in 1900.

This part of Fifth Avenue in the early twentieth century was lined with mansions of the new elite. The robber barons and their progeny had built edifices in the style of European royalty, proclaiming their wealth and power to the world through megaphones of limestone and granite. Classical statuary stood as sentries in front of homes the size of modern strip malls, winged gargoyles on every roof.

Ornate carriages rolled over cobblestone streets, and large chestnut horses stepped carefully around waistcoated pedestrians, horseshoes clopping above the din. The smells and sounds of the streetscape were overpowering and required a bit of getting used to for modern sensibilities. Visitors commonly remarked that this world seemed almost more real than their own.

Mark looked down at his own avatar and realized that the programming had already dressed him in the formal suit of a gentleman of the era. He could feel a top hat covering his head. He drew his hand across the brim and felt smooth silk so real that he almost gasped.

He had been surprised to realize that he was coming into this part of the network. While most people were satisfied with a networked existence not too dissimilar from the life they led in the real world, others wanted more. One group had put together an elaborate simulation of ancient Rome and lived in the network as though contemporaries of Caesar and Octavian. They had created a world where role-playing games had been transformed into something not too far from reality. In the network, they all could speak fluent Latin and understood the lore of the age.

Similarly, a group of enthusiasts had created a mockup of early twentieth-century New York, complete with gangs and tenements on the Lower East Side, wealthy sophisticates on the Upper East Side, and vaudeville palaces on Broadway. These worlds were not entirely populated by "real" people. Instead, artificial intelligence substituted as avatars, creating the impression that millions of real people filled the simulation. Such was the case here, with people of every kind and variety stretching out to the horizon as he looked north. On his left was Central Park, on his right a large stone house. He crossed the street, doing his best to avoid horse dung, pickpockets, and carriages. He walked to the elegant, richly carved wood door and knocked. Almost immediately the door opened. A man dressed in stiff, black, butler's livery stood in the entrance chamber, bowing slightly.

"My name is—"

"Yes, we know," said the butler in a starched voice. "Please follow me." He turned and began walking into the living quarters. Mark followed him into a sitting room covered with red damask wallpaper and filled with heavy silk settees.

"Please wait here," instructed the butler. "My employer will join you shortly." Bowing again, he slid backwards from the room.

Mark marveled at the cyber-rendering that had produced this room. Even in an age of super-realistic computer graphics, this room was an incredible technical achievement. Thousands of different textures and myriad fabrics had been drawn by powerful servers, mimicry so exacting that no human eye could distinguish fiction from reality. Velvet appeared soft and lush, while the loom-work of a tapestry on the wall was mesmerizing in its complexity, swirls of color composed of pixilated imagination.

Just as he picked up a circular, blood-red pillow to examine the hand feel of the woven fabric, he sensed another presence in the room.

"The technical specs on the pillow are indeed impressive."

Mark turned around and found himself face-to-face (or rather avatar-to-avatar) with Jackson Hronck.

"Mr. Hronck," he sputtered to the world's most powerful man. "It's a pleasure to—"

"Mark, we can dispense with the pleasantries." Hronck sat down on a large, intricately carved mahogany sofa. He had constructed his avatar to be of average size, but had given himself a strange luminescence that made it difficult to look directly at him for long periods of time. He was dressed in the clothing of the gilded age, with complex suiting, a double-breasted vest, and carved ivory buttons. His mustache was long and waxed, as was the fashion in this era. Hronck seemed somewhat more handsome than he did in photographs, but it was hard for Mark to compare when he couldn't get a good look at the man. "We need to discuss what you're going to do in order to convince this silly group in a van to turn around and go back to Kansas."

Mark gazed at him as long as he could stand it, then looked back at his feet. "Mr. Hronck, I'm not sure that will be so easy. You see, they think that—"

"I'm well aware of what they think, or *say* they think. I've heard the tapes you so graciously provided to me." Mark looked at Hronck again but found it almost painful. Hronck's opalescent skin grew more intense as his emotions rose. "They're convinced I can give them things they don't possess. They believe, or claim to believe, that they are from a different time." He was suddenly on his feet, his right fist pounding into his left palm. "This is clearly a scam, a story, nothing more. However," he said, and his voice lowered to a sudden whisper, "your friend Ms. Alter appears to have been taken in by these charlatans."

Mark nodded dumbly.

"I think your best move in this instance would be to convince your friend that these hoodlums cannot possibly be the individuals she believes them to be. Hope is a powerful drug." Hronck smiled in a manner that gave Mark the shivers. "But in the end it is just that: a drug. It can treat the symptoms of loss, but it cannot cure the disease. Those who are gone are forever beyond our grasp. I assume you understand this, don't you, Mark?" Mark did his best to meet Hronck's penetrating gaze. "I would not want to have a, shall we say, *negative* fate befall anyone. These girls are clearly the pawns of someone else, or perhaps poor souls suffering from one of the new viruses." He began to pace around the room. "You have heard about these viruses, Mark?"

It took a moment for Mark to realize what Hronck was talking about. He nodded his head in assent. "Yes, of course," he said, wondering where this conversation was headed. "I've seen the reports on the news. Pretty ugly stuff."

"I am particularly fascinated by the virus called 'The Sick Rose.' They found that one in the slums of Jakarta. It's a wonderfully poetic name for a virus, don't you think? If you've seen the reports, you know what is so odd about this new kind of sickness." Hronck paused and stroked his mustache. He had stopped next to a bookshelf that appeared to have been carved into the wall, covered with gold filigree and scrolling. He casually reached over and grabbed a book, examining the spine as he spoke again.

"These viruses appear to erase the line between our world of men and the world of the network." His lips curled into

what might have been a smile. "An infected avatar is something we have seen and understood for nearly a decade. It
is no different than any other kind of computer virus. The
idea, however, that an infected avatar could change the living person operating the avatar—well, that's quite unexpected, isn't it? Taking off your headset only to discover
that you have been altered...who would ever expect that?"

He began twisting the end of his mustache. Mark
squirmed under his gaze. "Of course, this is quite an
extraordinary development," Hronck went on. "Things in
the real world can now be affected by events of the network. Something has gone horribly wrong. A person on the
network could find themselves changed into someone else
entirely, against their will. Which brings me to our current
situation. Perhaps, given the state of things, an avatar created in the network could leak into our world. That would
be an interesting explanation for our bizarre apparitions.
Two dead girls? How likely is that?"

Mark absorbed this information for a moment, then his
mouth opened in shock. "Wait a minute. Are you saying
these girls aren't real? They're just avatars that have been
given—"

"Life," said Hronck evenly. "Yes, Mark, it appears to be
unprecedented. Avatars have been given life through the
agency of a virus. But unlike Pinocchio, they cannot become
real girls." His mustache twitched a bit at the corner as
he laughed. "That is my guess. And your friend should be
warned. Who knows what an enemy of mine might be willing to do in order to embarrass me? Danger seems to lurk
around every corner these days."

"Why are you telling me this?" asked Mark. "Why not
just have them disappear? I'm sure that Nick—"

"Mark." Hronck looked surprised and, if possible, a bit
hurt. "I have no interest in hurting people. I just want to

217

ensure that others do not hurt me. Who knows what the truth might be behind these faux girls and their quest?" He put the book back on the shelf. "But in any event, all of our interests are served by stopping them, and convincing them that this effort is both hopeless and potentially destructive. That will be your task." He gave Mark a hard look and then moved to the door. "I have my reasons for wanting them kept intact. I will probably want to speak with them myself at some point, but on my terms, not theirs. In any event, however, I suggest that you begin working on your presentation to Ms. Alter. You have only a few minutes before your plane arrives in New Jersey."

Without so much as a goodbye, the scene within Hronck's New York mansion dissolved, replaced by the interior of Hronck's drone aircraft. Mark apparently had been dismissed. He removed his headwork and stared out the window. The plane had begun to descend. He had perhaps twenty minutes until landing.

Could Hronck's story be true? Was Lisa really in danger? He had a difficult time deciding which was more improbable: (a) that Edie and Meg were computer programs, let loose on the real world to blackmail Jackson Hronck, or (b) that Edie and Meg were fugitives from the past, sent here against their will by Jackson Hronck. Neither explanation was even remotely believable, or even possible, as far as he could tell. Mark had always laughed at criminals who provided alibis half as ridiculous as either story. But then again, nothing else about this entire scenario made any sense.

He concluded that the only way to clarify things was to meet up with the van and talk things through with Lisa. He suspected he could learn the truth in no other manner. He watched the ground grow closer as the plane reached down to meet the concrete of New Jersey.

33

big decision

"So you basically just made a kitten out of thin air, and now you're spying on them in the car?" Jared had thought himself immune to amazement. Now he realized that Gluck was capable of surprising him at will.

Jared and Gluck were in New York City, sitting in a nondescript office in an older midtown office building. The window looked out at a brick wall, and the lighting in the room was artificial and dim. The only furniture in the office consisted of two beige plastic chairs and a large metallic screen. The screen was split between an image projected from the eyes of the cat currently sitting on Haley's lap in Sally's van, and a chart showing various different facts relating to Jackson Hronck. Most of these facts were simply lists of his assets in the "real" world. Clearly, Jared thought, Hronck was the most powerful, well-connected guy in this era. One fact, however, differed from the others: "fascination with popular culture."

"What does that mean?" he asked, examining the chart. "Why is he interested in our culture?"

Gluck had been sitting with his eyes closed, apparently elsewhere in the Mesh. He opened them and looked over at Jared.

"As Faktors, we are able to see many things in your world, but it is difficult to know what is important, and what is not, to the intentions of the Saan." His data cascade seemed almost wistful. "Many of us—and I am in agreement with Hronck on this point—believe that the iconography of your popular culture is highly significant, and may provide us with insight into the Saan and their ultimate plan. For that reason, we nearly always incorporate certain archetypes into our interactions with human beings."

"Archetypes? Like plotlines from books and movies?"

"Exactly. There is power in these archetypes, in these narratives. Part of our purpose is to locate the source of that power. Once you begin looking for these archetypes in your world, they appear quite often. Sometimes they occur naturally. Other times they indicate the influence of a Faktor. But they are important to recognize, and not only a source of what you might call déjà vu."

This was such a bizarre notion that Jared felt duty-bound to change the subject. Gluck had, at Jared's request, provided him with a hamburger several minutes before. Jared held a long french fry in one hand like a wand as he pointed to the screen.

"So what I don't understand is why Hronck didn't just snatch Edie, tell her to find the Root, whatever it is, and then go on his way," he said. "Why did this have to be such a long story? He must have started this whole thing decades ago. Why did he need to make this all so elaborate and complicated?"

"Ah, yes, Mr. Garber, this is something that we should discuss, as it relates to your role in all of this." Gluck was seated in the other chair but did not look comfortable. It almost seemed as though he was more comfortable with the *idea* of sitting than he was with actually sitting down.

But then again, thought Jared, *I guess he isn't actually sitting down at all. It's just his avatar.*

"Mr. Garber, the Mesh is, as I mentioned, mysterious even to Faktors. We have significant powers within the Mesh, and these powers may seem extraordinary to you. However, there are many holes in our understanding. There are things we cannot change, cannot alter. There are narratives within the Mesh that need to play out to their conclusions, and when we change them too much, the future does not adjust in the manner in which we necessarily expect it to. Unintended consequences occur. We must do things incrementally. I know this, and Hronck knows this."

"But when he moved to Kansas, didn't he do it because Edie was living there? Was this all planned out?"

"Yes. We believe that everything that has happened over the past several decades was in service to Hronck's plan. He felt that his own back story was necessary in order to snare Edie, and that he needed her willing participation in order to accomplish his goal. He wants her to come to him in New York, and he has set up everything in his own 'career' to ensure that result. I suspect that he is correct to take this approach." Gluck turned back towards his screen. "You must realize that to a Faktor, fifty years is only a moment. Our sense of psychological time is quite different than yours. We have lived for millions of your years. To Hronck, creating a new identity in your world for a few decades is a small price to pay for the potential benefit."

"Of finding the Root?"

"Yes. Of finding the Root. But as I said before, he does not know of your significance. He merely wanted to ensure that you did not disrupt his plan. Or perhaps he improvised, and after you vanished he decided to use the mystery of your family's disappearance to snare Ms. Boyd. It is all speculation on our part. But having made certain decisions, it is in his interest to allow them to play out. It is the only way he can find the Root."

"But why make a whole story for himself? What does he get out of that?"

"Hronck is different from Faktors such as myself," said Gluck. "I have spent my existence devoted to the idea of truth, to the operation of the Mesh, and to the questions of the Saan that remain unanswered. Hronck has chosen to develop himself in an entirely different manner."

"How is that?"

"Hronck has developed a *personality*. It is most unpredictable. We believe that he actually may experience something similar to the human idea of 'emotion.' We believe that he enjoys what he does, and yearns for power in an almost human manner. This is quite unlike other Faktors. Ah." Gluck looked up. "I see that Ms. Boyd and her colleagues are nearing their destination." The screen now showed a map of New Jersey. "It is time for you to become involved in this more directly."

"How? I still don't know what we're supposed to do here. In fact, *you* don't know what we're supposed to do here."

"I am going to alter your appearance and voice, such that you are not obviously Jared Garber," said Gluck, paying him no attention. "At the next stop they make, you will befriend them. It is up to you to determine how best to do that." Jared rolled his eyes as Gluck continued. "We need you to tell them what they need to know, but without them knowing who you really are, or Hronck's true identity. We do not want Ms. Boyd to become so concerned about being used by Hronck that she panics and stops their journey. And do not worry. I can communicate to you through the cat."

"I think you're missing something important," said Jared, surprised to find an angry edge developing in his own voice. He couldn't believe he hadn't noticed this before.

"You basically want me to lie to them. You want me to put them in danger that they don't understand, so that Edie can find something for you. Is that right?"

"Yes," said Gluck, oblivious to Jared's distress. "That is correct."

"Then how are you any different than Hronck? I mean, how can I trust you? How do I know that Hronck isn't the good guy, and you're not the bad guy? You can't even explain to me what it is that Edie is looking for, or what I'm supposed to do with it once we find it."

Gluck stood up and walked in front of the screen. He held out his hands as though conducting an orchestra. "I cannot prove to you our good intentions, nor demonstrate why you should help us at this point. I should merely note that, at this juncture, I am your only option."

Jared stared at Gluck and realized he was right. What else could he do? He was helpless without Gluck, and more than anything he wanted to find his family. What could have happened to them? Why were they invisible in the Mesh, even to Gluck? If he had any hope of figuring anything out, he had to play along. But, he decided, he was not going to trust Gluck completely. Not yet.

"Okay," he said, a reluctant note in his voice. "Where do you need to send me? I guess I'll figure something out."

"Good," said Gluck, already pulling his silvery handle from beneath his cloak. "That is the correct decision. You will not regret it."

34

the idea of truth

Lisa was no longer even making an effort to remain four or five cars behind Sally's van. Instead, she focused on remaining relatively inconspicuous. She floated closer and farther away from the van, as necessary, but tried not to seem as though she cared about the van at all. This type of "driving casual" was more difficult than some might believe, but it didn't take up every inch of her concentration. Thus, she had begun to daydream a bit when a call came through her comlink. She pressed behind her ear and immediately heard Mark's voice.

"Lisa, we need to talk. I—"

"Mark, I really don't have time now," she replied in an exasperated voice. "I'll talk to you when I get back."

"I know about Hronck." He spoke quickly, before she could hang up. "But you may not know everything. I think you may be in danger. Can we meet in your office, please?"

Lisa felt as though she had been sucker-punched. The last thing she had expected was a call from Mark. And how did he know about Hronck?

"What do you know?" she asked. "Can't you just tell me?"

"No. Please. I'll be outside your office in a minute. We'll talk then."

As the link disconnected, she considered whether she should meet up with him. Deciding that she had to at least hear him out, as part of her duty to protect Edie and Meg, she grabbed her headwork and cronked in.

Within a few moments she found herself in the familiar surrounds of her office. As though on cue, a knock came at the door. With a sigh, she said, "Come in," and Mark entered the room. His avatar, like hers, was dressed in full uniform.

"Lisa, I—"

"Mark, why are you here?"

"That's what I'm trying to tell you." He took a breath. "I know you think that Edie Boyd and Meg Karger are in the van you're following. I know you think that Jackson Hronck did something to them to send them into the future. But I'm not sure that's what's really going on."

"Oh?" She tried to conceal her shock that he knew the story. "Why do you believe that I think that is true? Have you been following me?"

"No," he said. "I've been contacted by Jackson Hronck's security people. They said—"

"Wait a minute." Lisa jumped up from her desk. "What do you mean? You've been talking to Hronck's people?"

"Yes." Mark tried to gain control of the conversation again. "I have. In fact, I spoke with Jackson Hronck himself."

"Did you?" she sneered. "Did you ask him why he ripped my childhood apart? Did you ask him why he took two girls away from their families? Did you ask him—"

"Lisa! Do you hear yourself? What happened to being a cop, eh? Are you going to just accept this crazy story without thinking about it? Somehow Jackson Hronck had a time machine twenty-five years ago, but has never revealed that fact to anyone? Somehow he was able to keep it secret all this time? And the only thing he used it for was to send two girls into the future?" He shook his head. "Does that make any sense at all?"

Lisa paused, struck at once by the fact that, yes, it made *no* sense at all. None whatsoever. At the same time, she could not deny the fact that Edie and Meg were in the van, and had spoken with her only a few minutes before. Her continued sense that this was some sort of twisted tale of faeries and magic was subtly reinforced.

"Mark, I don't know how Hronck, or you, know any of the things you just described." She tried to control her voice but found it difficult. "I do know, however, that I spoke to Edie and Meg a few minutes ago, and they are very much alive. They are still teenagers twenty-five years after their disappearance from our town. Can you explain that?"

He sat down on one of the chairs in front of her desk. "Are you familiar with the new cross-networked viruses?"

She was a bit taken aback by this change of subject. "Well, yes. I've heard about them."

"Pretty amazing stuff, right? I mean, you catch a virus on the network and your real body in the real world is affected. Your skin changes, or your mind changes. No one understands it yet, right?" She nodded, still wondering where this was all going. "So the line between the network and the real world is getting blurry, okay?" Mark rapped his fingers on the desk. "We can't just assume things that happen on the network stay on the network, right?"

"Mark, I don't see how any of this...," she started, but Mark interrupted her before she could gain any momentum.

"Just hear me out, okay? Jackson Hronck has a lot of enemies. A lot. What if they wanted to frame him for something he never did? What if they created avatars of young girls who disappeared from the town where he lived a quarter-century before? What if those avatars were allowed to 'leak' into the real world, where they could convince these girls' old friends to help bring them to New York, where they could be used to embarrass Hronck, and undermine his campaign for president? What if—"

"Mark, that's crazy." She began to pace around the office. Her hand tapping on the shelves that surrounded the room. A note of anger entered her voice. "You're telling me *my* story is nuts, but then you tell me what? Puh-lease."

"What I'm telling you is that *both* stories are nuts." He went over to her and considered whether to touch her arm, but decided against it for the moment. He was struck by how beautiful she was, even as her anger was palpable. "But aren't you accepting your version a bit too easily? If this didn't involve your friends, would you believe it? You're a cop, you know a crazy story when you hear it. Tell me the truth, would you believe it for even a single second?"

Lisa looked over at him. Her feelings for him, and her feelings for Edie, and the stress of the entire situation, began to froth her emotions. Without warning, she grabbed Mark and put her face into his shoulder. The tears that fell were tears of anger, confusion, and fear, and she could not control them, even as they flowed from her avatar's eyes.

• • •

Edie could see the towers of Manhattan in the distance as they drove over a rise in the road. New Jersey was, as far as she could tell, an endless prologue to New York. Each moment she spent in New Jersey seemed outlandishly long, as though time itself had slowed to a crawl. Her anxiety at the coming confrontation was immense, and she was unsure how things would turn out in the end. Lost in these fearful thoughts, she stared out into the horizon, at the green reflections of buildings still miles away.

The plan was to meet up with Kathrine and Melissa in Central Park. Then, if everything went according to plan, Amanda would arrive, having been tricked, somehow, into showing up. They would then try to convince her to help them to see Hronck. It seemed woefully skimpy, as far as clever plans went, and Edie wasn't even sure if it was a good idea anymore. There were so many things that could go wrong. In fact, only perfect execution of action items that none of them had even considered yet could make this plan work.

Edie looked over at Haley, who was playing with the cat. Ray had, for reasons of his own, named it Zeke. Although Zeke still seemed somewhat nervous, he was delighted to be receiving attention and food and water.

"I always wanted a cat," Haley said as she stroked Zeke between his pointed ears. "What a cute little guy."

Meg made a face at Zeke, who mewed contentedly. "I've always had dogs, always been a dog person. But there's no question that he's cute."

"I never had any animals, though I have them in the network," said Ray, turning away from the window. "On the network I got so many pets, you can't even believe it. I got a Komodo dragon I can ride with a saddle. His name is Joe. I got a penguin who can talk. His name is Bob. I got four muskrats that can sing—they can sing harmonies, man, it's incredible to hear."

Haley turned Zeke over and tickled him under his chin. "Yeah. But it's not the same as the real thing."

Edie could tell that Ray disagreed. "Haley," she said, looking back over at the group. "Why did you fall for your ex? No offense, but he sounds like he was trouble from the start."

Haley smiled ruefully. "I swore I'd never say something like this, but when you're a bit older you'll understand how stupid you can really get when you think someone likes you."

"Haley," said Meg, "you wouldn't believe how stupid *we* were and no one even liked us."

"Well, curiosity killed the cat," said Edie, a bit of sarcasm in her tone.

"Shh," joked Haley, covering Zeke's ears. "You'll scare him."

Edie rolled her eyes.

"I don't get how you're here." Ray looked between Edie and Meg. "I mean, it don't make sense that you're still young when you went away twenty-five years ago. That's clanzo, man."

"Clanzo?" asked Meg. "What's that?"

"You know," answered Haley. "New slang. You should hear the city kids, my god, nobody can understand anything they're saying. It's like a new language."

Ray began to bounce, excited again. "When you're on the network you run into these guys, the gangs, they got a presence there, and my fosters dealt with them sometimes too. Anyway, they talk in lingo, man, it's so hard to follow, even I can't do it, I got to get a translator module when I'm on the network to figure out what they saying. They talk with Spanish and Arabic and French, and English and Chinese and Japanese and jive, and like twenty other ways to talk, all mixed up. Then they do body modifications, different gangs, and if they looked in real life like they look on the network, they'd be pretty scary, pretty scary."

"What do they do to themselves?" asked Edie, interested yet mildly disgusted at the idea of body modification.

"I've seen it too." Haley made a face as though she was likely to get sick. "It's pretty grim. You see it on some of the new shows, too, the shows about cops." She noted the blank looks from Meg and Edie and made an exaggerated sigh. "It's like that thought-acting I was talking about. But not all of the shows are acted. They actually let you get into the head of cops while they're arresting people in some pretty sketchy areas. They edit it down, of course, so you don't get all of the bad thoughts—it isn't live or anything. But you see the people they're arresting and you can't believe it."

"What do they look like?" asked Meg. "The gang guys, I mean, not the cops."

Haley made yet another face. "Well, for one thing, they've all got those same stupid wristbands so it's like they're doing drugs on the network, which is totally gross." Edie could tell Haley was thinking about her ex-boyfriend, and shivered. "Then they put chips in their heads, and not comlinks like what Sally has behind her ear so she can talk on the phone. These guys do gruesome stuff, enlarging their heads sometimes to fit it all in. They've got massive computing power in their minds, so that they can do crazy stuff on the network when they cronk in. Then some of them get plastic surgery so that their faces are completely smooth. One guy I saw looked like he didn't have a nose or ears or hair. He had his eyes done so that they were mirrored. Totally freaky. Worst of all, he got his teeth shaped like little cones so he could bite people."

"Yeah," Ray continued excitedly, ignoring the looks of disgust on Edie and Meg's faces. "And different gangs do different kinds of body mods to make themselves look different. One gang in Atlanta gave themselves gills, like a fish, which is funny because there's no, like, ocean anywhere near Atlanta. Even I know that."

"That must look charming," Meg stuck her tongue out. "There must be lots of old people complaining about 'the kids today.' I'm a kid, and I feel like I should be complaining and I haven't even seen these people yet."

"Oh, you will," Sally suddenly chimed in from the front seat. They had forgotten she was even there. "You can't go to New York without seeing a bit of that kind of thing. And in different countries, people do different things to themselves, so you see lots of immigrants in the city with odd body mods that you haven't seen before. The only thing these gang guys have in common is that they all eat pizza, no matter what they look like. But don't worry," she said, noticing Edie's worried face. "It will be just like a circus, except for free."

"Great," Edie snorted. "I can tell you that I'm in the mood for many things right now, but the circus isn't one of them."

Just then, Sally's head began to ring. She turned back to face the front of the car, and the passengers returned to silently staring out the windows. Edie looked over at Meg and thought back to the two of them in second grade, locked in the closet. She remembered the thrill of adventure, and the edge of danger which had excited them to no end that day.

Now they were in real danger, and the thrill was gone. She missed her family, and while her friends had her back, they were grown, and in a different phase of their lives. It was as though Edie had been asleep for twenty-five years, only to awaken one day and realize that her whole life had been missed. It was awful.

"Guys," Sally announced. "We're going to pull over in a minute, at a restaurant in Fort Lee. Lisa wants to talk to us live, for whatever that's worth." She looked at a video map on her dashboard. "It sounds like it might be pretty serious, but let's assume that she's got whatever it is under control."

"Wonderful." Meg made a face. "Something more serious than this? I can't wait."

Zeke the cat looked over at Meg placidly, and closed his eyes.

35

under the bridge

The Original Pancake House in Fort Lee, New Jersey, was no different from the other Original Pancake Houses Edie had seen before, with two notable exceptions. In this time, the iconic sign of the little man dressed in white, flipping an enormous pancake, was seemingly alive. The chef actually flipped the pancake in a series of increasingly difficult moves, causing an apple pancake the size of a hubcap to spin, juke, and dive. It seemed as much like performance art as a sign advertising breakfast food, and she felt hypnotized by the image, and hungry.

Another difference was location. When Edie stood in the parking lot of this particular restaurant, she was only three blocks and a small park away from the Hudson River, and a different world. Physically, this was quite literal: the George Washington Bridge stretched across the river from Fort Lee, connecting the real world to New York City. But in a more spiritual way, Fort Lee was like a gateway, a door between one universe and another.

New York City had always seemed to Edie like a place where people went to realize their dreams, or fail in spectacular ways. So many movies and stories and songs began with a trip to New York that it felt like a second home to many who had never even made a visit. Certainly, her friends had all discussed moving there as adults in the same way that some children discussed a visit to Mars. Sure, it was possible, but not too likely.

Unlike her friends of twenty-five years before, however, Edie *had* been to New York as a child. The memory was incredibly strong, and even though she had been so much younger at the time, it felt as though it had just happened a few weeks earlier.

It had been her last family trip with her parents. Her mother and father, only two months before their own disappearance from her life, were dazzling. Edie was four years old and thrilled beyond measure to visit this alluring city. To be sure, she had visited cities in the past—smaller cities in Kansas, even St. Louis once. But nothing had prepared her for New York City.

To a four-year-old, the scale of the city was overwhelming. Canyons of buildings stretched out as far as the eye could see. Groups of people crossing Times Square seemed as enormous to her as a herd of wildebeests migrating across the savannas of Africa. Everything was lit up, and taxis marched through the streets like ants in an ant farm. The memory seemed so immediate to Edie, even years later, that it was as though she were watching a film in her mind.

She and her parents watched Broadway musicals, ate at restaurants serving unrecognizable food from around the world, and hired a carriage through Central Park. Her father looked like a movie star, dark hair swept behind his ears, piercing blue eyes glowing with the lights of the city. He was slightly unshaven and dashing. Edie could never read any book, nor see any movie, without imagining him as the hero. Her mother was glamour incarnate, with long brown hair cut far more fashionably than her neighbors in Kansas. When Edie looked at herself in the mirror, she had a difficult time believing that she was related to her mother, who moved with a grace Edie had not yet discovered.

Edie had never felt more loved, or safe, than she had in the arms of her parents in that carriage through Central Park. Or so she remembered. Now, as she sat in the parking lot of the Original Pancake House, staring at that animated sign, she barely believed that she was almost in New York once again.

It had been only a few days since she had been sitting at the breakfast table, listening to her uncle discuss the disappearance of the Garbers. Since that Thursday morning, she had been shot with a time machine, faced her friends as adults, learned that she was the victim of one of history's most powerful men, and traveled two-thirds of the way across the country. Moreover, this trip had been made with Meg, Sally, a cat, and two random people they'd met along the way. Now they were almost there, and she could see the towers of the bridge peeking over the tops of buildings and trees.

They did not wait in the parking lot for long, however, as two other cars joined them almost immediately. One contained Lt. Lisa Alter. As she left the car, Edie was struck by how much she looked like the fourteen-year-old Lisa. Yet growing up had been good her: what had seemed gangly in a teenager seemed lithe in an adult. Her brown hair, which had always been a bit unruly twenty-five years earlier, now framed her face attractively. Most important, thought Edie, her eyes seemed to reflect a sense of purpose, something that none of them had really felt while sitting in an eighth-grade classroom.

Haley was the first to notice the other car. Like the others, she was plastered against the window, transfixed by the half-empty parking lot. They were all expecting to see Lisa. Sally had already alerted the van to the arrival of their new visitor. A few moments later, however, another car, a black one shaped like a wedge, with silver piping around the edges, pulled up behind her.

"Hey, guys?" Haley piped up, a faint questioning note in her voice. "Who's in the other car?"

As one, the others turned to look at the other car. A man in his late thirties emerged. He was wearing a police officer's uniform, and a weapon of some kind was slung around his hips in a holster. His brown leather boots stretched nearly to the top of his calves, and he was wearing mirrored sunglasses. He walked up to Lisa, spoke a few words to her, and then turned to face the van.

"I have no idea," replied Sally. "But I don't like the feel of this."

"Last time I seen the cops, it was not fun." Ray sounded nervous. "My fosters talked their way out of it, but man, those cops were hardcore. Maybe we should drive away. Maybe they're coming to arrest me, or you. Maybe it's not legal to be in the wrong time."

"Lisa's with him," said Edie confidently. "It will be okay."

Meg looked skeptical as they watched the two police officers approach the van. Sally opened the door. "Don't say anything. Just wait until I tell you to come outside," she said, and stepped out of the van.

Normally Edie and Meg might have complained, but under the circumstances it seemed best to be cautious. Haley, Ray, and Zeke needed even less convincing. All of them hung back and listened to the conversation through the open van door.

Sally looked Mark up and down. "So. Who is this?"

"This," said Lisa, "is Mark Sullivan. He's also a lieutenant on the force, and he's been my boyfriend off and on for the past nine years." She touched his arm as though to make sure he was still there. "Mark, this is Sally Karger."

Mark reached out his hand. "Pleased to meet you, Ms. Karger."

Sally shook his hand a bit hesitantly, then turned to Lisa. "So what's up?"

"Well, Mark has a story to tell us, a story that's almost as crazy as the one I told him. His story also purports to explain why Edie and Meg have appeared on your doorstep." She looked down at her feet and shook her head. "Since neither story makes any sense, I figured it would be useful for all of us to discuss our situation before we get to New York."

"Oookay," drawled Sally, looking suspiciously back over at Mark. "What new tale do you have to tell?"

Mark was clearly feeling a bit uncomfortable, a sensation that was quite foreign to him. Normally, while wearing his uniform, he was the model of confidence, impossible to spook. The strangest circumstances never flustered him. Until now. Faced with Sally, who resembled a mother lion protecting her cubs, and with Lisa, a woman he still cared about deeply, Hronck's story seemed a bit less persuasive. But he felt as though he had no choice.

"Ms. Karger, this may seem like a shock," he began, cautious to sound as official as possible, "but others are aware of your current cargo, and—"

"Cargo?" exploded Sally. "*Cargo?* Is that what you call kids in trouble? Lisa, I don't have time—"

"Please, Ms. Karger," said Mark. "Please hear me out. Are you familiar with 'The Sick Rose'?"

Sally seemed surprised at this turn in the conversation, and calmed down a bit. "The computer virus?"

"Yes" Mark was relieved that she no longer seemed prepared to bite off one of his limbs. "Are you familiar with the symptoms?"

She thought for a moment. "Isn't that the one you get online but somehow affects your body in the real world?"

"Bingo," said Mark. "That's the one."

Sally looked a bit puzzled. "Not to be rude, but I don't see what this virus has to do with anything going on here."

He took off his sunglasses to look at her more directly. "Well, think about it. Things that take place *on* the network can come to life *off* the network. Pretty amazing, eh?"

"I still don't—"

"It has been suggested by people a lot smarter than me," he continued, now gaining some momentum, "that other things can be ported from the network as well." He leaned forward a bit, as though to emphasize his point. "Other things like avatars."

Sally was initially struck dumb by the idea. Finally, after a moment of silence, she recovered. "Avatars leaving the network? That makes no—"

"Right. It makes no sense. Just about as little sense as, say, teenagers dead for a quarter-century coming back to life."

Edie could see where this conversation was going, and she had heard enough to realize what Mark was suggesting. "Wait a minute," she yelled, bursting out of the van and rapidly crossing and uncrossing her arms across her body as though she needed to physically say *no*. She was followed almost immediately by Meg, who looked just as outraged. Haley and Ray hung back inside the van door.

"Are you saying that we're not real, that we're just, I don't know, *cartoons* brought to life?" Edie shook her head angrily. "You've *got* to be kidding me."

"Lisa, why did you bring this bozo to talk to us?" snarled Meg, pointedly looking away from Mark. "Don't you think we're real? Do you think we're lying?"

Lisa looked thunderstruck. Mark was clearly not expecting the "avatars" to start arguing with him about whether or not they existed. But without missing a beat, he came right back at Edie and Meg.

"You can understand my suspicion. I'm only trying to figure out what's actually going on here. But imagine how I feel: one person I trust has suggested that you two are avatars, controlled by somebody else. Meanwhile, Lisa, whom I also trust, claims that you're actually dead girls brought back to life by a time machine. My primary concern, to be frank, is Lisa." He grew more animated, pointing at Edie as he spoke. "I don't want her to get hurt. I don't care which of these crazy stories is true, I just want to make sure you aren't using Lisa to try to hurt someone else."

"Who told you that we were avatars?" asked Edie, now genuinely curious. "I mean, that has to be the craziest thing I've ever heard."

"Jackson Hronck."

It was as though he had thrown a match on a pool of gasoline.

"What?" yelled Meg, stepping forward towards Mark, rage eliminating any fear she might have had about confronting a police officer. "You *talked* to that guy? He did this to us! Why don't you ask your buddy why he destroyed our lives, or why he erased the Garbers? Ask him that! Ask him how he can run for freaking president when he has blood on his hands, my blood, and Edie's. It's not fair, and you're standing there like it's some kind of game?" She spun around to face her sister. "Let's blow this place before I do something stupid."

"Look," Mark insisted. "I'm not saying anything is true. But I'm a police officer. I'm trained to be skeptical. And the story Lisa tells me is just as crazy as Jackson Hronck's. So I'm doing what any reasonable cop would do: investigate."

"Meg." Lisa spoke as though suddenly remembering that she could talk. "I believe you. At least I think I do. I'm not really sure of anything anymore. But given the fact that Mark has already talked to Hronck, we need you guys to convince him. He could help us."

"Lisa," snapped Edie, with a bit more bite than she'd intended. "Are you sure we don't have to convince you, too?"

Lisa's face was flush with emotion, and her voice was ragged. "Edie, there is nothing in my whole life that I want to believe more. I want to believe that you guys are alive, that I can get my childhood back. I want to believe that fairy tales are real, and that if you wish hard enough and long enough, you'll get your fondest desire, just like a movie. But it's hard." She stared at the ground as if to avoid looking at Edie. "I've spent so many years dreaming about this...." She wiped her eyes on her sleeve and returned her gaze to the girls. "It's hard to explain, but I used to imagine that the faeries had taken you away to another world, and that I would rescue you. I would fall asleep dreaming that I could do it, that maybe when I became a cop I'd find you, all grown up and living in another place." She suddenly walked up to Edie and grabbed her arm, seemingly hugging her and simultaneously testing to see if she were real. "I've felt like a failure my whole life because you were still gone and I couldn't find you. Can you forgive me for doubting you? But I have to doubt, I need to prove it so that I can forgive myself for letting you get lost."

Edie was now openly crying herself. "I don't know how we can prove it, except to say that I remember sitting with you under a big maple tree in your backyard when we were nine." She wrapped her arms around her chest as though to hug herself. "Your collie, Elwood, had just died, remember? He was tied out back by your brother, who was always careless about the dog. Elwood saw a squirrel, he ran for it, and he snapped his neck. And you were crying for days,

239

almost like you're crying now, like I'm crying now. And you said you couldn't believe you'd loved anything as much as you had loved your dog. And I told you that you were lucky. Do you remember that?"

"Yes." Lisa was now almost impossible to hear through the tears. Mark had put his arm around her and was holding her against his shoulder. She didn't even seem to notice as Edie continued.

"And I said that you were lucky to have been able to love your dog and have your dog love you back. And that I was jealous you had been so happy, when my whole life had been a disaster. And you told me—do you remember what you told me?"

"Yes. I told you that if you had felt like I did when Elwood died, I finally understood what it was like to lose something important." She paused to wipe her eyes once more. Meg touched Edie's shoulder.

"And I said that I'd make sure that you were never hurt like that again," said Lisa. "And here we are."

"Yes." Meg now had a bit more empathy in her voice. "Here we are. Do you believe it now, Lisa?"

"Yes. I do."

Mark looked down as Lisa moved out from under his arm and turned away. Abashed, and as though he suddenly understood the truth of what had transpired, he began walking silently towards his car. As the rest of them watched, he got in and carefully drove back out to the street. Within a few moments, his car had disappeared into traffic.

Edie suddenly was aware that she was standing in the parking lot of a restaurant, and that other people were passing by, watching them, trying to guess what this motley crew was doing together. Just as she began to feel spied upon, she heard Ray's voice from the van.

"If you believe her, Lisa, then why don't we all go get some food in the restaurant? I'm hungry, and I want a pancake."

"Well," said Sally, visibly still trying to calm herself. "I guess I could use some pancakes too."

As they walked through the parking lot into the restaurant, Edie smiled, but then was struck by an odd thought: if they succeeded in going back to their own time, perhaps Lisa would never meet Mark. Perhaps Sally would never meet Jim. Perhaps many of the children alive in this new time would never be born. Happy people would never get the chance to be happy, and the world would move forward in unpredictable ways. As she entered the restaurant and was accosted by the smell of cinnamon and sugar, she wondered whether it was selfish of her to want to go back. What if, in going back to her own time, she ruined the lives of so many other people?

Meg looked at her and nodded, as though sharing the same thought. "Don't worry. We'll get back. I know it." Meg's voice was reassuring, but she was clearly not convinced herself.

Edie felt skeptical, too. "That's what I'm afraid of now. Maybe this world is better than the one that would have happened if we had never disappeared."

Meg looked surprised at this thought but then shook her head. "We can't worry about that." She put her hands on her hips as though trying to look authoritative. "We don't belong here. And we're going home soon."

Edie tried to smile. Just then, a boy with blond hair and a lopsided smile approached them. He seemed to be around their age, dressed in what even Edie and Meg could recognize as hip clothing of this time: jeans with animated bleach stains and glowing metallic rivets. His shirt was striped, with an orange aura surrounding the arms. He had been standing in the entrance foyer of the restaurant, slouched easily against a wall, his boots shiny and new. But now he leaned over towards them, and his smile vanished as he spoke in an urgent whisper.

"I know you don't belong here," said Jared, discomfited at the sound of the new voice Gluck had given him as part of his disguise. "I know you belong in another time. I can't explain everything right now, but can we talk? I think I can help."

Edie was shocked. How could this random guy know what was going on? Was Hronck already onto them? She was astounded to find Meg smiling. Meg looked at Jared appraisingly and shook her head with amusement.

"I have no idea why I think this is a good idea, but nothing surprises me anymore. Come on inside." She put her arm on Jared's shoulder and guided him towards the restaurant. "We can talk over some pancakes, and you can explain it all to me."

"Meg," hissed Edie, "you heard what Mark had to say. How do we know this guy is okay? He really could be some kind of sick rose, or whatever it was."

"Edie," said Jared, startling her. "I know you were raised by your aunt and uncle in Kansas, and I know that Meg's sister, Sally, was best friends with Josie Garber. I know that Mrs. Besicka was the best teacher in your school, and that Jackson Hronck sent you here. I know more about what's going on than you can even imagine. You don't have to trust me, just listen to what I have to say."

Now it was Meg's turn to be shocked. For once, she seemed unable to even respond. Edie, however, was now the one to smile, as though everything suddenly made sense.

"Yup, sounds like we need some pancakes." She looked again at Jared's snazzy clothes and raised an eyebrow. "But you're buying."

36

queen of the city

A manda Sheppard had accomplished a great deal in her young life, but she still felt as though her story had only just begun. She was the youngest Manhattan borough president in the history of the city, and one of the few who had not been born there. After arriving in New York for college, she'd become involved in local politics almost immediately. Her first job involved volunteering for a party boss focused on the Lower East Side. She had spent nearly as much time walking door to door soliciting voters in the district as she had attending classes. By the time she graduated, there was not a single person in the local party organization who did not know Amanda, like her and depend on her.

She had been elected to the city council at the shockingly young age of twenty-four and became a powerhouse almost immediately. She was a master at horse-trading and soon leveraged herself into a position of real authority within the council chamber. Political analysts discussed her as a "phenom," the way sportswriters discussed a basketball player of rare talent and superhuman focus. Her election to borough president at the age of thirty-three was impressive but was widely considered an interim step, a way of gaining more citywide name recognition in preparation for her future run for mayor. A close ally of Mayor Hronck, she was deemed by politicos across the city as a shoe-in to succeed him. Her fundraising acumen, combined with Hronck's support, gave her an aura of inevitability. Her children, at the direction of her husband, had jokingly referred to her as "the Mayor" since they were old enough to talk. But as the years went by, their joke increasingly looked like a prediction.

Amanda had initially remained in touch with her Kansas friends, especially Melissa, who also lived in New York. Yet she saw each of them less frequently as her time became more precious. And over the past five years, her time had become quite precious indeed. Between two children, her job as president of Manhattan, her charitable duties, and the stresses of daily life, she had barely seen or spoken to Lisa or Kathrine. Only their occasional visits to New York provided her with a chance to talk to her childhood friends, and those trips became rarer as the years went by. Amanda's own family had relocated, so she herself never found herself back in Kansas, and even Melissa—a cardiothoracic surgeon living less than a mile away—was often too busy to talk. Her days in Kansas felt more distant with each passing year. Her childhood rarely crossed her mind.

Thus it came as a surprise when she received an urgent, cryptic message from Melissa: "Need to talk. Urgent. Central Park, by the boathouse @ 8 this evening? Mel."

This was so thoroughly out of character for Melissa that Amanda's initial instinct was to dismiss it as a misdirected message. She was sitting in her office, looking out her window at the view of City Hall Park, when she received the call. Her office was aggressively masculine, filled with mementos from the fire department, the various unions she dealt with, and assorted honoraria. Conversely, she herself tended to dress in the latest fashions, with exotically feminine touches like video-enabled blouses with flowers opening and closing, matching the circadian rhythms of the day. She wanted her constituents to feel the power and the gravitas of the office, while being blinded by the glamour of her personal style. That way, she figured, she could cover maximum territory in the public mind. Her political consultants agreed. She could be an attractive feminine presence and a hard-edged political power, without compromising on either image. She was particularly proud of that accomplishment.

Today, however, her gaze was focused on a bird circling high above the park. It was a peregrine falcon, wafting on currents of air, looking for a pigeon to snatch. Amanda had been imagining herself as a raptor, graceful yet deadly, when Melissa's message came in. She clicked behind her ear and the message was displayed visually on her optic nerve. The words were clear, but the message was not. Why would Melissa want to meet so urgently? It was already 6:30. Why would she want to meet in a public place?

Amanda had last seen Melissa over dinner nearly five months ago, and they had not spoken since. It had been a perfectly friendly dinner, with spouses and one other couple as well. But it was during that dinner that Amanda had recognized that her circle of friends was getting smaller, and became aware that Melissa was getting close to the perimeter of that circle. The inevitability of this estrangement saddened her. After all, Melissa was one of her oldest friends. But she guessed she wouldn't see Melissa again for a very long time.

With this message, however, it appeared that her guess had been wrong. Curious, Amanda thought out her reply, which appeared immediately in her field of vision: "Are you okay? I'll be there, but tell me what's up." She tapped herself behind the ear. She glanced over at her calendar, noticed that for once she really had nothing pressing that evening, and tapped her head once again.

"Honey, what's up?" asked a male voice suddenly in her ear.

"Barry, I got a message from Melissa. Sounds like she needs to talk. I may be a bit late for dinner tonight." She tried to sound matter-of-fact about this change of plans, but a worried note in her voice betrayed her feelings.

"Is everything okay? What kind of message?"

"Pretty minimal, actually. Which is why I'm worried. She wants to meet at the boathouse at eight tonight, and—"

"Honey, why don't you bring someone from your security detail?" suggested Barry, now sounding somewhat concerned himself. "Just ask them to hang out. I don't like the idea of you standing around by yourself at night in the middle of Central Park."

"Thanks for worrying, Barry," she said, irritated that she hadn't thought of it herself. "I'll do that. And I'll let you know what's up when I get home. Love you."

"Love you too."

The line went dead, and Amanda immediately pressed a button on her desk. A disembodied voice emerged.

"Yes, Madam President?"

"Nick, can you get me a car and a driver for this evening?" She always felt a bit silly asking for security, especially in this day and age, but sometimes it was necessary, and Mayor Hronck made it so easy for everyone in her office. "I need someone to watch over me a bit. I have to meet someone at eight tonight. Do you have people available?"

"Certainly. I'll have Dimitri come over. What time do you want him?"

Amanda was pleased. She'd always liked Nick, and she was glad he was so solicitous of her needs. "I'll be downstairs at 7:30, sharp."

"We'll be ready, Madam President. Don't worry about a thing."

37

resurrected friends

Earlier that day, Melissa had received a shock of her own, a shock that had led directly to her mysterious message to Amanda. Melissa had just arrived home after a particularly grueling bit of emergency heart surgery. These days, surgery was performed at such incredibly fine levels of magnification that her eyes ached more than her hands, which had robotic assistance. Nonetheless, the surgery had been performed in the very early morning, and she was now sitting at home during the middle of the day. Her kids were out of town with her husband, Dave, and she was staring blankly into space as she tried to re-engage her exhausted mind.

Just then her comlink went off, indicating a call that she knew from caller ID was Kathrine. *How strange,* she thought at once. *I haven't heard from Kathrine in so long.* She tapped herself behind the ear.

"Hey, Kathrine, long time no speak!" Melissa was always excited to talk to her. As the only other science-oriented girl amongst her friends growing up, Melissa had felt particularly close to her fellow math geek, and had experienced Kathrine's absence most pointedly.

"Melissa," Kathrine intoned in her typically unexcited voice. "Are you sitting down?"

Melissa laughed. "Wait, let me guess. You're getting married? Pregnant? Won the Nobel Prize in physics?"

"Close," said Kathrine. "It's about Edie."

Melissa, tired joints and all, leapt to her feet. "What? Are you serious?"

"Incredibly serious. But we need to talk somewhere secure. You still have the same office coordinates?"

"Sure," said Melissa weakly, still in shock at the unexpected topic of conversation.

"I'll meet you at your office on the network in, say, five minutes," said Kathrine in her insistent monotone. "We'll talk then."

Melissa felt as though she were sleepwalking as she went over to her desk, slipped the headwork over her hair, and cronked in. She must have misheard Kathrine, thought Melissa. Edie...it couldn't be....

Once she had cronked in, she found herself sitting in her private office. The design was hypermodern, with glass shelving and sleek lucite furniture scattered around the room. Almost as soon as she had oriented herself, she heard the knock on her networked office door. She ran over, opened it, and physically pulled Kathrine's avatar inside.

"Okay." She felt as though her avatar was out of breath from excitement. "What are you talking about?"

"When I tell you this," Kathrine warned, "you're going to have to rely on the fact that I'm a scientist, and unlikely to be persuaded by crazy things without evidence. Okay?"

Melissa paused. "This is going to be a really strange story, isn't it? Because you never warn me before telling me normal things."

Kathrine smiled. "Well, yes, that's true. Okay, I'll be blunt. Edie Boyd and Meg Karger are alive. I've seen them and I've spoken with them. I'm currently trying to help them get back to their own time."

Melissa stared at Kathrine. Melissa's avatar, like Melissa herself, was the height of New York sophistication. It wore a sleek black wrap dress and strappy high heels. It had chiseled features out of a beauty magazine, with dramatic cheekbones and blazing eyes. She suspected, however, that her avatar's jaw was currently on the floor. "Their own *time*?"

"They were sent here by Jackson Hronck, who shot them with what I can only describe as a time ray. To them, they were sitting in Mrs. Besicka's class a few days ago. To us, they've been dead for decades." Kathrine paused. "I told you it was crazy."

Melissa rolled her eyes. "Be serious. Enough with the jokes, Kath. Are they really alive or not?"

Kathrine shook her head. "I'm being completely serious. A couple of days ago, Sally Karger opened her door to find her sister, Meg, and Edie Boyd standing on her stoop. They had been investigating the disappearance of the Garbers when they accidentally saw Jackson Hronck in his back-yard, playing with his time machine. He turned it on the girls and sent them twenty-five years into the future. To our time."

To Melissa, this was not too different from hearing Kathrine tell her that purple elephants and polka-dotted zebras were storming New York with the assistance of one-eyed aliens from Venus. She stared at Kathrine, wondering if she had lost her mind, whether she might need to per-form some kind of intervention or emergency brain surgery.

"Oh, and one other thing," added Kathrine mischie-vously, noting Melissa's look of shock. "Lisa is with them too. They're headed to New York as we speak and should be arriving here in a few hours. I will be there shortly, as well.

It will be a big reunion." She looked directly into Melissa's eyes. "Melissa, we need your help."

Melissa stared right back. It began to dawn on her that Kathrine might, in fact, be sane after all. "You are serious, aren't you? You've talked to Edie?"

"Yep. She even asked me about the toothpick sculpture I never finished." Kathrine grinned. "Melissa, she looks the same. Just like we remember her, like she disappeared yesterday. Meg too. If I hadn't seen it myself, I would swear it was a trick, or a dream."

Melissa felt her eyes grow large with amazement as she digested the news. "Okay, so maybe you're right, and maybe this is real. But how did it happen?"

"I don't fully understand the science involved, which is pretty amazing in and of itself." Kathrine smirked. "But it turns out that Jackson Hronck was the Garbers' neighbor. Oh, and he probably sent them into another time, too." Melissa continued to stare, but her avatar started stroking her chin as though in thought. In actuality, she was just trying to do something with her avatar's hands while she tried desperately to make sense of this astounding new information.

"Anyway," continued Kathrine, "Edie and Meg were snooping around, the way they always did—to Hronck, they were the classic 'meddling kids' from every bad cartoon we saw after school—and he sent them into the future. That's why nobody ever found a body. They aren't even dead, never were dead. Jim and I are still working to try to figure out how this all works, but it's clear that the only person who can help us is Hronck himself. Which means..."

"Which means that you need to talk to Amanda. Who will never believe this. And even if she does, Jackson Hronck is responsible for her career, so I don't even know if she'd help us anyway." Melissa shook her head. "You already thought of all that, I assume?"

"All that and more," replied Kathrine, a grim look on her face. "Hronck's her patron. Unless we can really overwhelm her emotionally, we have no shot. We need to arrange that reunion in a public place, in a context where she can't, and won't, run away." Kathrine sat down on a bright red foam chaise shaped like a women's pump, the stiletto heel made from glowing black lacquer. "Do you have any ideas?"

Melissa began to pace the room. "We really haven't been seeing much of each other. We had dinner with her and Barry months ago. It won't be easy to just get her to show up somewhere at the drop of a hat."

"Can you fake an emergency? If you told her it was urgent, would she show up?"

Melissa shrugged. "I have no idea." She tried to search for an explanation, then seemed to give up on her effort. "But when you're a surgeon, sometimes you just have to try something to see if it works. We'll give it a shot, and hopefully Amanda shows up."

"It will work." Kathrine sounded confident. "After all Edie and Meg have been through, it *has* to work."

Melissa smiled. "I'm glad you're so confident. Then again, you haven't seen Amanda lately. She's our next mayor, you know."

Kathrine sighed. "Does that mean she can get us in to see Hronck?"

"Sure." There was a perceptible edge to Melissa's voice. "As long as there's something in it for her."

"Maybe you're underestimating her," mused Kathrine. "After all, she was one of our best friends."

"I hope so. But maybe that's why I'm underestimating her. Anyway, we'll try for Central Park. That's probably the safest place in New York these days."

less than jake

Edie's mind was racing. On one level, she was madly obsessing about the confrontation with Mark. The pure terror she'd felt when Mark described his online discussion with Hronck had failed to dissipate even twenty minutes later. Hronck's easy lies had been chilling. Moreover, the fact that Mark had been so willing to believe those lies, as incredible as they were, had persuaded Edie that Hronck was likely to convince others as well. The fact that he knew they were coming only made it worse.

And then there was this mysterious boy who had approached them in the restaurant. Who was he, and why did he know so much about Edie? She was both disturbed by his secret knowledge and oddly excited.

As far as she knew, she had never been the subject of any whispers or gossip, and had lived about as boring an existence as she could imagine. While for the most part she was fine with that state of affairs, she could not deny the feelings she had now. Suddenly, she was important. Sure, she was terrified and confused, but there was no question that something was going on, and that she was in the eye of the hurricane. People were talking about her, and that was a radical change for Edie. She was not yet sure how she felt about it, but she was intrigued to learn about this new boy and why he had taken an interest in her.

She saw Sally's look of surprise as she approached the table with this mysterious new visitor in tow. Sally mouthed, "Who?" Edie answered her with a wink and guided Jared towards the table. He gulped at seeing a woman he recognized as the cute girl from his history class, the one he had been thinking of asking out, now an adult.

Haley and Ray were deep in conversation, barely aware of anyone else at the table. Haley was fascinated by something Ray was describing, her eyes wide with wonder as he gesticulated wildly with his arms, nearly knocking over his glass of water in his enthusiasm. Lisa was beaming at Edie, a look of profound wonder on her face. As everyone arrived, Edie cleared her throat to get everyone's attention.

"Everyone wants to talk to us today," she began, smiling over at Lisa to indicate that hurt feelings had been dismissed. She then pointed over to Jared. "So I guess I shouldn't be surprised that someone else wants to chat as well. I don't even know your name." She looked over at Jared. "Why don't you introduce yourself and tell us how you know so much about me, and what you know."

Jared took a deep breath. He had been working on this story ever since Gluck had made it clear that he really had no choice. He knew that this was important, and he hoped he could pull it off.

"My name is Jake," he said, trying to keep his frayed nerves out of his voice, "and I don't belong here either." He looked over at Edie and Meg, and tried to focus on them. "As I already told Edie and Meg, I know a lot about them, and about how they got here. I also know about Jackson Hronck."

Sally looked as though she had just been pinched, and Jared found it difficult to look at her when he spoke. "I don't know everything that's going on, but you don't know as much of the story as I do, and I think you're going to need some help."

Meg spoke up, sarcastic. "I think I speak for all of us when I say that we *do* need all of the help we can get."

Jared smiled. "Good. Let me tell you something about Jackson Hronck. He isn't from this time."

"We guessed that," said Edie.

"But what you may not have guessed is that he isn't even human."

At this new bombshell, everyone, even Ray, who had been busily scanning the menu, snapped to attention.

"Hronck is not from our world, and he is trying to manipulate things in order to achieve certain results. I don't know exactly what he's trying to do," he added quickly, sensing another interruption and thankful that he had been able thus far to avoid any outright lies. "But he thinks you're important. You're not here by accident."

"What do you mean he's not from this world?" asked Lisa. "And if he isn't human, what is he?"

"I'm pretty much in a state right now where I'll believe almost anything," cracked Meg. "But that's too weird."

"Hronck is some kind of energy being. And no," he added, before Sally could interject, "I don't know what that means, either. But I can see it." He tried to find the right words to describe his unusual ability. "Like a lot of you," he said, nodding at Haley and Ray, "I have a special power. I can tell when the people you see on the street aren't really people. I can tell—"

"Are they aliens?" asked Ray, suddenly excited and bouncing in his seat. "I got a beef with aliens, they are so *not* cool with me. They killed my parents, see, and—"

"Yes," said Jared patiently. "They're kind of like aliens, but not really. They're from here, not from another planet.

But they can take the form of people, and do things to us. Like send us into the wrong time."

"How do you know about this?" Lisa sounded skeptical. "I mean, you said that you're not supposed to be here either. Who are you?"

"I was sent to another time by Hronck, too, but I don't think it was on purpose. More important, while in that other time, which was something like 4,000 years from now, I met up with someone else, another being like Hronck. He told me all about it. While a lot of it is over my head, I think I understand the basics. In short, they're at war, he's trying to stop Hronck, and now I'm helping him do it, because I think it's the only way I can get back to my family." He looked over at Edie and Meg, feeling a bond with them he could not have explained. "And that's how I know we're supposed to help you. You're a big part of this, and without you, I'm stuck here permanently."

"Okay," said Edie warily. "That sounds great. What are we supposed to do?"

"That's the hard part," said Jared, earnestly trying not to say more than he had promised Gluck. "I'd like to get back to my own time, and I'd like it if everyone else was back where they all belonged too, but I think that the only way to do that is to confront Hronck. I think you're doing the right thing by trying to see him. But you need to understand, you won't be talking to some regular person. He's much more powerful than that."

"So who's this person, or being, or whatever that you're working with?" asked Haley. "Are you sure you can trust him?"

"No," he said, and Haley looked surprised. "Not really. I don't know who I can trust, any more than you do. I do believe that Hronck needs Edie; otherwise he would have already killed all of you. I don't think he really has any problem doing something like that. Right now, I'm trusting people only as much as I have to. But I want to see my family again, and I want to get back to where I belong, and I don't think that it's a coincidence that all of you are together right now in the restaurant."

Now it was Edie's turn to look surprised. "What do you mean?"

"Don't you think that it's strange that you just happened to run into a boy who can manipulate his avatar on the computer network to make impossible things happen? And then you met a girl who can pretend to be anyone on the computer network, even to the extent of changing her thoughts?" Sally dropped the menu to the floor and appeared to be in no hurry to pick it up. "Yes, I know all about your friends. I know that Kathrine and Melissa are waiting to meet you in New York, and that you're going to try to use another friend to get at Hronck. But don't you think all of this is too convenient?"

Meg frowned. "Well, it is strange."

"And Sally, don't you find it odd that you picked both of them up without hesitation? They're strangers. You're taking your little sister to New York on a dangerous mission. Don't you think that's all kind of peculiar? Do you normally do that type of thing?"

"Wait a sec," chimed in Ray. "You don't think we're trying to pull one over, do you? These folks saved me, and Haley too!" Haley nodded. "What are you saying about all of us? We didn't do nothing."

Jared sighed. "I'm saying that Hronck is manipulating things, trying to make things happen, including all of you. You aren't trying to trick Edie and Meg. Hronck is trying to trick all of *you.*"

"But all of this is happening in the real world, not in a computer," said Haley. "How could he make all of this happen? We're real people, not avatars."

Jared knew that this would be the most difficult part. How to explain all of this without giving everything away?

"I told you that Hronck isn't human. To him, everything is inside the network, including us. Look, to us, there's real life and a network. We get on a computer to see the network. We live through avatars on the network. To us, the world of the network isn't real. Our bodies, where we sit in a restaurant—that's real. With me so far?"

His audience nodded, although Lisa looked like she was getting ready to ask a question. He continued quickly before he lost his momentum. "To Hronck, there's something called the Mesh, where *we live*. It's like the network, except we live inside it. Just like Ray here can change the computer network you know so well, Hronck can alter our own world at will. To him, the 'real world' is just another computer game. To him, our real bodies are no different from avatars. He can do all sorts of things we can't even imagine. He doesn't know everything, and he can't do everything, but he can do a lot. Far more than any of us can imagine."

Edie now felt sick to her stomach and began shifting in her seat. "If that's true, how are we supposed to get home? If he's so powerful, why are we even bothering with this trip? Doesn't he know you're here talking to us?"

"I don't know if he knows I'm here talking to you, but I doubt it. As I said, he doesn't know everything—he can find things out if he wants to know them, but he can't know everything at once." He looked down at the table. "But as for the rest, if you think about it, he must want you to do this. He's bringing all of you together to do something, and I have no question that this is part of some plan."

He looked directly at Edie, who squirmed under his gaze. After a moment, she had to look away, and he continued. "But while he wants you to look for him, and wants to make it hard for you for some reason, he's also giving you tools, and giving you help. Isn't that strange? You have to ask yourself why. Why the big game?"

At that point, the waitress approached with menus, and Jared stopped talking. Apparently able to detect that her presence was not wanted, the waitress, a young woman with her hair pulled up into an age-inappropriate bun, distributed the menus, promised to return in a few minutes, and hurried away. As soon as she was out of earshot, Jared went on. "Think about it: Hronck could have destroyed you, but he didn't. He could have sent you somewhere else, where you had no friends, and where Sally wasn't around. But he didn't. This is all a set-up, sure, but if we have any hope of figuring out what he's up to, or how to stop him, we have to play along."

Edie thought about this and silently agreed that this was deeply puzzling. It did all seem oddly prearranged. But before she could add her own thoughts into the mix, Meg began to speak.

"Jake, you'll have to excuse me, but the fact that you've shown up here like this seems a bit too perfect, too." She pulled a strand of hair from behind her ear and began twisting it around her finger, her eyes tightly focused on Jared. "I mean, just before we get to New York, you show up, announce that you're from a different time, tell us that Hronck is some kind of energy whoosit....What are we supposed to think about all of this?"

Jared tried to look as earnest as possible, but the strain of the day made it impossible. His voice began to break with emotion. "I wish I had a better answer. I don't like the fact that I have to trust strangers in all of this, either." He struggled for a moment with what he wanted to say next, until it came out in a rush. "Over the past two days I lost my family. I lost the life I had. I found myself alone and completely confused. I'm stuck here just like you. You don't have to trust me. You don't have to like me. You don't even have to pay any attention to anything I'm saying. I just want to help. I'm telling you things you need to know. I don't know what's going on any more than you do, but I've learned some things that should make you think. I can tell you what I know, and then you can decide what to do with it. But I want to get home, and I think I'm probably stuck here too until you figure it out."

Meg looked stricken as she listened to Jared's rant, as did everyone else at the table, their expressions hovering between fear and confusion. Kathrine in particular seemed to be struggling with the implications of what "Jake" had just told them, and she felt her mind was whirring like a machine as she ran through proofs in her head.

Edie, however, felt strangely impressed and, if anything, even more inclined to follow this boy after listening to his speech. As Meg was about to say something, Edie grabbed her arm. "Let's go to the bathroom. Sally, why don't you order some pancakes for us or something. We'll be back." And before Meg even seemed aware that anything had transpired, Edie had half-lifted her out of the chair and steered her towards the restroom. By the time the door closed behind them, Meg had snapped out of it and begun to giggle. Then she peered under the stalls, one by one.

"Okay, we're alone," she whispered. "I have no idea what's going on, but if nothing else, that guy is cute."

"Great," said Edie, surprised to feel a twinge of jealousy which she quickly banished. "Glad to hear you've got your priorities straight. What do you think about what he *said*?"

Meg turned serious. "I have no idea. I do think he's right that we don't have much of a choice here. Hronck isn't even human? What else are we supposed to do?"

Edie looked in the mirror as she listened to Meg. After everything that had happened over the past few days, she expected to look older or more weathered. But she looked no different than the girl who only a few days before had imagined herself to look like a praying mantis. But she didn't feel the same anymore. She felt as though something had changed.

Edie had been so focused on her appearance that she almost lost track of Meg's monologue.

"And that," concluded Meg with a flourish, "is why I think that things are going to turn out okay."

Edie smiled as she bent over the sink to splash some water on her face. "Glad to see you're still optimistic about it."

"Actually, I'm not, but I feel like I have to be the one to fake it. You aren't as good an actor as I am."

"So we keep on heading down the road, eh?"

"I don't see any other options, do you? Although there are some parts of this that are probably going to be harder than we thought."

"Like what?" asked Edie, now arranging her hair in the mirror. "I thought all of this was going to be pretty much impossible. Can it get much harder?"

"I think that getting Amanda to help will be a problem. I think that getting Hronck to see us will be a problem. But Jake is right, a lot of this seems like a set-up. Heck, even *Jake* seems like a set-up."

"This does all feel like a movie. I just wish I could look up the ending." Edie turned back to Meg. "But for whatever it's worth, I think Ray and Haley are going to be the key here. Maybe that Jake guy, too."

"Ray and Haley, really? Why do you say that?"

"I got a feeling about them." She moved back to the sinks to splash some more water on her face, but really just to have something to do while they talked. "These talents they keep talking about—I think that could be our ticket out of here."

"How?" asked Meg, trying to envision a scenario when this incomprehensible kid and traumatized young woman might actually prove useful. At this point, she thought, the cat might be more helpful.

"Well, remember when I said that it seemed like the network knew who I was, and understood our problem?"

Meg thought for a moment. "In the library, you mean? With the picture in the book? I'm still not sure I understand what you were talking about there."

"It was like the network told me to grab a certain book, and turn to a certain page." Edie realized how ridiculous this sounded, even as she said it. "And then it was that picture of a looping waterfall. When the water came to the bottom, it flowed back to the top, which is impossible, right? But there it was. That's sort of what we're in here—a loop. I sent myself notes from a different time, and because of those notes we got sent to that different time. And because I was in that different time, I could send myself the notes. It's almost like that future me was trying to get us sent to another time. Man. That's confusing, isn't it? I can't—"

"Edie." Meg looked uncomfortable. "Why do you think you would have sent yourself notes like that? Do you have any guesses?"

Edie could tell that Meg was still mad at her on some level. Without knowing what else to say, she decided to confront it directly. "I have no idea. I'm sure I must have had a good reason for it. And since you were probably with me when it happened, I'm sure you approved or I wouldn't have done it. For all we know," she added, smiling, "this could have been your idea."

Meg laughed bitterly. "Unfortunately, you're probably right. It does sound like the kind of dumb idea I might come up with. I guess I'll blame myself too." She looked in the mirror and examined what looked like the beginnings of a blemish. She then turned and entered a stall. "So tell me more about the library. You think that the network was trying to communicate with you?"

"No," said Edie, a bit more insistently. "I'm saying that the network *was* communicating with me. It knows who we are and why we're here. And it's explaining our problem through that picture."

"Okay." Meg's voice echoed in the stall. "Now you're just repeating yourself. What do you *mean*?"

"Think about those notes." Edie was adamant, but was now examining her own face in the mirror again. *I never liked my cheekbones,* she thought. "We sent those notes to ourselves. Because we got them, we investigated and got sent back in time. But the only reason we were able to send them was because we had been sent back in time in the first place. Don't you see? It's a loop, we got caught in a loop. Remember back when we were looking up 'time' on the computer? One of those sites talked about loops in time. That's where we are—we've slipped into a time loop."

"Does that mean that *everything* we've done was planned for us?" Meg sounded horrified. "Does that mean we never had a choice? Did Hronck send those notes?"

Just then, the door to the bathroom opened and a large, middle-aged woman walked in. Her smock-like dress was covered with small pink poodles, which were performing nineteenth-century circus tricks across the front. As the dress was video-enabled, the dogs were actually moving. She noisily walked into a stall and closed the door. Figuring it was just as well, Edie found an empty stall and did the same.

She heard a flush and then water running. "I'll see you back at the table," Meg said.

• • •

By the time Edie returned, Jared/Jake seemed to have befriended everyone. As she sidled up to her chair, she could see him deep in conversation with Sally. Lisa was listening intently, while Ray and Haley tossed in random thoughts like hecklers at a show.

"So wait a minute," said Ray. "Hronck can change me, like I can change the network? Why don't he just make us do what he wants?"

"I don't know," said Jared, apparently struggling to find the right words. "I'm not sure I understand it either, but I guess there are rules, like in a computer program, and you can't break the rules."

"This does explain many things," said Sally. "But why did he have to shoot Edie and Meg? What is he trying to do?"

"Yeah," said Edie. "Couldn't he have just snatched us?"

"I guess he has to use certain types of tools from the human world to accomplish certain types of things," said Jared. "Again, I don't know. I don't even know why he wants you."

"But does he want us to find him, or not?" asked Lisa. "Why is he making up these stories for Mark?"

"My guess is that he's trying to make sure that we have no choice," said Edie. "I mean, if we think that no one else will believe us, then Hronck's our only option."

"*Isn't* he our only option?" Meg chimed in. "We're pretty much stuck otherwise."

"I think that Hronck is playing a long game, and we don't even know the rules," said Jared. "Whatever he needs you to do, he must think that this trip out to see him is important for you, or necessary. I have no idea. But from what I understand, the guy is incredibly dangerous in just about every way you can imagine."

"Wonderful," sighed Sally. She turned to Meg with watery eyes. "Meg, I've been thinking. You don't have to do this. You could stay with me and Jim. It won't be the same, but you'll be with family, and you can just live your life starting now. I don't want to lose you again."

Meg looked tempted for a moment, but then she made eye contact with Edie, and a look or resolve replaced any uncertainty.

"Sally, I'd love to, and maybe I even want to, but we have to change things." She looked around, everyone's face reflecting her disturbed expression. "We were meant to do this, Sall. Jake is right, this is part of a big game. The only way for us to win is to play it."

"I think Jake is right about something else," added Edie. "It's pretty clear that all of us were meant to do this together."

"Well," said Sally, still flushed. "I'm beginning to think this is a big mistake, and I may not be done trying to convince you to change your minds. But as a book I read somewhere once said, 'There are no coincidences.' Maybe I'm the one who's mistaken."

Just then the waitress arrived, both arms covered in plates of pancakes, stacked on top of each other like a fan of cards.

"But right now," said Jared, breaking the spell, "we're meant to eat. Ray, can you pass the syrup?"

39

in hronck's city

Ray was beside himself with excitement, bouncing against his seat belt like a toddler hopped up on heavily frosted birthday cake and juice boxes. In contrast, the rest of the passengers seemed almost nauseated from the heavy food. As they drove onto the George Washington Bridge, with New York glimmering on the other shore, Ray could not stop talking.

"This is so far beyond amazing." He looked as excited as he sounded. "I've always wanted to go here, to see this place, you know, I've been here on the network. You been here on the network, Haley?"

"I've been here a bunch of times. I grew up not too far—"

"I been here loads of times. But on the network, you don't get all the detail. Once, though, I built a building right in the center of Manhattan, it was so—"

"Wait a sec," said Meg, awakening a bit from her food coma. "You built a building in Manhattan?"

"On the network," explained Ray patiently. "Remember, I can do lots of things on the network that other people can't do. Of course, somebody noticed, and they took it down, but we made a lot of money in rent until they did. Or at least, my fosters made a lot of money." He stopped and became suddenly forlorn. "Guys, where am I going to live now? I mean, my fosters don't want me anymore, and I got no place to go, exactly...."

"Don't worry," said Sally. "We'll figure something out when we get back to Kansas. Right now we just need to get you a passkey. Everything else will take care of itself."

Jared stared out the window, watching the scenery float by as though projected onto a screen. Phase 1 of his plan had worked. He was in the van, and he had given the travelers a sense of what they were up against without telling them the full story. He had even managed to speak to the adult version of a girl he'd had a crush on twenty-five years earlier without making a fool of himself. Now *that* was strange.

How the next phase would play out, he had no idea. As he closed his eyes to contemplate his situation, and to think about his missing family, Gluck's kitten jumped onto his lap. Surprised, he looked down to see the cat staring deeply into his eyes as though they were endless pools of blackness. Without warning, he suddenly found himself sitting next to Gluck in the midtown office they had adopted as their headquarters.

"Wait, how did you do that? No, don't tell me. Am I still in the van?"

"Yes, Mr. Garber, you are still in the van. You will appear asleep to the others, and while this conversation will take as long as necessary, it will seem to be but an instant to your companions driving into Manhattan."

He looked down and was pleased to see that he no longer looked like "Jake," but appeared to be himself again.

"What's going on?" he asked. "I warned them, but I didn't tell them about the Root, or any of that stuff. Not that it would have mattered, since none of us have any idea what the Root is, or what it does, or what we're supposed to do with it even if we found it."

"I am pleased to hear your initial efforts were success-ful," said Gluck, blithely ignoring Jared's distress. To Jared, Gluck once again appeared as a cascade of code, with empty eyes and flat features. Being away from Gluck for a few hours had allowed Jared to forget how distract-ing it could be to talk with someone with a moving digital surface instead of skin. "However, when the van comes to a halt, I will need you to leave your compatriots behind. They must approach Hronck without you. Instead, I have another task for you. This will require travel to yet another time, while Ms. Boyd and Ms. Karger attempt to achieve their goal." With that, Gluck once again pulled out his sil-very handle. Jared sighed.

"Where are we going this time? Back to the time of the pharaohs?"

"No, we will return back to your own time. Or to be more exact, shortly after your disappearance. I will need you to place some items for me. Everything will be clear when we get there. As soon as you say your goodbyes in the van, we can depart."

• • •

Sally was talking on her comlink as they drove into Manhattan, and the rest of the van couldn't hear much. Just as the car turned itself down the FDR along the East River, she turned around and smiled.

"Guys, we're going to stop by Melissa's house and pick up her and Kathrine. It will be a bit crowded in the backseat, but we won't be driving too long. We're meeting Amanda at 8:30 in Central Park."

"When do I get to get my passkey?" Ray piped in. "I mean, I know I can help, but I can't do nothing right now."

Sally was all business. "Tomorrow morning. Everything from the government is going to be closed by now, and it isn't like we're going to see Hronck tonight, anyway. We're going to stay the night at Melissa's and hopefully get everything done tomorrow."

Meg looked over at Haley and gave her a significant look. Haley nodded, then turned to Sally. "Sally, I really don't have any place to stay, and I don't have—"

Sally laughed. "Haley, don't worry, you're still with us, part of this whole sick crew. We're not abandoning you here."

Haley smiled. It was a big, glowing smile, radiating pure joy, and it reminded Edie of why Haley must have thought she could get a job in show business. But as big a smile as it was, and as genuine as the emotion may have been, there was something missing. Haley had stage presence, even sitting in the back seat of a van, but there was emptiness there, too. *I guess that's what happens,* Edie thought, *when someone breaks your heart.*

"Guys, when you stop by Melissa's house, I have to leave," said Jared. "I have some other things I have to do, and it's important that Hronck not know I'm here."

"What?" exclaimed Edie and Meg at once.

"You can't leave," said Sally. "You've got all sorts of information we need. We can't just go get this guy blind."

"Before I met you guys a couple of hours ago, you were going to do exactly that," he said. "Look, I'll be back. It's just a bad idea if I'm with you when you go to meet with Hronck. Or even while you're trying to meet with him. It could be dangerous for me, and dangerous for you."

The van became quiet. Edie was disappointed but couldn't quite put her finger on why. She supposed she had become used to the idea that everyone who was joining up with their crew was doing so for the duration of their journey. She also admitted to herself that she liked Jake. For that reason, his departure was doubly unsettling.

The silence in the van was short-lived. As they drove across Manhattan, "oohs" and "aahs" from Meg, Edie, and Ray peppered the air. They stared at the buildings alive with lights, with mirrored glass in residential skyscrapers covered in multicolored LEDs. To Edie it seemed as much like an underwater fantasia filled with crazy sea coral and lighted fish as it did like as a skyline. The skin of one building was covered with advertising: the image of an attractive Japanese woman 200 feet tall and clutching a soft drink was rapidly replaced by dogs leaping over immense hurdles in order to snag treats from their masters. It was bright, overwhelming, and nonstop.

Sally exited at 96th Street. Finally, as they left the highway, the lights began to diminish, and what appeared to be normal residential streets emerged from the chaos. Within a few minutes, they had pulled up alongside an enormous, stately, and impossibly old apartment building. An awning covered the sidewalk from the door all the way to the curb, and a doorman in fancy livery and gold epaulets stood like a soldier at attention. He reminded Edie of a character from the Nutcracker, and she smiled. Not too far behind him were Kathrine and, Edie guessed, a woman who must have been Melissa.

Melissa had been the girl who'd developed first, the one who'd grown taller than all the boys in fourth grade, gangly and uncomfortable. When Edie had known her as a girl, this early growth spurt had rendered Melissa awkward, shy and perpetually nervous. Edie remembered how Melissa had stared at the floor as she walked, hunched over, afraid to make eye contact with anyone except for Lisa, Amanda, Edie, and Kathrine. Now, like Edie's other friends, Melissa was a confident adult, her head high as she walked up to the van. She was dressed like a Manhattan sophisticate, in all black and high heels, towering over Kathrine, who was quite tall in her own right.

Edie wished she felt as assured as her friends all looked. She knew she'd have to draw on their confidence if she had any chance of surviving this ordeal.

She saw the look of anticipation on Melissa's face as she opened the door and climbed inside.

"Edie, is that really you?" Melissa squeaked, grabbing Edie and squeezing her so hard that she was certain she was going to break a rib. "I can't believe it!"

Edie laughed. "It's amazing how you all miss me like I've been dead or something. I can't believe how much you guys have changed over the past few days."

Melissa was barely able to hold back her tears. "You can't even imagine how big a shock it is to see you alive." She looked over at Meg and shook her head. "When you disappeared, it changed our lives so much. Now you're sitting here like fourteen-year-olds..."

Edie sighed. "Barely fourteen."

Kathrine closed the door behind her. "You're still obsessed about that, aren't you? You could never stand the fact that you were the youngest."

"Sorry," said Meg, patting Edie's arm in a show of faux comfort. "You're still the youngest."

"Enough of the melodrama," said Sally, a bit of snark in her voice as the car drove away from the curb. "Do you guys have a plan for what we're going to say to Amanda?"

"Nope," said Kathrine, looking back at Edie and Meg and grinning malevolently. "I suspect these two will do all the talking we need."

"This is where I have to leave you," said Jared. Kathrine and Melissa looked over with surprise to see "Jake" sitting in the van next to Ray.

"Before you leave, I should probably introduce you to Kathrine and Melissa," said Edie. "Guys, this is Jake. He's lost in time, too. He told us all sorts of things about Hronck, and we can talk about it in a few minutes, but he has to leave now."

"So hello and goodbye," he said, shaking hands with Melissa and Kathrine. As he started to open the door, Kathrine held out her arm to bar his progress.

"You're lost in time, too?" she asked, her voice already locked into an analytic tone. "Who sent you here? Where are you from?"

"It's a long story. Edie and Meg can fill you in. I'll be back, but it's important that Hronck doesn't see me with you guys." He opened the door and jumped out. "I'll see you soon." And with that, he ran down the street and disappeared around a corner.

"That was strange," said Melissa. "I expect a full explanation, after I hug you again, of course."

Sally drove them around the Upper East Side, and as they wended their way south, Edie and Meg told Kathrine and Melissa about Jake, and Hronck, and the fact that all of this had been prearranged for their benefit. Both were suitably appalled. But soon Edie was forced to stop talking and simply stared out the window instead, trying to control the emotional turmoil she felt. This time, however, the wonders she saw were human, rather than architectural.

As they turned down Fifth Avenue, she saw a group of teenagers walking down the street, south towards the museum. Each one of them was more deformed than the next: several of them had enormous heads, like melons, while others had what appeared to be alligator skin. Still others had transformed their skin into large, video-enabled screens, with images of death and disease scrolling across their faces.

"Are those the body mods you were talking about?" Edie asked Ray, disgust coloring her voice. "That's pretty nasty stuff."

"Yeah. You stay away from them, on the network or in real life. The stuff they do online is pretty harsh, not fun at all."

"We'll stay away from them, don't worry about that," said Meg, also looking out the window, horrified at what she was seeing. "I just hope they stay away from us."

part five

the secret root

40

amanda's surprise

A manda's regular driver, Dimitri, drove up in her official car. She had worked with him for several years and he was a wonderful asset to the office, well beyond his skills behind the wheel. He had an encyclopedic knowledge of ethnic food in New York and was always ready with a tasty recommendation. He knew how to make anything happen, whether it required a plumber or an accountant, and had capable friends in every profession imaginable. He knew what was actually going on in every precinct, and could make calls to uncover any fact. It was almost like magic.

Amanda suspected he might be tied into unsavory elements of the city—what other explanation could there be for his vast store of knowledge?—but she had come to rely on him so completely that she had long ago decided not to inquire. Sometimes, she thought, it was best not to know the answers.

"You are going to the boathouse, yes?" asked Dimitri in his rumbling, Slavic voice, as they drove towards Central Park, many blocks ahead.

"Right, yes, I'm meeting a friend." She decided not to be more specific. After all, she didn't even know what Melissa's emergency might be. It could be personal, or embarrassing. "I just didn't want to be out by myself at night."

"Do you want me to be staying with you at meeting?" He turned to look at her and the car continued forward. She suddenly realized that they were driving about 90 miles an hour up the West Side Highway.

"No," she replied, with a touch of nervousness in her voice, "but I would like you to hang back and watch from a distance. It's a private conversation, so I don't want her to feel like someone else is there, too."

"Understood. Just set your comlink for me. I watch from trees."

As they hurtled north towards Central Park, Amanda became concerned again. What could possibly be such an emergency for Melissa? Was she getting a divorce? Why would she want to meet at the boathouse? Not even in the restaurant *inside* the boathouse, but *at* the boathouse. Suddenly she was glad she had Dimitri there, for this was all very odd indeed.

Amanda's feeling of disquiet did not decrease as they pulled into the boathouse parking lot a few minutes later. There were a number of nondescript cars parked in the lot, but it seemed otherwise deserted. The darkness of the park, even through the streetlights, created a feeling of foreboding and nonspecific danger. She took out her electronic compact, which expanded out to a holographic mirror. After examining her face to ensure that her makeup was right, she paused a moment to gather her thoughts. She saw her hard, brown eyes glaring back, and her still-youthful face framed by shoulder-length hair held in an iridescent blue headband. Satisfied that she looked appropriate for whatever might happen, she opened the door.

"Thanks, Dimitri," she said, climbing out of the car. "Just watch me without seeming to watch me. You know what I mean?"

He smiled through the open window. "I watch casual. Don't worry, and call me on comlink if there is problem."

She wasn't sure where exactly Melissa would be, but she decided the easiest thing to do would be to head towards the front door. She had barely gone five steps, however, before she heard Melissa's voice.

"Amanda." Melissa stood next to a van parked a couple of spaces away from her, looking quite serious in the darkness. "Over here."

Amanda walked over to the van. "Melissa? What's wrong? What's the emergency? Why did we have to meet here in the middle of the park?"

Melissa bent forward, almost bowing to her friend. "What I am about to show you is going to be difficult to take, but I need you to promise me you aren't going to panic or run away. Can you do that?"

Amanda didn't like the way this was developing. "Since I don't know what you're talking about, I don't know what I can promise. But I trust you, you know that. I always have." She noticed that Melissa was holding the van's door handle, as though to open the door. "Is it in the van?"

"Yes," said Melissa haltingly, "but it is more in the nature of a 'they' than an 'it.' But this kind of suspense isn't fair. Amanda, here's the scoop: Edie Boyd and Meg Karger are alive. And they're here, inside the van." With a flourish, she opened up the sliding back door, and Edie and Meg jumped out onto the pavement.

Nothing could have prepared Amanda for this. As she stood there, flummoxed and unable to conjure any sort of coherent response, Edie and Meg gently took her by the arms and led her into the van. Melissa looked around and climbed in herself. A moment later the van started and turned out of the parking lot.

• • •

Back in Amanda's car, Dimitri leaned forward and began speaking over his comlink. "Yes, it is van. Yes, I am sure license plate is correct."

"Follow them," instructed Nick through the link. "Be sure not to lose them."

"Don't worry. I not lose."

• • •

As Dimitri pulled away, another car left the parking lot as well. As Lisa carefully observed Dimitri pursuing their friends, she crossed her fingers. She hoped that the plan—hatched only five minutes before the meeting—would work.

41

past as present

When Jared arrived back in his own time, with Gluck and his silver handle now familiar companions, he was startled to find himself inside his own school, at night. The buiding was just as he remembered it, with red brick covering every visible surface except where blue doors or green metal lockers intervened. The floors had been shined to a high gloss by janitors using floor buffers that swirled patterns of wax into vortices spinning as far as the eye could see.

The halls were silent in a way he had never experienced before, and the absence of the typical chaos of a school day was tangible. Except for a handful of emergency lights, it was dim. The brightly colored lockers he had walked past so many times before seemed dull in the gloom, and shadows created pockets of darkness every few yards. He found the entire scene disconcerting.

Unlike his prior experiences traveling with Gluck, this time he had received some limited warning of his destination. After leaving Edie and the rest of her entourage at Melissa's house, he had walked morosely back to midtown Manhattan and Gluck's temporary headquarters. Jared found it odd that a higher being like Gluck wanted or needed a 'headquarters,' but he figured it was probably for his benefit rather than Gluck's. After debriefing Gluck on what had transpired (Gluck's spy-cat had, for obvious reasons, not been in the restaurant), Gluck explained what would happen next. As usual, he left out important details, but Jared would not recognize those omissions until much later, when it was far too late.

As Gluck described it, Jared and he would travel back to Jared's school, during the evening right after the Garbers' disappearance had been discovered. Gluck wanted to drop off some items, some physical things, at the high school. He explained that it would be useful to have Jared perform these tasks, as he (in his physically transformed state as "Jake") would be able to more easily fit in with crowds of teenagers. It didn't occur to Jared until they arrived that there would be no crowds of teenagers filling the hallways late at night.

As they stood in the vacant hallway, he waited silently for Gluck to say or do something, anything. Their last conversation had taken place only a few minutes before, but to Jared time had become meaningless. What did it mean when something seemed to occur only a few minutes before, but in fact took place twenty-five years later? Everything was flowing together into a seamless river of time, but flowing in all directions at once. Even though he was rested, the lack of formal sleep had led him to lose track of what day it was, or whether it was time for breakfast or dinner. It took every ounce of his concentration to keep up with what was happening from moment to moment. Everything was simply a series of nows, with no future and no past to grasp.

This left Jared feeling exceptionally disconnected from what was going on around him. His chaotic emotions were still present at all times, and his fear for his family was undiminished. But even those passionate concerns began to seem distant, as though experienced by someone else, far away.

Yet even in this numbed state, he wished with every cell in his body that he were a student again, and could forget about avatars and networks and Faktors. Running his hand along the familiar walls of the school corridor, he didn't want to think about Gluck or Hronck, and what they wanted with him or Edie. He wanted to be yelled at by his father or sneered at by his sister. He wanted geometry homework and a date with Sally. He didn't want to think about the Saan or why they'd created this world.

With that last thought, however, something new occurred to Jared. After puzzling over it for a moment, he decided to break the silence. "Gluck, do you actually know *anything* about the Saan? You said they created you, and created the Mesh. But how do you know who they are, or that they created you at all? Didn't you say they were around millions of years ago?"

"That is an excellent question," replied Gluck, looking around as though uncertain of his location. "Ah." He moved towards a bank of lockers on the right. "The Saan left behind many clues for the Faktors to unravel. Moreover, they did so intentionally. You may recall that I described the Mesh as a great computer. I was not speaking in metaphors. The Mesh is, quite literally, a large computer. Each particle in every atom in your body is engaged in a massive quantum calculation spanning millions of years. You are, so to speak, no different than a transistor in one of your laptops. But in order for this computer to work properly, the Saan needed a plan."

"What type of plan? They couldn't control everything that happened in the future, could they? It isn't like everything we do has been planned out for us, is it?"

"Oh no. In fact, the Saan quite explicitly did *not* want to control everything. They wanted the Mesh, and each of its component universes, to grow and expand organically. Their calculations required it. But for some reason unknown to us, they decided that the Mesh alone was insufficient. They required another level of programming layered upon the Mesh in order to achieve their goals. For that reason they created Faktors as agents within the system, and gave us some limited insight into the Mesh and their intentions." He began to examine the numbers on each locker, apparently searching for one in particular.

"So you have no idea what they were trying to figure out?" asked Jared, peering over Gluck's shoulder. "Do you have anything they wrote, something like that?"

"No," said Gluck flatly. "Ah, here it is. Mr. Garber, please place this notecard in this locker through the vent at the top." He suddenly held a piece of paper in his glowing hand.

"What's this? What do you want me to do?"

"This is a note composed by Ms. Boyd. I have two others. We need to place them in Ms. Boyd's locker at designated times so that she finds them. It is not strictly necessary for you to place this first one, as this school is empty now, but the others must go in while school is in session, and therefore you must do it, as I cannot do so in a form that would be acceptable. I will disguise you appropriately, of course."

"Um, can you explain what you just said a little better?" asked Jared. "I mean, if Edie wrote the notes, why are you putting them in her locker?"

Gluck spoke without any audible emotion. "These are the notes that will compel Ms. Boyd and Ms. Karger to enter your home two days from now. I do not know if they discussed any of this with you during your brief visit at the restaurant, but Ms. Boyd and Ms. Karger were investigating your disappearance when Hronk transported them into the future."

"Why were they doing that?" asked Jared incredulously. "I mean, they're kids, not the police."

"They were inspired by these notes, which purport to be clues to your disappearance. These notes will convince the two girls that you and your family have fallen into a time trap. Which is accurate, in a manner of speaking." He handed the note to Jared, who examined it. "The girls proceeded to enter your home, where they were seen by Hronck, who then used his time device to place them twenty-five years into the future."

"Wait a minute, hold it—was Hronck there on purpose? How did he know that Meg and Edie would be there in my house? That seems pretty convenient."

"I told him, of course," said Gluck. "Faktors are quite powerful, but we are not omnipotent. He could not have known without advance warning. But once he became aware that Ms. Boyd and Ms. Karger would be in the house, he arranged himself accordingly."

Jared was so unprepared for this turn of events that it left him dumbfounded and without a response. He stood motionless, the note still in his hand, which was now visibly shaking. Apparently unaware that anything he had said was controversial, Gluck continued.

"Later on, as I understand it, Ms. Boyd and Ms. Karger discovered that these notes were composed by Ms. Boyd herself. For that reason, they believe themselves to be in some form of time loop, a chicken-and-egg problem, if you will. This is incorrect, but for our purposes it is an acceptable point of view."

"*Our* purposes?" Jared could barely control a rage growing inside him. "You told Hronck that they would be there, so he could send them back in time? *You* did this?"

"Of course," said Gluck patiently. "He did not realize that the information came from me, of course. I planted it in a manner that could not be traced to me or my faction. If he had known of my involvement, he would have been suspicious, and may have refrained at that time."

"So they didn't even write the notes? This was all fake?"

Gluck seemed disturbed only at that particular aspect of Jared's accusation. "Oh, no. The notes themselves were truly composed by Ms. Boyd, but in, let us say, a different context. We can discuss that at a later time." He began looking more closely at the locker, as though fascinated by its construction. "As I perceived it, Hronck was going to transport Ms. Boyd into a different time eventually, and perhaps quite soon. It was clearly the best way to manipulate the situation to Hronck's advantage, and it's what I would have done in his place. Therefore, given the inevitability of Ms. Boyd's disappearance, I wanted the incident, which I had forseen, to take place in a manner more suitable for my purposes and, quite frankly, her safety."

"You couldn't have stopped Hronck?" Jared's voice was now raised just short of a yell as he began walking away from Gluck. "You had to arrange this all to be more 'suitable'? That's ridiculous. You tricked them and now they're stuck like me!"

"May I remind you, Mr. Garber, that without Ms. Boyd's disappearance, and without her presence in the future, you would have no chance of ever returning home or seeing your family again. So let us be clear: you will assist me. And you will do it simply because you must. If you don't, Hronck will succeed, and we shall all be subject to his power eternally. So please understand: not only does the Mesh and all life within it depend on your success, but if you refuse, you will be alone permanently." He paused and looked around. "I also caution you to keep your voice at a more muted level. I do sense that there are security guards within the building."

Jared felt completely trapped. He was now being asked, by a being he did not trust or understand, to do something that would render him complicit in the disappearances of Edie Boyd and Meg Karger. If he slipped these notes in Edie's locker, it would begin an inexorable chain of events that would lead to the girls' getting ripped from their families and taken bodily to another time. But what if he didn't do it? Then would the disappearance of his own family be for naught? Would Hronck just snatch Edie at some other time, but without Meg there to support her? And was that unfair to Meg?

His head hurt from all the possibilities, and he felt sweat begin to run down his neck. If he didn't do anything, he might be responsible for the destruction of millions of people he had never met, in worlds he could not even imagine. What if Gluck was right, and Hronck was eventually able to take control of the Mesh? Would the blood of infinite lives be on Jared's hands? Yet there was no question that by putting the notes in Edie's locker, he was responsible for the lives of two very real people—girls he had met and liked. He was reminded of something Mrs. Besicka had once told him, a quote from some writer a long time ago: "Nobody ever did, or ever will, escape the consequences of his choices." He had never really understood her point until now.

He took another look at the note gripped in his clammy hand. The note read "TIME IS A TRAP" in careful block letters. He sighed and considered bitterly that the note could not have seemed more accurate had he composed it himself. Then he walked over to Edie's locker, took a deep breath, and carefully slid the note through the vent.

42

the many faces of
jackson hronck

Jackson Hronck was a busy man. His staff would often joke that he seemed to be in several places at once, at all times. As difficult as it was for the average person to imagine how Hronck accomplished as much as he did, for those who worked closely with him it was nearly impossible to comprehend.

According to the engineers in his labs, he often spent several hours a day with them, explaining his newest ideas and providing them with design prototypes of his newest inventions. His political advisers, meanwhile, swore up and down that he was with them, talking strategy and devising ways to win the presidency. The folks who managed the city told a different story, with Jackson Hronck controlling the minute details of New York City with a mastery never before seen in any prior administration. He was at a fire station on Staten Island in the morning and a school in Chinatown after lunch. He was glad-handing voters in the evening at a midtown hotel, and inspecting night repair crews on the Brooklyn Bridge.

Jackson Hronck was everywhere.

This morning, however, Jackson Hronck was in his office at City Hall, speaking with Nick, his security chief. Both were dressed casually, in matching black Hronet jumpsuits with neon orange piping and dark green accents around the lapels, and seemed at ease in each other's company. Only when they spoke could any hierarchy be perceived.

"Mr. Hronck, you're sure about this? I can pick them up whenever you say…"

"Yes, Nick," said Hronck, the left side of his mustache turning up in a slight grin. "I am quite certain. They are persistent, though, eh? I really have to admire that type of determination. It is something I value in myself." He spun his chair to look out the window. "When Amanda contacts me, as I have forseen, she will try to get an appointment. The only surprise will be that we will go along with it: we will let them see me. But let us have the appointment at my home." He looked back at Nick, his eyes glinting in the morning light. "It will be far easier there."

"I'm surprised that you're even letting them meet with you," said Nick, a slight grin of his own now curling the outsides of his mouth. "I assume you have a plan in mind?"

"Yes, but that is not something you need to worry about. The fact that they grabbed Amanda is enough proof of their intentions, and of their value to me. They want to use her to get to me. And I am going to let them do it."

• • •

As predicted, Amanda was more resistant to the truth than were any of Edie's other friends. They drove around the city for hours, talking, offering up every piece of evidence they could muster. Meg had grown so mad at one point that she nearly came to blows with Amanda, and had to be held back by Ray and Haley. Zeke the cat huddled in Edie's lap, apparently upset at the angry voices.

It was a strange reunion indeed, and reminiscent of the way they had argued as kids many years before.

"Look," declared Amanda, shaking her head as though trying to erase the images of Edie and Meg from her mind. "I'm sorry. I've worked with Jackson for—"

"Amanda, look at us!" insisted Edie. "How do you explain this? How do you explain the fact that you're all adults, you even have kids, for goodness' sake, and we're still teenagers?"

Amanda still looked shocked. "I *can't* explain it, but I also can't believe that Jackson would hurt you guys."

Meg spoke up, calmed a bit from her earlier explosion. "He's responsible for the Garbers disappearing. He lived right behind them. Who knows what year he sent them off to—maybe they've been eaten by dinosaurs. He shot us into the future because we saw his ray gun in the backyard. We're lucky to be alive. I don't care if he's your best friend. He's a bad guy. Period."

"Amanda," said Melissa cautiously, "I realize this is difficult, but you've got to help us here. Hronck is the only one who can send them back. He's the only one who can make things right. And you," she added, poking her thigh for emphasis, "are the only one who can get us in to see him."

Amanda remained skeptical, but in the absence of any other explanation, she concluded that having the group meet Jackson Hronck was probably for the best. He was, after all, the greatest scientist of his generation. Perhaps he might have a solution to their problem, regardless of whether or not he was responsible for Edie and Meg's appearance a quarter-century after their deaths. Even if she couldn't quite believe what she was hearing, Amanda was sure that Jackson could help. He always had the answers.

• • •

After Sally had dropped Amanda off at her apartment, with a promise that they would talk further in the morning, the group departed for Melissa's house, where they planned to sleep soundly, piled into a guest bedroom with a king-sized mattress and three sleeping bags. Edie was so tired that she barely took notice of the apartment as she dragged herself into the bedroom to sleep. She hoped to be asleep within minutes, if not sooner, and based on the snores that rapidly filled the room, the others in their party had beat her to it.

Yet the best-laid plans, thought Edie as she lay sleepless on the floor, rarely worked out as you intended. That was what Aunt Judy had always said, and it was certainly true tonight. There was no way, even as exhausted as she was, that she was going to fall asleep any time soon, no matter how much she longed for dreams. There was far too much to think about, and far too many decisions to consider.

But it was the images of Aunt Judy and Uncle Pete that she could not erase from her mind as she lay on Melissa's floor. Aunt Judy making pancakes, Uncle Pete's diatribes about the modern world... all of it was so perfect, and so comforting. It was the only world she had known. Now she wasn't sure she would ever see the two of them again, ever have the opportunity to tell them how much she loved them, and how thankful she was for the life they had given her after the death of her parents.

It had always bothered Edie that she had such a small family. Many of her friends had siblings, and passels of cousins and grandparents and aunts and uncles. She had once been invited to attend one of Melissa's family reunions (at Melissa's insistence, Edie suspected) and had been amazed at the number of other kids filling the house. She wanted to feel as though she were a part of something larger. Without a family, she felt alone.

This train of thought, based on some confused logic which only made sense when one was two heartbeats short of sleep, led Edie to consider Mark and Lisa. In the van, Lisa had told her the story of their many breakup, and insisted that this was the last one. According to Lisa, they were now done. Edie was the last straw. But given their history, Edie was not so sure. Lying in her sleeping bag, reviewing the events of the past few days, she thought she understood the forces that might cause Lisa to return to Mark, regardless of whether it was a good idea.

The things you do with your friends are shared memories, thought Edie. You never fully remember the details of your life's experiences yourself; you need your friends to fill in the gaps to completely experience the memory. Otherwise the depth and power of that memory gets lost to the passage of time.

Thus, when your friends are denied to you, part of your past life is shut away forever. When you lose a friend, she thought, you lose part of yourself—which is why it was so easy to remain friends with people who weren't right for you at all. Edie felt comforted by this insight.

Perhaps Lisa could find herself in a better place once Meg and Edie got back to Kansas, and everyone could start their lives over again. It was one more reason to go back to where she belonged—so that Lisa could be happy. At least Edie hoped that was the case.

And what of Jake and his warnings about Hronck? This was the greatest mystery. She had never even asked Jake where he lived, and how Hronck had transported him to this time. Did his failure to explain things render his information suspicious? She had come to like him and thought he had provided some useful insights. But if what he had told them was true, and Hronck was some kind of otherworldly being, then what hope did they have of convincing him to help them?

Perhaps, as Jake had suggested, Hronck wanted Edie and the others to find him. Perhaps this whole thing was a set-up, part of Hronck's plan. But why? And what of Ray and Haley—were they part of this great plan, too?

As she considered the image of Hronck, half-remembered from the documentary she had watched with Meg in the van, she finally fell into a deep and dreamless slumber, and the blackness felt like a comfort.

• • •

Unsurprisingly, Ray was the first one up at the crack of dawn, bouncing around at the thought that he would get his passkey back today.

"Passkey! Passkey!" he chanted, running around the room and waking everyone up. Edie yawned, sat up, and promptly bumped her head on Meg's head as Meg turned to the side to stretch.

"Ow!" yelled Meg in mock indignation. "First you get me stuck here in the future, and now my head hurts."

Edie rolled her eyes. "Ha, ha. Very funny."

Everyone slowly hauled themselves awake and dragged themselves into the kitchen. Edie noted that the bedroom itself looked pretty much like every bedroom she had ever been in, except that the bed was apparently floating two feet off the ground, and Zeke was sleeping underneath it. She shook her head as though the image were faulty, but still the bed remained suspended in the air.

She tapped Sally on the shoulder. "So where do we get him a passkey?" she asked, trying to ignore the fact that a king-sized bed was about to squash a cat.

Meg smiled, watching Ray jumping on Melissa's bed, oblivious to the kitten underneath. "Yeah. It may be the only way to shut him up."

"I don't know where we go," replied Sally. "I was going to ask Melissa. Hey, Melissa, do you—"

"Yes, I know the place." Melissa emerged from the bathroom, tying a bathrobe around herself. "It's downtown, near the old financial center. Right off West Street, across from the Battery."

"Sounds good. I'll check the map in the van." Sally closed her eyes to picture it. "I'll take Ray, and I'll grab him some new clothes while I'm at it." Ray turned at the sound of his name and squeaked excitedly. "I also want to look into his foster parents. We need to figure out something permanent for the kid."

"Can I come too?" asked Haley in a voice that sounded nearly despondent. "I don't have any money right now and I need a job. I need to start looking for something quickly, since I don't know how long it will take."

Edie thought that Haley, who had been in good spirits yesterday, looked pretty forlorn, as though the enormity of her situation had just hit her. Haley went on. "I also need to borrow some clothes. I—I probably can't find a job in this dress. At least not a job that I'd want to take. I promise to bring it back."

"Of course." Melissa went back into her room and disappeared into the closet. She emerged a moment later with a set of clothes more appropriate for a job search, which in this particular era consisted of a shiny black tracksuit with illuminated lapels. "This should be fine for most jobs. What are you looking for?"

"At first, I'm thinking just a waitressing job while I try to get into acting. I just need something where I can get started immediately." She looked at the floor, abashed. "Can I also—I mean, I'd also like to borrow some money so I can get by until my first paycheck, assuming I can even get a job. I'm good for it, I promise, and—"

"Haley," said Sally with a kind of maternal finality, grasping her by the shoulder as she spoke. "Don't worry about it. Seriously." Edie thought Haley's smile could have lit up a large city. "We'll take care of everything. But I suspect that if Jake is correct, we may need your help, too. As long as you're willing to promise me that you'll help Meg and Edie if they need it, whenever they need it, you have my word that you'll never again find yourself sitting on a suitcase in the middle of nowhere."

As Haley ran up to hug Sally, Meg looked over at Edie and pointed at the doorway. They both walked through quickly and into another room. Once they were alone, Meg turned to Edie with a look equal parts fear and determination.

"I've been thinking about all of this," she said. "I woke up about an hour before Ray and just lay in that sleeping bag trying to figure out how this will all play out."

"Did you figure it out?" asked Edie sarcastically. "Because I'd really like to know that myself."

"Very funny," said Meg, as if biting back something stronger. "But seriously, think about it. What if Amanda gets us in front of Hronck today? What do we say to him?"

"Tell him to send us home, I guess. But I think he wants something from us. At least that's what it sounds like."

"But what could he want from us? We're two teenage girls. It sounds like he's not even a human being, and if he were a person he'd be the richest one around. And he knows we're coming. We don't have much to bargain with here."

"I don't know about that. He's rich, he has a time ray, and he possesses incredible powers that we don't even understand. But *we* have a kitten." Edie looked down and saw Zeke padding across the floor. "See? Things are pretty even."

Meg snorted. "Yeah, Zeke ought to intimidate him. If Hronck's really a mouse."

Edie laughed. "Look, I know what you're saying, but we have no idea why we're here, or if this is actually part of some big plot. We're just going to have to play it by ear." She sighed, watched Zeke for a moment more, and then took Meg's arm. "Come on, let's head back. I want to know what the others are up to."

As they walked back into the room, Sally was preparing to leave, with Ray and Haley in tow.

"Melissa," said Sally as she opened the door, "you'll stay here with Edie and Meg and wait for Amanda to call?" Melissa nodded. "Great, let me know immediately when she does. Lisa, you'll be okay here, too?"

"Absolutely," said Lisa, finally emerging from the bedroom, with Kathrine following close behind. "I'll be security." She patted her holster, which Edie had not previously noticed. "And we can talk strategy."

"Yes," said Kathrine. "There's a lot we still need to discuss. Including Jake's theories."

"That sounds good," said Edie as the others left through the front door. "But I'm still nervous. Things are moving so quickly, and Amanda could call any minute now."

Melissa shook her head. "She won't. I know Amanda better than any of you, and she is currently sitting in her office, staring out the window and trying to build up the nerve to call Hronck. It will take her hours of second-guessing and dilly-dallying before she does it. She probably believes us at this point. How could she not? But she *is* worried that she's about to throw her career out the window. And—"

"—and Amanda is all about her career," finished Edie. "I'm definitely getting that vibe. But she'll help us get in. I can feel it."

Meg turned to Kathrine, Lisa, and Melissa. "I hope you're right. Because no offense, guys, but Edie and I have got to get out of this place. Soon."

43

memories can wait

Amanda sat in her office, staring out the window, her head in her hands, trying to figure out what to do next. Seeing Edie and Meg had been a stunning experience. When she'd finally realized that yes, it was truly them, *back from the dead*, she was thrilled. But tempering that excitement was the fact that they wanted to meet with her friend Jackson Hronck. They blamed him for their predicament. They thought he was a bad guy, an evil man. This was, unquestionably, a problem for her, and something she wasn't sure that she could believe.

Amanda's entire life was inextricably tied to her future with Jackson Hronck. She was a politician in a town where he was an incredibly powerful, popular mayor. But more than that, he was her patron, her long-time supporter, and, if the polls were to be believed, the next president of the nation. Calling him up and saying, "You sent two of my friends from childhood forward in time, and they want their lives back" was unlikely to accomplish much. She needed a suitable pretext.

She looked up and stared from a distance at the books on her shelves. As she stared, she found herself, suddenly and subtly, drawn to the books, as though something inside her was suggesting that the books might be a good thing to examine right now. She rose from her chair, almost as though in response to a magnet in the wall, and went over to the shelves. Why, she wondered, was she walking over to the books? But it seemed evident to her that she should do so, must do so.

She ran her hands across the leather- and cardboard-bound spines of her books, her finger tapping against them like a stick on a picket fence. So few people still kept books in their houses, but Amanda loved the way they looked on her shelves. She found herself looking at a large and impressive volume with a vivid, animated cover. It was a book about Jackson that had come out last month, an authorized biography in a limited-edition physical copy. She had purchased it because she herself was mentioned in the index, and she always bought books in which her name was mentioned. At some point, she figured, she would make a scrapbook and collect all of her clippings. That way, when she was older and needed to jog her memory a bit, she'd be able to easily call up her recollections from an earlier time. She didn't need to clutter her mind with useless memories. Those memories, she thought, could wait.

She had not read much of the book, however, beyond looking up her own name in the index. Now, though, nothing seemed as important as this book. She began to flip through it, amazed as usual at Jackson's varied accomplishments. She found herself stopping at one picture in particular. It was of Jackson at a small dinner party, on July 24 of the previous year. He was dressed formally, in a magnificent tuxedo, at a small table in a large, modernist house in Palo Alto, California. The other people at the table were fellow scientists, also dressed to the nines in ballgowns and elaborate formalwear. They seemed to be enjoying themselves as they celebrated the anniversary of Hronck's development of the fusion drive.

There was only one problem with the picture. On the evening of July 24 last year, Jackson Hronck had attended a small birthday party for Amanda. July 24 was her birthday. He had arrived early at her party and stayed late. They had discussed his candidacy for president, and her upcoming run to replace him as mayor. It was a memorable night. There was no way Jackson could have been at someone else's dinner party on July 24, let alone a party on the other side of the continent. There must be a mistake. She examined the caption more closely:

> Counterclockwise from the left, Jackson Hronck, Leif Osmondson, Harald Kjellander, and Louise Hopp celebrate the twentieth anniversary of the fusion drive. Every July 24, the original team of scientists who worked on the problem of small-scale fusion energy gather privately to toast their achievement, but this anniversary was something special....

Amanda shook her head and rubbed her eyes, certain that she must have misread the date. This wasn't possible. How could Jackson be in two places at the same time?

She put the book down on a small table and numbly returned to her chair, her hands tightly balled into fists. Something about all of this was horribly wrong, and she couldn't get her mind around it. Old friends presumed dead for twenty-five years had suddenly appeared and claimed that Jackson Hronck was responsible. They had also alleged that Jackson was behind the disappearance of the Garber family, another trauma of her childhood. Finally, she'd been drawn mysteriously to a book that suggested Jackson had been in two different places at once. As she rolled the facts around in her mind, she concluded that there was only one thing to do.

She tapped herself behind the ear and dialed. Hronck answered on the second ring.

44

into action

After the first note had been slipped between the vent slots in Edie's locker, Jared hid himself in a maintenance closet next to the bank of lockers and waited. Gluck had provided him with a watch and a designated time to deposit the second note, though for the life of him he couldn't figure out why Gluck hadn't merely transported him to the next point in time. But while he didn't fully understand Gluck's rationale, he figured he didn't really have much of a choice.

Jared first slept, and then listened to the voices of his classmates as they arrived for school. In that fashion, and for the first time, he heard the deeply disconcerting story of his disappearance. It made him feel physically ill.

He heard his sister's friends in tears, wild speculation about his parents' finances, and terror at who would be taken next. Worst of all, he heard Edie and Meg find the first note, and knew that the nightmare had begun. The girls sounded so innocent, so different from the cynical and weary teens he would meet only a few days later.

"Meg, do you know this handwriting?" asked Edie.

He heard Meg's fear melt into excitement as Edie showed her the note, and felt his stomach turn to lead as they left for class. He felt like he was watching a car crash in slow motion.

After the girls left for class, Jared easily dropped off the second note. During class the hallways were as empty as they had been at night. Almost instantaneously, Gluck had reappeared.

"You have one more note to deliver. Then we can deal with Hronck."

"Deal with Hronck?" Jared was surprised enough that the guilt he felt momentarily lifted. "How are we going to do that?"

"Jackson Hronck will meet with Ms. Boyd and Ms. Karger in a few short hours in our current temporal frame. Our moment here is limited. We do not know what Hronck plans to do with these girls, and we do not know where they will be sent. We cannot follow them into Hronck's house, and we cannot spy on them in the normal fashion." Jared noted that Gluck nearly sounded concerned. "We *must* discover where they are going. They could discover the Root at any time, whatever it might be, and then all will be lost. Wherever they go, you must be there too. After they meet with Hronck, you must travel with them no matter where they are sent."

Jared's skeptical voice echoed in the closet. "How are we supposed to do that? Do you, I don't know, have a plan?"

"We will discuss our next tasks after you have deposited the final note, which must be done tomorrow. We will go there now." At that, Gluck once again produced his silver handle. After grasping it, and feeling the now-familiar tug behind his ribcage, Jared found himself standing in the same maintenance closet. He presumed that Gluck was correct, and it was in fact the next day. Jared peeked out of the room and saw that class was in session. Gluck nodded. At that signal, Jared quietly walked over to Edie's locker and slipped the note between the vent slots. When he returned, he grasped the handle once more, and shortly found himself transported back to Gluck's office in midtown Manhattan.

Upon arrival, without speaking a word to Jared, Gluck promptly walked over to a long, matte-black instrument of some kind. He seemed to be absorbed with whatever he was doing. This left Jared with an opportunity, for the first time in a while, to think about what had just transpired without exhaustion or nervous tension to distract him.

He stepped over to a mauve wingback chair with undulating green rubber legs and sat down, swinging his own legs over one of the arms. He closed his eyes and tried to picture his twin sister, Josie. He realized, with a start, that this was the longest time they had ever been apart since their birth. He had once read that twins could sense danger and discomfort in each other, even when separated by hundreds of miles. He had occasionally experienced that feeling, especially when they had been younger. However, he felt nothing right now, and hoped that simply meant that twin ESP couldn't communicate across time.

He wondered where Josie was, what she was doing and what she was feeling. She had been so looking forward to some party on Saturday, surrounded by her people. Now she was probably alone somewhere, maybe even without their parents. He hoped that she'd found a friend, or someone like Gluck, to help explain things.

But that, of course, was exactly the question. Was Gluck a friend, or secretly an enemy? It was difficult to say anymore what those terms even meant. Gluck had rescued him from an incomprehensible future, long after any civilization he might recognize had been replaced several times over. Gluck opposed Hronck, the man who had ripped Jared from his life.

Or had he? It occurred to Jared that he had never seen Hronck actually do anything. Other than the one vision of Hronck on the street, Jared had never even laid eyes on Hronck in person. Why would Hronck care about the Garbers? According to Gluck, Jackson Hronck wasn't even aware that Jared had any significance whatsoever. The only being with a notion that Jared might be important was…Gluck.

He suddenly felt nauseous. He couldn't believe he hadn't noticed it before. He stood up slowly, rubbing his temples as his head began to swim, and walked over to Gluck. The data man was still focused on his mysterious instrument and seemed to have forgotten that anyone else was in the room. Jared tapped him on his data-laden shoulder, momentarily surprised to realize that Gluck actually had physical substance that could be touched.

"Yes?" Gluck asked.

"Jackson Hronck didn't send me here, did he?" asked Jared, though there was very little inquisitive about his tone.

Gluck looked blankly at Jared, his code-laden lips pursed as though with distaste.

"I see that I was correct about you," he said in what might have been an admiring tone. "That was quite perceptive. You are the one I was looking for."

"You haven't answered my question," insisted Jared, though he felt certain that Gluck might have done so. "Jackson Hronck didn't do it. You did. Isn't that correct?"

Gluck stared directly into Jared's eyes, his blank expression a luminous, swirling surface of coded activity. He held that gaze for what seemed to be several minutes. Finally he spoke, his voice flat and nearly mechanical. "You are, indeed, correct. It was necessary." Jared was amazed that he felt so little surprise or emotion at hearing this revelation. "You had seen Hronck coming out of his house, and he had seen you. It was only a matter of time before he learned the truth about you. Something had to be done."

Jared's toes curled inside his shoes in impotent rage. "Where is my family? You have them, don't you?"

"Your family is safe, far safer than they would be if Hronck knew where they were," replied Gluck, as though his statement were self-evident. "I have no illusions that at some point in this journey that Hronck will not realize what exactly is happening. When that happens, you and your family will be in enormous danger. Any person who might give Hronck leverage over you will be in a desperate position indeed."

"Again, you haven't answered my question." Jared's voice was beginning to develop more of an edge, as he had increasing difficulty containing his temper. "Where are they? When can I see them?" He felt almost frantic as the truth began to weigh on him, pulling him down with apparently unstoppable force.

"It is best that you do not know where they are. And it is best that you do not see them at the present time. Hopefully, if all goes well, you will be reunited. But there are many tasks before us." He turned back to his mysterious instrument, indicating that the conversation was over.

"We're not done!" yelled Jared, knocking a chair over as he swung his arms around. "This is not acceptable! You lied to me, Gluck. You kidnapped me—you're holding all of us against our will. You can't do this!"

"Actually, that is incorrect. You have had every ability to leave and always have. At no point have I required you to remain with me or to assist me with this journey."

Jared threw his hands in the air. "Choice? At any point in all of this, did you tell me what really happened? When you 'found' me, I was stuck in a different time, with no friends and no idea what was going on. You were the only one who was ready and able to help. What choice did I have? What choice does my family have now? Why didn't you tell me the truth?"

"Quite frankly, I did not believe that you would respond properly," said Gluck in what Jared assumed must have been his idea of a patronizing tone. "Moreover, this conversation confirms the accuracy of my assessment. In any event, your tirade does not change the facts. You are in real danger. Not the danger of movies or books, real danger. The entire Mesh is imperiled. Jackson Hronck is currently in the process of using Ms. Boyd in order to obtain the means for our enslavement, or even extinction." He turned back to his instrument. "You are incorrect that you have no choice. You most certainly do. But in truth you only have a choice if you do not value your own existence, or the existence of everything you care about."

Jared stared at Gluck, who was now busily fiddling around with levers and buttons on his oddly shaped device as if nothing of note had just transpired. Gluck was right, he thought, but that didn't make him feel any better. Jared had been lied to, tricked; worse, he had now tricked Edie and Meg in almost the exact same way. But that was done. Now he needed to figure out how to make things right.

"So what do we do next?" asked Jared, resigned to his fate and disgusted with what he could not decide was his own helplessness or cowardice.

"Ah, I am glad you have seen reason in this matter. You will need to make contact with the other individuals traveling alongside Ms. Boyd and Ms. Karger. The boy known as Ray, and the young woman known as Haley. Hopefully they can assist you."

"And if they can't? What if we can't think of something?"

"In that case," said Gluck matter-of-factly, "all will be lost."

45

true confessions

Edie and Meg sat and talked with Melissa, Lisa, and Kathrine for hours while the others were away. Melissa had called in sick at the hospital. "If I told them that I'd seen you guys, they'd assume I was sick anyway," she joked. In the meantime, they discussed Melissa's, Lisa's, and Kathrine's adult lives, the changes the world had experienced over the past twenty-five years, and how happy Edie and Meg would be to get back home. But while Edie and Meg found the other topics fairly interesting, it was Melissa's life as a married adult that most fascinated them.

"So," asked Meg, "when did you meet Dave? How long did you guys date before you got married?"

A faraway look settled across Melissa's face. "In medical school. I wanted to be a surgeon; he wanted to be a psychiatrist. We dated for about three years before we got married, but we didn't see much of each other while we were residents. Thankfully," she added, smiling wickedly, "we still liked each other when we actually hung out together, years after we got married."

"I think *I'm* going to be sick," said Kathrine, a sarcastic smile forming on her lips. "Good thing you're a doctor, eh?"

Edie laughed softly. "You know, I find it amazing that you *really* ended up as a doctor, and Lisa *really* ended up as a cop. Of course, Kathrine as a math genius and Amanda as a politician were always obvious." The grin slid off her face. "You guys always knew what you wanted to be. I never did."

Melissa turned serious. "Maybe. But you were our leader, Edie. You know that, don't you?" Kathrine nodded in agreement. "We may have known what we wanted to be, but you knew what we should be doing right that minute. And we listened to you. When you were gone, there was a big hole in our lives."

"I have a confession to make," said Meg, her hand on her forehead in mock distress, but then her eyes drew together in a more somber look. "I used to think you guys were losers and I tried to convince Edie to hang out with my other friends instead." She paused and pulled on her hair. "Obviously I had no idea what I was talking about. Now I wonder what happened to all of my 'cool' friends from eighth grade. I can't imagine they ended up any better than you, and probably a lot worse." She frowned, and her voice was surprisingly earnest. "In any event, I just thought I would let you all know that I was a moron."

Kathrine smiled benevolently at Meg, as though granting her forgiveness. "Well, some of the popular kids did turn out to be middle-manager types and life-insurance salesmen. But not all of them. And some of the 'losers' turned out pretty well, I think. But not all of them. There's really no way to know when you're a kid. And now," she added, a significant smile playing about her lips, "when you get back to your own time, you can make your choices with that in mind."

Edie sighed. "Now you sound like a motivational speaker."

Melissa laughed. "Well, maybe you should stay in this time and hang out with us to get motivated."

Just then, the phone rang and Edie jumped. Melissa tapped the back of her ear.

"Hello? Yes, Amanda, I...." Melissa squinted as though concentrating. Then she sprang up, waved her hand, and began scribbling down information on a holographic screen that suddenly appeared, floating in the air. "Okay, four o'clock?...Really, at his house?...Are you going to be there too?...Fine, we'll...Yes...And Amanda, thanks again, I can't tell you how much...I understand...Yes, of course... Okay, we'll talk later."

Melissa turned to Meg and Edie, who were sitting on the edges of their seats, waiting to hear what Amanda had said.

"Well, kiddos, Amanda got us an appointment this afternoon. We need to get you girls cleaned up. We're off to see Hronck, and then to get you guys back to where you belong."

Edie was stunned. "You mean it actually worked?"

"Seems like it." Melissa touched the back of her ear again. "I'll let Sally know. This is great news, great news."

Melissa stood up and began talking as Sally answered her own comlink. Meg and Edie could hear her chattering into space as she wandered into the kitchen. As soon as she was gone, Edie turned to Meg, Lisa, and Kathrine, troubled.

"I've got a bad feeling about this," she said quietly. "That was too easy. Jake was right, Hronck really does want to see us, and that can't be good."

"Maybe he realizes that he *has* to see us," responded Meg. "I mean, we're not exactly good facts for his campaign, are we?"

"True," Kathrine mused. "But we need to be careful. You heard from Jake that Hronck might not be human, and given how many rules of the time-space continuum he breaks each day before breakfast, I think that may be right. In any event, Amanda got us into the throne room, but we need to make sure there are no trapdoors in the floor, no boogiemen behind the curtains."

"And we'll be there, we'll protect you," said Lisa triumphantly.

"This is going to work," insisted Meg. "There's something wrong here, but I can tell that it's going to work anyway."

Edie grinned. "Meg, this is awful, but I'm glad you're here with me."

Meg returned her smile and rolled her eyes, "I'm not glad to be here at all."

• • •

They spent the next few hours taking showers, putting on new clothes, and, after he returned with Sally and Haley, talking to Ray about his new passkey.

When he'd flown through the door, Ray had begged Melissa to use her headwork. Smiling indulgently, she'd let him slide them on, and then watched as he sat in one spot for half an hour trying it out. When he finally slipped them off, a massive smile dominated his face.

"I can't tell you how much I missed this." He looked as though he might explode with excitement. "Now I can get back and do my thing. I felt like I couldn't use my head anymore, you know what I mean? It was brutal."

Sally sidled up to Ray, a curious look on her face. "Can you check out Hronck's schedule today on the network? Can you tell us what he's doing?"

Ray nodded vigorously. "Sure, it won't take more than a few minutes." He slid the headwork back on and was soon staring vacantly into space underneath his visor.

Haley had also been out, looking for a job. She had interviewed for a position as a waitress at a low-end, mid-town theme restaurant.

"Isn't that the cliché?" she joked to Edie. "Don't all aspiring actors have to work as waiters?"

"What kind of theme is the restaurant?" asked Meg. "Do you have to dress up as a pirate or something?"

Haley laughed. "No, but close. It's a princess-themed restaurant. Every waitress is dressed up like a different kind of princess, and every male waiter is dressed up like a prince. Very retro."

"Great way to support positive girl images," said Edie sarcastically. "But as long as they tip well...."

Haley giggled. "Yeah, I know. But since it's all tourists, I don't know. Hopefully they'll tip okay. At this point, I'm fine with anything that pays."

"Pretty weird," interrupted Ray, pulling off the head-work. "According to Hronck's schedule, he's in Florida today."

"Florida?" Edie said. "Hronck? That must be wrong."

"Not wrong," insisted Ray. "At least, that's what his official schedule says. I don't know if something else is going on."

They all sat quietly for a moment. "Don't we have to assume that he's coming to the meeting?" Sally asked.

Kathrine's eyes shifted over to Edie. "And more important, what's our plan for this meeting? Who's going? How are we getting there?"

When no one spoke, Sally stood up from the couch and launched herself into the silence. "Okay, then, let's talk it through. We probably don't want too many people going there, and we probably want people who can protect Edie and Meg from Hronck, if necessary."

"I'm thinking Lisa." Kathrine looked as though she had just answered a math problem. "She's the one with weapons and a badge." Lisa nodded vigorously in response.

"I agree," said Melissa. "Amanda is going to be there at the house to introduce the girls, but Hronck wants to meet with them in private. We probably don't want to crowd it up, but we do want someone there who can help them if things get sticky."

"And let's have Ray monitor everything online," added Sally. "He should be able to see if anything odd is going on and alert us. After all, he already broke into Hronck's house."

Haley looked a bit chagrined. "Is there anything for me to do?"

Meg smiled at her. "I'm sure that before we're done with this, there will be something for you to do. We didn't pick you up for nothing."

Edie wondered about that once again. Jake was right: it did seem strange that they had run into these particular people along the way to New York. Haley, who could mimic the thoughts of others on the network; Ray, who could be anywhere on the network. Edie's faith in coincidence was fading fast and she presumed that there was an important role for these random cohorts yet to come.

• • •

Lisa was downstairs in front of the building at 3:45 sharp. She had left the apartment a few minutes before to get her car, an unmarked police vehicle that had a few special toys and tricks built in, as all police cars did. It could drive underwater, and had jet inserts below the chassis in case the car needed to levitate like a hovercraft. An injection gun attached to the wheel well could shoot a stream of intelligent nanobots at a target at several times the speed of sound, where they could disassemble a truck in under five seconds. Lisa had occasionally hoped for more opportunities to use that hardware. Most of the time, however, she was glad that she rarely needed to do so.

Sally, Kathrine, Melissa, Ray and Haley came down to the lobby with Edie and Meg to wish them luck. While Edie appreciated the show of support, it also made her feel as though they were headed off to war, or a long trip to the moon.

Kathrine gave her a big hug. "Be careful. Hopefully when I next see you, we'll both be teenagers again."

"I hope so," said Edie, hugging her back. "I just wonder whether I'll remember all of this."

"If you do," said Melissa, in mid-hug with Meg, "don't tell us, because we'll never believe you."

Meg laughed. "Hey, it happened to me and *I* don't believe it." Then she hugged Sally, and turned to address the rest of the group. "Seriously, though, we really appreciate all of your help. Without you, we would have been completely lost. Or at least more lost than we are right now."

"Of course," added Edie, "if this doesn't work, you'll see us again in an hour, and then, Kathrine, you have to promise to get us custom avatars. I can't stand looking like a lame cartoon online any longer."

As they climbed into the car, Edie realized that this journey was coming to an end. She had traveled across time and then across most of the country in order to meet with one man. Now, if all went according to plan, they would see him in a few minutes.

"Are you nervous?" asked Meg, sitting in the backseat next to Edie "Because I'm shaking like a leaf here."

"You guys will be fine," said Lisa confidently from the driver's seat. "You've come this far, this has to work. He's even agreed to see you. You'll be heading home within the hour, I'm sure of it."

"I'm glad someone thinks so," said Edie. "I just hope you're right."

As Lisa drove them through the streets of Manhattan, with skyscrapers so high they seemed to arc above their heads like a rainbow, no one spoke. There was nothing to say, really. Edie stared out the window at the canyons of concrete, steel, glass, and plastic that soared in every direction. The buildings seemed alive, as though they were talking to each other, flashing their lights in Morse code to discuss the day's gossip about a building downtown. Everything in this world felt like it was alive, she thought. She wondered whether this meant she was noticing something significant, or whether it meant she was losing her mind.

46

pretzel logic

Once Gluck and Jared agreed that Jared should speak with Edie's friends, the next issue was one of strategy. Gluck believed he should simply appear inside Melissa's apartment and start talking. Jared thought this was a poor idea for a variety of reasons, and that it demonstrated Gluck's complete inability to understand human behavior. Had Jared not been so irritated by the entire situation, he would have probably found Gluck's cluelessness amusing.

Instead, after several exasperating minutes of explanation regarding the concept of personal space, he had convinced Gluck that a better option would be to appear right outside Melissa's front door. And then to knock, politely, before entering someone else's home.

Therefore, it came to pass that with an almost soundless "pop," Jared materialized in the twelfth-floor hallway of Melissa's New York City apartment building, about three feet from her door, disguised once more as "Jake." He could tell that his face had been altered and harbored a strange suspicion that he himself would appear as a cascade of information had he looked at himself in a mirror. Great, he thought, now I'm like a vampire, afraid of mirrors. Or of being like Gluck.

But Jared felt as though he had a card up his sleeve. It wasn't much, but it appeared that Gluck was not able to read Jared's mind. Thus, Gluck was unaware that Jared had already decided not to abide by the "rules" Gluck had insisted upon during their earlier encounter with the girls. He didn't trust Gluck in the slightest, and had concluded that he must act independently if he had any hope of escaping with his life, or the lives of his parents and sister. He would no longer hide his true identity, and would no longer pretend that everything was a simple matter of the girls meeting up with Hronck. At this point, he wasn't even completely certain that Gluck was a "good guy" in any traditional understanding of the term.

And Gluck knew nothing of Jared's plan.

Thus, when Jared knocked on Melissa's door and heard footsteps padding behind it, he had already prepared a short statement to break the ice.

"Hello?" said a voice from behind the door. It sounded like Melissa. "Who is it?"

"I'm Jared Garber, and I really need to talk to all of you. Edie and Meg are in trouble, and it's partially my fault, and we have to save them, because the whole world depends on it."

The silence on the other side of the door was total. He felt Melissa's eyes through the peephole, trying to figure out why this person who had been briefly introduced to her before as "Jake" would now claim to be Jared Garber. *The* Jared Garber.

Slowly, and with evident uncertainty, a variety of locks were clicked open, and the door swung open to reveal an ashen-faced Melissa.

"Are you really Jared Garber? I don't remember Jared looking anything like you. Not that anything surprises me anymore, I guess. Is Josie with you?"

"I wish she were, but she's not. It's a long story, and the idea was to trick you, but I don't want to play that game anymore. You guys really need to hear what I have to say. Can I come in?"

Melissa hesitated. If Lisa were still there, armed and ready to perform violence in support of her friends, letting Jared in would have been an easy decision. Without Lisa, it was not so simple, and Melissa was not nearly so confident. She was aware that all of them were in danger somehow, but she could barely even understand what was going on, let alone identify the threats. There were no longer any obvious choices.

"Can you hold on for one minute?" She carefully looked Jared over from head to toe. still unsure of what exactly she was trying to see. "I need to speak with my friends."

Jared tried to sound as adult as possible. "I understand. If you'd feel more comfortable, I'd be happy to tell you my story from the hallway." A smile played briefly on his lips, then vanished. "But you really need to hear what I have to say, and quickly. We don't have much time."

Kathrine's face suddenly appeared behind Melissa's shoulder. She had apparently been listening to their conversation from behind the door. Melissa was looking closely at Jared too, as though peering at a specimen under a microscope.

"You don't look like Jared Garber," said Kathrine slowly, now staring directly into Jared's eyes. "And if you are Jared Garber, why the nonsense at the restaurant?"

"And how did you get into my building?" added Melissa. "What did you tell the doorman? They don't let just anyone up here."

"I promise, I can explain everything. Even how I'm standing in this hallway right now. But please, you have to believe me, we really need to talk."

Melissa remained suspicious, of this and everything else she had experienced recently. But more than that she was curious, and she desperately wanted to protect Edie. If there was any chance that what this boy had to say would help Edie, it was a chance worth taking.

With a deep breath, Melissa opened the door all the way and guided Jared into the living room, Kathrine close behind, on guard against any sudden movements. As he entered the room, he saw Haley, Ray, and Sally talking quietly together on a couch, their faces shadowed by the bright lights that had been painted onto the ceiling. Sally was sipping some orange juice out of a spiral-shaped cup, while Haley and Ray were munching on neon-colored chips of some kind.

"Folks," said Melissa, as the others turned to face her. "I give you Jared Garber."

The name meant little to Ray or Haley, but Sally nearly dropped her drink. She looked at Jared, who had previously been introduced to her as Jake, and her look of surprise quickly turned to confusion. She went over to Jared. "Isn't this Jake? From the restaurant?"

"Actually, I'm really Jared Garber. I'm sorry about not coming clean about that earlier, but I've been changed to look like someone else. I can explain everything, but we all need to talk. Edie and Meg are in danger, and it's my fault, and we have to do something. Oh," he added blithely, "and the future of the whole world may depend on us helping them."

Sally raised an eyebrow and shook her head. "You'll have to excuse me, um, *Jake*, but how do I know you're Jared Garber when you don't look anything like him? I knew Jared pretty well, and I'm sorry, you'll have to prove it to me before we talk."

Jared had been ready for this and didn't even pause before beginning. "Sally, you were one of my sister's

317

best friends. You and Alexis Steinrhone, remember?" He sounded almost wistful, as though this had really been a lifetime in the past. "I remember when the three of you would lock yourselves in Josie's room, and I could hear you laughing for hours at a time. Last week, a few days before I disappeared, you guys were being incredibly loud. After a while it got annoying, so I put my ear to my bedroom wall and listened to you talk, wondering what could possibly be so funny." He smiled and closed his eyes, remembering the moment vividly. "It turns out you had a crush on me, and had finally admitted it to Josie and Alexis. Josie, of course, thought it was the most ridiculous thing she had ever heard, because why would anyone have a crush on her *brother*? Alexis was daring you to knock on my door and ask me to go to a movie. You were embarrassed, but you laughed and said you would, but only if Josie asked Griff Thomas to go to the same movie on a double date. Josie cracked up and said she would, but only if Alexis asked Dylan Miles. And Alexis said *she'd* do it, but not until next week." Sally's mouth was frozen in shock. "I'm sorry we never went on that date. I'm sure we would have had a good time, even though that Miles kid was always such a smart-aleck." He smiled once more. "I can't imagine why Alexis liked him."

"Oh my god," said Sally, her voice trembling. "It *is* you. That was just last week?"

A hollowness entered Jared's voice from some previously unknown wellspring of emotion. "To *me* it was just last week. So much has happened in the past few days, I feel as though I've lived three lifetimes. But we don't have time to relive the past right now, and given the fact that you have kids, I'm guessing that you don't want to go out on a date anymore...." He smiled briefly. "Do you believe me, Sally? Will you listen to my story now?"

She stared at him for so long that he began to wonder whether she was going to respond. He tried to read her face, but her hair had fallen over her forehead and was veiling one of her eyes, just as he remembered from when she was a teenager. He swallowed hard at the thought.

"Yes," she said finally, a catch in her voice. "I believe you." She gave him a hug, which he found himself returning, if uncomfortably. Once she broke away to look at him again, as though a silent signal had been shared between them, Kathrine and Melissa went up to Jared and Sally and led them back to the couch, where they each sat down on either side of Haley and Ray. Haley and Ray had watched the drama unfold before them as though it were a play on stage, both seemingly puzzled by this entire conversation. In fact, neither one had made a sound since Jared had entered the room.

Kathrine plopped herself down on a chair opposite the couch. "Well, now that you've been properly identified and ripped Sally's guts out, let's hear your story. In particular, I'd like to know why Edie and Meg are in danger, and why you lied to us before about who you were."

Jared took a deep breath and began. "For several years, I've been seeing things. Code and symbols would pop up in the surface of almost any random thing I was looking at—objects, animals, people, it could be almost anything. It was as though the world was made of code."

Kathrine narrowed her eyes and began to focus more intently on Jared, as though trying to assess his sanity.

"Do you mean like computer code?" asked Ray. "That's what I see on the network, that's why I got that talent. I can see that too." He stopped. "But you can see that in the real world?"

"Yes. If I look closely at any of you, you might begin to fade, and code might become visible at the edge of your shoulder, or the tips of your fingers." He struggled a moment, as though trying to decide how best to describe the experience. "It doesn't happen every time, but pretty often. It's almost as though nothing in the world has any substance. Nothing is real."

"Have you seen anyone about this?" asked Melissa in her concerned doctor's voice. "I mean, this could mean all sorts of things, hallucinations that—"

"At first I thought they *were* hallucinations," interrupted Jared, a bit impatiently. "But they didn't seem to be much of a problem, so I basically ignored them. Clearly, that was a mistake. But then, last week, or whenever it was, I was walking home from school with Josie, and I saw something that made me think something else was going on." He looked back over at Sally this time, who was now listening with rapt attention. "We passed the house behind ours, and a man walked out. He was literally made of bright, glowing code and symbols. Every inch of him. Later I learned that this man was Jackson Hronck."

"What?" asked a chorus of voices.

"Hronck was made of code?" asked Kathrine.

"What does that mean?" said Melissa.

"At the time, I didn't know who he was, or why he looked like that. I had no idea what was going on. Later that same evening, however, while we were eating dinner, a bright light flashed and I suddenly found myself several thousand years in the future."

"Several *thousand* years?" asked Haley, wide-eyed. "How do you know? What was that like?"

"Let me tell you, there's no way you wouldn't know it. I guess by that point most people have left here and are living someplace else. Earth is basically just a place where people go to college, or a big national park, or something like that. But before I got too panicked about where I was or how to get back, I ran into another guy entirely made of code. This guy was named Gluck. Lasho Gluck."

"Gluck?" said Sally. "Was this the person you were telling us about at the restaurant?"

"Yup. Except I didn't realize what was really going on when I first met him. You see, Gluck and Hronck are both something called Faktors, these things that can move around through time and across worlds." He took a deep breath and looked directly at Kathrine, figuring that she would handle this best. "They can do this because the world, and all of us, are part of something called the Mesh that I mentioned at the restaurant. No," he added, as Ray started to ask a question. "I'm sure this isn't the same network you use. It's much bigger. All of us are in it, but it's the same basic idea."

"Wait a minute," said Kathrine, suddenly grasping the implications. "Are you saying we're all inside a computer of some kind?"

"Actually, it's worse than that. We are all *part* of a giant computer. That's what the Mesh is, and it was created by this race of other beings called the Saan. Apparently—and this is just what I was told, so who knows if it is true—they disappeared millions of years ago, but they left the Mesh in place to solve certain problems, or do certain things, even after they were gone." He paused dramatically and looked around at the group. "Our entire universe is all part of that calculation."

He was unsure where to go next with the tale. The others appeared to be teetering between bewilderment and outright refusal to accept what he'd said. They were all staring at him. Everyone, that is, except Ray, who was already bouncing on the couch with excitement.

"So hold it, I see, we're all part of a computer program, or maybe we all *are* computer programs, and we're all solving a problem by just being alive, even if we don't realize it?" He was now hitting his knee with the back of his hand in a steady rhythm. "I can *totally* see that! So none of us are real? What we think are our real bodies are actually avatars? So do we have real bodies somewhere else, like one of those movies?"

"As I understand it, no, we don't," answered Jared, surprised that Ray understood so easily. "We're all just computer programs inside a huge simulation. But I've got a special talent, I guess just like you, Ray. Inside the regular network, Ray can see the code, and he can make things change. Inside the Mesh, I can see the code, too, just like Ray. I haven't learned how to change things yet, the way Ray can when he's an avatar, but from what I've heard from Gluck, I'm guessing that I may be able to do that at some point."

"You realize what you're saying?" asked Melissa, sounding thoroughly horrified. "We're all just imaginary people? We're all just programs solving a problem without realizing it, or knowing what we're doing?"

Sally's face went slack. "If that's the meaning of life, then it sounds like there's no meaning at all."

"Well, it's more complicated than that," said Jared, trying to steer the conversation away from the depressing conclusions that could be drawn from his story. "Apparently we're all part of a great effort to reach some larger answer, some bigger truth, and we're almost there. That's why we were made in the first place. But Edie is the important key to all of that. She's special. She doesn't know it, but she didn't even have real parents—"

"What?" interjected chorus of voices.

"You have got to be kidding," started Lisa, but Jared broke back in.

"She was created by the Mesh out of nothing. Seriously, I'm sure of it. I talked with her aunt and uncle. They're really special computer programs created by the Faktors to protect Edie. They've been dormant at the nursing home all this time. Edie's memories of her parents were implanted so she would think she was a normal kid, not a person with, I don't know, a *destiny*."

The painful silence that settled over the conversation lasted for nearly a minute. "So why did Hronck send you and your family into the future?" Haley finally asked, though she had said nothing for most of Jared's narrative. "If Edie is the important one, why are you here?"

"Good question," said Kathrine, a hint of snark returning to her voice. "And what exactly is Edie supposed to do? What is this 'destiny' she has?" Kathrine made air quotes around the word "destiny," as though the entire notion was laughable.

Jared sighed. "I'm not sure I understand Edie's destiny, and I'll get to that it a minute, but let me tell you one more thing about my story first, and hopefully that will explain some of this. You see, Gluck is really the one who sent me into the future." Kathrine eyes opened wide with surprise. "And then he manipulated everything so that Hronck could get to Edie. Gluck isn't the good guy I originally thought he was. I don't know that he's a bad guy either. It's all pretty confusing. He's just trying to do everything he can to stop Hronck. And if that means taking my family hostage so that I'll cooperate with him, he'll do it. If it means giving Edie up so he can figure out how to stop Hronck, he'll do that too."

"So what does Hronck want with Edie?" asked Sally. "And why does Gluck want to stop him?"

"And you still haven't said what Edie is supposed to do," added Kathrine.

"And why you're important," said Melissa, still suspicious. "You haven't said that either."

"Hronck wants something called the 'Root.' If he gets it, he'll become, like, the supreme overlord of everything in the Mesh, and we'll all basically be serving him and what he wants forever, or something like that. Edie is apparently destined to be the one who can find the Root. She was created for that specific purpose by the Mesh. It's all part of the answer to the calculation it's been doing for millions of years. According to Gluck, and assuming that Hronck doesn't get at it first, I'm destined to be the one who can use the Root, with Edie, and do something important with the Mesh. I don't know what it is yet, but it sounds like it might free us from the Mesh and make us all real."

Jared paused and looked at his audience. Ray was still bursting at the seams after learning that everything was a network, finally giving him hope that he could regain control over his own life. Melissa, Kathrine, and Sally were aghast that their fruitful, successful lives were apparently nothing but an illusion. Haley was staring into space, deep in thought, trying to come to terms with what this all meant to her. How could they think of a solution when he couldn't even get everyone to focus? Jared wondered. They didn't have much time.

"If it sounds like I don't know what I'm talking about," said Jared, hoping he could now bring his story to a logical conclusion, "it's because I don't know what I'm talking about. I have no idea what this Root is, or where it is, or what I'm supposed to do with it once we find it. I do know that Hronck is desperately trying to find it, and is setting everything up in our world so that Edie *can* find it. He's been spending the past several decades playing all of us like a piano so that this all ends up the way he wants it to."

Kathrine put her head on her hands and stared intently at Jared once more. "So why don't you look like Jared Garber?"

"And how did you end up outside my door?" added Melissa.

"None of that's important." Jared wished once again that he had a watch. "But Gluck changed me because he didn't want me to tell you the truth. He wanted me to pretend that I was someone else, because he was afraid that Edie, if she knew the truth, might not try to find the Root."

A maternal note came into Sally's voice. "And why should she? So this Gluck guy and Hronck both want Edie to find the Root, whatever it is—why should she do it?"

"Well that's the point, isn't it?" said Jared. "She's going to meet Hronck right now. Gluck thinks the only way to get the Root before Hronck does is to follow her. But she's about to go to see Hronck, and who knows where he'll send her?" He wondered if he should tell them about the notes but decided against it. There was too much for them to absorb at once, and knowing about the notes might make them even more suspicious and angry.

"So what can we do?" asked Kathrine. "She's probably already there at this point."

"Wait a minute," said Ray, a realization dawning in his eyes. "If the real world and the network and the Mesh are all part of the same thing—which is totally weird, but whatever—I'll bet I *can* do something." He looked up as though examining something on the ceiling, and then began to nod. "Melissa, can we all cronk in? I have an idea."

"Sure." She rose and ran over to a drawer, where she began rummaging through various wires and headwork. "What do you have in mind?"

"We're all going to Mr. Hronck's house," said Ray, a happy glint in his eye. "Through the back door."

47

walking towards
another time

A large mansion dominated the east side of 5th Avenue, only a few short blocks from the Metropolitan Museum. The grey limestone masonry reflected the light as though made of glass—a special treatment invented by Jackson Hronck himself, creating the illusion that the building materials themselves were illuminated from within. Massive wrought-iron gates with twisted images of lions, bears, and tigers woven into the metal surrounded the property, which at first looked rather more like an apartment building than a house.

As Lisa, Edie, and Meg pulled up to the address provided by Amanda, they noticed that a small driveway was attached to the side of the house behind the gate. As Lisa pulled up to the driveway, a thin red laser scanned the car, and the gates swung open. "Nice," she said under her breath, and drove inside. She pulled up alongside a fountain where a dozen different tiny animal figures leapt through the water at regular intervals, near what looked like the formal entrance to the house.

She turned to face Edie and Meg in the back seat. "Ready?"

"No, but that hasn't stopped us so far," said Edie, trying to look brave. "Are you coming in with us?"

Lisa shrugged. "Hopefully. Assuming that Hronck lets me. If not, I'll wait outside. And guys—if I haven't heard anything from you an hour from now, I'm coming in."

"That's reassuring," said Meg in a mock-serious voice, eyeing a secondary security fence near the door. "Not."

Lisa rolled her eyes. "Whatever. Just keep your cool and ask him nicely."

"Yeah." Edie elbowed Meg in the ribs. "Don't get him mad this time."

Meg shook her head, and the three of them slid cautiously out of the car. They walked up to the blood-red front door, a heavy wood double door with a knob the size of a Frisbee. Edie was about to knock when the door swung open as if by magic.

A butler in formal, old-fashioned livery stood at the door. He wore an emerald green vest, black topcoat, and highly shined patent leather shoes. Nothing on his outfit was video-enabled—perhaps the first person Edie had seen in this era without moving images projected onto his clothes, although the buttons on his vest were so shiny she could see her face as clearly as in a mirror. He bowed slightly. "Ms. Boyd and Ms. Karger, please come in." All three began to enter, but he held up his hand. "Ah, Lt. Alter, Mr. Hronck would prefer that you wait outside, please."

Lisa took another step forward and placed her arm in front of the girls. "I'm here to protect them. Where they go, I go."

"I am sorry," said the butler. "But Mr. Hronck will not see anyone except Ms. Boyd and Ms. Karger. If you choose to stay with them, none of you shall pass."

Lisa turned to Edie. "Are you okay with this? You don't have to go in, you know."

"Yes we do. We have to try. You know where we are, and if we don't come out, you know where to look."

Lisa nodded and reached over and hugged Edie, then Meg. She watched as the two girls stepped into the Hronck's massive home and the door closed behind them.

I have a bad feeling about this, she thought as the door clicked shut. But Edie was right. Lisa needed to wait in the car and see what happened.

Having no alternative, she walked back to the car, climbed inside, and prepared to wait.

48

a clever plan

Jared had never actually cronked into the network before. He had traveled using Gluck's silver handle in the "real" world of the Mesh, but had not personally entered the human network as an avatar. Thus, when he felt that familiar tug but suddenly appeared in generic avatar format in an imaginary room, rather than another time, he was astonished.

Melissa, Lisa, Kathrine, Sally, Haley, and Ray each resembled idealized version of themselves. They and Jared were sitting in Melissa's hyper-modern office, where much of the furniture appeared to be constructed out of clear, nearly invisible Lucite.

"Doesn't Jared need a passkey?" asked Haley, her already impressive beauty nearly blinding in avatar format. "How is he going to leave this room without one?"

"As long as I'm on the network and *I* have a passkey," said Ray with pride, "he won't need one of his own. Trust me."

"So where are we going?" asked Kathrine. "How are we getting into Hronck's house?"

"I told you, we're going in the back door. Or at least some of us are." Ray snickered and looked over at Haley. "But first I need to have a talk with the network." Without further explanation, Ray he his arm directly into and through the wall, which reacted like gelatin, at first resisting and then accepting and surrounding his hand and arm up to his shoulder. He pulled himself into the office wall and disappeared with a pop.

Kathrine, who had more experience with and understanding of the science of the network than any of the others, winced with shock. "How did he do that?" she gulped, almost swallowing her words. "That's not possible."

Sally gave a resigned sigh. "Kathrine, I've given up on being shocked at anything anymore."

Just the, Ray reappeared, holding some odd contraption shaped like a large cone attached to a rod that arched down onto a stand. He promptly attached the device to one of Melissa's office chairs. It became obvious almost immediately that the cone on the machine was designed to fit directly over a person's head.

"Haley," said Ray. "You're a good actor, right?"

"I guess," said Haley cautiously, eyeing the machine with some concern. "What do you need me to do?"

"Sit in the chair and put this on. We're going to make a fake avatar, and you're going to be it."

Now it was Melissa's turn to be surprised. "You can't do that. She's already an avatar right now, and we're already on the network."

"Don't worry," replied Ray. "I got this figured out. Haley, trust me, I just talked with the network, and we're totally cool."

"What does this do?" asked Jared, helping Haley get underneath the strange device that soon engulfed her head in what appeared to be melon-green plastic.

Ray adjusted the cone over Haley's avatar's head. "The network will make another avatar, and it will be controlled by Haley from here in Melissa's office. Haley, are you ready?"

"I still have no idea what you're doing." Haley's echoed inside the device, which covered her avatar down to its shoulders. "But I'll do what I can. Who am I supposed to be?"

"You're going to be Lisa's friend Mark," said Ray, to a chorus of surprised voices.

"Why Mark?" asked Kathrine, disgust apparent in her tone. "That guy was a real piece of work."

"Hronck's already met with the guy. And when he shows up with some important information, Hronck may actually let him in."

"What information?" asked Jared, wondering about his own role in this plan.

"Information about that Gluck guy," said Ray, smiling. He pointed at Jared's chest. "And of course he'll believe Mark because Mark'll have captured *you*." Jared suddenly understood where this was going and did not like it one bit. "Jared, you'll be Mark's prisoner, just like in the movies. Don't worry, I got this all figured out."

49

lies

Edie and Meg were led through a foyer into a series of narrow passageways in Hronck's real-world home. Each wall was covered with art, some of it interactive, much of it of the more old-fashioned, static variety. Most were portraits of Jackson Hronck himself, completed in a variety of different styles ranging from classical to Byzantine to Renaissance to cubist. Small spotlights in the ceiling illuminated these paintings and video art installations, but not the hallway itself, which was oddly dark.

Finally, after several minutes, they reached a large formal drawing room, which branched off into several other large spaces. On one side of the room was an elevator, and the butler silently led them towards it. The elevator itself was covered in twisted bronze, sculpted into a fantasia of cherubs and angels, connected by bars of metal that looked like prison windows. The butler pushed the call button, which initiated a whirring noise behind the gate. He stared straight ahead as though the girls were not even there. While they waited, Edie looked around and tried to get a sense of where she was.

Even from an examination of just this one room, it was obvious that this was the most spectacular and bizarre home she had ever seen. The walls of the room were, again, covered with art from every era, from Dutch masters to crazy abstract patterns, and the leather furniture looked as though it had been ripped from the mind of an eccentric, colorblind designer. Every surface and every fabric was alive with movement and motion, as images from nature moved across chairs and chaises, sofas and walls. One coffee table had holographic images of bears drinking tea etched into the side, while a sideboard was covered with realistic-looking forest scenes and leaping squirrels.

Finally the elevator arrived, and the three of them stepped inside. It was a surprisingly large elevator, with enough room for at least ten people. Edie looked over at the elevator destination buttons. She noticed that there were buttons for four floors above the ground, and nine for floors below. She guessed, correctly, that the butler would press the lowest button, and the elevator began a slow, even descent nine stories beneath the surface of Manhattan.

When the doors eventually opened, Edie and Meg were faced with a large room with high ceilings and walls paneled in matte stainless steel. The floor was textured like a tire tread and the ceiling was a maze of small lights interspaced with winches and pulleys. A series of tables filled the room around its edges. In the center was a large, polished-metal desk. Behind it, wearing a plain white lab coat, was Jackson Hronck.

"Mr. Stevens, thank you for bringing our guests down." Hronck switched to a voice of authority. "You may return to your station now."

With a bow, the butler backed into the elevator and shoed the girls into the room in a single gesture. As they turned around, the elevator door closed, and Edie gulped as she realized that they were now alone with the man who had sent them into the future.

"Please, girls," said Hronck in what he probably assumed was a charming voice. "Have a seat." He pointed to two well-worn, brown leather chairs set in front of the desk.

Edie and Meg looked at each other; Meg raised her shoulders as though to say "why not?" and they stepped down into the room. As they approached the chairs, Edie realized that the room was even larger than she had originally thought. It was not only cavernous but long, perhaps forty yards from end to end. Some of the tables were covered with machines smoldering with some kind of green, internal fire; some stretched far into the room, while others disappeared into recesses in the walls. She shivered as she noticed that two of the tables nearest to them contained machines in various stages of assembling themselves, as though they were performing a form of particularly delicate self-surgery.

"Girls," announced Hronck with a flourish, as Edie and Meg finally sat down. "I have been watching your approach with some interest. Your journey here appears to have been quite eventful. You were even able to convince your former schoolmate Amanda to call me and make an appointment with you." He smiled ironically. "I am most certainly impressed. I am sorry, however, that she will be unable to make it to our little discussion this afternoon. I informed her that her presence was unnecessary." He paused, as though preparing to tell the punchline to a joke. "I gather from all of this effort, however, that you wish to ask me a question?"

Edie was stunned by Hronck's even manner and didn't know where to start. Meg, however, was seething.

"Yes," she snarled, trying without success to control her voice. "You sent us here twenty-five years ago, and we want you to send us back. This isn't right. Our families think we're dead. We need to go back to where we belong."

Hronck shook his head. "Oh, I feared you might be here to ask me that." He looked almost sad as he continued. "I am so sorry if you came all this way to ask me to send you back to the past. I am afraid that, for obvious reasons, I cannot do that."

Edie suddenly found her voice. "You can't send us back?" she said, her fists clenching automatically. "Or *won't* send us back?"

"Ah yes, Ms. Boyd, that is such an important distinction. Can't versus won't. Cannot versus will not." He looked down his nose at them deviously. "So many books have been written about the difference. In this case, however, it is an easy divide for me to bridge. The answer is: both."

"Both?" asked Edie and Meg at once.

"Yes," said Hronck, and an exaggeratedly innocent tone entered his voice. "Both. I cannot send you back, and even if I could I would not choose to do so. You see, you want to get back to where you were in time, and slip back into your old bodies as though nothing ever happened. I am afraid that even I cannot do that. There would be too many implications for this future which I so humbly dominate. Why would I wish to alter this wonderful outcome? You would still remember what had transpired here, in this time, and that cannot possibly be good for me.

"You see," he continued, still smiling as though discussing a fine meal, "if I sent you back, you would know a great deal about the secrets of my success in this life. That type of knowledge could prevent me from achieving what I have now. Thus, even were I capable of such a thing, I would refuse."

Edie stared at him, bug-eyed, hardly believing what she heard.

"Then why are you even bothering to see us?" demanded Meg. "I don't understand."

"Well, young ladies, I decided to allow you to visit me here so that I could offer you a deal." Hronck stood and began to walk around towards Edie's chair. "You see, there are ways that all of this can turn out well for you, and there are ways it can be enormously unpleasant. I want you to understand your options."

"Our options?" Edie spat. "You mean other than us telling the world what you did in order to—"

"Oh, temper, Ms. Boyd, temper!" He shook his head like a disappointed parent. "This is *exactly* the type of behavior that could cause all of us to lose in the end. You could, of course, try to do share your information, but I can assure you that my people will be able to discredit your efforts quite effectively. You will be quarantined as living viruses, and—"

"Living viruses?" Edie was incredulous.

"Oh, I'm sure that Lt. Sullivan has already revealed my conversation with him when he met with you at the restaurant, in New Jersey. You recall the transhuman virus from Indonesia?"

"People are not going to believe that we're some kind of escaped avatar," said Meg. "That's ridiculous."

"But they'll believe that two girls were shot into the future by a time machine twenty-five years ago when, as we all know, there is no such thing as a time machine?" Hronck laughed. "Come, girls, you must realize that I am in a position of strength here. I can have you quarantined so easily.... Everyone, with the exception of your friends, will believe that you are rogue avatars. And your friends will be discredited as either well-meaning cranks or fools."

The girls went silent, allowing Hronck's threat to sink in.

"You said we had multiple choices...." Edie trailed off, considering her every word. "What are the other choices?"

"Ah yes. That *is* the spirit! Do not assume that the pessimistic path is the only one open to you. There is a world of opportunity before you!" His enthusiasm was oily in its transparency. "Your other two choices are simple. Option one: I provide you with identity papers and you walk out the door. You live your lives from this moment forward, never breathing another word of our meeting or of your past life twenty-five years ago. If any problems ever arise due to your, er, unconventional birthdays, you need only contact my security chief, Nick, and he will provide you with whatever you need in order to correct the record. But you may never speak of this again."

"And option two?" Trepidation turned Meg's voice into something like a croak.

"Ah, option two. To be frank, this is the reason I wanted to see you this afternoon." He circled back behind his desk, now visibly excited. "As you can tell, I would be perfectly happy if you accepted option one, though it will mean a degree of surveillance on my part, in order to ensure that you keep your side of the bargain. However, option number two may permit us to solve all of our problems, yours and mine." He smiled more widely, revealing impossibly white teeth.

Meg rolled her eyes. "All of 'our' problems? What problem do *you* have?"

"That is the question, is it not?" Hronck had suddenly stopped smiling. "You see, girls, if you are willing, I have a task for you. A difficult task, certainly, but a task which carries with it a wonderful reward."

Edie could barely believe her ears. "You want *us* to do something for *you*? After what you did to us?"

"But Ms. Boyd, this task carries with it the opportunity to go back home, to Kansas." He leaned back in his chair. He did not even look at the girls as he continued. "If you are able to successfully obtain for me this object which I desire, it would permit me to send you back home to Kansas without fear of repercussions."

"So what is this thing you want us to do?" asked Meg, glancing nervously over at Edie slunk down in the next chair. "You're making this sound pretty difficult, whatever it is."

"Oh, it is quite difficult! But rest assured that you are far better suited to obtain it than I am. You see, in other times I am—how shall I say this?—easily recognized." He laughed, a weird, forced laugh that contained no mirth. "There are people, and others, who would be rather displeased to see me, and that would render my efforts difficult, if not doomed. You, however, are not well known to the authorities who monitor such things, and can travel with impunity."

"Authorities?" asked Edie. "You want us to do something illegal?"

"No, of course not! That is the irony of it all. But let me explain." He leaned forward on the desk, looking intently at them. "Are you familiar with the concept of a root?"

"Like on a tree?" asked Meg.

"No. As in a computer." He thought for a moment. "Let me describe it like this: in the old days of your world, when computers were less complicated, there would be something called the 'root privilege.' The root privilege was quite powerful, and whoever who possessed it was in charge of the entire system. He was a super-user, like a god within the system, able to do whatever he wanted to the computer. He could change files or force the system to do things it was otherwise unable to do. He could eliminate other users, or transform their access privileges, or alter the software in any manner he so desired. Other users were restricted in what they could do; the root user was not."

"I still don't see—" said Edie, but Hronck spoke over her.

"The root user can do many things that regular users of the system may not. The root user can make the system move like his own personal marionette. If he wants it to dance in one way, suddenly, Edie Boyd can no longer access the system! If he wants to access the operating system and change the very code that serves as the blood of the network, he may do so with abandon. Thus, a root user can also be dangerous to any system. The root user can, if unchecked, or sloppy, cause significant harm."

Hronck began drumming his fingers on the table and appeared to be thinking intently. "In the future, where I am from, the world as you know it and the network as you know it merge together into a seamless whole, into a system of unlimited size and scope. No one individual can tell the difference between their networked life and their life as a physical being. Your great-grandchildren effectively live with headwork grafted into their souls! As babies they learn language from their mothers while cronked into the network, cuddling as avatars. The network becomes of paramount importance to anyone and everyone."

Edie was still trying to figure out where all of this led, but Meg seemed to be making some initial strides in comprehension. "Let me see if I understand," she said. "In the future, we'll exist inside computers...."

"Yes. With some limited interaction in the physical world."

"So, anyone who could get this root privilege..."

"*Yes*, Ms. Karger! Excellent! Full marks for you. That is correct: a user with root privileges could accomplish infinite things in this merged world. There is a difficulty, however." He suddenly looked distraught. "The wise individuals who constructed this system of networks devised it to be free of root privileges. It is purportedly a system run from billions of different nodes. It has no super-user, and it has no root. But I believe that there is a secret root privilege within the network."

"And that," asked Edie wearily, "is what you want us to find?"

"Exactly! I want you to get this secret root for me."

"But how will this get us home?" asked Meg. "I don't understand how this makes any difference to us."

"Oh, Ms. Karger, do not allow your imagination to fail you now!" He was smiling malevolently again. "I can send you back to your own time without fear of change if I know that I can have the root. Your activities in the past—*my* activities in the past—are irrelevant if I have complete control of the network in all of its forms."

Edie and Meg looked at each other, and then Edie spoke. "Where is this root? What do we have to do to find it?"

"Ah, well, yes, that is the trick, isn't it? I believe I know when it can be obtained. But I am not sure. Until you try, I cannot be certain. But I believe it is in the hands of someone you know, many years in the future from now."

"Who?" Then, suddenly, she understood. "Wait a minute..."

"Your friend Ray, in your van. Let us just say that he becomes quite a significant figure in the future. I suggest you reacquaint yourselves with him when you get there. Assuming that you accept the challenge." He laughed again, this time with a bit more humor.

"Can we talk about this first?" asked Meg. "I'd like to discuss our options before we make a decision."

"Go ahead, go ahead!" He got up from the desk and stepped away from the girls. "I'll stand over by the elevator while you talk between yourselves. I am certain you will make the correct decision." He beamed at them insincerely and then strolled towards the elevator, where he immediately began consulting an unrecognizable hand-held device of some kind. Once he was out of earshot, Edie turned to Meg and began to whisper frantically.

"I don't trust this guy. I don't trust him at all."

"Me neither, but I also don't think he's going to let us go if we don't do this. Do you? I think he may just kill us if we don't."

Meg thought for a moment, kicking the ground in frustration. "I think that's right. I don't think we'll really have a choice here." She bit her fingernail and looked back at Edie. "Maybe if we get sent into the future, Ray will be able to help us, especially if he's as important as Hronck says he is."

"Yeah, but we may just get stuck again there, too. This is so totally not a good choice." She felt just as helpless as she had when they'd first arrived in this time, and just as then she could feel tears welling in her eyes. "Even if he was going to let us go, I don't want to live now, I don't belong here. And I don't think he'll let us go anyway."

Meg stared at the floor, and a determined look formed over her features. "Is there any other option? We have to think this through."

"Well," said Edie slowly, wiping her eyes, "if we say no, we're stuck in this time, and we have to start our lives all over again here. Assuming he isn't lying and doesn't just get rid of us."

"And if we say yes, we're still stuck, but at least we have a chance of getting home."

They stared at each other, as though each hoped that the other would make this impossible decision for them.

"We've got to do this," said Meg finally. "We can't give up. We've got to keep on trying to get home."

Edie nodded. "I don't trust him, but we have to keep going. I want to go home too, and I can't think of anything else to do."

Meg sighed. "Who knew Kansas was such a great place, until we couldn't get back there?"

"Mr. Hronck," said Edie, waving him over. "We've made our decision."

"Yes, girls?" he asked, his voice betraying a bit of nervousness as he approached. Something about his attitude only confirmed for Edie her suspicion that they had little choice in this decision.

"We'll help you find this secret root thing," announced Meg. "But we need more details. What year are you sending us to?"

"I am sending you thirty more years into the future," he said triumphantly, clearly pleased at their decision. "I am also going to suggest that, before you meet up with Ray, you meet up with some other acquaintances from your past."

"Other acquaintances?" asked Edie. "Who?"

"You will need all the help you can muster to accomplish this task," Hronck oozed in a particularly greasy voice. "Perhaps the girl, the actress."

"How do you know about her?" asked Meg.

Edie shivered. "And how can you do this to people? Aren't you human?"

Hronck chuckled. "The more difficult questions will have to remain unanswered for today. Now, I do have something for you both to carry." He reached behind the desk and picked up two small watches, each with a matte metal bracelet.

"You should wear these at all times." He handed one to each of them. "If you press all three buttons on the right side of the dial at the same time, it will allow me to locate you and bring you back here. Please do not use this device unless you have either obtained the Root, or concluded that it is not present in the time where you have been sent."

The girls began strapping on the watches. "I cannot provide you with too many details beyond what I have told you, because I do not know more myself." Hronck looked almost pensive. "I believe, based on things I have learned in other times, that the root exists. I do not know the form it takes, nor do I know how it relates to the network."

"So," Edie said slowly, as though trying to figure out a math problem, "you're sending us into the future to get something you can't identify from someone you can't identify, at a location—"

"—I cannot identify. Yes, you have summed it up quite nicely! As I said, I would do this myself, but it is too much of a risk for me. And the two of you are the only other people in this time who know that I can move through time in this manner. We can help each other."

"What about Lisa?" asked Meg. "She's waiting outside for us. What are you going to tell her?"

Hronck thought for a moment, then smiled. "I will tell her that I have sent you back into the past, but into a different branching of the timeline, so that this one continues unabated. You will be missing in this timeline, but may continue your lives in another. This is not true, and it is not how time works in your world, but I will be quite convincing, and your friends will have no reason to disbelieve me. Everyone will return to their lives, pleased to conclude that everything has turned out perfectly for all of us."

Edie wasn't sure any of this was going to work, but she had decided to go forward. She turned to Meg. "Are you ready to do this again?"

"No," replied Meg, her voice now somewhat hoarse. "But I'm guessing that we're going to have some pretty good stories after this is done."

Edie laughed. "True. But I'm also guessing that no one will believe us."

"Girls," called Hronck, waving towards the far left corner of the room. "Please come over here."

There, on a table near the wall, was the same machine Edie and Meg had seen from the window of the Garbers' house. It was still shaped like a French bread on a tripod, and it was now pointing towards what looked like an archery target that had been painted on the wall.

"Please stand in front of the target." Hronck put on a pair of shaded lab glasses. "I suggest you close your eyes, put your heels tightly together, and stand as close to the wall as you can. Also, please grip your hands together; without contact, I cannot guarantee that you will travel together, or arrive at the same destination."

The girls did as they were instructed.

"I will count down from five," Hronck said over the sound of the machine warming up. "When I reach zero, I will engage the machine. Are you ready?"

They nodded silently, and Hronck began to count down.

"Five," he intoned. "Four...three..."

Edie and Meg grabbed hands.

50

the battle is joined

The wall behind the girls opened up like a mouth, and Lt. Mark Sullivan emerged through it, holding a generic boy avatar in some form of military handcuff restraint. Even Hronck was so taken aback by this unexpected development that he stopped the countdown and stared, his arms held stiffly before him near the button.

"Mr. Hronck," said Mark. "I think you may want to hear what this boy has to say before you continue."

Hronck smiled despite himself. "Lt. Sullivan. How on earth did you just do that?"

"Perhaps this 'Jake' kid can explain it to you."

Edie and Meg gasped. "Jake?" whispered Edie. "What are you doing here?"

Mark sneered. "Oh, he's not really Jake. Is he, Hronck?"

Hronck nodded at Jared in recognition. "No, he is not. He is Jared Garber." Edie's and Meg's mouths each turned into a silent O of shock. "But he is merely an avatar, as is Lt. Sullivan, and this—this is not possible. Unless..."

As Hronck trailed off, Jared stared back at him, wondering how this was going to play out.

Haley had downloaded a huge amount of information about Mark into her mind through Ray's strange conical device, and Kathrine had provided more background on Lisa's former boyfriend. Jared hoped that Haley had enough material to fool Hronck by pretending to be Mark. As for Jared, he wasn't even sure whether he himself was an avatar or a "real" person anymore, and it wasn't until he looked down at himself that he could confirm that he was still in avatar format, albeit an avatar now interacting in the real world.

Jared was still a bit confused about how all of this worked, but Ray seemed to be on top of things. After recognizing that the human network was merely part of a larger network, and that there was no "real world" at all, Ray had used his talent to break through that artificial barrier between these dominions. Just as the transhuman viruses had leaped from cyberspace into "reality," Ray had created a "Mark" avatar which had taken Jared's avatar into the real world, even as the "real" Jared was just a few blocks away.

"Doesn't this mean that I'm in the 'real' world twice?" Jared had askedwhile they discussed their approach. "I mean, I'm in Melissa's apartment wearing that head-work stuff, and I'll be in Hronck's house as an avatar. That doesn't make any sense."

"Yup," said Ray, adjusting something on the Mark avatar as he spoke, an excited rhythm in his voice. "Just stick with the story, and don't go looking for yourself."

Now, finally confronting Hronck, Jared hoped he could act as well as Haley, even just for a few minutes.

"Mr. Hronck, I understand that this person has some information of value to you," said Mark. "I made him take me here immediately so that you could hear it. It would appear that I got here just in time."

"You're with Gluck, aren't you?" said Hronck to Jared quietly. "That's how you got here." The last statement was emphatically not a question.

"Yeah," agreed Jared weakly, trying to sound despondent and hoping that he wasn't overdoing it. "With Gluck I could do all sorts of things. He's as powerful as you are, you know. And we could have stopped you, too, if it wasn't for this guy." He appeared to struggle against the handcuffs, gesturing to Mark with his nose.

Hronck shook his head as though learning of particularly tragic news. "I am afraid you have been exposed to all sorts of untruths from Gluck, Mr. Garber. Do you not suppose that he wants the root as much as I do?"

"I'm sure he does," said Jared, "but he doesn't want it to do what you want it to do."

Hronck's eyes twinkled with malice. "Really? And what did Gluck tell you about my intentions?"

"That you want the root for yourself, to make yourself all-powerful," Jared said defiantly. "You don't care about the Saan and what they were doing, that's what he said. We'd all be your slaves."

Hronck stared at Jared for an uncomfortably long time, until Jared finally had to look away from the power of his gaze.

"You know nothing of the Saan," said Hronck, almost under his breath. "And you clearly know nothing of Gluck. Why do you think that he wants the root? Did he tell you that *you* were important?"

"He said that he wanted to figure out the answer, that he wanted the calculations of the Saan to continue," said Jared, now a bit less sure of himself.

Hronck shook his head. "You are so very naïve, Jared Garber. Do you not realize that the so-called 'final calculation' of the Saan imperils your world? The fact that Ms. Boyd has appeared"—Hronck pointed at Edie, who cringed as though he were about to throw something at her—"is evidence that the Mesh is nearing the end of its work. When that happens, *all* of us may disappear. All of this"—he waved his arms—"will disappear. We shall fade into nothingness. Gluck knows this and is trying to protect *himself.* Faktors will receive no special dispensation if the Mesh comes to an end."

"Okay, what are you guys talking about?" said Meg. "I mean, none of this makes any sense."

"There's a lot to explain," said Jared. "But I need to come with you, wherever you're going next. I need to help you find the root."

"Ah, yes, well, that is a wonderful sentiment, Mr. Garber," said Hronck contemptuously. "But thanks to Lt. Sullivan—and please be aware, Lt. Sullivan, that you will be amply rewarded for your service in this matter—you will be going nowhere. I look forward to hearing the details of your capture, Mr. Garber, after Ms. Boyd and Ms. Karger are sent off to perform their task on my behalf."

"Wait a minute," said Edie. "Didn't you send Jared Garber into the future, too? What's going on?"

"I most certainly did not send the Garber family into the future," said Hronck. "Someone else, someone by the name of Lasho Gluck, was responsible for that."

"Hold it, hold it!" said Meg. "You didn't send the Garbers here? We did all of this for nothing?"

Hronck pushed a button on the silver console on his right. "That is a long tale, which I am afraid must wait until another time, Ms. Karger." Large liquid metal restraints popped out of the floor and grabbed onto both Meg and Edie like vines, immobilizing them on the spot. While they could move their arms, they could not bend or step in any direction.

"This has been an interesting, though in the end distracting, interruption. We will now continue our countdown."

Then the wall opened a second time, this time revealing Lasho Gluck. To Jared, he looked the same as Hronck—a pulsing icon of cascading symbols. To Edie, he looked like an aging history professor, with leather patches on a tattered tweed jacket. Yet even she could sense a strange power just barely visible beneath his skin, as though lightning had been captured inside him.

Hronck stepped back from the console. "This now grows tiresome. Gluck, you must let me proceed. It is the only way."

"Where are all of these people coming from?" whispered Meg.

"No idea," replied Edie. "Is that really Jared Garber?"

"Doesn't look like him," said Meg as Gluck approached Hronck, "but who knows anymore? I just can't believe we've been chasing the wrong guy all this time."

"Were we? It sounds like Hronck really did send *us* into the future, for whatever that's worth. But this other guy was responsible for making the Garbers disappear, I think." She watched the two beings, their eyes locked on each other with something similar to hatred, but less human.

Finally, once he stood only a few feet away from the console, Gluck made a strange salute with his hand, putting his pinky and thumb together in a circle with a snap. It seemed to Jared like a sarcastic greeting. It also seemed—for Faktors, at least—that appearing out of a solid wall was a fairly typical social situation.

"Hello, Hronck," said Gluck, a slight smile playing across his lips.

Hronck returned Gluck's salute with reluctance. "Ah. Gluck. I thought you might wish to drop in at some point this evening, but I am surprised that you were able to get inside my home. How on earth did you manage that feat?"

"Mr. Garber was quite effective in providing me with the means to get here. I merely followed him and his compatriots into the Mesh through the network. Their friend Ray is becoming quite accomplished, as you know."

Hronck made a noise of impatience. "Yes, but as we both know, he will become quite a bit more accomplished later. He will be far more interesting to me then." His finger hovered over a red button on the console. Neither Edie nor Jared dared breathe. "What do you want, Gluck?"

"We both need the Root." Gluck went up to a table and tapped on its stainless steel surface. "And we both know that only Ms. Boyd can find it. Why do we not cooperate?"

"What good would that do me?" asked Hronck irritably. "We both know why *you* want the root, and we both know why *I* want it. Either you must defeat me, or I must defeat you. There can be no compromise."

Gluck shook his head. "You speak of the battle that must occur in the end. Yet neither of us can do anything until the root is discovered. Before then we are at a stand-off, and neither side may triumph."

"Excuse me," said Edie. "Only *I* can find this thing? What is that supposed to mean?"

Hronck glanced briefly in her direction. "It is your destiny. It is the reason why you were created." Gluck nodded in agreement

Edie struggled against the liquid metal restraints on her legs. "My parents had *me* to find some stupid secret root thing for *you*? That's completely stupid."

"You go, girl," whispered Meg fiercely.

"Ms. Boyd," said Hronck, as though explaining the idea of a nap to an exhausted toddler. "You *had no parents*. You were created by the Mesh. Your memories of your parents were implanted, and you were raised by artificial intelligence agents developed by Gluck. You are the result of millions of years of complex calculations, and now is the time for you to fulfill your purpose."

Before Edie or Meg could object or seek clarification, Hronck moved to press the button. Just before his finger could reach the console, in what seemed to Jared to be mere fractions of a second, Gluck leaped onto Hronck like a cat. The two of them began to pummel each other, but their fists and their bodies never actually touched. Instead, blinding bolts of energy shot from their hands as though they had each become cannons of light.

Seeing his chance, Jared turned to "Lt. Sullivan" and spoke urgently in his captor's ear. "Haley, let me go. We need to do something *now*."

It seemed to Jared that he could see Haley's eyes inside of Mark's avatar face as she reached over and released the handcuffs. Jared immediately ran over to Edie and Meg, who were struggling to get out of their own restraints.

"Can you get these things off of me?" said Meg, trying to pull herself out of the leg braces.

"I'm trying." He tried to lever them off with a metal pole that had been sitting on one of the tables nearby. But nothing seemed to work. He looked over at Edie, who seemed frozen in terror, still staring blankly at Hronck and Gluck as they glowed ominously with green and blue radiance, viciously grappling with each other without any apparent contact. Meanwhile, "Mark" was at Hronck's console, examining the controls, which were themselves lit up like a Christmas tree.

Jared realized quickly that he would never be able to get the restraints off of Edie or Meg with his hands. The cuffs were too tightly coiled around their legs. He ran over to join Haley's "Mark" avatar at the console and was immediately faced with an impossibly confusing series of screens and entry fields.

"Do you know what any of this is?" he asked. "None of it has any labels."

"No idea," replied Haley, running her hands over the touch screens as though trying to summon a message from the dead at a séance. "I've never seen anything like this."

Then Jared saw Gluck fall backwards. Hronck moved with almost unimaginable speed towards the console, pushing Jared and Haley out of the way with a violent shove. With a look of satisfaction on his face, he pushed the red button.

With sudden force, Edie felt a jerk behind her ribcage. Before she could scream or even react, she swirled into a vortex. As her body was consumed with almost unbearable pressure, she thought about her home. She remembered her aunt and uncle, how much she loved them, how she so desperately wanted to see them again, and how it couldn't possibly be true that they weren't real. That must have been a lie. Her parents were real, her life was real—only *this* was all a dream. Maybe she would wake up in her bed as though nothing had ever happened. She thought about small worries from her past, of how she had looked in the mirror in another lifetime. She thought about larger worries, about what she wanted to be when she grew up. If she grew up.

She could tell, somehow, that all of these other concerns had been replaced by an unknowable future. But at least she would have friends in the future, she thought, friends she understood and appreciated so much more than she had before. She wouldn't be alone. She wondered if she would ever see Jared Garber again. He had tried to save her, and she had so many questions to ask. She hoped he would be okay.

And as she spun through the darkness, she hoped Meg's hand was still tightly clenched in her own. She could not remember if they'd been holding hands when Hronck pushed the button, and she could no longer feel anything.

She thought about how important it was that she not let go. "Don't let go," she tried to say, but nothing came out of her mouth in the darkness as she spun back towards another time.

epilogue

many happy returns

Clara had no memory of her parents, but she did have an image of her mother. She had saved a copy of that likeness to her implanted headwork and thus carried it around with her at all times. The image showed her mother as a young woman, perhaps in her mid-twenties, with a pretty oval face and long black hair tied into a plait. She was sitting at a desk of some kind, leaning forward in her chair as though she had been interrupted in her work.

The woman in the image had been examining something on the table, and Clara imagined that her mother had looked up in surprise when the photographer had called her name. Her mother seemed amused, and had a broad smile on her face that made Clara almost unbearably sad. There was no question in her mind that her mother loved the photographer, and Clara liked to think that the photographer was her father. She had never known him, either, and had no idea what he looked like.

Clara would sometimes sit outside, under a real tree, and stare at her mother's eyes in the image. They looked so much like her own, kindly and warm, but filled with drive and purpose. Her mother seemed to be the type of person who accomplished things, important things.

Or so Clara believed.

She also looked into her mother's eyes hoping to see a reflection of the photographer, but she could never make out a face, even with every technological enhancement she could find on the network. So hers imagination was free to invent the appearance of her father, who inevitably looked dashing and suave in her own mind.

Clara was fourteen years old. She had been raised in foster homes for as long as she could remember, but she had no bad feelings towards the people that had raised her. They were good people, working hard to help those less fortunate than themselves. According to her current foster parents, the ones who had housed her since her sixth birthday, she had been found alone at the doorstep of a hospital when she was a baby. In an envelope attached to her blanket had been a memory device with the image of her mother, and a handwritten note. The note had been cryptic:

This little girl is named Clara. She is in terrible danger. Please take care of her. Her birthday is on January 1. I love her more than I can possibly express. I must protect her, and she cannot stay with me if she is to remain safe. I will return when she is fourteen, and although this will not make sense to you now, I will not remember anything when I return. Tell her that I am sorry, and that I will need her help when I return. I love you, Clara, and I will see you again someday. I promise.

While she had been shown the picture as a little girl, Clara had never before been allowed to see the note or even know of its existence until earlier this year. As she approached the age of fourteen, however, her foster parents, Stacey and Steve Teinowicz, began to worry.

The Teinowiczes loved Clara as though she were their own daughter. He worked as a paralegal and she worked in a bank, and their own children were grown. They had been tempted to adopt Clara formally on more than one occasion, and only their own precarious financial straits had stopped them from doing so. Nevertheless, they wanted to protect her as best they could, and hiding the note no longer seemed like such a good idea to either of them. What if her mother really did return? Shouldn't Clara be warned? Perhaps her mother was dangerous, or a kidnapping risk. Her mother, quite frankly, sounded mildly insane in the note.

So, with some reluctance, Clara had been shown the note several months ago, amidst much handwringing and many excuses. In fact, after she had been presented with the note, her foster parents sat nervously on the couch next to her, waiting to see if she would be frightened or disturbed or unreasonably angry at having this key piece of evidence withheld from her for so long. Much to their surprise, however, Clara barely batted an eye.

Instead, she remembered feeling an overwhelming sense of déjà vu, as though she had always known the contents of the note. It occurred to her that even though the details of the note were new, she had always felt that her mother might return, and could not imagine the woman in the picture abandoning her child forever. There had to be a reason for her disappearance, a good reason, and soon she would have a chance to discover it.

• • •

Five months to the day after her fourteenth birthday, Clara sat in her backyard watching a bird searching for food. The bird hopped back and forth across the ground, pecking at invisible worms and grubs, speeding quickly across the yard as though pursued.

Unlike most of her friends, Clara did not spend every waking minute burrowed within the warm embrace of the network. It was possible, of course, to live your life almost entirely as an avatar, but that lifestyle held little appeal for her. She enjoyed the physical sense of sitting outside in the real world, of listening to birds and watching squirrels. She also liked to talk—a lot—and enjoyed the sensation of speaking words in real life. For some reason, it was never the same on the network.

On this day, however, she was speaking to no one, and saw no squirrels. In fact, the only living thing in her presence was the bird, but even it flew away when a small *crack* echoed near the patio door. She turned back towards the house and was surprised to see a girl in old-fashioned clothing standing unsteadily on the patio, leaning face-first into the wall.

"Hello?" Clara got up. "Are you okay? Can I help you?" She began walking towards the girl, who seemed to be recovering, and who pushed herself back from the wall just as Clara approached.

"What's your name?" asked Clara, concerned about this girl who had suddenly appeared in her yard. "Can you talk?"

Edie turned around to face a girl who appeared to be about her same age, dressed in clothing that seemed even more astounding than the outfits she had just experienced. The girl wore a form-fitting jumpsuit that seemed almost like a second layer of skin. The only clue that she was wearing clothing at all was the fact that she was covered in advertising from her neck to her toes, a waterfall of liquid information morphing from one slogan into another. Edie quickly looked around, hoping to see Meg nearby, but she already knew that she was alone.

"My name is Edie." She looked directly at Clara. "What year is this?"

Clara, who was so rarely silent, had been struck dumb from the moment that she saw Edie's face. There was no question in her mind who this girl was, or why she had suddenly shown up on Clara's patio.

"Edie," said Clara, finally developing the nerve to speak. "My name is Clara. And I've been waiting for you my whole life. I am so glad to see you."

And before she even finished speaking, she had wrapped her arms around Edie and gave her a deep, emotional hug. Startled, Edie pushed her away.

"Excuse me. Who are you? I mean, how do you know me?"

Clara calmly pushed a button behind her ear and a holographic image shot out of her outfit into the space between them. The image showed a young woman sitting at a desk, looking up. It took Edie no more than a moment to realize the woman's identity: it was Edie herself, perhaps a dozen years older.

"Edie," said Clara, and happiness glowed in her eyes like hot coals. "That's you. You are my mother. Or at least you will be. And you told me you would return, and that you would need my help."

Edie stared gape-mouthed at the shimmering image of her older self.

"So," Clara said. "Let's get started."

acknowledgements

This book has had a long gestation, and could not have been completed without the assistance of a whole crew of great readers and good friends. While I can't mention everyone, I would like to thank the Gofen and Mora families for their invaluable input, and the reading group that included Grace Hildebrand, Caroline Chu, Kathryn Garrett, Madeline Sachs, Devin Rosen and their very generous moms. I would also like to thank Ray Silverman, Laurie Holmes, Randy Stearns and Stacey Bashara, Jillisa Brittan, (who read the very first draft before anyone else), Dorothy Grunes, Sammy and Rachel Pesick, Mark Mitten, Ira Kalina, Bev and Dick Bernstein (on whose computer the first few chapters was composed on a Thanksgiving weekend many years ago), my parents and sister, and of course Jill and Ian, to whom this book (and pretty much everything else) is dedicated.

18577615R00198

Made in the USA
Lexington, KY
12 November 2012